Praise
Dark E...

"Written in a compelling voice, *Dark Embers* introduces a sexy and intriguing new world. I'm looking forward to seeing where Tessa Adams takes her dragons next."

—Nalini Singh, *New York Times*
bestselling author of *Archangel's Consort*

"*Dark Embers* is a blistering-hot, fast-paced adventure that will leave readers breathless. Dylan and Phoebe have great chemistry and a romantic story that will captivate you and keep you turning pages long into the night. I'm really looking forward to the next book in the series!"

—Anya Bast, *New York Times* bestselling author of *Jeweled*

"This darkly seductive tale will have you longing for a dragon of your very own."

—Shiloh Walker, national bestselling author of *Veil of Shadows*

"A fantastic debut to a new erotic paranormal series that will take you on a scorching-hot adventure and leave you wanting more."

—Among the Muses

"If you're looking for a fast paranormal read featuring suspense, hot shifters, and even hotter sex, then look no further."

—Smexy Books Romance Reviews

"A wonderful shape-shifter tale."

—*Midwest Book Review*

ALSO BY TESSA ADAMS

Dark Embers

Hidden Embers

FORBIDDEN EMBERS

A DRAGON'S HEAT NOVEL

TESSA ADAMS

HEAT

HEAT
Published by New American Library,
a division of Penguin Group (USA) Inc.,
375 Hudson Street, New York, New York 10014, USA
Penguin Group (Canada), 90 Eglinton Avenue East, Suite 700, Toronto,
Ontario M4P 2Y3, Canada (a division of Pearson Penguin Canada Inc.)
Penguin Books Ltd., 80 Strand, London WC2R 0RL, England
Penguin Ireland, 25 St. Stephen's Green, Dublin 2,
Ireland (a division of Penguin Books Ltd.)
Penguin Group (Australia), 250 Camberwell Road, Camberwell,
Victoria 3124, Australia (a division of Pearson Australia Group Pty. Ltd.)
Penguin Books India Pvt. Ltd., 11 Community Centre,
Panchsheel Park, New Delhi - 110 017, India
Penguin Group (NZ), 67 Apollo Drive, Rosedale, Auckland 0632,
New Zealand (a division of Pearson New Zealand Ltd.)
Penguin Books (South Africa) (Pty.) Ltd., 24 Sturdee Avenue,
Rosebank, Johannesburg 2196, South Africa

Penguin Books Ltd., Registered Offices:
80 Strand, London WC2R 0RL, England

First published by Heat, an imprint of New American Library,
a division of Penguin Group (USA) Inc.

First Printing, October 2011
1   3   5   7   9   10   8   6   4   2

LIBRARY OF CONGRESS CATALOGING-IN-PUBLICATION DATA:

Adams, Tessa.
Forbidden embers: a dragon's heat novel/Tessa Adams.
p. cm.—(Dragon's heat; 3)
ISBN 978-0-451-23470-4 (pbk.)
I. Title.
PS3623.O57F67 2011
813'.6—dc22   2011020487

Set in Minion Pro
Printed in the United States of America

For Jenn

ACKNOWLEDGMENTS

As always, there are so many people to thank—at NAL and at home.

First off, I have to thank my amazing, wonderful, fabulous editor, Jhanteigh Kupihea, who is incredible to work with and who always has time for me, no matter how small the question or crazy the idea. You're the best, Jhanteigh, and I am so grateful to have you.

I also must thank everyone at NAL who helps create such amazing books for me. I am so lucky to write for such a wonderful, talented house.

Thank you to Shellee Roberts and Emily McKay for the fun, companionship and chocolate cake. Not to mention all the emergency brainstorming sessions, when I was certain I wouldn't find the way to Logan and Cecily's HEA.

As always, thanks to Emily Sylvan Kim, who truly is the best agent and friend anyone could ever ask for.

And to my fans, thanks so much for your enthusiasm for this series. I appreciate all your e-mails and encouragement and suggestions more than I can ever say.

FORBIDDEN EMBERS

PROLOGUE

He was dreaming. He knew it, understood it, yet could do nothing to wake himself up.

In the world of his mind's creation, it was already too late. But then, it always was. Part and parcel of his gift, these little trips into dreamland were his psyche's way of foretelling the future. His future. And as the dreams were never wrong, he knew within a few minutes of falling asleep exactly what he had to do.

Even as the *idea* came to him—even as he continued to sleep—Logan Kelly searched for a way around it.

But there was none, just as he'd known all along. Better minds than his had been working on this for months now. Years. All to no avail. The thought that had snuck into his dreams, and expanded until it already felt like reality, really was the only rational solution.

That didn't mean he had to like it.

As he slept, the walls and ceiling of the cave seemed to be closing in on him, the stalactites closer and sharper than they had ever been before. Without conscious thought, he reached up and broke off one of the very sharp ones and shoved it into his pocket before using a burst of preternatural speed to go outside.

Under the stars.

Amid the sand and cacti.

In the middle of the desert that had become more of a home to him than the rolling green hills of Ireland had ever been.

The thought destroyed him, made him dizzy. Nauseated. Not the knowledge that he'd forsaken Ireland, but the sudden recognition that he would soon be forsaking the endless caves and deserts of New Mexico, as well. And with it the only men and women he'd ever considered friends. Family.

Bending over, he braced his hands on his knees and sucked huge, gulping breaths of air deep into his lungs. One after another, until the world around him stopped spinning. One after another, until the burst of short-lived panic receded.

I will do this for them, he told himself, *because I am the only one who can.* That realization was enough to steady him, when just moments before he'd been certain that nothing would ever be able to do so again.

Unable to bear his thoughts—his own stillness—for one second more, he began to walk. Around him, the desert teemed with life. Night predators searching out prey. Prey searching out new and better hiding spots. In the distance, an owl swept down toward the still-warm sand at an amazing speed. Seconds later, a small animal squealed in pain.

He refused to let it get to him. Predator, prey. It was the way of the world. Certainly, the way of *his* world, and after a decade of watching his clan mates living in fear, he was sick of being the quarry. Sick to death of hanging around and waiting for the next attack, the next wave of sickness, the next horrifying death of someone he loved and was sworn to protect.

He was ready to strike. It was the nature of the beast, after all. The nature of *his* beast, and those of his closest friends. He would find his enemy's weak spot; hit fast and hard. Whatever damage he sustained— whether fleeting or absolute—would be more than worth it if he could finally find a way to neutralize the enemy.

He snarled at the thought of the Wyvernmoons, his long legs eating up the miles as he walked off his frustration, his pain. Inside, his beast thrashed and snarled in an effort to get out, but Logan kept it on a very short leash. One slipup, and the dragon would burst free. He couldn't afford that, not now, when logic and reason had to be everything.

Not now, when the hot-tempered screams of the animal would do nothing to advance the case he knew he had to make.

As he walked, he memorized the feel of the desert at night. After more than two hundred years, he should be able to call it up at will, but he wasn't taking any chances. South Dakota in the wintertime was as different from New Mexico as one could get and still be in America. And God only knew how many winters he would have to endure in that hell-hole of a compound before he would once again find his way back here.

If he ever did.

The pragmatist in him knew that there was more than a passing chance that he would die on this latest quest, knew that after he left here in a few days, he might never see his beloved stretch of desert again. And while he didn't fear death—at 397 years old, he had faced that enemy many times before—he did regret that he might never again enjoy the peaceful solitude of a walk over the land, his land, while a blanket of stars stretched as far as the eye could see.

He broke into a run then, all but flying in human form across the forty or so miles that separated him from the small house he kept in town. But that was the thing about dreams—fiction and reality could mix until it was impossible to tell one from the other.

The closer he got to the small city that was the heart of the Dragonstars' home, the more voices and thoughts crowded in on him. They pressed down from every side, nearly blinding him. Almost making him insane with the fear and worry and pain that threaded through so many of his fellow dragons.

He could feel walls closing in even though he was outside. Could feel time ticking away from him like the sand of his beloved desert through an hourglass.

It was exactly what he needed to cement his resolve. Usually his psychic abilities drove him nuts. Though they made things easier in battle, the rest of the time they were nothing but a pain in the ass.

An ability to eavesdrop on thoughts and conversations that were never meant to be public.

An invasion of privacy that, even after almost four centuries, he sometimes couldn't block.

A knowledge of people's most embarrassing moments and deepest, darkest secrets.

It sucked, big-time.

His psychic ability was one of the reasons he spent so much of his free time deep in the desert, away from the other dragon shifters. It was often the only way he could give the civilian dragons of the clan any privacy. The only way he could quiet the nonstop chatter in his head. It was also the reason it had taken him nearly three centuries to find a home.

He shied away from the thought and the emotions that were still too raw, even after all this time. Then he slipped silently into town, nodding to his friend and fellow sentry Ty as he passed him on the street. It was Ty's turn to patrol the town boundaries, and though he looked like he wanted to talk, Logan didn't stop. He couldn't afford to, not now, when his plan was only half-formed. It would still be too easy to talk him out of it.

No, there was a council meeting in a few days, a gathering of the other sentries like him, and that was where he would reveal his plan. It wasn't much time, but he was determined to be prepared.

To be resolute.

To be unshakable. Otherwise, his peers would never go along with what he wanted to do.

They still might not—that fact was what had driven him toward town before he even knew where he was heading. He needed to talk to Dylan before the meeting, needed to talk him into the idea that was still not fully formed in his own head.

It shouldn't be that hard to convince the Dragonstar king, a little voice inside Logan's head whispered. Dylan had to go along with it.

They were running out of time. Even with the Wyvernmoons' last attack party decimated, it wouldn't take long for them to regroup and head back to New Mexico, looking to wipe out the Dragonstars once and for all. And while they couldn't beat the Dragonstars in a fair fight, the Wyvernmoons had much greater numbers and an amorality that gave them a firm advantage. After all, they were responsible for the disease that had ravaged his clan for more than a decade.

He wouldn't let them destroy the Dragonstars. He couldn't. Not when this clan, *his* clan, was the only one who had taken him in after long centuries of searching. Not when these people, *his* people, had given him the only home he'd ever known.

That generosity was one of the many reasons it was so difficult to contemplate leaving. And one of the many reasons he had to.

After checking around his house for signs of disturbances, he opened the door and let his senses flood the place—searching for the thoughts, the presence, of any intruders. He found none, but that didn't stop him from making the rounds, checking every room to make sure no enemies lay in wait. As he did, he cursed the Wyvernmoons and the fact that such hyper-vigilance was even necessary when he and his clan mates wanted nothing more than to live in peace.

It wouldn't be for long—not if he had anything to say about it.

When he was convinced his house was clear, Logan strode into the kitchen and yanked a pair of scissors out of one of the drawers. Then went into the bathroom and, without thought or remorse, cut off the long, flowing hair that had all but been his trademark for centuries. Amid the Dragonstars, almost all of whom were dark, his too-long blond hair and amber eyes were legendary.

After the hair was gone—and he was barely recognizable even to himself—Logan reached into his pocket and pulled out the stalactite he'd shoved in there earlier. He studied it for a moment, made sure it was strong enough and sharp enough to do what had to be done.

Then, without pause, he reached up and raked the hard, sharp tip of it down the right side of his face, from his eye to the corner of his mouth.

They had reached the point of no return. As he watched blood flow freely down his face and neck, he knew that nothing else mattered.

His clan would be safe. He would make sure of it.

He woke up a few minutes later, shivering and huddled up on the couch in his living room in town, though he had fallen asleep in his cave. He blinked a few times, brought the world around him into focus.

And realized that the pillow he'd been sleeping on was coated in his blood.

His fight had already begun.

CHAPTER ONE

The murmurs started the second Logan walked into the War Room. He ignored them as he headed to the front of the long, underground cavern that Dylan used as a meeting and strategizing room for himself and his sentries, but that only made the sounds—and the worry that fueled them—more insistent.

The room wasn't even close to full. After finding a traitor in their midst a few weeks before, Dylan had tripled patrols around their territory. Everyone was suddenly being very careful about what they did and who they trusted, but still, the emotions of his closest friends pressed in on Logan from every side.

He refused to acknowledge them, instead choosing to keep his eyes on his king, who stood at the front of the room, waiting for him. The look in Dylan's eyes was a mixture of fury, concern and resignation. Logan recognized it because they were the same emotions that had been flooding him for far too long, as he'd watched clan mate after clan mate die around him.

"What the hell did you do to yourself?" Quinn, the Dragonstars' number-one healer, jumped up from his spot next to Dylan and crossed the room so quickly he was nearly a blur. "You should have called me right away."

"I'm fine."

"You're patently not fine," Quinn answered, reaching for his face. Though the healer had yet to touch him, already Logan could feel the warmth emanating from his fingers. The promise of healing that would make the ceaseless ache in his face finally go away.

He shrugged Quinn off and shouldered his way past the other sentries who had gathered around him to lend support and inquire about his health. They were his friends, his family, the only people he had cared about in his long, long existence, and he was afraid if he spoke to them now, he would let them change his mind about what he planned to do.

It wasn't that he was uncertain of his choice. He wasn't, and the support of his king had only made him more resolute. It was simply that none of those closest to him were bothering to shield themselves and he was too worn down, his mind in too much turmoil, to do it for them. Their emotions were coming at him from every side.

Concern from Paige, the sentry he had been involved with for nearly half of the previous century.

Rage from his closest friend, Shawn.

An ice-cold need for revenge from Gabe, who had lost his wife and daughter to the Wyvernmoons' machinations less than a year before.

And from Dylan, his king and one of his closest friends, a resigned and resolute sadness that very much matched his own feelings. Strange that with everything floating around the room, his were the emotions that came closest to breaking Logan.

"What happened to you?" Shawn demanded, flashing across the cave in an instant to block his path. The look in his best friend's furious gold eyes would have felled a lesser man, but Logan just stepped around him.

"I'm fine."

"Not to echo Quinn, but you don't look fine. You look like you went a full ten rounds with a weed whacker. And lost."

Even though that had been the point—the scar was raw and ugly enough to draw even the most discerning attention away from his features—he still took exception to the implication that he couldn't hold his own in a fight. "I think you have me confused with yourself," he said, bumping his shoulder into the other dragon shifter as he passed.

"Yeah. Because I'm the one who didn't even bother to call for help when someone messed with *my* pretty-boy face."

"That's because you're so ugly no one would try to mess with your mug. Any scars would be an improvement."

"Yeah, well, I can't say the same about you. You look like shit. And what the fuck happened to your hair?"

"Enough!" Dylan's voice echoed through the cavern. And while theirs wasn't a council that stood on ceremony, the five sentries currently in the room froze. When Dylan used that tone, it meant business—usually of the bloodiest, most serious kind.

Logan worked his way around Shawn and Quinn and kept walking through the cold, underground cave. But instead of taking his normal spot in the War Room on the large, flat rock against the side wall, he continued to the front of the room, where Dylan, Quinn and Gabe, the king's seconds-in-command, always sat in huge, heavy chairs.

Quinn followed him, and Logan was aware that everyone in the room was staring at him, their cagey, intelligent minds casting around for a reasonable explanation for his appearance and Dylan's obvious lack of worry over his wound.

Paige, one of only two female shifters on Dylan's council, hit on the answer first, but, then, she knew a side of him that no one else did. It had been years since they'd been together, but some things you didn't forget. He still knew all her weak spots, as well.

Her understanding cut like a beacon of light through the murky gray that surrounded the others' thoughts. "Don't do it, Logan," she pleaded from where she was seated on one of the large black couches in the center of the room. "You don't look nearly different enough to pull it off."

Confusion continued to press in on him, and Logan made a belated effort to slide his psychic shields into place. If he spent much more time in this room without their protection, he'd be crushed under the weight of his fellow sentries' concern.

"Pull what off?" demanded Shawn, his voice little more than a growl of frustration. "Will someone please tell me what the fuck is going on here?"

"It won't work, Logan. You're one of us," Paige continued. "You've been one of us for two centuries. You won't be able to hide that."

"I'm the only one who *can* hide it," he answered. "Because I wasn't born Dragonstar. The clan's magic isn't as deeply imprinted in me, and what little there is, I can shield."

"All the time?" Paige asked skeptically. "Even you're not that good. And if you slip, even for a second, then you're dead. You know that, right?"

"If I don't try, then I'm dead, anyway. We all are. If the virus doesn't get us, then their damn war parties will. We can't fight the Wyvernmoons forever, not if they keep finding a way to turn our clan members into traitors." He paused, started to run a hand through his hair before he remembered that he had cut almost all of it off. "They turned Callie, for God's sake, Paige. If they could get to her, they could get to anyone."

"Bullshit." This time it was Dylan who answered. "Yes, the fact that they turned Callie was a blow. But that doesn't mean I don't trust the rest of my sentries implicitly."

"Then you're a fool," Logan growled, frustrated at Dylan's interference just when he was trying to make a point.

Other kings would have bitten his head off for that comment, but his simply inclined his head. "Maybe you're right. I'm going along with this scheme of yours, aren't I? Despite my better judgment."

"Are you kidding me? You're just going to let him walk into the lion's den?" Paige sprang to her feet and walked toward Logan. "That's the stupidest thing I've ever heard. Logan, you can't possibly believe a scar and a haircut are going to keep them from recognizing you, even if, by some miracle, you manage to strip yourself of your Dragonstar affiliation."

"That's suicide!" Shawn exploded as the light finally dawned.

"Completely insane," echoed Quinn. "We're making huge progress now that we know some of us have natural antibodies to the virus. It's only a matter of time before we find a way to immunize against it."

The three of them looked to Dylan for support, but the king just shook his head. "If he can infiltrate, we'll have a spy in the heart of Wyvernmoon territory. Someone who can get close enough to the lab to destroy the virus once and for all, not to mention warn us of an impending attack. Too many Dragonstars are getting hurt or injured in this stupid campaign of theirs. It has to stop."

"And if Logan doesn't pull it off, we just leave him there to die?" Shawn demanded. "Fuck that."

"It's not your choice," Dylan answered. His face mirrored his concern—concern that Logan appreciated, but also that he refused to accept. Especially since Dylan's mate, Phoebe, was pregnant with the heir to the Dragonstar throne. If it was in his power to keep her—and Dylan's baby—from falling victim to this damn virus, then he was more than ready to step up and do whatever was necessary.

"Yeah, well, it is yours, and you're making the wrong one," Shawn told him. "I never thought I'd live to see the day you sent one of your sentries out to be slaughtered like a sacrificial lamb."

Ice-cold silence slammed through the cavern, and Logan turned just in time to see Dylan swing around. He grabbed Shawn by the back of the neck in a gesture of absolute dominance that demanded absolute obedience. The fact that Shawn didn't lower his eyes, didn't apologize, didn't do anything but meet his king's gaze with complete aplomb spoke louder than any words could have. And while Logan appreciated the support—especially because he appreciated it—he couldn't just sit by and watch his friend being used as a dragon-sized chew toy.

"It's my choice, Shawn. I went to Dylan with the idea." His voice was loud and strong and it echoed off the jewel-encrusted walls. It filled the entire cavern and had Shawn finally bowing his head. Dylan released him with a low growl.

"Sure, I might die there if someone finds out what I'm doing," Logan continued. "But I'll go crazy if I stay here and watch everyone I care about die around me from that goddamn virus. I'm the only one of the sentries who isn't genetically Dragonstar. The virus doesn't affect me the way it affects the rest of you.

"I can get in there, find a way to destroy the thing and, if we're lucky, maybe even find out some of the Wyvernmoons' battle plans. You know as well as I do that this is only going to get worse. We're on the brink of full-scale war, and if this damn virus continues annihilating our strongest members, we'll be hard-pressed to win."

Shawn looked like he wanted to protest more—as did Quinn—but both stopped when Dylan held up a hand. "This isn't something Logan is going into blindly. He and I have spent most of the last four days talking over the pros and cons. The time for discussion is finished."

"Nice that you didn't let us in on the discussion," Shawn said bitterly.

Dylan's face darkened, and for a second it looked like he was going to take up where he had left off and rip Shawn a new one. Logan took a cautious step forward, put himself between Shawn and their king. But the movement turned out to be unnecessary, as Dylan contented himself with simply saying, "Don't mistake the fact that I look to you for counsel on most matters as a requirement. *I* am king. The responsibility for this clan falls on *my* shoulders, and I will do whatever I have to do to ensure that my people are safe. Even if it means sending a man that I like and admire very much into the very heart of darkness."

"You're not sending me," Logan argued. "I'm choosing to go."

"Then you're a lot stupider than you look," Shawn muttered. Before Logan could answer, Shawn was gone, flashing out of the cavern in the blink of an eye.

"I hate it when he does that." Paige shook her head and looked at Logan through narrowed eyes. "When are you going?"

"Tonight. As soon as possible, actually. We can't afford to wait."

"Shawn's right. You are a moron." But even as she said it, she threw her arms around his neck, holding on tight. "Take care of yourself." The last part she whispered in his ear.

"That's what I'm planning on," he answered as his arms went around her. For a second, he just stood there, absorbing the soft, female scent of her. There was nothing sexual between them anymore, hadn't been in more than a decade, but that didn't mean he couldn't appreciate the feel of being held by a woman who cared about him. It was something he'd never take for granted—not after spending the first three hundred years of his life without the sensation.

When she pulled away, he let her go reluctantly. It was hard to believe he might never see her again. He wasn't suicidal, but he was practical. He needed to hold on to the belief that whatever happened to him after he left here would be worth it if he could keep his people safe.

His good-byes to Quinn and Gabe were brief—there wasn't anything left to say after all, and he and Dylan had already said everything they'd needed to the day before. With a smile and a halfhearted wave, he gathered up his pack and headed out of the cave, his footsteps growing heavier the farther away from them he got.

This is it, he told himself. It was time to put his money where his mouth was. Time to do what had to be done.

He'd climbed steadily upward and could see daylight ahead of him. He would shift as soon as he got out and then head to South Dakota. If things went as planned, he'd be in his new home by nightfall.

But the second he set foot out of the cave, Shawn grabbed his shoulder. "Why are you doing this?" his oldest and closest friend demanded. "You don't have anything to prove to anyone."

"I have something to prove to myself," he answered fiercely, shrugging off the hand. "You guys took me in when no one else would have me. You gave me a family and a home and a life. How can I do anything less for you?"

"We're not keeping track, you know. And besides, any debt you might think you owe, you paid back a long time ago."

"It's not a matter of paying back a debt! It's a matter of doing what's right. If there's even a chance that I can do this, that I can stop this, I have to try."

Shawn snorted. "You're not superdragon, you know."

"And you're not my keeper."

"I should be. God knows you fucking need one."

"Look who's talking. You've spent your entire life doing one reckless thing after another."

"Yeah, well, there's reckless and there's suicidal. It's a thin fucking line, and you're skating right down the center of it."

Logan inclined his head. "Then I guess it's a good thing I have an impeccable ability to balance."

"You'd better." Shawn's look turned serious, and Logan shifted uncomfortably. Smart-ass, he could do. Real emotions were another thing altogether.

He took a few steps back, was totally unprepared for Shawn to follow him and grab him in a huge bear hug. Of all the dragons, Shawn was usually the least demonstrative—and that was saying something, as most of the male Dragonstars viewed showing emotion right up there with getting a root canal without anesthetic. They didn't mind putting their anger on display, but anything else was pretty much off-limits.

"Don't get dead." Shawn's voice was low and fierce. "I'm going to be really pissed off if I have to waste time building your funeral pyre."

"I'll do my best."

Shawn pulled back, punched him in the chest. "You'd better do more than try." He took a few steps back, putting distance—physical and emotional—between them. Then glanced very deliberately up at the sky, where rain was rolling in from the east. "If you're going to go, you'd better get started. That storm promises to be a real bitch."

"You calling me a pussy?" It was Logan's turn to shove him, desperate to put things back on an even keel. Back to how they'd been before he'd undertaken this nightmarish mission. "You think I can't take a little rain?"

"I was more concerned about the lightning, but whatever. You get down with your bad self."

He grinned and looked at the sky. "Don't you mean up?"

Shawn groaned at the terrible pun. "Whatever. But I mean it. Take care of yourself.

"I plan on it." The lie tripped easily off his tongue.

"Yeah, right." Shawn's look was sardonic, as if he knew exactly what Logan was thinking despite his lack of psychic ability. Despite his disbelief—or maybe because of it—he muttered, "May your life flow like the sands in the desert, infinite and unending. May you be as strong and untamable as fire, as cunning and as sly as the beast that resides inside you. And may you return to us, your flame forever undimmed."

The formal words of the Dragonstar blessing slipped inside Logan, twisted up his insides when he'd been so sure that he was relaxed and ready for whatever came. "Shawn, I—"

His friend just shook his head. "Bye, Logan." And then he was gone, flashing out between one breath and the next.

And Logan was alone, just him and the beast inside of him. *I'm used to it,* he told himself. *Prepared for it.* It was how he'd lived for nearly three centuries of his existence, how he would remain for the indefinite future. Why, then, did it feel so fucking lonely this time around?

Refusing to dwell on it—or anything that didn't have to do with the mission he needed to accomplish—he stripped down.

Shoved his clothes and shoes in the backpack he'd packed early that morning.

Began to shift, relishing in the dark pain that swept through him as his beast took over.

Long, curved nails burst out the ends of fingers and toes already elongating and curling into talons.

Bones broke and reformed in a combination of agony and ecstasy that took his breath away every time.

His skin changed, thickened, turned red and scaly and cool, while his vision took on the incredible acuity of the dragon.

Long, sharp spines poked up along his own spine, while huge wings broke through the skin and muscles of his upper back.

The beast roared, screaming in euphoria as Logan released the last of the hold he had on the creature. He felt the change deep inside himself—not just the physical one, but the mental one, as well. The usually sharp, omnipotent control of the human was gone, and in its place were the all-consuming instincts of the dragon.

Pride in the animalistic power sweeping through every cell in his body.

Joy in being fierce and free and strong.

A need to meet this newest Wyvernmoon threat head on, to rip apart the ones responsible limb by limb. To hell with secrecy and caution.

In the back of his head, the human within warned of following plans and being careful. The dragon roared back an impatient response before launching itself into the sky with one powerful thrust of its legs. Then it began to fly due north, straight toward a destiny that would be Logan's absolute downfall or his clan's eventual salvation.

As he flew, he prayed with everything inside of him that it was the latter. He owed that much to the Dragonstars, and even more to Dylan.

CHAPTER TWO

"Excuse me, Your Highness. You cannot go in there."

Though every ounce of training she'd been given held with the rightness of those words, Cecily Fournier forced herself to ignore them. After all, she'd known someone was going to try to stop her. She just hadn't figured it would be a maître d' who looked more like a stressed-out penguin than he ever would a dragon. *Ah, well. Live and learn,* she figured. But she didn't allow her stride to falter, not even when the small man hurried to get in front of her and then attempted to bar her path.

"This is a gentleman's club," the little twit said in a French accent that was as pretentious as his hairstyle—and as fake. She'd known Antoine since he was a child, had gone to school with him. Knew he'd been born here in South Dakota half a century ago, the same as she had. But none of those ties—nor the fact that she was the only living member of the Wyvernmoon royal family—kept him from throwing his arms wide in an attempt to ensure that she didn't try to scoot around him.

She finally stopped walking, but only to avoid running into him. She didn't like touching people any more than she had to.

He sighed in obvious relief, but she had no intention of letting him off the hook that easily.

"I know exactly what this place is, Antoine," she told him in her haughtiest tone. It wasn't one she employed often, as it was about a

million times too snooty for her, but she hadn't been raised by Silus
Fournier for nothing. Observing her father's interaction with his subjects had taught her very early on how to put someone who needed it in
his place.

Antoine flushed with embarrassment at the obvious disgust in her
tone, but, for once, she couldn't bring herself to feel bad about humiliating someone. She was too annoyed that he'd felt the need to remind
her what the Dracon Club was. Like she was some imbecilic twit who
had come down from her ivory tower for a spot of tea.

What an idiot. But he was an idiot who was slowing her down—
something she couldn't afford. With each second that passed, her already
less-than-steady resolve only got shakier. She stepped to the side, but he
followed her, refusing to get out of her way.

Anger welled up inside her. Could he possibly believe her decision
to breach these hallowed halls had been made lightly? That she hadn't
spent the better part of a week agonizing over what she knew she had
to do? Could he actually believe that she *wanted* to be here?

If so, he couldn't be more mistaken. Her father had come here every
day of his long, 605-year life to deal with his *Conseil*, his council, and the
business of running a clan. Her brother, Jacob, had done the same from
the time he'd reached adulthood. While she, on the other hand, had
been barred from its doors every day of her forty-seven-year existence.

But, then, she was still a baby by dragon standards, only a few
years beyond her adolescence. Jacob had tried to tell her that things
would change when she got older, more mature, and she hadn't bothered arguing with him. It hadn't been worth it, not when she'd known
the truth all along.

Yes, most of the business of running the clan happened in here.
But she was a *woman*. A princess, yes, but still just a woman in her
father's eyes. She didn't need to know anything about how the clan was
run because she would never have control of it.

Of course, that had been before her father and his son died within days of each other, leaving her the only living member of the royal family. And though clan law and thousands of years of tradition clearly stated that she would never be able to rule the clan, she was here to change that. Not because she wanted to. Not because she was power hungry. But because she had no other choice.

The months between her family members' funerals and the present had been rife with the kind of infighting and posturing and power struggles that, if left unchecked, could very easily bring the Wyvernmoons to their knees. That was the last thing her father would have wanted after his years of hard work, and she was determined to ensure that it didn't happen. The strong dragons might be able to survive on their own, but what about the submissives? Or the civilian dragons who'd never had to learn to fight? What would happen to them if the clan's power structure fell down around all of them?

She'd kept out of it as long as she could. She had been trained to be seen and not heard, after all. But she couldn't do that anymore, couldn't afford to just sit around and be shut out any more than the clan could afford for her to—not if it wanted to survive another decade.

The thought of the Wyvernmoons' ultimate destruction made her cringe, especially considering just how long her clan had been around. More than three millennia now, and ruled by a member of the Fournier family for every day of those three thousand and some odd years. The idea that all of her ancestors' hard work might have ended with her father made her sick to her stomach—almost as much as it frightened her.

Feeling her shoulders start to sag under the weight of everything before her, Cecily locked them in place. She couldn't afford to show a moment of insecurity—not to Antoine, the mealymouthed maître d', and certainly not to the much more forceful dragons who had been her father's *factionnaires*—his sentries—for much of his rule.

No, her family's rule wasn't going to end with the annihilation of the clan they had sacrificed so much for. She wouldn't let it. *Couldn't* let it. Just as she couldn't let the fact that she knew less than nothing about the day-to-day business of running a clan stand in her way. She was a fast learner when she had to be, and today she would find a way to do what she should have done five months earlier. And she would start with the clan member currently blocking her path.

"Get out of my way, Antoine."

"I'm afraid I can't do that, Your Highness."

"I'm afraid you are going to have to do exactly that. I'm not leaving before I see my *factionnaires*." She very deliberately used the first-person-possessive pronoun. Then waited to see if Antoine was smarter than he looked.

For one long minute, she was convinced that he wasn't. That he was really going to force her to bully her way past him. She'd never used physical violence in her life—and wasn't looking forward to doing so now—but she *was* going to get into the room at the end of the hall. And no one was going to tell her she couldn't.

At the last second, though, the maître d' stepped aside, and Cecily was left facing a long, empty hallway. Now that the impediment to her path had disappeared and there was nothing barring her way, she couldn't ignore the bowling ball weighing down her stomach. For a second, she was desperately afraid she was going to vomit all over the black Aubusson rug she was currently standing on.

She forced the sickness down, took several deep breaths through her mouth as she walked slowly toward the private room at the end of the hall. Each step had become an effort, and she couldn't help feeling like she was going to her execution rather than her first *Conseil* meeting.

And could the hallway get any longer? she wondered distractedly. It stretched before her like the Black Hills she liked to fly over late at night—dark and silent and seemingly infinite, at least now that she was walking down it. She started to turn back more than once, but she knew if she did, she'd never again be able to look herself—or any of her clan members—in the eye again.

She prayed she was going in the right direction. She wasn't sure she could work up the courage to do this again if it turned out she'd chosen the wrong hall to walk down.

She didn't think she had, though. While she'd never been inside the Dracon Club before, Jacob had told her enough about it when they were children that she had a pretty good idea of the layout. The dining room was in the front of the club, with several small, private rooms off each side of it, while her father's meeting room—Throne Room, really—was all the way at the back.

She paused when she got to it, spent long moments doing nothing more than staring at the huge, carved mahogany doors that barred access to the most exclusive place on the Wyvernmoon compound. How many pictures had she seen of her father standing in front of these doors? How many times had she wondered what was behind them? The fact that she was about to find out . . . it sent chills down her spine, and not in a good way. She might be inexperienced, but she was smart enough to know that she was in for the battle of her life—today, now, and in the weeks and months to come.

The deep breathing she'd started on her walk down the hallway hadn't worked. But, then, she hadn't really expected it to. How could she calm down when the arguments against her being here were lined up in her head like soldiers on a bloody field of battle?

She was not supposed to step into the breach.

She didn't know a thing about actually running a clan.

She was well under one hundred years old—little more than a child in the eyes of most of the clan.

She was female in a clan that had always been extremely patriarchal.

She had no business even thinking of trying to hold on to the throne. That right belonged to the husband she had yet to choose.

The confidence she'd spent most of the day working up deserted her, and yet again, Cecily contemplated turning around and going back to her father's house. It would be so much easier. Wiser, even. Or at least that's what most people would say.

But they would be wrong. How wise was it, really, to sit back and watch her entire clan—three millennia of work and compromise and survival—just fall apart around her? How wise was it to stand by and watch as the *Conseil* destroyed itself?

No. Despite what everyone would say, she had to do this. Had to interfere, and to hell with whether it was her place. She was the last surviving member of the Fournier line, and though women couldn't rule in her clan, she figured all those days and years and decades of observing her father had to count for something.

I can get them through this, she told herself as she closed her eyes. *I have to.*

It was her duty. And more, it was her right. She'd spent almost her entire life being used as a pawn by her father—being dangled like a prize in front of the men he wanted to do his bidding. Was it any wonder his *factionnaires* had continued treating her the same way after his death?

It was her fault that she'd let them, but all that stopped here and now. It was time she stepped out of her sheltered existence and figured out how to be not just a princess, but the queen her clan so desperately needed.

She reached for the huge doorknob before she could change her mind.

Twisted it and pushed the door open halfway.

Then slipped silently inside, hoping to have a few minutes to observe the proceedings before drawing attention to herself.

She should have known better. Dragons had keen senses, even in their human forms, and the second the door opened every man in the room turned to stare at her. Within seconds, she was nearly drowning in the weight of the disapproval rolling in waves off most of the room's occupants.

The heaviness in her stomach got even worse, but she refused to acknowledge it. Just as she refused to let her hands clench in nervousness or her eyes to drop in submission. She might not be able to ascend to the throne, damn it, but she *was* a princess of the royal family. No one could take that away from her.

"Cecily? What are you doing here? Is something wrong?" Julian, a dragon shifter who was one of the highest-ranking *Conseil* members left, and who had been in the front of the room speaking when she walked in, headed down the aisle toward her, a frown on his too-handsome, too-boyish face.

She tried not to be offended by the fact that he had called her by her given name and not her title, as her father had always insisted that the *factionnaires* do, but she couldn't help it. The look on his face said the slipup had not been an accident. Not that she was surprised—as one of the main dragons jockeying for the position of Wyvernmoon king, it was only natural that he try to claim an intimacy in their relationship that just wasn't there.

Still, it irritated her, and when he reached to cup her elbow, she very deliberately turned away. From the way his mouth tightened, she knew he had caught the slight—and was aware that the others had, as well.

"I'm fine, Julian. Thank you for asking." Again she surveyed the room, made sure she let her gaze fall on every man in the hugely ornate space. These were her father's *factionnaires*, after all, his *sentinels*. Which meant, for all intents and purposes, that they were hers, as well. She was here to lay claim to them, and that was exactly what she would do.

Better late than never.

Acel and Remy, two of the oldest clan members, sat rigidly on a pair of uncomfortable-looking chairs positioned in the front of the room. Though both were pushing six hundred, they still looked like young men—as long as you didn't spend too much time staring into their eyes. If you did, you could see every one of their years—and every one of their prejudices—reflected there. She had always figured their attitudes, like her father's, came from being born in a totally different age. But right now she couldn't afford to care about what had shaped them, only that neither was happy she had crashed their little party.

Too bad for them, because she wasn't going anywhere until she'd had her say.

Dashiell, Dax and Wyatt, on the other hand, looked almost pleased to see her. Three of her favorite *factionnaires*, each was lounging indolently on a huge sofa in the back of the room. When she looked at them, they smiled, especially Dash, who gave her a subtle thumbs-up.

She felt the tightness in her stomach begin to relax just a little bit. It was nice to know that someone was in her corner—or three someones, for that matter. It made what she had come here to do just a little bit easier.

Of course, that was before she got a look at Luc, Garen, Eriq and Blaze, all of whom looked like they had swallowed something particularly distasteful. Too bad for them. If they thought her presence here was distasteful, she couldn't wait to see their reaction to her words.

Even Thierren, her oldest friend, seated in the center of the room, wasn't looking particularly welcoming.

"Hello, gentlemen," she said, forcing a smile she was far from feeling. "It's so nice to see all of you again."

"As always, it's nice to see you, as well, Cecily," Julian replied smoothly. "Although I must admit to being a little surprised by your choice of venue. The Dracon Club is not really the place for the likes of you."

She raised one brow and gave him the most regal look in her repertoire. "The likes of me? You mean, royalty?"

Wyatt laughed, and she glanced at him out of the corner of her eye. He caught the look and winked at her, despite the disapproving frown on Julian's lips. Her stomach relaxed even more.

"Of course," Julian lied smoothly. "With your heightened stature, I'm not certain that you belong here. The only women to ever enter this club before have been . . ." He let his voice trail off, then smiled insultingly at her. "Well, let's just say they serve a purpose quite different from your own."

Her dragon roared and thrashed inside her, and Cecily had to bite her tongue to keep from lashing out at him. She carefully considered her next words. How was it that her father's golden boy had just plainly said that she *wasn't* a prostitute, and yet she felt a lot more insulted than she would have if he had actually called her one?

Perhaps it was the smarmy look on his face. Or the fact that, no matter how hard he tried to ingratiate himself, she always got the distinct impression that he found her lacking. As a member of the royal family and as a woman. And this was the man her father had wanted her to marry.

She felt the old, familiar stirrings start to undermine her confidence. God knew her father had pointed out her failings to her more times than she could count—usually whenever she opened her mouth to voice an opinion that didn't agree with his. And she might despise Julian, but there was no doubt in her mind that he knew more about what was going on with the Wyvernmoons than she ever would.

"I hope you don't mind me asking, Cecily darling, but is there a purpose to your visit? Or did you just stop by to say hello? I know I've been remiss in my attentions lately, but there've been a number of things here that required my input of late. I was certain that you'd understand."

There it was again—the implication that their relationship was more than it had ever been. She saw Dashiell and Garen stiffen, saw Dax shoot a speculative look between Julian and her. Many of the others had varying looks of disappointment on their faces, as if they believed completely that she and Julian were involved in some kind of relationship.

She looked at him, at his too-cold smile and the leer of triumph he didn't even try to hide, and knew that she was going to have to tread softly. She was the interloper here, the one who definitely didn't belong. And if she hoped to make any progress at all, she would need his cooperation to do it. Antagonizing him was a bad idea. This time, when he moved to cup her elbow, she let him.

Swallowing the bile that rose in her throat, she smiled at him.

Opened her mouth and began to give her prepared speech. The one she had practiced for hours in front of the mirror in her bedroom. The one she had painstakingly crafted over the past three days to ensure that she didn't overstep her boundaries or unduly offend anyone.

But she couldn't get the words out. They might have been political and smart and savvy, but they weren't what the clan needed right now. They weren't what her father's *Conseil*—her *Conseil,* damnit—needed right now.

And they sure as hell weren't what her relationship with Julian needed right now.

Which was why when she saw Gage leaning indolently against the wall, she knew she wasn't going to give her speech. The much-older dragon was the only one in the room besides Julian who didn't look concerned. Of course, he was the one here who knew her best. He was the one who had taught her to fly, the one who had helped her learn to shift, the one who, for all intents and purposes, had been the older brother to her that Jacob had rarely wanted to be.

She knew Gage was unhappy with the way things were going in the clan—with the unprecedented raids on the Dragonstars and Shadowdrakes, the infighting and jockeying for position amid the clan's strongest dragons, the overall lack of leadership. He'd been by the house often enough in the past few months with dire reports of how the *Conseil* was falling apart. As she met his cool, black eyes across the room, she found herself swallowing the rehearsed phrases and saying the only words that really mattered.

"We can't go on this way." She paused, waited until she was certain every eye in the room was on her. "We can't keep fighting battles on every front—not if we have any hope of remaining a strong, united clan. All of the pettiness, all of the positioning, is doing nothing but destroying us, and it has to stop. It *will* stop, from this moment forward."

Julian started to speak, to ridicule her in his soft, it's-for-your-own-good tone, but she cut him off. The floor was hers now, and she would not yield it until she had said what she'd come here to say. "There are things I don't know about this *Conseil*, about this clan. A lot of things, as you all well know. That, too, has to stop. I may not be queen yet, but I will be someday, and I will not be just a figurehead like all those queens who have come before me. The time for that is gone."

A low murmuring started in the front of the room, but she ignored it. She had bigger things to worry about. Like the fact that Julian appeared on the edge of a furious outburst.

"I know that you are all waiting for me to choose someone to marry, someone to make the next king. That is what much of this infighting is about. But that, too, has to stop.

"Yes, it is my duty to marry. And yes, I will fulfill that duty. But I will do it on my timetable, and I will choose the man that I want." Every man in the room straightened, looked a little more alert—except Thierren, who was leaning against the wall, arms and legs crossed in front of him. His eyes were inscrutable, and she found herself wishing very much to know what he was thinking.

They had been friends for decades and there was no one in the room whose opinion she valued more, save Gage's. More important, he was one of only two dragons in the room whom she truly believed had no desire to rule.

"But I don't plan to marry for a long time. That does not, however, mean that I do not have a say in how this clan is run, in what we do, and how we do it. I am the last living Fournier heir, and I will not stand by and watch us fall apart. The more we fight, the more we end up hurting the clan."

She gestured to the lot of them. "Look at yourselves. Look at what you're doing to the *Conseil*. At this time, when we should be most united, we are desperately divided, and it is getting worse every day.

"Part of it is my fault. I take full responsibility for it. As things have gotten worse, I have done what everyone has always expected of me: absolutely nothing. I have stayed in my father's house and watched as you fought each other for the right to be king. As you led war parties on the Dragonstars and the Shadowdrakes, war parties that seem to have no purpose other than to distinguish you as leaders. War parties that have failed abysmally, and have done nothing but weaken our clan when we can least afford it.

"All of that stops here. All of that stops now. I have been to too many funerals in the past five months. I have watched too many of my clan mates burn. Enough is enough."

She paused, took a deep breath and gave her words time to register as she looked straight in the eyes of every single man in the room. Etienne and Luc both looked like they were going to have a stroke, their black eyes blazing with a fiery hatred neither even attempted to hide. Acel, Remy, Eriq, Nicolas and Blaze didn't look like they were faring much better. But the others—Thierren, Dashiell, Dax, Gage and Garen— all looked surprisingly calm. And Wyatt looked downright gleeful. But, then, he'd always been the thorn in her father's side, his inability to take anything seriously nearly getting him removed from the *Conseil* more times than any of them could keep track of through the years. He was probably reveling in the thought of total and complete anarchy.

As for Julian, his face was such a bright pink that she couldn't help wondering if a stroke was imminent. She should probably feel worse about that prospect—after all, he had been her father's favorite for centuries—but she couldn't bring herself to care. Getting him out of the way would make things run that much more smoothly.

Besides, it felt good to know she wasn't as alone as she'd feared when walking in here a few minutes before. But, then again, the fact that the *Conseil* had not condemned her out of hand didn't mean that they supported her, either. While many of them enjoyed watching her pull Julian's tail, she had no idea how many of them would actually back her when push came to shove. It would take a lot of work on her part to win them over.

She couldn't let them know that she cared about their opinions, however, not now when she really couldn't afford to care one way or the other. If she even looked like she was backing down now, any clout she had would disappear and her clan would suffer. That was the last thing her people needed, the last thing she would allow to happen. They had already suffered more than enough.

She cleared her throat, made sure her voice was as firm and irrevocable as her will when she started to speak again. "From this day forward, you are *my Conseil* and you will do *my* bidding. I may not be queen yet, but make no mistake, from this day forward, I *am* in charge. There will be no king until I say so, and if you think I'm going to choose my husband from a group that is acting like spoiled little boys, then you all have another thing coming. I will be back in the morning, and we will get to work fixing the mess you all have made."

Head held high, spine ramrod straight, she turned and made a beeline for the door. She may not have ever had the chance to rule while her father was alive, but she'd learned something from him. And that was how to make an entrance—and an exit.

Voices exploded behind her in a mixture of English and French, and she fought down the smile that very much wanted to bloom across her face for the first time since she'd set her course that morning.

Oh yes, she had given them something to think about. The next move was theirs, no doubt about it. But if they weren't careful, they would find that she wasn't above wresting control away from them— any way she had to.

CHAPTER THREE

As she swept through the club and into the street, Cecily was hyperaware that half of the men in her father's *Conseil* were following her and the other half were cursing her heavily, even as they refused to join the others. She didn't let anyone's reaction bother her, however, even when she realized Julian was one of the shifters hot on her heels.

Not letting their reactions bother her wasn't the same as being stupid, though. And since Julian was only a step or two behind her, she knew if she didn't hustle, he was going to catch her. *Not that I'm afraid of him,* she assured herself. Because she wasn't. She had just proved that she could hold her own against him or any of the others.

But at the same time, she'd pretty much used up her quota of courage for the day. Maybe even the whole week. She'd need to get some back, and quickly, but she just didn't have anything else left in her today. The idea of another confrontation left her shaky—especially one with Julian, in front of all the other *factionnaires.*

Still, she didn't shrink when his hand closed around her elbow. Instead, she stopped and looked down at where his talons had punched through his fingertips. His nails were digging into her skin, drawing blood, but she'd be damned if she let him know how much it hurt. In the game they were playing, whoever flinched first lost. And she so was not going to spend the next five hundred years bowing and scraping to Julian. She would rather be dead.

"You're going to want to get your hand off me," she said in the most frigid voice she could muster.

"And you're going to want to be very careful about whom you challenge in public," he answered, leaning in so close that his lips were just a hairsbreadth from her ear. To the casual eye, it looked like a lover's embrace, and though dragons had incredible hearing, he was being very careful to keep his voice pitched so low that even she had to strain to hear him.

"You may think you're ready to play with the big boys, *ma chérie*, but you're still just a spoiled little girl at heart." He reached into his pocket and pulled out some money, then forced her clenched fingers open enough to take the thick wad of bills. "Why don't you go buy something pretty and leave the real work for those of us who know more than which fork we're supposed to use at dinner?"

His words hit far too close to home, and it was only the years of experience with her father's cruelty that allowed her to keep her face serene as she scrambled for an answer that would not make her sound weak.

Nothing brilliant came to her, so she had to settle for mildness. "Yes, well, I figure I'm a step above you, as from what I've observed of your table manners, you don't even know that much."

Julian's face flushed and his fingers tightened on her elbow until the talons pierced almost to the bone. At the same time, he angled his body so that none of the men watching from the front of the club could see the blood that had started to drip down her arm. "You need to be very careful, Cecily. People who cross me once don't normally get a second chance. I'm being more generous with you because I respected your father and because I believe we could be very good for each other. But don't mistake my generosity for weakness. I will not tolerate another display like the one you just put on."

Her heart was beating uncomfortably fast, and the pain of his attack was getting to her. But she absolutely refused to back down—not now, not in front of the others and definitely not to him. Besides, her beast wouldn't allow it. The dragon was snapping and scratching at her insides, desperate to get out and go for Julian's throat.

She controlled it but just barely. It helped that instead of bowing her head in the sign of submission he and the others were so obviously waiting for, she simply smiled sweetly and said, "I'm sorry you feel you have the right to tell me anything, let alone threaten me. I'm going to assume you've forgotten who you're talking to."

"I haven't forgotten anything," he all but snarled.

"Really? Well, that's a shame, then, because it means you really are as stupid as you look." He had clamped his second hand around her fist, keeping her fingers closed and the money in place. Through sheer strength of will, she uncurled her fingers. As she did, she let her own talons scrape against his palm where it squeezed hers.

Julian's eyes widened, and she continued. "You'll do well to remember that you aren't the only powerful dragon in this clan. Just because I've been content to sit back and let the *Conseil* muck around for the past five months doesn't mean that I am weak."

She let the money flutter to the ground, then watched as the early autumn wind caught it and blew it away. "Perhaps it's time I remind you of just how strong I am."

With that, she wrenched her arm out of his grip, ignoring the tearing she felt. Knowing he wouldn't let her go easily—and knowing that a show of strength from her was more necessary now that she stood there bleeding than it had ever been before—she started to change.

There were at least twenty pairs of eyes on her—twenty pairs of male eyes, at that—so she didn't bother to strip. While nudity was fairly common in the shifter world, by necessity, the absolute last thing she wanted at that moment was for Julian and the rest of the *Conseil* to get an eyeful of her bleeding, naked human form. The last thing she wanted to do was to flaunt the fact that she was female.

So instead, she let the clothes simply rip away as she shifted. Normally it took even the most accomplished shifters at least a few minutes to go from human to dragon or back again, but that had never been a problem for her. From the time she had first learned to change, she had been able to do it quickly. Like, a-few-seconds quickly. Like, blink-of-an-eye quickly.

It was not a talent she had ever bragged about—or one she'd let anyone but Gage ever see—but it was a talent she now used ruthlessly to her advantage.

Throwing every ounce of power she had behind the change, she grew talons and a tail.

Her skin turned purple and became thick and scaly.

Her head grew, her nose and mouth elongating.

Her belly turned hard as her legs and arms grew in length and width.

Her clothes split at the seams, fell to the ground in a forgotten heap.

The entire transformation took less than fifteen seconds, and though the pain of it lashed through her like hellfire, she ignored it. Pain was a small price to pay for the freedom to be a dragon so quickly. Conscious of the men getting closer, their murmurs louder, she launched herself straight up into the sky. It was another show of dominance and power, as most dragons, including her father's *factionnaires*, required a running start to fly.

And then she was soaring through the skies, leaving the ugly meeting and the condemnation of her father's *Conseil* far behind. At least for a little while. She knew running wasn't the answer—it couldn't be—but right then she felt so uncivilized, so raw, that the only help for it was hanging in her dragon's skin for a while. Somehow the beast always helped her put things in perspective. Not to mention the fact that it was about a million times braver than she was, and after spending the last few minutes going head-to-head with Julian, she could use the comfort.

She drew from that strength now, gave her beast its turn to spin and flip and somersault through the air. She cloaked herself, making herself invisible, as all dragons could, while she zoomed above the Black Hills that had made South Dakota so famous.

Her dragon shuddered in delight, exulting in the freedom to flex its talons and exercise its wings. Before today, it had been far too long since she'd let herself shift, far too long since she'd given herself permission to do anything else but be the sweet, dutiful, and *useless* princess she had been raised to be.

It felt good to shake off that persona. Really good. And as she spiraled lower, she reveled in her ability to be—even for a little while—the woman she had always wished to be. Flying low, she sped across the pine-covered mountains, soaking in the delightful smell and feel of the place she had called home for her entire life.

The air rushed by her face, and she sucked it inside her, tasted it— and the liberty that came with its freshness—with a joy she had no desire to deny or hide. Not here and not now.

But even as her beast delighted in the magnificence of the ride, she knew deep inside that her headlong flight couldn't last. She had things to do, responsibilities back at home. And while part of her longed for nothing more than to fly away from the oppressive life she'd always led, another part of her, the part that had been raised royal, understood that she would never have that option. Now that her father and brother were dead, the Wyvernmoons were her people, her responsibility. And no matter how fractious they were, she couldn't leave them to fend for themselves, especially under Julian's obnoxious, perilous and self-serving leadership.

It killed her that her father had really wanted her to marry that man. Julian was dark and dangerous, and while neither of those things bothered her particularly—show her a dragon who wasn't—he also had a mean streak a mile wide. And that she just couldn't tolerate.

She didn't think her father had ever seen it, though. Julian only messed with people he considered weaker than himself. Besides, she wasn't sure Silus would have cared even if he had been aware of Julian's proclivities. It wasn't like her father had been known for his kind heart and pleasant personality.

A spurt of guilt assailed her at the thought, ruining the last bit of pleasure she'd been taking in her flight. Her father was dead, murdered by the new Dragonstar queen, and Cecily had never been one to talk ill of the dead. At the same time, though, she'd never been a hypocrite. While she had loved her father very much, she hadn't been blind to his faults. Silus had been arrogant in the extreme, diabolical and, more often than not, amoral.

But he'd still been her father. And, for the most part, he'd been a hell of a king to the Wyvernmoons. She might not have agreed with everything he'd done or every decision he had made, but that didn't mean he hadn't had the clan's best interests at heart through it all. He had just gone about it differently than she would have.

Not that anyone had ever asked her. Then again, why would they? She might be a member of the royal family, but she was also a woman and in some ways—many ways—the Wyvernmoons were a clan stuck hundreds of years in the past.

It was why her father had wanted her to marry Julian, after all. Or at least one of the reasons. Julian's family had provided *factionnaires* and *Conseil* members for the royal family for millennia. They were one of the richest, most powerful families in the clan, and they were probably the only family with strong enough magic to wrest the throne away from the Fourniers by force, if they put their minds to it. Oh, it had been a long time since they'd tried—at least four or five hundred years—but her father had had a long memory. And while he ruled with an iron fist, in the years before his death, his sovereignty had been called into question more than once. The last thing he'd wanted was a challenge from Julian's family, so in exchange for their loyalty, he had promised her to Julian.

It had nearly killed her when she'd found out what he'd done, and for the first time in her life, she'd contemplated leaving the compound. Leaving the clan. Her whole life, she had longed to be useful, longed to have some sort of responsibility, the way Jacob had. To have some sort of role to play that would help her clan in a meaningful way.

But when she'd been confronted with what her role was to be—marriage to a man she despised—she'd balked. Hugely. Had refused to even consider it. Her father had been furious, and she'd felt the considerable force of his wrath. She hated that her father was dead; hated more that he had died while they'd been completely at odds. The fact that she'd never have a chance to make things up with him haunted her.

Shuddering at the hard truth, Cecily dropped lower and lower until her feet were on the ground. She winced when her sore front leg touched down, annoyed that Julian had managed to injure her arm so severely that a shift to dragon had not alleviated the wound.

How could he possibly think that bullying me is going to get him what he wants? she wondered furiously as she tested the leg's ability to bear weight. All he'd done was piss her off to the point that she could barely see straight. But, then again, Julian had watched her interact with her father for half a century, knew that intimidation was Silus's favorite weapon to wield against her. What he hadn't understood was that just because she'd bowed to her father didn't mean she would ever do it for another man, and certainly not one as horrific as Julian was turning out to be.

Cecily shifted back to human form so she could get a better look at the damage done to her elbow. What she saw made her curse. The bleeding had stopped, thanks to her first shift, but the skin was pretty torn up—as was the muscle beneath it. Though she healed quickly, she figured it would be a day or two before the arm was back to normal, especially if she didn't get to Simone, the Wyvernmoon healer.

She knew that was exactly what she should do—head back to the compound and let Simone look at her arm. But she wasn't ready to go back there yet, didn't want word of how Julian had savaged her to get around the clan. That she'd let him do it would be just one more strike against her.

Confused, annoyed and in pain, she headed across the clearing for her favorite tree. This spot atop the highest of the Black Hills was *her* spot, and she'd been coming here for years to think or just to escape the darkness of her father's house. In the past few years, she'd come so often that she'd hidden a secret stash of clothes inside one of the trees.

It made things easier for her, especially now, when the last thing she wanted to do was land naked in the middle of the Wyvernmoon compound. She didn't think anyone would harm her, but without a father and a brother, the protection of her station extended only so far, especially with the higher-ranked families in the clan. She hated it, hated that she no longer felt safe in the only home she had ever known, but she knew she wouldn't be able to change it. At least not until she had amassed enough power as queen that they would be afraid to take her on, or until she finally decided on a husband.

The fact that she was now considering getting married only made her regret harder to bear. *And yet it might be worth it,* she thought for the first time. Might be worth it still to accede to her father's wishes, though everything inside of her rebelled at the thought. Ambition was too rampant among the dragons, and letting them continue to compete for the title basically meant declaring open season, and she couldn't do that. Wouldn't do that. Most everyone knew of her father's plans to marry her off to Julian, though. If she chose him, if she married him, the infighting would stop. Julian was one of the strongest dragons in the clan, no doubt about it. If she elevated him to royalty, the clan might finally have a chance to heal, even as it doomed her to life with a sadistic asshole.

But isn't that the price of royalty? she mused. The price for all the riches and respect and perks that came with being a member of the ruling family? The absolute determination to do what was right for your people, despite the personal cost. And in this case, the personal cost would be almost unbearable. She had no doubt that marriage to Julian would leave her broken, no matter how hard she fought to stay whole.

Absently, she reached into the knotty hole in the huge spruce tree where she always kept a change of clothes in a waterproof backpack. Her hand met nothing but air. Frowning, she reached for a branch and hoisted herself up so she could peer inside the opening, in case she had somehow shoved the bag farther back than usual the last time.

But no, there was nothing there. She glanced around at the landscape, made sure she had the right tree. She did. So where the hell was her backpack?

She shoved her hand deeper into the tree. Had one of the animals run off with it? The idea seemed more than strange. What would a squirrel or even a bobcat want with her old backpack? But she had a hard time coming up with another alternative. She was high enough in the Black Hills that few tourists ever came here, and she'd made sure to hide the backpack far enough off the ground that the few who did wander this way would never find it.

The other Wyvernmoons didn't come up here, either. They much preferred the caves and caverns down below to the heavy woods up here. All the trees hemmed them in, made it difficult for them to stretch their wings or fly, as most of them couldn't take off or land without room to speed up or slow down.

Frustrated, she continued feeling around in the hole, certain that she must simply be missing her bag. Her next hidey-hole was nearly two hundred miles away, and while that was only an hour and a half by flight, she was tired and cold and more than a little grumpy. Not to mention the fact that her arm hurt.

Damn it! Where were her clothes? Could nothing, absolutely nothing, go right today?

"Are you looking for these?"

At the words, spoken in a deep and darkly amused voice, Cecily whirled around. Only quick thinking and her dragon reflexes kept her from tumbling out of the tree and landing on her very naked ass at the speaker's feet.

Why the hell hadn't she thought to scan? It was the first rule of safety, and she'd completely ignored it.

In the middle of berating herself, it took her a second to realize that he'd made no move toward her. Raising her eyes to look at him for the first time, she found him halfway across the clearing, watching and waiting for her to get her bearings.

Too bad that might take a while, as her first glimpse of him had her brain freezing and her mouth nearly hanging open. Dressed only in worn, faded jeans and a pair of tan work boots, the man standing in front of her just might have been the most beautiful creature she had ever laid eyes on. Not to mention the largest. And seeing as she'd spent her entire life around dragon shifters, that was saying something.

A quick sniff of the air—about five minutes too late—told her he was dragon, too, though unlike any dragon she had seen before. She'd always considered the men in her clan pretty tall at a little over six feet, but this man made even the Wyvernmoon *factionnaires* look like malnourished children. A quick measurement of his eye level with the branch she was currently sitting on told her he was at least six-and-a-half feet tall, though another look down at the ground told her he might be even taller.

And he wasn't just tall—he was broad, as well. His shoulders were so wide that they actually spanned the distance between the two trees he was currently standing in the middle of. It was a distance that would have fit her three times over, and she'd never considered herself small.

The fact that he was so big should probably have intimidated her—would probably intimidate her once she got past her utter amazement at his size. Not to mention his good looks. No two ways about it, the man was gorgeous, with very short, dark blond hair and long-lashed, whiskey-colored eyes. He had a strong jaw with just a little bit of stubble on it, bronze skin and a series of complicated-looking black tribal tattoos covering most of the left side of his body.

For a second, she had a vision of running her lips over those tattoos. Of letting her tongue linger on the warm, tanned skin between the thick black lines. The vision was so real—as was the answering response in her body—that it had her snapping out "Who are you?" before she had thought better of it.

"The dragon who currently has possession of what I'm guessing are your clothes," he said with a grin that changed his face from a work of art into a study in mischievousness. But when he shifted, turned, she saw that the entire right side of his face was marred with a long, angry-looking scar.

She knew she should look away; he was probably self-conscious of the injury. But she couldn't do it. Yes, it was ugly, but somehow that only emphasized the incredible beauty of the rest of his face.

He didn't flinch from her examination of him, just stared at her with those odd-colored eyes. As he did, her breath caught in her throat and she felt a strange tingling along her nerve endings, one that made it almost impossible for her to sit still.

Out of self-preservation, she forced herself to look away from him. Immediately his words sank in. They were easier to understand when she wasn't blinded by his insanely good looks, and for the first time, she noticed the dark green backpack dangling from his fingers.

Outrage filled her. "Hey! Give that to me!"

"Why should I?"

"Because it's mine!" she said. "You said so yourself."

"Are you sure? Because from where I'm standing, things look a little different. Possession is nine-tenths of the law, after all."

"You can't be serious," she said with a quick roll of her eyes. "What would you do with them, anyway? It's not like my clothes will fit you."

"Maybe not. But it turns out I'm particularly fond of the blue lace bra and panty set in the front pocket. If you want it back, I'm afraid it's going to cost you."

His smile grew even wider, and the weird tingling spread through her entire body. She knew it was stupid to be so overwhelmed by his sheer physical beauty, especially considering the fact that he was doing his best to torment her, but she couldn't help herself. There was something about this strange, unfamiliar dragon that got deep inside her— even when she was beyond annoyed that he'd pawed through her stuff.

Still, if she was honest, it wasn't like she could really blame him for it. If she'd found a strange backpack in a tree in the middle of nowhere, she would have opened the thing up, too. She wouldn't hold it for hostage, as he seemed hell-bent on doing, but she definitely would have checked it out.

Still, it wouldn't pay to let him know how much leeway she was willing to give him on the subject. Feigning boredom, she finally told him, "Never mind. It's not like I need it, anyway."

He shrugged. "Well, if that's how you really feel . . ." He slung the backpack over his shoulder and started walking in the opposite direction.

Cecily stared at his retreating back in shock. *He isn't really going to take my clothes,* she assured herself. *Any minute now, he'll stop and hand them to me.* She waited and waited. *Any minute now. Surely—*

"Hey! You can't just disappear with my things!" she shouted after him. His steps didn't so much as falter, though she'd pitched her voice as loud as she could, amazed at how much ground he'd managed to cover in a few seconds with those crazy-long legs of his.

"Come on! I need my clothes. Please."

He paused then and feigned surprise, but those damn amber eyes of his all but shouted *Gotcha!* when he turned back to look at her. The bastard. "I thought you said you *didn't* need them."

She narrowed her eyes at him. "Are you always this perverse?"

"You call this perverse?" he said with a laugh. "Darlin', I haven't even gotten warmed up."

"Well, before you get too hot and spontaneously combust, could you please toss me the stupid backpack? It's not fireproof."

He tilted his head as he considered. "I could toss it to you. But I don't think I'm going to."

At his cocky grin, she lost the battle to hold on to her patience. "You're a real jerk. You know that?"

"I am, but I'll tell you what. Since the clothes mean so much to you, I'll make you a deal. You come over here and get the backpack, and I'll let you have it." The look in his eyes said he didn't believe for one second that she was going to leave her perch on the branch, where she was safely covered by a strategic arrangement of leaves.

Never one to resist a challenge, Cecily was scrambling down the tree before she could think better of it, and headed straight for him with her hand outstretched. Maybe it was stupid to let him goad her into it, but she'd had about enough of his attitude. It was time he figured out that she gave back as good as she got.

It took only a minute for her to cross the distance between them. As she got closer, she realized with a grim sort of delight that he was no longer smiling. He was too busy staring at her naked body. And while she wasn't normally self-conscious of her nude form around anyone but her father's *Conseil*—it was hard to be a shifter and be uncomfortable with nudity—his single-minded regard for her form made her nervous in a way that Julian's disgusting leers never had.

A shiver worked its way up her spine, and as she felt herself start to tremble, she thought briefly about shifting. After all, it was beyond stupid to stand out here, completely vulnerable, in front of this man. She didn't even know who he was, only that he was another dragon. And not one from her clan. She knew every single male member of her clan, at least by sight, and she knew very well that this behemoth was not one of them. What was more, he didn't smell like one of her kind— on a physical or psychic level.

Add in the fact that he hadn't come to the Wyvernmoon compound and introduced himself—as was expected of dragons visiting the area— and she was suddenly more than a little suspicious. Of course, it was kind of late for that, and she wished the thought had occurred to her before she'd dropped out of the tree to parade nude in front of him.

C'est la vie. What was done was done. At this point, she had no choice but to brazen it out.

Showing fear—or anything else—isn't an option, she told herself, even as an unfamiliar heat started in the pit of her stomach and sizzled its way through her blood. Dragons were wild animals, after all . . .

CHAPTER FOUR

Logan watched in appreciation as the woman in the tree headed straight for him. She was completely naked, and while he knew that the gentlemanly thing to do was to hand her the backpack, he couldn't quite bring himself to do it. Not when it meant that she would cover up that delectable body he'd been getting glimpses of ever since he'd realized she was in the tree.

He looked his fill as she got closer, impressed and awed by just how beautiful his little tree dragon was. Curved in all the right places, she was a little rounder than most of the women he knew. Her breasts were full and high and rosy tipped, her thighs soft, her belly just a little curved. But her waist was slender enough for him to span with both hands, and her legs were long and shapely.

As she walked toward him with smooth, gliding strides, his gaze was drawn unerringly to the shadowy area at the apex of her thighs. He did his best not to look—doing so would step over the invisible line of conduct most shifters adhered to with members of the opposite sex— but it was a lot more difficult than it should have been. He found himself wanting to spread her legs, to see if she was as soft and pink there as she was everywhere else. His cock hardened at the thought and at the certainty that she would be.

He was used to the Dragonstar women, who were gorgeous, no

doubt about it. But they were all tall and toned, with muscles nearly as hard as his. This dragon, this woman, looked like something he could sink right into. Like she would make the most comfortable of resting spots.

The thought of stretching out above her and burying his face in the sweet curve of her neck while her long blond hair wrapped itself around them aroused him even more. He wasn't sure why, as that had never been one of his fantasies before. But looking at her, he couldn't get the picture out of his mind. Maybe because he was so deep-down tired. He hadn't realized just how exhausted he was until he'd landed up here the night before and had a few hours free from any and all forms of mental intrusion.

It had been an incredible gift, one he hadn't even known he needed.

God, he was getting tired of his psychic gifts. Even with his ability to block, four centuries was too long to live with other people's thoughts crowding into his head.

Knowing her thoughts wouldn't be a burden, though, he figured, as he dropped the shields he'd slammed into place the second he realized another person had invaded the mountaintop he had begun to think of as his. For the first time in as long as he could remember, he wanted to know what someone else was thinking.

When he wasn't immediately flooded by her feelings and imaginings and desires, he deliberately arrowed his consciousness toward her mind, trying to get inside her head to see what was up. It didn't work. Her shields were rock-solid, impenetrable. At least by his first, relaxed foray. Her mental strength intrigued him, turned him on even more, and suddenly he found himself really wanting to know what was going on inside that brain of hers. He was just about to start digging a little, to launch a more aggressive foray into her brain, when a stray thought slipped through her defenses.

She felt uncomfortable, on display, not nearly as relaxed with her nudity as her initial behavior had led him to believe. It was a strange reaction for a shifter, but, then, she wasn't just any shifter, and this wasn't just any situation. She was a woman completely alone with a strange man, and a small woman at that. If he had to guess, he would say she stood about five-five or five-six. A perfectly normal height for a human woman, but tiny for a shifter—at least by Dragonstar standards. At home, most of the women stood close to six feet tall. Still not as tall as the men, but within half a foot or less of most of the male clan members.

If the same held true of the Wyvernmoons—and he had no doubt that it would, based on the war parties they had sent into New Mexico—she must feel dwarfed by the men around her all the time. And his height, which was unusual even for a dragon shifter, could definitely be making her uncomfortable. Plus, if she was as soft as she looked, she was pretty much defenseless against him. She probably knew that, as well.

The beast inside him let out a low, mean growl, began scratching at his insides in an effort to get out. Not to harm her, but to protect her. The vulnerability of this delicate little shifter obviously upset his dragon as much as it did him.

He yanked the old, worn backpack he'd found in the tree off his shoulder and held it out to her with what he hoped was an innocuous smile. The last thing he ever wanted a part of was making a woman feel vulnerable—at least not in that way. And though he knew the shifter in front of him had claws and fire and probably some other powers when she was in dragon form, he didn't know what she could do as a human. Or even if she could do anything at all.

She looked surprised when he held the bag out to her, her big violet eyes going wide as a little bit of the fight—and fright—drained out of them. The surprise didn't last long. Tossing her hair over her shoulder, she reached for the bag. The second her fingers closed over it, she whirled away, speeding toward the nearest clump of trees.

She moved quickly, gracefully, nearly soundlessly, and he found himself straining to hear where she stopped. Was that it, then? Was she done with him, having gotten what she wanted? He wouldn't blame her if she was, but the thought was strangely disappointing.

Not so strange, he told himself forcefully. It was all part of the job. After all, when she'd gotten close to him, he'd scented Wyvernmoon on her. His guess when he'd first seen her had been right on—she was a member of the enemy clan. Maybe, if he played his cards right, finding an in wouldn't be quite as difficult as he'd originally anticipated.

But not if she left him standing there, with his brain empty and his dick hard. Shaking his head at his own stupidity, he headed for the clump of trees at a dead run. She probably didn't have much of a head start. He could catch up to her and—

He froze as she stepped back into the clearing. Though he was glad to see her, he was a little disappointed to find that she was now dressed in a pair of worn jeans and a long-sleeved gray T-shirt that was a little too big for her. Somehow she looked even more vulnerable like this than she had naked.

His conscience smarted at the realization, but he shoved down the misplaced guilt. She might not have been one of the dragons that attacked his clan, but that didn't mean she hadn't known about it or had something to do with it. Besides, even if she hadn't, she was part of the clan that had done their best to wipe the Dragonstars from existence. He couldn't afford to feel anything for her—and he sure as hell had nothing to feel guilty about.

After all, he'd come here for exactly this purpose—to infiltrate the Wyvernmoons and find a way to bring down the clan once and for all. Dylan had told him to content himself with finding a way to destroy the virus, but that wasn't what he was after. No way were his friends going to spend the rest of their lives looking over their shoulders, waiting for the next nightmare the Wyvernmoons could dream up. He was going to finish the bastards completely or die trying.

Forcing a smile that he was far from feeling, Logan told her, "You look different with your clothes on."

She blushed. "Yes, well, I don't think naked is my best look."

"Oh, I don't know about that. Not that the jeans don't look good or anything. It's just, you're one of the few women I've met who doesn't need adornment."

Her eyes narrowed, and he wondered if he was laying it on a bit thick. Not that he was lying to her—she looked damn good naked. But telling her that might be too much too soon. Maybe he needed to pull it back a little. He was pushing awfully hard.

When she finally answered him, though, it wasn't to call him on his cheesy lines. Instead, she simply said, "I think you're the first man to see me naked before we've even exchanged names." She held out an elegant hand. "I'm Cecily Fournier."

The name sent him reeling, so much so that it was a few seconds before he could get himself together enough to take her proffered hand. "I'm Logan Kelly."

"It's nice to meet you, Logan."

Could it really be this easy? he wondered frantically. Could he really have just fallen into a meeting with the Wyvernmoon princess? Shaking his head to clear it, he murmured, "You, as well, Cecily."

Then, watching her closely, he added, "Or should I say, Your Highness? I have to admit, I'm a little rusty on protocol when dealing with royalty."

Her face fell and he felt guilty all over again, but this time he didn't have any idea why. "It doesn't matter." She took a few steps back. "I suppose I should be going now."

"Already?" he asked, determined not to let her get away so easily. "I thought we could spend a few minutes getting to know each other."

"Is it me you want to get to know, or the princess of the Wyvernmoon clan?"

Shit. Talk about a loaded question. He spent a minute observing her, noting the way she held her breath as she waited for his answer.

The way her pupils contracted and her fists clenched. Then told her the truth—or as much of the truth as he could risk admitting.

"Would it be a completely bad move for me to admit to a little of both?"

Cecily weighed Logan's answer, looking for any hint of guile or dishonesty. She didn't find any, but, then, maybe she wasn't looking hard enough. When she was standing this close to him, it was difficult to concentrate on anything but his broad, tanned chest and the rich, sexy smell of him. Inhaling slowly, she took his scent deep inside herself.

He smelled like the ocean her mother had taken her to when she was a little girl, like the wild, salty sea just where it tumbled over the sand.

Like the peppermint candies she went through by the dozen.

Like freedom—or the closest thing to it she'd ever experienced.

For that reason alone, she wasn't going to push him away, at least not just because he admitted to being curious about her royal status. After all, she had yet to meet a dragon who wasn't.

Still, she had to ask one more time. "Is that the truth?" She lifted her chin so that she was looking him point-blank in the eye.

"It is, aye."

"Okay, then. Since the truth is rarely a bad move, I'll go along with you on this one."

His grin flashed, wide and brilliant, and her heart started to beat just a little bit faster. "Excellent. So, where should we go?"

"What?" She replayed his words in her mind, trying to figure out the strange segue in their conversation. Nothing came to her, so she added, "I'm afraid I don't know what you mean."

"You said you were willing to go along with me. I was wondering where you wanted to go."

"Oh, I just meant—"

"I know what you meant, Cecily." He reached out and gently tugged one long strand of her hair. "I was just teasing you."

"Right. Of course." She felt her cheeks warm, but was wont to do anything to stop it. She couldn't remember the last time someone had teased her. It had been years, certainly—maybe decades. Gage had played around with her when he'd been teaching her how to fly, but that had been eons ago. Besides, his comments had never made her feel like this.

A little scared, a little excited and completely shaky inside.

"Come on," he said, slowly dropping her hair. "Take a walk with me."

She knew she should refuse—the Crown Princess of the Wyvernmoon clan didn't take walks with strange men, let alone give them permission to touch her. But up here, at the top of the Black Hills, so high that she could see clouds when she looked down, she didn't feel like a princess. She felt like plain old Cecily. It was such a novel feeling that it took her a little while to understand it.

But once she did, she liked it, almost as much as she liked the way his hand rested lightly on her back as he guided her around a curve that could loosely be called a trail.

"Where are we going?" she asked, shocked at the sudden breathlessness of her voice. Because she hiked these mountains regularly, she knew it had nothing to do with her athletic prowess and everything to do with the man standing next to her.

"I spent the morning exploring. There's a lake a mile or so down this path."

She knew the exact spot he was talking about. Small but crystal clear, the lake seemed to pop up out of nowhere, like so many of the water sources in and around the Black Hills. It was also fed by an amazing waterfall—one that she had showered under more times than she could count.

She snuck a glance at Logan, wondering if he had put the waterfall to good use earlier in the day. Just the idea of it made her entire body tingle in a way she'd never experienced before. Her nipples hardened beneath the thin fabric of her T-shirt, and she pulled away from him a little bit so she could casually cross her arms over her chest.

She'd thought she'd been subtle, but the wicked gleam in Logan's eyes told her he knew exactly what was going on.

Her cheeks warmed again and she nearly groaned. In the real world, in *her* world, she could go days and weeks without blushing. But up here, with Logan, it seemed like every three seconds something new was setting her off.

So much for being the strong, powerful leader her clan needed. She could barely talk to one unfamiliar man without hyperventilating. He was a hell of a man, no doubt about it, but still. It was completely humiliating.

Putting her embarrassment aside, she turned to him with a frown as common sense belatedly kicked in. She was far from defenseless, but still, she couldn't just go wandering into the woods with a dragon she barely knew. Not without asking him the question that had been bugging her since she had first laid eyes on him. "What are you doing here, Logan?"

"Talking to a beautiful woman whom I find very intriguing," he answered. "I guess I must not be doing it right if you haven't figured that much out yet."

She wasn't going to fall for smooth lines and the wicked flash of his grin. At least not yet. "You know what I mean. You're not part of the Wyvernmoon clan."

It wasn't a question, but he answered, anyway. "No, I'm not."

"So why are you here? It's not like South Dakota is that high up on the list of places for a dragon shifter to visit. It's pretty boring out here if you aren't aiming to do the tourist stuff. Which, I assume, you aren't."

"You assume right. But that doesn't mean I'm bored." His smile was friendly and almost harmless. "I'm finding a lot out here to keep both me and my beast occupied."

"Logan . . ."

"All right, all right." He backed off a little, but strangely his retreat didn't make it any easier for her to breathe. Not when it gave her such a good view of his tantalizing tattoos. "I'm just passing through on my way up to Canada. I have some friends up there I want to visit."

"Canada?" she asked, surprised. "There's only one clan up there. The—"

"Nightfires. I know."

"And you actually have friends in that clan?" She didn't mean to look skeptical, but the dragons in question were notoriously close ranked—and so suspicious they made Julian look like the most inclusive guy on the planet.

He didn't take offense at her skepticism. Instead, he just shrugged. "I have friends everywhere."

"Really? What clan are you from?"

"I'm from the Flamedancers. They're in Ireland."

"Oh, right." She relaxed a little at the name of the familiar clan. "That's where the accent comes from."

"What accent?" He looked startled.

"You've slipped into an accent twice since we've been talking. It's subtle, so I had a hard time placing it, but of course it's Gaelic."

"You must be mistaken. I haven't had an accent in more than two hundred years."

She was a little surprised at his obvious discomfort. "It's no big deal. I kind of like it. The words roll off your tongue so beautifully."

"That's not the point—" He cut himself off, but it was obvious that her casual words had upset him, though she didn't know why.

Seeking a way to learn more about this dragon who intrigued her on every level, she rested her hand on his forearm, waiting for him to look at her. "Why does the idea bother you so much? There's nothing wrong with people being able to identify you by clan."

"They're not my clan!"

"I thought you just said—"

"I said I was from Ireland, and I am. But I haven't been back in nearly three hundred years and don't plan on returning anytime soon."

"Oh. But if you're no longer a member of the Flamedancers, then you must be . . . I mean, are you a . . ." She hesitated, not wanting to use the insulting term.

He didn't seem to be having the same problem, as he said roughly, "Yeah. I'm rogue."

Now she knew that she should run, that she should get away from him any way she could. There was a reason calling someone a rogue was an insult in the dragon community. Despite popular fairy-tale representations, dragons were a social species by nature, and very few ever chose to leave the protection of their clans. It was dangerous, even in the twenty-first century, to be without family at your back. Which meant that most rogue dragons were either extremely antisocial or had been banished from their clan for committing a terrible offense.

And since Logan didn't seem the least bit antisocial . . .

"You don't have to look like that, you know. I haven't kicked a puppy in at least a decade."

Mortified that her thoughts were so plainly discerned, Cecily suddenly didn't know where to look. It didn't seem right to look him in the eye when she was thinking so badly of him, but at the same time it seemed ridiculous to pretend an interest in the landscape that she was far from feeling.

In the end, she settled for staring at her fingernails. At least they distracted her for a second as she wondered absently how long it had been since she'd been to the salon. Too long, judging from the jagged edges of her nails and the peeling polish.

"You can look at me, you know. I didn't say that to embarrass you."

Her eyes shot to his before she could think better of it. "Yes, you did."

"So you *can* give as good as you get. I wondered." He inclined his head. "You're right. I *was* hoping to embarrass you."

She waited, but he didn't say anything more. "And?" She finally asked.

"And what?"

"Aren't you going to apologize?"

"Why should I when I'm not sorry?"

Her cheeks flamed yet again, but this time it was more indignation than discomfiture that made her blush. Maybe she'd been wrong. Maybe he was antisocial after all.

She wasn't sure what to say to that, so she kept her mouth shut—until he moved a little closer and ran a finger down her cheek. "I like the way you look when you blush."

Of course, his words only made it worse. "Yeah, right. Nothing like looking like a tomato to really impress a guy."

"Do you want to impress me?" he asked.

"It was just an expression," she stuttered.

"Was it?" His voice had dropped, deepened, and his eyes seemed to glow as the shadows lengthened around them.

"Yes!" Cecily glanced around. The sun was setting and it would be dark soon. She needed to leave, to head back to the compound, but she was finding it difficult to move when he looked at her so intently. In all her life, she'd never had a man look at her quite like that before.

Oh, a number of her father's *factionnaires* and business allies had studied her intently for years, but their looks were usually loaded with avarice. They saw her as a means to an end, a way to gain power in the clan—especially now that her father and Jacob were out of the picture. They wanted her, but only because of what she could bring them.

The look in Logan's eyes, the way he angled his body toward her, the way his heat wrapped around her, told her more clearly than any words could that he wanted something else entirely from her. Maybe it was stupid to believe that—he was rogue, after all—but she found that she didn't care.

So what if she was being stupid up here on the top of this mountain?

So what if she wanted to believe that this one dragon wanted her, Cecily, not just the Crown Princess of the Wyvernmoon clan?

So what if for once she wanted to act like a woman and not a puppet in her father's quest to keep his *Conseil* in line?

No one would know if she didn't tell them. And for this moment, right now, she wanted to say to hell with her innate caution. To hell with her innocence. To hell with everything but the heat coursing through her body under his steady perusal.

"Logan." She took a step toward him, told herself to reach out to him, but she wasn't that brave. Not yet. She wouldn't run away if he wanted to kiss her, but she couldn't bring herself to initiate it.

She didn't know how.

"Cecily." This time when he smiled, it didn't hold a trace of mockery. Instead, it was warm and enticing and just a little bit feral. For the first time since she'd met him, she could see the beast that lurked deep inside him—intelligent, cunning, determined.

The knowledge made her chest tighten, made the act of drawing air into her lungs almost impossible. Deep inside, her own dragon stirred. Stretched. Even preened a little under the regard.

He must have seen the beast, because his eyes darkened and his breathing grew shallower. Harsher. Then he lifted a finger to her mouth, toyed with her lower lip.

She gasped and he took instant advantage, stroking his finger from her lip to the inside of her mouth. He traced the sharp edge of her teeth with his fingertip before brushing against the very tip of her tongue.

Instinctively, she bit down, nipping at the warm, resilient flesh.

He groaned and she started to apologize, more than a little shocked that she'd bitten him. But the look on his face told her he'd liked it, that she had nothing to apologize for. So she did it again, then laved her tongue against the small wound to soothe away the sting.

"Cecily." This time when he said her name, his voice was low and gravelly and so tempting that she found herself leaning toward him without conscious thought.

She didn't have far to go. He stepped forward, closing the distance between them until her breasts skimmed against his bare stomach. He was hot, burning up, the fire that raged within him stoked to the highest degree.

Her nipples hardened at the feel of him—at the all-encompassing warmth of him—and she arched her back without conscious thought. She wanted to feel more of him against her, ached for it in a way she hadn't known was possible before she met him.

That movement—and the permission implicit in it—must have been what Logan was waiting for. For the second she pressed herself against him, he slid his hand up her cheek to tangle in her hair.

He tugged gently—not enough to hurt, but definitely enough to let her know he considered himself in charge—and tilted her head up, up, up, so that their gazes met and locked. Then he moved his other hand to the small of her back, guiding her even closer, until their bodies were plastered together.

He lowered his head so slowly that she nearly screamed with the agony of waiting. Her body jerked against his as every nerve ending she had cried out for more. More contact. More pleasure. More everything.

And then he was there, so close that she could feel his warm, peppermint-scented breath against her cheek. She closed her eyes. Parted her lips. Waited for him to kiss her. And waited. And waited.

But he didn't do it, didn't move that last crucial inch, and her eyes flew open. "What's wrong?" she breathed, her hands coming up to clutch at his shoulders. "Why won't you kiss me?"

"I'm going to kiss you," he answered, and her heart jerked painfully.

She closed her eyes again, tilted her face even more. And still he didn't do it.

"What are you waiting for?" she demanded, her eyes opening for a second time.

"For you to want this as much as I do," he growled.

"I do!" she all but wailed, her nails digging into his heavily muscled back. "I need—"

She never finished. His mouth slammed down on hers and she nearly screamed at the heat of it. The sexiness of it. The downright deliciousness of it.

He tasted like he smelled—of rich, tangy peppermint candy and an untamed Irish sea in the middle of a powerful storm.

He tasted of sex and satin sheets and long, sultry nights.

He was delicious and she wanted more, so much more than the meeting of their mouths could give her.

Her hands crept up his neck to bury themselves in his cropped hair. It was cool and silky against her fingers and felt so good she couldn't help grabbing on. Tugging a little, so that his lips were pressed even more firmly against her own. And then she surrendered completely, giving herself over to the lightning flashing between them.

It was nothing like what she thought kissing him would be like, nothing like anything she had ever experienced before. Though she hadn't kissed that many men, she had dated a few. Had let them kiss her and hold her, even if she hadn't given them her virginity, and never had it been anything like this.

This was wicked and wild and so wonderful that she never wanted it to end. His lips were hard against hers, firm but just a little out of control. And his tongue . . . It was everywhere. It swept over her bottom lip, nuzzled at the corner of her mouth before darting inside and stroking against her own tongue. Back and forth, over the roof of her mouth, down her cheek, along the inside of her upper lip before delving deep to explore her most hidden recesses.

She gasped, and he pulled back a little, a questioning look in his eyes. But she refused to let him go—not yet, not now when she had barely gotten a taste of him and the pleasure he could bring her. Instead, she pressed her advantage and sucked his lower lip between her teeth.

He groaned, and the hand at the small of her back slipped lower to cup and knead her ass. It was her turn to moan, and as she did, he lifted her with one strong hand until the bulge of his cock brushed against the thin fabric of her jeans, barely separating him from her sex.

She saw stars—there was no other word for the blinding flashes of light that pulsed behind her closed eyelids—and her hands slipped down to clutch at his neck, his shoulders, his back.

Being held by him was unlike anything she had ever felt before, and she never wanted it to stop. Wanted to stand right here in this little copse of trees, the only sounds their heavy breathing and the waterfall behind them, forever. Wanted to forget about the mess her clan was in and the duty she had to somehow steer them through it.

The sudden reminder of her clan was like cold water dumped over her head. She couldn't forget them, couldn't hide away like she always had. They needed her down there with them, not up here with the hottest dragon shifter she had ever seen, let alone kissed.

She pulled back reluctantly, and for a second she wasn't sure Logan was going to let her go. His hands tightened, squeezing her more firmly against his very aroused body.

"Logan, stop." She whispered it, and even though a part of her knew the last thing she wanted him to do was stop, she forced her hands to let go of him and push against his chest.

He relinquished his hold on her instantly, stepped back and shoved his hands in his jean pockets. She did the same, figuring it was safer, as the look on his face was so aroused, so intense, that she wanted nothing more than to latch on to him again and pick up where they'd just left of.

Only common sense kept her rooted to her spot. That and the knowledge that if she kissed him again, neither of them would stop until they were naked and rolling around on the ground. It was a strange thought. Highly arousing, but still strange, as she'd spent her entire existence thinking of her sexuality as some entity completely separate from herself.

She'd had to, if she'd had any hope of surviving. Like most other shifters, dragons were highly sexual creatures. But while her girlfriends had indulged themselves after they'd reached a certain age, steeping themselves in sex with young, sexy males of the clan, she'd been stuck in her father's house, her virginity bartered like that of a highborn lady of old. Except *bartered* wasn't exactly the right word, was it? Not when her father had refused to ever relinquish her to anyone, instead holding her up as a prize that he would give away to the man who most impressed him.

The result was that she had gone through her life without ever being touched. Alone and lonely and sometimes aching so badly that she could hardly stand it.

I can change that right now, a little voice in the back of her head told her. Logan was ready and willing, and judging by the hard bulge in the front of his jeans, more than able. Her knees trembled at the thought, and for a second she fantasized about what it would be like to reach out and touch him there. To have the right to stroke his aroused cock with her hand, her body, her mouth.

Heat slammed through her, and Logan made a sound halfway between a groan and a laugh. "No offense, Cecily, but if you want to call a halt to this, you need to stop looking at me like that."

"How am I—" Her voice broke. "How am I looking at you?"

"Like you're a kid on Christmas morning and I'm the last candy cane on the tree."

She thought of his peppermint scent, of the warm, fresh peppermint taste of him, and felt everything inside her melt. *Does he taste like that everywhere?* she wondered. *Or are there other amazing tastes in store for me as I explore his body?*

Her breath came out in a strangled gasp, and his laughter changed to a growl that shot straight through her. "I'm serious, Cecily. You need to stop, or I'm going to end up taking you where you stand."

Though it was the last thing she wanted to do, she forced herself to back away slowly. Much as she wanted Logan, much as she wanted him to make love to her and melt the frozen core that had been within her for as long as she could imagine, she knew that she couldn't let that happen.

Not when she was trying to get her clan back on the right path.

And not when she might very well have to marry one of her father's *Conseil* members to do it.

"I need to go," she whispered, but from the way his eyes turned almost black, she knew he'd heard her.

He didn't say anything, didn't try to convince her to stay, and a little part of her smarted at the omission. Not because she would have been able to stay with him, but because she wanted to—and wanted him to feel the same way.

"I guess I'll see you around," she said with a shrug, and started backing up the trail. She wanted to turn around and flee, but years of experience with Julian and Acel and Remy had taught her not to turn her back on a dragon with that pissed-off look on his face. Not that she thought Logan would really hurt her, but sometimes it paid to be careful . . .

He was beside her in a flash, so fast that she wasn't sure she'd even seen him move. He didn't block her path as Julian might have, didn't try to bully her or use their obvious attraction to get her to stay. Instead, he just walked beside her back to the clearing where she'd first seen him.

"Will you come again?" he asked, and she wasn't sure if the impatience in his tone was for her or for himself.

"If you want me to," she answered.

He brushed a hand down her cheek. "I want you to."

"Okay." She cleared her throat. "How long are you going to be staying up here?"

"A couple of days. Maybe a week."

"All right, then. I'll try to come back tomorrow or the next day."

"I'll look forward to it." His smile was surprisingly gentle, considering the fire lurking in the back of his eyes. He leaned down to kiss her again and she raised her lips, waiting for the spark to consume her one more time.

She expected the heat, had braced herself for it, in fact. But what she got was so much more—and less—that she didn't quite know how to process it. His lips brushed softly, sweetly against hers before sweeping up her cheek to her forehead. Once there, he pressed a kiss right above her left brow, then dropped his hands and let her go.

"I guess I'll see you around, then," he said with the cocky grin she had first seen from him.

"I guess you might," she answered, then watched as he turned and headed back into the forest he had come out of right after she'd landed. As she watched him go, she told herself she should be grateful that he'd taken the initiative and walked away. Because after the tender way he'd just kissed her, she wasn't sure she would have had the willpower to do the same.

CHAPTER FIVE

What the fuck had just happened? Logan stared after Cecily for long minutes, wondering how he'd gone from thinking about using her to just thinking about her so quickly. It was crazy, but from the second he'd touched her, he had forgotten what he'd come here to do. Had forgotten everything but the way she felt in his arms.

Jesus, he really was an asshole. If Cecily hadn't called a halt to it, they would have had sex. Hell, what was he thinking? They would be having it still. If she hadn't stopped him, he would be balls-deep in her right about now.

The thought only made his already-hard dick harder, especially as he imagined what it would feel like to be inside her. She had tasted so fucking sweet—like strawberries and caramel and fresh, rich cream—that he had wanted to devour her.

His beast had clawed at him from the inside, raking sharp talons down his skin in an effort to get to Cecily. To feel her and touch her and taste her. God, he'd wanted to go down on her, to thrust his tongue deep inside her and see if her pussy tasted half as good as her mouth.

Somehow he knew it would, which only made the fact that she had left him a million times worse.

Trying to shake off the desire that was a knife in his gut, Logan grabbed a shirt and pulled it on. Then he started hiking down the steepest side of the mountain, figuring if he couldn't exhaust himself with sex, he could at least do it with another, less pleasurable physical exertion.

But fifteen minutes into the hike, he knew it was no use. He didn't want to climb up and down a mountain. He wanted to fuck, and for the first time in his very long life, not any woman would do. He wanted to fuck a specific woman. He wanted to fuck Cecily.

Shaking his head as he scaled down a particularly sharp cliff face, Logan called himself every name in the book. And then made up a few for good measure. It worked, and by the time he'd made it to the bottom of the sheer rock drop, he was feeling almost like himself again. Except, of course, for the raging erection that came back every time he thought about Cecily.

He'd have to get that under control—get himself and his dragon under control—because meeting Cecily had been a gift from the gods. Oh, he'd had a few ideas on how to get inside the Wyvernmoon compound, but none of them were without risk of discovery. Not of his actual presence, because, really, being accepted as a guest of the clan had been the whole point. He couldn't do what he had to do by spending months skulking around in the dark.

But presenting himself to the clan council, asking for amnesty for a while—that came with certain risks, especially because the Wyvernmoons were bound to be more paranoid than other clans, considering what they'd been up to.

Being invited in without asking for an invitation, however, would be a huge plus in his favor. He had already figured that out before he'd met Cecily, but talking to her—kissing her—had only solidified his plans. If he played his cards right, the princess herself would be his ticket into the compound. And once he was in and an accepted escort of the princess, it would be a hell of a lot easier to destroy the clan.

The thought grated a lot more than it should; he should be overjoyed that he'd hit on an almost-foolproof entrance to the clan. It was stupid to be worried about it, stupid to feel that niggling bit of guilt at the thought of using Cecily so blatantly. Yes, she'd been nice—a lot nicer than he had ever imagined she would be. But that didn't mean anything. A lot of people had different faces. It was more than possible that she had been involved in the Wyvernmoon attacks but could seem like a genuinely nice person on the surface. Look at how many sociopaths were able to fool the people in their lives for so long.

Not that he was calling Cecily a sociopath, but he couldn't help wondering if she was amoral. How could she not be if she sanctioned the vicious, bloody, terrible massacre of innocents with that stupid virus? How she could be anything but a coldhearted bitch if she had anything to do with what the Wyvernmoons had been doing to his clan?

And, not to put too fine a point on it, what the fuck did it say about him that he could still want her when he believed that she was somehow involved in destroying his clan?

Even if he gave her the benefit of the doubt, even if he tried to tell himself that it was her father and brother who had spearheaded the whole viral attack, they had both been dead for a number of months. Someone had to be carrying on the work in their stead, and if it wasn't Cecily, then it was someone close to her. And if she really didn't know, well, then, she was a lot stupider than she'd come across today. Because the woman who had met him quip for quip, who had stared at him out of those shrewdly sexy purple eyes, had been anything but stupid.

Still, he could use the desire he felt for her to his own advantage. Could play on the desire she felt for him just as easily. And if he ended up in bed with her . . . His cock jumped at the thought, telling him that ship was already headed for port. So, fine. *When* he ended up in bed with her, it would just be sex. Not pure, not simple, definitely not uncomplicated—at least not with the agenda he was determined to push forward—but it would just be sex. He just had to get a grip on himself and on Cecily, and then everything would be fine.

He would get into the compound.

Destroy the lab and the virus.

Find a way to bring the Wyvernmoons down once and for all, and then get the hell out of Dodge.

He couldn't afford to take his eye off the ball, not at this late date. Dylan and the other Dragonstars were counting on him. It wasn't in him, after everything they'd done for him through the years, to let them down. Not for anything.

Happy now that he'd worked things through to his satisfaction, Logan started the long climb back up the mountain. This time, with his mind relatively settled, he could focus on the beauty of his surroundings instead of on the maelstrom of thoughts and feelings that had been whipping around inside him on the way down.

South Dakota was beautiful, or at least the Black Hills were—a lot more beautiful than he had anticipated when he'd been walking his desert back at home. Oh, the sunrises and sunsets were different here, the landscape nowhere near as barren and mystifying as what he looked out at every day in New Mexico, but it had its own brand of charm.

The trees were gorgeous, full and green and towering much higher than anything in the flat deserts of New Mexico. The hills themselves were rocky and filled with colors ranging from gray to brown, red and gold. And the lakes . . . Coming from a state where water availability was a huge deal and where they could sometimes go years without a good rainstorm, it was amazing to know that there were lakes and rivers and waterfalls around many of the twists and turns of these mountains.

Still, they weren't all that tall compared to the Colorado Rockies that he, Shawn and Ty liked to climb at least once a year, just to prove they still could. Logan was at the top of his mountain—Cecily's mountain—in no time, without even having broken a sweat.

Still, Cecily's unexpected arrival had forced him to skip the dip he'd planned in the lake earlier that evening. Though it was getting dark—or maybe because of it—he thought now might be a great time to remedy that. None of the wildlife up here would bother him. His

dragon was by far the fiercest, biggest thing around, and local predators were usually smart enough to recognize that, even when he was in
human form.

He took a quick detour through the camp he'd set up after a visit to
one of the local camping stores. Stripped off his shirt and grabbed a
towel out of his pack before heading down to the lake he'd been dying
to try since he'd first found it.

Once there, he stripped down and dived in. The water was cold—
freezing, really—but he'd been expecting it. This was South Dakota,
after all. And it was fall. In a couple more months, right around the
time of the first big snowstorm of the year, he figured he'd be longing
for the warmth of this water.

He'd been in the water about fifteen minutes, had swum a few laps
across the small lake and back, and had just started lazing around
under the waterfall when he felt her creep into his mind.

Slamming his feet down onto the rocky floor of the lake, he stood
up and looked around, letting the dragon peer out of his eyes. Using his
beast's sharp eyesight, he studied every inch of the shore around the
lake, looking for her. His beast growled with pent-up sexual frustration.
If she'd come back, he was going to take her here and now. To hell with
guilt, to hell with his plan, to hell with everything about the Wyvernmoons. He wanted inside her in the worst way, and he was going to
get there.

Except after a few minutes, he figured out that Cecily was nowhere
to be found. Somehow, some way, his mind had managed to connect to
hers over a pretty decent distance. And while he'd always been able to
do that with the Dragonstars, he'd never been able to pick up on the
thoughts of anyone else miles away before. At least not without some
serious effort.

Not sure what was going on but determined to figure it out, Logan
settled down to listen to whatever it was Cecily wanted to tell him.
Which, as it turned out, was a singularly bad idea. Because within two

minutes of eavesdropping on her thoughts, it was like the hike and the swim had never happened. He was back to being hot and hard and raging for release.

Pissed off, out of sorts, and so aroused that breathing had become an Olympic event, he fisted his hand around his cock and willed Cecily to let him in just a little more.

She was twitchy. There was no other word for it. She'd been home for nearly three hours and despite being exhausted, she couldn't settle. Instead, she prowled through the house, her eyes focused on the blackness of the night beyond the huge picture windows her father had put in years before.

She wanted to be out there, racing through the cool darkness as the wind wound itself around her body.

She wanted to relax, to let go of the control that had stifled her for so long, and just be.

She wanted . . . she wanted Logan. She wanted to be back in the mountains with him, holding him again. Kissing him.

What was wrong with her? She'd dated men before, had kissed a number of them, but none of them had left her feeling like this. Like her skin was too tight and her blood was too hot and every other part of her body was screaming for relief.

Unable to take being cooped up in the house one second longer, she threw open the back doors and walked out to the patio. Immediately, a cool wind brushed against her, but instead of relieving the heat that was burning her from the inside out, it just stoked it. Made it worse, until she could barely think.

Why had she walked away from Logan that afternoon, when it had been obvious that he would have been more than happy to give her what her body was begging for? She didn't prize her virginity, didn't plan on using it to bargain for power or position, as her father had always planned to do.

So why hadn't she followed through with what both of them wanted? Sex wasn't a big deal to most shifters—or, at least, not that she could tell. With their animal natures, it was just one more need to assuage, one more itch to scratch.

Annoyed and achy, she flopped down on one of the big chaise longues that overlooked the pool and tried to concentrate on something, anything, besides the emptiness she felt inside her.

It didn't work.

She glanced up at the sky, at the stars that were specks of gold and silver against the blanket of night, and thought of Logan. What it had felt like to be touched by him, held by him, kissed by him.

It had been hours, and her lips still felt swollen and well used. She'd never been kissed like that before, like a man was ravenous, starving for her.

And not just any man, but Logan.

Let me in, Cecily. Let me touch you.

The voice came out of the night and into her head so naturally that it felt like it had always been there. Though she knew it was only fantasy, knew her lonely mind was conjuring up the contact, she reveled in it. Wrapped it around herself as she closed her eyes, stretched out on the lounger, and let the sound of his voice—of her fantasy—spread through her.

That's it, A stor. His voice was as rich and delicious as the caramel syrup she put in her coffee every morning. It burrowed inside her, lit her up from the inside out. *Just relax.*

She almost laughed. She was so wound up, so needy, that relaxing was out of the question.

But she needed Logan, needed something if she couldn't have him.

Then take it, the voice in the back of her head said. *Take what you need. I want to pleasure you.*

She gasped at the words, at the realness of the fantasy she was building for herself. Reaching up, she stroked her fingers lightly—so lightly—over her forehead, down her temple, across the bridge of her nose before sliding them down her cheek and pausing at her mouth.

She parted her lips, sucked her finger a little inside. Imagined it was his again and he was staring at her with that narrowed, intense amber gaze. Just the thought of his look—so wicked, wild—had her back arching, her breasts aching until she thought she would go crazy.

Touch them, then. There was that voice again—his voice—encouraging her to take what she so desperately wanted. *Lift up your shirt,* A Ghra, *and feel yourself. Run your hands over those beautiful breasts.*

She did as her fantasy lover asked—as Logan asked—and slid her hands beneath her shirt and cupped the heavy weight of her breasts. Then nearly whimpered at the relief of it, at the feel of her flesh, firm and resilient beneath her palm and fingers.

Her fantasy lover groaned a little and the sound shot straight to her sex, made the hurt and the heat just a little bit worse.

Fuck, you're so goddamn sexy, her lover told her in a low, gravelly voice, and she nearly laughed out loud at the absurdity of her own imagination. She'd never been called sexy a day in her life, had never had a man look at her as anything more than Princess Cecily. The fact that her fantasy lover told her what she'd always wanted to hear spoke so much louder than his words. But, then again, that was kind of the point of creating a fantasy in her own head, wasn't it? He could say or do whatever she wanted him to.

Right now, if you don't get back to it, I'm going to throw you across my lap and spank you until you scream for relief, the dark voice in her head bit out.

Fire spiraled through her at the image, and she started to obey him. But something stopped her, some part of her that she hadn't known existed before tonight. She waited, breath held, to see what her lover would do.

So it's going to be like that, is it? For one brief moment, she swore she could feel his hands on her.

His fingers gripping the back of her neck in a sign of painless but obvious dominance.

His body resting above hers, the rough fabric of his jeans brushing against her bare stomach.

His mouth sucking roughly on her nipples, bringing them to hard, painful points.

She moaned, trembled, and he laughed—low and hot. She felt his hands brush over the skin of her abdomen and she spread her legs, whimpered. But the tangible aspect of him was gone as suddenly as it had come. Only his voice was left.

I love the feel of your skin, Cecily. So soft and creamy, like the petals of a flower just on the brink of opening. Touch it for me again, he whispered. *Touch your breasts and those cherry red nipples I swear I'll never get enough of.*

Aroused, out of control, desperate for the feel of his mouth on her again, she never even thought to disobey. She brought her hands to her breasts again, kneaded them slowly, softly, then harder as pleasure streaked through her like lightning.

Touch your nipples, he told her again. *Brush your fingers against one and then the other.*

She did as he asked and felt sweat bloom on her skin, despite the coolness of the evening.

Good girl. Now do it harder. Pinch them; play with them. Imagine my mouth is on you, licking and sucking and tasting you.

She whimpered—she couldn't help herself. The picture he had painted was so real, so devastating, so arousing that she was swept up in it. Swept away by it even as she obeyed him.

Oh, God, she moaned inside her own head. *Logan—*

Do you like that? he demanded.

She didn't answer, couldn't answer; she was too caught up in the sensations cascading through her body. Though all she was touching were her breasts, she could feel the sparks streaking through her from her breasts to her stomach to her sex.

Answer me, he barked. *Tell me what you're feeling.*

Her cheeks flushed at the order, embarrassment sweeping through her. What was she supposed to say—that she felt empty, aching? That she could barely keep herself still when every instinct she had screamed that she needed to be filled.

Yes! Fuck, yes. If that's what you're feeling, say exactly that. Tell me.

I already did, she wailed.

Tell me again. His voice was deeper, shadowy and brooked no disobedience. For a second, she wondered about this fantasy, about the dominance and darkness of it. It was so different from anything she had ever experienced before, anything she had ever thought she wanted.

You don't like it? her fantasy lover asked. *I can go.*

No! She all but screamed the objection. *Don't leave me.*

I'm not going anywhere. She could almost see his fallen-angel smile. *I just needed you to know it, too. Now tell me what you're feeling.*

I need more. It feels like I'm being ripped apart from the inside. I need . . . I need—

What do you need, Cecily? Tell me. His voice snapped like a whip across her consciousness, stoking the flames even higher.

I need you! she wailed.

Where do you need me? On your breasts? For one, hot second she felt his teeth on her nipple. She clutched at him, tried to keep him there, but came away with only air.

In your mouth? He was there, his tongue thrusting past her lips and tangling with her own.

Or do you need me lower?

His lips skimmed down her neck to her shoulder. Then it felt like he was beside her, his lips trailing sweet, hot kisses down her shoulder to her hip. She was trembling with the overwhelming pleasure of his touch, shaking apart from it.

Do you need me here? he asked.

She gasped, barely able to hold back a scream as his finger slipped beneath her and circled her anus before slipping inside.

She clenched around him as threads of pleasure shot through her in all directions. What he was doing was wicked, was nothing she had ever imagined before. But the feel of it, the sensations, were incredible. Unbelievable. Like nothing she had ever dreamed existed.

Is this what you want, sweet Cecily? he demanded, and his voice was a growl, barely recognizable now. *Or do you want more?*

More? There's more?

Oh, A stor, there's always more. And then he was between her legs, his mouth on her hot, wet sex.

She did scream then, arching and struggling against a pleasure so overwhelming that she was certain she would shatter at any moment. She started to cry, great sobs shaking her body as her fantasy lover—as Logan—took her higher and higher.

Baby? Cecily? Are you okay? For the first time since this whole, crazy roller-coaster ride had started, he sounded uncertain. *Do you want me to stop?* The pressure and pleasure eased, but its absence only made her crazier.

No! No, no, no. Don't stop. Please— She thrashed against the chaise, arched and trembled and begged. In those moments, nothing mattered but him and the pleasure—the incredible, overwhelming pleasure— that he could bring to her.

Are we there already, A Ghra?

Yes! Oh, God, yes! she answered him, desperate for some relief from the agony and the ecstasy of her arousal.

All right, then. He lowered his mouth to her again, thrust his tongue deep inside her sex, and she went insane, bucking and twisting and pleading with him for more. For everything.

One of his hands came down on her abdomen, held her in place as his tongue stroked her from the inside. Once, twice, then again and again before he pulled out.

No! She clutched at his hair, held him in place. *Please—*

But she'd misunderstood. He wasn't going anywhere. He was just readjusting, changing position.

Suddenly she was on her knees, facing the tall back of the lounger and he was lying beneath her, one hand on her hip and the other on her ass as he sucked and licked and nibbled his way from the bottom of her pussy to her clit.

She screamed when he touched the little button for the first time, her hands clenching the chair as she rocked against his chin, his mouth, his nose. *Logan, Logan, Logan.* It was a chant, a mantra, a prayer. The only word she could hang on to in the crazy maelstrom of pleasure that surrounded her.

Wave after wave of ecstasy swept through her, took her away, as orgasm hit—huge and wild and totally overwhelming. It enveloped her totally, swamped her, and still he didn't stop. Still, his tongue fluttered and circled her clit. Still, his finger flexed inside her.

The pleasure was insane, all-consuming, and it went on and on and on, one orgasm running into another until she was blind and deaf and dumb with it. Until her body had dropped away and she was nothing but pure, absolute sensation. And still he didn't stop.

No more! she gasped finally. *I can't take it—*

You'll take it, he growled. *I need more. I need everything.* He pulled her clit between his teeth and bit down softly.

Logan! Her body convulsed again, harder than it ever had before, and suddenly it wasn't enough. She wanted to pleasure him, as well, wanted him to feel just a little bit of what she was experiencing.

Believe me, A stor, I feel it. Touching you brings me more pleasure than—

She took one hand off the chair she'd been gripping, reached behind her and rubbed him through the thick fabric of his jeans. He groaned, thrust against her palm, and then he was naked, his cock hot and hard and satiny against her palm.

She wanted to take her time, to explore him—even if it was just a fantasy—but his mouth was still on her, his tongue fluttering against her clit and her labia before thrusting inside her.

She cried out as another orgasm hit, her hand sliding up and down his cock as she thrust herself against his mouth.

Fuck, damn, shit. A stor, *you can't—* His hand came over hers, started to unwind her fingers, but she whimpered and tightened her grip. Not enough to cause him pain, she hoped, but enough to let him know she wasn't giving up.

He didn't take much convincing. Suddenly, his hand was moving over hers, lifting and lowering her palm and fingers on his cock as he taught her what he liked and how to pleasure him.

She was leaning back now, her back arched, her thighs trembling a little with the strain. She started to move so that she could pleasure him better, but his hand came back to her hip, held her in place directly over his mouth. One flick of his talented tongue and she was coming again, spiraling out into the night, head over heels, floating, floating, floating . . .

But then it didn't matter because he was coming, too, his big body jerking beneath her as he spurted, warm and wet and silky, against her hand.

When Logan came back to himself, he was standing thigh deep in the lake, his hand fisted around his dick and the remnants of a powerful orgasm still working their way through him.

What the hell was that? he wondered when he could finally think again. *What the hell had just happened?* One minute he'd been thinking about fucking Cecily, and the next minute he'd been right there, his mouth on her breasts and his dick aching for relief.

He'd made love to women with his mind before—hell, he had to get what joy he could out of this gift. But never one he had not already been with in reality. And never had it been as powerful, as earth-shattering, as what he had just experienced.

After quickly rinsing himself off in the lake, he climbed out and reached for a towel. As he settled onto his sleeping bag—he hadn't bothered to set up the tent—he stared up at the myriad stars that were just as bright here as they were back in New Mexico. He wondered if Cecily was looking up at the same stars right now, and if she was, if she was thinking of him as he was thinking of her.

A quick mental zap against the barriers he'd hastily erected told him that she was, indeed, doing the same thing he was doing. Which left only one question: what the hell had he gotten himself into?

CHAPTER SIX

Cecily came awake slowly, shocked to find herself lying outside by the pool, her nightgown around her waist. Memories of the night before—of her fantasies about Logan—bombarded her, and she sat up, hastily yanking her gown back into place.

What came over me? she wondered, pressing cold hands to her suddenly hot cheeks. She'd masturbated before—she was more than forty, a shifter and untouched, which pretty much made masturbation a requirement, especially when her dragon's hormones got the best of her—but never had she experienced anything like what had happened last night. Never had her fantasies felt so real. Never had her imagined lover felt so hot and hard and ready.

A picture of Logan rose in her mind, his eyes glowing with sex and need and pure, unadulterated wickedness. An arrow of heat shot through her and she nearly came again, just sitting there imagining all the things he had done to her body last night.

In my dreams, she reminded herself as she climbed shakily to her feet. *In my fantasies.* None of what had happened last night had been real, no matter how it had felt at the time. She needed to remember that. As it was, she wasn't sure how she was ever going to face him again.

When she'd left him yesterday, she had told him she would return. After the way he'd kissed her—and after what her mind had conjured up the night before—she was more than eager to do just that. But at the same time, she was embarrassed by her imagination, shocked by the creativity and reality of her own fantasies. What would Logan think of her if he knew what thoughts she'd been having about him? Would he like her fantasies or be disgusted by them? Last night had been raunchy and raw and more graphic than any fantasy she'd had before. In the light of day, it shocked even her. How could he fail to feel any differently?

And yet I want to find out, she realized as she walked into the house and straight for a hot shower. She wanted to know if the reality of Logan would live up to her fantasies, or if she was just setting herself up for disappointment. He was the first man she'd ever fantasized about. Usually, her dream lovers were shadowed, faceless men who pleasured her but whom she could never quite connect with.

Last night, she couldn't have been more connected with her fantasy than if they had been handcuffed together. The thought brought on a whole new kind of heat, and Cecily nearly died. What was wrong with her? Why was she suddenly thinking and behaving like a sex-crazed fiend? And why wasn't she more upset by the fact that she had masturbated in the middle of her backyard, where any dragon flying by could have seen her?

Who was this woman she was becoming, and what had happened to the old Cecily, the little mouse who hid in her father's mansion and never dared to make waves?

A glance in the mirror told her she even looked different after last night. Her eyes were wide and glowing, her mouth swollen, her skin flushed a rosy, satisfied pink. Her nipples were standing at attention, stiff and tight beneath the thin cotton of her nightgown, and her muscles felt weak and achy, like they did after she'd overtaxed them with a particularly long flight.

Even her hair was different. Instead of flowing down her back in its usual straight style, it was completely out of control. Wavy, curly, snarled in some places, it looked like someone had spent hours plunging his hands through it. Immediately, her mind jumped back to Logan and their kiss by the lake. He had grabbed on to her hair, had wrapped it around his fist, and she had loved every second of it. And now, standing here, she loved knowing that in doing that, he had marked her in a tangible way—even if a shower would take care of it.

Her sex clenched at the thought of being marked by Logan in a more permanent way, and she heard him whisper again—as her fantasy lover had the night before—that he would spank her if she didn't listen to him. Her knees turned to jelly at the memory, and she would have fallen if she hadn't grabbed on to the counter to catch herself.

God. She was insane. Absolutely crazy. This whole thing with the *factionnaires* was driving her completely around the bend. What other explanation was there for what she'd been thinking and fantasizing about?

Can the real Cecily Fournier please stand up? she demanded, shaking her head as if doing so would get her sluggish brain back on the right channel. She had a meeting today—probably the most important meeting of her life—and she couldn't afford to be muddled, sex-drunk, horny. She needed to be sharp, to focus, or the *Conseil* would walk all over her. That was something that Cecily—new or old—would never allow.

Stripping off her nightgown, she dropped it in the hamper against the wall and stepped into the steaming hot shower. She washed quickly, refusing to be distracted by her tender breasts or the ache between her legs. Last night had been strange, fantastical, fantastic, but it was daylight now and she had much bigger things to worry about than her nonexistent sex life. It was time to get her head in the game.

Six hours later, she wasn't nearly so sure she wouldn't have been better off lying around the house and fantasizing about Logan. If she thought the meeting had gone badly yesterday, when they'd been unprepared for her, then she was sorely mistaken. Because now that they'd had twenty-four hours to think and strategize and unite, the *factionnaires* were coming after her—and they were loaded for bear. Or dragon, as the case may be.

"With all due respect, Cecily, you don't know what you're talking about."

Julian's voice rang, loud and clear and condescending, through the meeting room. Just the sight of him earlier that morning had set her teeth on edge, and nothing he'd done since had endeared him to her.

Not that he cared. The more time she spent around the narcissistic asshole, the more she realized he cared about nothing but his perceived position in the clan. How he failed to realize that alienating her was not going to get him what he wanted, she didn't know. But, obviously, he was nowhere near as shrewd as her father had given him credit for. That, or he really didn't think she had any power.

Of course, on that point, he was dead-on, but that didn't mean it was going to stay like that. It wasn't. She really didn't care what three thousand years of tradition and fourteen *factionnaires* said; it was more than time for her to have an active role in the *Conseil*. After all, not one person sitting in this room cared more about the future of this clan than she did.

Not trusting herself to answer Julian's latest put-down—it was the sixth or seventh of the day—she counted to ten, then back down to one, then to ten again before she felt it was safe to open her mouth. And even then she wanted nothing more than to kick him out of the room, off the *Conseil* and out of the clan.

She couldn't do that, though. Not now and probably not ever. Especially not with the way Remy, Acel and Etienne were backing just about everything he said, looking for any chance to kick her out of the room once and for all. Which meant, for a while, anyway, that she would be better off working with him instead of against him. It grated—God, did it ever—but she had no doubt she would have to do worse for her clan than make nice with Julian before this nightmare was over.

"I understand that I have a lot to learn," she finally told him in the calmest voice she could manage. "That's why I'm here, asking to be filled in on the clan's inner workings. I've been watching things since my father's death, and I'm not nearly as inept as you all seem to think I am."

When no one butted in to tell her they thought differently, Cecily buried her hurt and anger behind a layer of unbreakable ice and told herself that it was okay. If she was at rock bottom in terms of their trust, then up really was the only way she could go.

Shrugging off the fact that none of the men she'd considered her friends—not even Gage or Thierren—had come to her defense, she said, "Let me tell you a little of what I've figured out since my father died."

She held up one finger and began ticking off her observations. "One, we're on the brink of a full-scale war with both the Dragonstar and Shadowdrake clans. In the past five months, we've lost nearly a hundred dragons in battles with them—including my father and my brother. Jacob was killed in what I'm assuming was a raid on the Dragonstar compound."

"They don't actually have a compound," interjected Wyatt. She stared at him, unsure if he was trying to make her look even more ignorant than she was or if he was genuinely trying to help. Either way, she didn't stop him, as she wanted to know, to learn as much as she could. "It's more of a city in the middle of the New Mexican desert. They're a lot less war oriented than we are—or, at least, they're set up that way. Their behavior lately, however, couldn't be more at odds with peace."

She let his last comment go, as she had her own theories about it and wasn't quite ready to discuss them yet, and focused instead on what he'd said about the way the Dragonstars lived. The news that they had a civilian setup instead of a military one surprised her, especially considering how much violence had passed between the Wyvern-moons and Dragonstars in the past couple of years.

"Where are they located exactly?" she asked.

"A little outside of Las Cruces, New Mexico. They have a town out there, along with a huge network of underground caverns that they live in."

She nodded, jotting yet another note in the journal she'd brought with her to the meeting. They'd been talking for only an hour and already she'd filled close to twenty pages with things she should have known but hadn't. Things she needed to know if she had any hope of keeping the Wyvernmoons from extinction.

"And where is the Shadowdrake clan from? I know they're in California, but—"

"San Diego," Gage said, in the slow, deep drawl that always reminded her of her childhood. "They're about an hour and a half outside of the downtown, and they live on a compound similar to ours."

"Thanks." She shot him a quick smile. He didn't return it like he normally would have, but he did nod, and there was a gleam in his eyes that none of the other dragons had. It made her feel a little better, though she couldn't have said why.

She added the information he'd given her to the notebook and then turned to Wyatt. "And thank you," she added, before continuing with her earlier train of thought. "So, Jacob *was* killed on some kind of raid of this town in New Mexico?"

"Yes." This time it was Dash who spoke up. "He took twenty or so dragons with him and attacked the woman who is now the Dragonstar queen."

"Why?"

"Excuse me?" She didn't think he could have looked more surprised if she had asked him to strip naked and crow like a rooster. Which told her a lot more about the Wyvernmoon state of mind than she wanted to believe.

"Why did he do it?" she repeated. "It's not like we don't have enough problems here at home with years of bad crops, poor food distribution to the civilian clan members and a war brewing with the Shadowdrakes. Why would he deliberately go down and antagonize the Dragonstars? Have they been attacking us and I'm just not aware of it?" she demanded.

"Noooo—"

"Yes." Acel interrupted Dash with a fierce frown. "Cecily, we've been engaged in skirmishes with both of those clans for decades now. You know that. Trying to understand one battle in the overall war is almost impossible."

"So now it's a full-scale war?" she demanded. "You actually consider us at war with these clans?"

"No, of course not," Remy said at the exact moment Julian responded, "Of course."

She raised an eyebrow and looked in astonishment at the other *factionnaires* in the room. "Well, which is it? Are we at war or aren't we?"

They all began talking at once, and after a minute, she gave up trying to follow a conversation that resembled a three-ring circus much more than it did a rational discussion. Instead, she reviewed the notes she had already taken for the day and waited for everyone to wind down so they could pick up where they'd left off.

Withdrawing from the conversation also gave her a chance to process the absolute shock she'd felt that half of the *Conseil* really believed that they were at war. How could that be? What had her father said to make them believe that he felt like war was a viable option at a time when they could barely feed their people?

And if he *had* said something, how could the rest of the *factionnaires* not pick up on it? How could they believe that the clan *wasn't* at war? She would've wondered if all this confusion—all these different definitions of war—had come about after her father's death, except for the fact that he had died in battle. As had Jacob. Which she had to believe meant he'd truly thought they were fighting for something important, so important that he was willing to risk his life and the lives of his son and his *factionnaires* to obtain it.

But what was it? What had he been trying to gain—or defend? she wondered as she concentrated on listing her thoughts in her notebook, no matter how random some of them were. This was how she thought things through, how she saw evidence of emerging patterns, by recording—by hand—all the information and ideas she ran across.

She was totally aware of the condescending way most of the *Conseil* had looked at her when they'd seen her pen and paper, as if she'd barely entered the twentieth century, let alone the twenty-first. She knew from the looks they'd shot one another that they thought her lack of computer savvy meant she was stupid.

It didn't, any more than her use of a notebook meant she didn't know her way—intimately—around the various computers and equipment that lined one long wall of the meeting room. She did. But this was her party, and she would do things her way. If that meant they underestimated her, well, then, they had nobody but themselves to blame.

As she kept her mouth shut and continued writing, she picked out a few choice phrases from the argument her *factionnaires* were still waging—just enough to let her know that there were two main schools of thought on the current issue. Either the Dragonstars and Shadowdrakes were provoking them and the Wyvernmoons were simply responding in kind, or the Wyvernmoons were doing the provoking.

She weighed the probabilities of both scenarios in her head, based on the information she currently had—which, she had to admit, was sorely lacking. She looked at them in combination with the things she'd already written down throughout the day and didn't like the conclusions she came to.

"Why have we been provoking them?" she asked when the room finally fell into a seething kind of silence.

"We haven't—" Julian started again, but she held up her hand to cut him off.

"I'm not aware of any raids from either of those clans on our compound in the past year. Longer, really, but let's go with the past twelve months, just to be clear. Except for the one where my father was killed."

"Like that wasn't enough?" Luc demanded. "They came here and killed our king. We should already be at war, instead of just contemplating it behind closed doors. What kind of a message does it send if we don't avenge Silus's death?"

"We've tried," Remy answered. "Brock got his neck snapped for the privilege, as have numerous others."

"That's because we're going at this piecemeal," Julian said firmly. "Everyone is doing their own thing, leading their own little faction. Whether it's Wyatt's group or Acel's or even mine. We all have our own agendas and we're not working together, when what we should be doing is uniting under one leader and going after them full force. This cloak-and-dagger stuff is ridiculous, especially considering the fact that we have the numbers to do it."

"But why do we want to do it?" Cecily demanded again. "I know they killed my family. I understand that, believe me. Nobody in this room misses Jacob more than I do. But I keep trying to figure this out, and every way I look at this, the blame is on us. *We* attacked *them*."

"That's not strictly true," said Garen. "Remember, they came here and killed Silus."

"Because we had Dylan MacLeod's mate!" Thierren answered. "Are you forgetting that?"

"The whys aren't important," Remy said with a wave of his hand.

"I beg to differ," Cecily objected. "The whys are everything here. Are we responsible for the situation we find ourselves in? Did we *cause* this enmity with the Dragonstars?"

An uncomfortable silence, one that had her stomach sinking as her worst fears were confirmed, filled the room. "And what about the Shadowdrakes? Did we also kidnap Rafael's mate?" she asked, referring to the Shadowdrake king.

"He has no mate," Devin answered.

"Because he hasn't found her yet, or because we killed her?"

"Cecily! You're being ridiculous!" Julian burst out.

"Am I, Julian? Am I, really?" Taking a deep breath, she spent a long minute trying to figure out what she wanted to say—and how she wanted to say it. Their battles, their raids, their war—whatever they wanted to call it—had systematically been weakening the clan for years, taking money and resources away from the civilian dragons in an effort to gain . . . what? She didn't have a clue, but whatever it was they were hoping to achieve, it hadn't happened so far. All they'd done was hurt themselves—hurt the clan—almost beyond repair.

But she couldn't say that, not now. After all, there really was no good way to accuse the men in the room—and her father—of treason. Or, at least, the closest thing to it. Because the longer she sat there looking at the evidence, the more it began to seem like that was exactly what had been going on.

Letting that fight go, for the moment, anyway, she asked, "What did we do to get the Shadowdrakes all worked up? They're pretty reclusive over there in California, and I have trouble imagining them killing sixty or so of our clan mates without provocation."

"It's not that simple," Nicolas said.

"On the contrary, I think it is exactly that simple. I have a hard time believing that two formerly peace-loving clans, acting independently of each other, suddenly have it out for us. Not for each other, not for anyone else, just for us. If we haven't done something to provoke this, then what the hell is going on?"

No one answered her, and no one looked her in the eye. Even Gage suddenly found his shoes a lot more interesting than her words. "Come on," she added impatiently. "Until I know exactly what caused all of this, how am I supposed to be able to stop it?"

"You think *you're* going to stop it?" Acel burst out incredulously. "When your father couldn't? That's—"

A well-placed elbow from Remy shut him up, but as she looked around her, she realized that nearly every man in the room was staring at her just as dubiously.

"Cecily, darling." Dax spoke up for the first time. "While we all very much appreciate your desire to be involved in the clan politics, the fact of the matter is, you're out of your depth here. You don't know all the history, you don't know the particulars and you don't know the players beyond the most superficial level. How, exactly, do you propose to devise a strategy to extricate us from this mess?"

His voice was soft, his body language nonconfrontational, but she knew when she'd been put in her place. Her father had certainly done it to her often enough.

The blood drained from her face as embarrassment filled her, along with a hopeless fury. Dax was her friend, had been for nearly her entire life. If he didn't have any faith in her, how was she supposed to win over the other dragons like Remy and Acel and Luc, who had been around for well over half a millennia and who didn't believe she had any right to even be in this room, let alone planning strategy for the clan?

For a minute, she reeled under the weight of just how much she had to do. A part of her wanted nothing more than to run back to her house and hide, never to be seen in this room again. She didn't need this—didn't need the suspicion and the sarcasm, the maliciousness and the doubts. She'd gotten more than enough of those things growing up as Silus's daughter.

But she couldn't just leave them to their own devices, either. With the route they were going, the clan would be under a full-scale attack in a matter of months. After all, you could pull a dragon's tail for only so long before it showed you its teeth. She had a feeling Dylan MacLeod and Rafael Vega were on the brink of doing more than just showing their teeth—the two kings were about to gobble up the Wyvernmoons once and for all. And while the *factionnaires* would pay—more than likely with their lives—so would the clan's civilian dragons, who would be dragged into the fight.

That she couldn't tolerate, not if there was any way she could stop it.

She had to try, had to say something profound right now, or any progress she'd made—which was, admittedly, almost nonexistent—would disappear and she'd end up even further behind than she had been when she'd marched in here yesterday.

"Diplomacy." She groped for a better explanation, something that would prove she at least had a clue about how this game was played. "We need to reach out to Rafael and Dylan, show them that we're not—"

"Reach out to the man who murdered our king?" Julian's fist banged down on the huge cherry table they were gathered around. "Are you insane? That will never happen!"

"I thought it was Dylan's wife who killed Silus?" she asked, determined to get the facts straight once and for all. Bad enough that she was, for all intents and purposes, fumbling around in the dark here. The least she could do was make sure she knew what she was talking about when she did open her mouth.

"He was there, and he would have killed your father if his mate hadn't gotten to Silus first. Besides, as anyone knows, the king is ultimately responsible for what his people do—particularly those in the royal family."

He was absolutely right. She knew he was, but he was twisting things around to suit his own agenda. That responsibility he talked of worked both ways. Yes, the king—or queen—was responsible for the actions of his or her clan members. But at the same time, he or she also had a responsibility to those same clan members, and it seemed to her that this two-way street was something her father and his *factionnaires* had completely forgotten through the years.

Yes, Dylan was responsible for his wife's killing of Silus, but Silus was responsible for having put her in a position where she felt murder was the only answer. They could go round and round for days, but whatever was said, whatever was thought, the fact remained that this problem belonged firmly on the Wyvernmoons' doorstep.

And since, according to the *Conseil*'s own beliefs, she was now responsible for what the Wyvernmoons did, there was no way she would sanction any more raids or attacks or battles or whatever the hell the *factionnaires* wanted to call them, unless she really believed they were necessary and in the Wyvernmoons' best interest. And she didn't, not now when they had so many other pressing issues to deal with. And maybe she never would.

But when she said as much to the *Conseil*, they looked at her as if she were insane. Even Thierren and Gage, whom she'd believed were at least mostly on her side, didn't seem to agree with the moratorium she was asking for.

"*Mon Dieu*, Cecily," said Julian, outrage in every line of his body. "I know you weren't close to your father, but I can't believe his death means so little to you that you want us to just let it go. 'Put it behind us,' didn't you say the last time we spoke?" He shook his head sadly, and she wondered if she was the only one who saw the gleam of triumph in his eyes. "I'm afraid I can't do that."

"None of us can," Remy agreed. "We need to avenge the deaths of your family and show both the Dragonstars and the Shadowdrakes that the Wyvernmoons are a force to be reckoned with."

"But we aren't. That's the point, isn't it? We're losing power with every one of these ill-advised raids. Soon, we'll be less than nothing." As soon as the words were out, she wanted desperately to take them back. They were exactly what Julian had wanted her to say—hell, he'd even led her there like a sheep too stupid to know what was about to happen.

Looking around, she saw that every man in the room wore a look of affront, as if she had just cast aspersions on his very manhood. And maybe she had, though that certainly hadn't been what she'd intended. But all dragons took the protection of their families, and their clans, very seriously, and that seriousness was doubled or tripled when dealing with the *factionnaires*. The most dominant of the clan's dragons, they lived—and died—to protect their people.

By saying that the Wyvernmoons couldn't stand up against their enemies—no matter how true that statement was—she had basically told the men sitting around her that they couldn't be trusted to take care of the clan. While she might believe that, saying it straight out was a rookie mistake and one she wouldn't soon recover from.

Once the significance of what she had done sunk in, she tried to backpedal as fast as she could. She knew it was too late, but she had to try to salvage a little bit of this disastrous meeting. "I'm sorry. I didn't mean that you—"

"I think we're done here," Thierren interrupted her. "It's been a long day. Let's say we'll pick it back up here tomorrow morning at nine."

The other men nodded, started gathering their things, and she knew if she didn't do something right then she was going to lose any hope she had of ever winning them to her side.

"Wait! I'm not done yet. There are still a number of things we need to consider. I want to talk about—"

"No offense, Cecily," Thierren said with a grin that was all sharp teeth and razor blades. "But I don't think anyone in this room really gives a shit what you want right now."

"Damn straight," said Dash as he headed for the door, the others right behind him.

And that was that. In less than a minute, the room was empty of everyone save her, and Cecily wanted nothing more than to lay her head on the huge cherry table and bawl her eyes out.

How could they just walk out on her like that? Yes, she'd said one wrong thing, but they'd been attacking her for two days and she was still there. She was still willing to work to save the clan. But she insulted them—accidentally—and they were through with her. It was bullshit, especially when she knew they never would have done it to her father.

But she wasn't her father or her brother. She was just stupid little Cecily, and what she wanted didn't matter. Just like it hadn't mattered to them that they were being manipulated by Julian. She knew that most—if not all—of them were aware of it, could see it in their faces and the way they'd responded to him at various times throughout the day. And yet they'd chosen him. Chosen his subterfuge and veiled insults and selfishness over her desire to get the clan going in the right direction again.

How could that be? How could they care so little about the clan they professed to love that they would rather rally behind an asshole with an agenda than behind her, simply because she was a woman? Even worse, she hadn't been able to do anything to stop it.

What it all boiled down to—what it always boiled down to—was that she had no authority to ask them for anything, let alone to enforce it. She was a member of the royal family, yes, but she was powerless.

Useless.

Her opinion of no import whatsoever.

They could walk away from her any time they wanted, and she had no way to stop them because she had no authority and she never would. She meant nothing to them, her opinions even less. The only reason the *factionnaires* had bothered to listen to her this long was out of courtesy—and respect for her dead father. But she'd killed that when she'd accidently said she didn't think they were up to the task of protecting the clan.

Furious with herself, with Julian, and with the entire *Conseil*, for that matter, Cecily slowly gathered her things while her mind went over the day's discussions again and again. By the time she headed out the front door, she had the need to cry under control, but her fury had become a wild, uncharted thing.

She wasn't wrong, damn it. That's what was so damn frustrating about this whole thing. She was right. She knew she was, and if they'd stop thinking with their dicks and egos for a few minutes, they'd see the truth, too.

The time for action, for fighting, for *war*, was over—if it had ever even existed to begin with. They needed to find a way to reconcile with the Dragonstars and the Shadowdrakes or they were doomed. Maybe not this month or even this year, but soon they would find themselves too weak to fight or even to make a stand.

She had run the numbers. Had looked at the percentage of healthy males in her clan, compared it to numbers she'd found in her father's study from the other two clans, and known that it wasn't possible for them to win a war against the two clans at the same time—especially if they were the aggressors. The term *home-field advantage* existed for a reason.

That wasn't even taking into account the fact that their people were currently overworked and on the brink of going hungry. Silus had put much less stock in his people than the kings who had come before him, and, as such, had not dealt with crop or employment issues for far too long. He'd funneled all the money he could into defense, and a few pet projects she had yet to get to the bottom of, while his people suffered.

She couldn't live with that, and she ached, physically, with the need to somehow help her people. But without the *Conseil's* support, her hands were tied. She could do nothing, not even access the clan's money to invest in resources. And after this afternoon's demonstration, she doubted that any of the *factionnaires* were going to come around to her point of view. But if they really did refuse to help her . . .

She shook her head as she walked slowly through the streets to her father's house. If they really did refuse to see her side of things, then she would have a lot more to worry about than whether the Wyvern-moons could win a war. They all would.

Survival would be their only goal, and it would be a frail and nebulous one at that.

CHAPTER SEVEN

He felt like a stalker. It had been less than twenty-four hours since he'd used his psychic gifts to seduce Cecily, and here he was, skulking around the outskirts of the compound while trying to pick up whatever he could about the Wyvernmoons. And while he obviously had motives for being here that had nothing to do with her—and he needed to concentrate on them if he was going to set his plan into motion—a part of his brain was constantly tuned to her, constantly searching for her on the psychic plane. And not because she was the Wyvernmoon princess.

It was a stupid move, damn near suicidal, and one he told himself to stop even as he sent his senses out in a wider circle to try to locate her. There was nothing to say that the Wyvernmoons didn't have a psychic dragon or two of their own, and the last thing he needed was for them to sense him out here. He'd planned on keeping his scan very light—*had* kept it very light—but even he couldn't go unnoticed forever. His chances of being discovered were growing exponentially the longer he stood out here searching for Cecily.

Why am I so determined to find her? he wondered. Was it what he'd told himself before he'd come on this little sojourn—that he wanted to parlay the momentum he'd gained with her the previous afternoon to get access to the Wyvernmoons? Though it made him feel like a total louse, he really hoped that was all it was. Because anything else, particularly the idea that he wanted to find Cecily because he'd enjoyed talking to her and kissing her and psychically fucking her the day before, didn't bear thinking about. Talk about what could easily become a disaster of epic proportions. Not to mention leave him feeling like a complete and total traitor.

Giving up on the spot he'd been lurking in for the past fifteen minutes, Logan began working his way along the outskirts of the compound. Situated in a kind of natural bowl, the Wyvernmoon headquarters were surrounded on all sides by craggy hills and mountains. Add to that the protection safeguards that enveloped the entire thing, and it should have been nearly impossible to breach the safety of its walls.

But he'd already found one way in and he hadn't even been looking for it. Not how Dylan had gotten in a few months ago when they'd come to retrieve Phoebe, but a viable place nonetheless. More viable, really, as he wouldn't have to transform into smoke to fit through it—which was a good thing, as that was definitely not a talent in his skill set.

Sneaking into the compound wasn't exactly the point, though. He could take the hole in the safeguards, could even use his extra senses to help him unravel them if he really needed to, but none of that would get him into the heart of Wyvernmoon society.

He needed to ingratiate himself with someone—preferably Cecily—and get invited into the center of the Wyvernmoon clan. Otherwise his entire plan would fail. An intruder showing up inside without an invitation would be shot on sight. And knowing the way the Wyvernmoons operated, the shots fired wouldn't be meant to wound.

Which was why he was pretty shocked that he'd been out here for nearly half an hour and had remained undetected. He knew he was good. Among the skills he'd learned as a rogue dragon, what Dylan had taught him through the years and his own psychic powers, he knew it was almost impossible to catch him if he didn't want to be caught. That wasn't arrogance talking, just simple fact. Camouflage, blending in and sneaking around were major talents of his, and when he'd left his spot on Cecily's mountain, he'd figured he would have to use every ounce of those skills to avoid the Wyvernmoon sentries.

Instead, he'd all but gotten an engraved invitation. As it was, he'd been allowed to work his way around the perimeter of the camp completely unbothered. While he'd taken the added precaution of staying invisible, that alone wouldn't protect him. Because it was a tool all dragons had, it was one that they were all trained to pick up on. He'd been prepared to flee at the first sign of trouble—or to ask to see the king. He'd concocted an entire story about seeking asylum for a little while, had practiced it on his flight down the mountain.

But, so far, none of his planned subterfuge had been necessary. It made the spot between his shoulder blades itch as he picked his way around the base of the mountain.

Where were the sentries, the famed Wyvernmoon *factionnaires* who for millennia had been almost impossible to defeat?

Where were the guards on patrol?

Where was any sign of self-awareness, any sign that they understood they needed to guard themselves against the outside world—particularly considering their extracurricular activities of late?

Sure, the safeguards were impressive, but safeguards were unraveled every day. Yes, each clan—and each dragon, even—had his own special safeguard weave, but that didn't make them impenetrable. Especially to Logan. One of the abilities that came with his psychic talents was being able to see other people's safeguards and the patterns they used to weave them. It gave him a huge advantage when he went to unweave them, an advantage he had planned to use to sneak on to the Wyvernmoon compound if absolutely necessary.

His beast roared at the thought of Cecily being unprotected. Its protectiveness alarmed him a little, but probably not as much as it should have, as his brain was having a nearly identical response. Cecily was vulnerable, open to attack, and he didn't like it.

His reaction was stupid—he knew it even as he was having it. He planned to use her, planned to bring down her clan however he could, and yet the idea of hurting her was abhorrent to him. The whole thing was ridiculous, especially considering what her family had done to the Dragonstars. Caring about her safety was absurd when he didn't know what she knew—and what she didn't—about the virus and the war parties.

Though Silus was dead, the virus continued to be manufactured. War parties were still sent to other clans. Treachery abounded. All of that could be starting with her. Probably was starting with her, if he wanted to be honest about it. She was the only living member of the royal family, after all.

He kept walking as he tried to puzzle out exactly what was going on. Part of him swore he was—that he had to be—walking into a trap, and yet he'd used every ounce of power he had and he still couldn't sense anything out here. He started to send out another psychic wave to see if he could find anyone, but if there were any dragons close by that he hadn't picked up on, they would feel the burst of power. And he'd be surrounded before he so much as had a chance to shift.

No, better to keep going as he was, using his regular senses, instincts and training to determine what he was facing.

He'd hiked about twenty miles around the compound—maybe one-fifth of the way around the massive enclosure—before he decided that he really was the only one out there. More than once he'd slowed down to regular human speed, making sure to make enough noise to attract the attention of the laziest sentry. But nothing had happened.

Shaking his head at this newest proof of the stupidity of the Wyvernmoons, Logan finally decided it was safe to dig a little and see what he could find out about the inner workings of the clan. It had been months since he had been here on the rescue mission for Phoebe, but he still had a pretty good idea of the layout of the place. Largely because when they'd gotten back to New Mexico, the group had gotten together and mapped out as much of the compound as they could remember. When he'd decided to do this, to come here, Dylan and he had sat down and gone over every inch of those maps until his king had been satisfied that he knew them like the back of his hand. He had copies in his bag, as well, but neither of them had been content to limit his knowledge to a piece of paper.

Orienting himself with the help of the landscape, the mountains and the stars that shone so brightly overhead, he called up a mental picture of the map. If he was right about where he was standing—and he was so sure that he didn't bother to pull the GPS out of the backpack he had slung over his shoulder—the laboratory was directly in front of him.

It was at least ten miles inside the compound, but it should be a straight shot from where he was standing. And if the lab was there, then he was close to one of the main defense areas in the compound. Loaded with weapons and usually having seven to ten soldiers and sentries guarding it, at least according to the intelligence some of the Dragonstars had been able to gather when they'd spied on the compound a few months before, it was one of the most sophisticated places in the whole operation. The fact that he was standing so close to it without sending off any alarms made him wonder just how bad the state of the Wyvernmoons was.

Not bad enough, obviously, as the attacks were still coming and the virus was still infecting some Dragonstars. If they were really in as bad a shape as this reconnaissance mission implied, wouldn't they be pulling back? Gathering their resources and trying to save what they could instead of antagonizing other clans?

But then again, nobody ever said that Silus had been sane. Cagey, yes. Sly, absolutely. Amoral, without a doubt. But sane? That was a whole different ball of wax, and the longer Logan stood out here, the more convinced he became that the Wyvernmoon king had lost his marbles sometime in the middle of his whole planned attack.

For the first time since he'd left New Mexico, Logan let himself breathe. If things were as bad here as he suspected, then this whole thing was going to be a lot easier than he had originally planned. He just might get out of this with his scales intact after all. Realizing that felt strange, especially after he'd spent so long preparing himself for death.

Feeling a little more secure than he had since he'd started on this journey, Logan finally let loose the stranglehold he'd been keeping on his psychic abilities for the past two hours. Instantly, his mind shot onto the psychic plane, his consciousness streaking out in different directions to cover the 180 degrees straight in front of him. He couldn't cover the whole compound, obviously, but he could cover a semicircle of about fifteen miles from where he was standing, as long as the area was on the psychic line that extended out from him in both directions.

As he went seeking, he braced himself for an onslaught of psychic noise—people thinking and talking and going about the actions of their daily life. That was the problem with opening himself up like this: to try to pick up a few important facts, he had to leave himself completely vulnerable to everything else out there.

Surprisingly, the chatter wasn't nearly as bad as he'd expected it to be for a clan of this size. He picked up a few stray thoughts—a woman trying to decide what to make for dinner, a few men playing a poker game (one had a really good hand, but was too new to the game to understand that) and some Wyvernmoon children trying to organize a basketball game of three on three. Most of them were thinking about the game, but one of the boys was concentrating a lot harder on trying to find a way to impress the girl who was watching him. He was hoping he'd have an on day, that the strange body he was still getting used to wouldn't betray him at an important point in the game.

Curious, Logan delved a little deeper, trying to figure out why being dragon was new to him when he was at least fifteen or sixteen. Most dragons were born with their beasts as sentient beings inside them. By the time they were toddlers, they were fully aware the thing was there.

When he streaked into the kid's mind, however, he came out grinning. It wasn't the dragon the kid was worried about—it was the long, gangly arms and legs that he was still getting used to. Though it had been nearly four hundred years, Logan remembered that feeling well. He'd been barely sixteen when he'd shot up to six foot seven, and for a while nothing had been safe—least of all his own pride. He'd knocked things over, crashed into walls, done any number of crazy things as he'd tried to get used to the body that had seemed to change overnight. He hoped the kid had better luck with his girl than Logan had at his age.

He frowned as soon as the thought came to him. Why did he care about some Wyvernmoon kid and whether he impressed the current girl of his dreams? He'd come here to cripple the clan so badly that it would take centuries for them to recover—if they ever did.

He couldn't afford to worry about the children or the other innocent members of the clan any more than he could afford to worry about Cecily. If he did, he would never be able to do what he'd come here to, and there was no way he was leaving the Dragonstars vulnerable to this kind of threat. Not after everything Dylan and the others had done for him.

Leaving the boys behind, he shifted his focus a little. Lowered the very last of the internal shields he kept between his brain and the rest of the world. Immediately, he was bombarded from all sides, so hard and so fast that for a moment he thought his head was literally going to explode.

Dropping to his knees, hands to his head, he struggled to get control over all the feedback that was flooding into him. He was tempted to raise the blocks again—at least the first one—and had actually started to reconstruct it when a stray thought got through the mishmash, one that had excitement thrumming in his veins even as it concerned him.

What can I say to convince Cecily that I'm right? That she has to go along with me?

He focused on the thought, did his best to sort through everything else to find the person it belonged to. For a couple of minutes, he found nothing. Under normal circumstances, he might have been tempted to give up. His headache was so bad it felt like his head was going to shatter into a million different pieces.

But he hadn't expected this to be easy. He forced himself to ignore the nauseating pain and to remain open as he divided the area he'd been focused on into a series of manageable groups. Then he started scanning the groups one at a time. It took precious minutes that he didn't have, but he refused to stop until he'd combed every quadrant. Maybe it had just been a passing thought, but then again, maybe it had been—

He hit pay dirt on the fourth of the seven quadrants he had set up in his head. A voice, deep and self-assured, was running through a bunch of arguments in his head. Arguments that Logan knew were destined for Cecily.

With a frown, he settled onto a nearby rock and prepared to listen to everything this guy wanted to say.

"Hey, Cecily, wait up!" Thierren's voice sounded behind her, but she was too frustrated and too hurt to deal with him right then. She quickened her pace, hoping that if she moved fast enough she'd make it inside the house before he caught up with her. Normally, it would be a ridiculous goal—he was a *factionnaire*, after all—but her house was close and he was still a ways back. One more minute and she'd make it.

A hand closed around her elbow and she mentally cursed, even as she turned to the man she'd always considered one of her closest friends. Amazing the difference a day made. Making sure she kept a cool, impersonal smile on her face, she said. "Yes, Thierren? Can I help you?"

He groaned, tried to pull her into his arms for a hug, but she refused to give in. Not this time. Not only had he embarrassed her in front of the entire *Conseil*, but he had also been largely responsible for their walking out on her in the middle of the discussion. That was something she could not forget or forgive. Not at this delicate juncture in time.

"Come on, Ceece. Don't be like this."

"I'm not being like anything, Thierren. It's been a long day and I'm tired. I want to go home."

"Good. I'll come with you." He started to walk, his grip on her arm firm enough that she didn't have a choice but to follow along with him. It burned her ass, especially since he was holding on to the same arm Julian had savaged the day before, but she absolutely refused to engage in a power struggle out here in the middle of the street for everyone to see. She wouldn't give him the satisfaction.

Besides, she was smart enough to know that the whole world was watching and waiting for just such an occurrence. Julian would love if he had public proof of a break between her and any of the *factionnaires* who might actually support her. Of course, that was assuming any were left after the debacle earlier that afternoon.

Still, she couldn't just let the manhandling pass without at least making a comment. "You're not invited," she snapped.

"I should be. Because if you want to get out of this disaster alive, I would strongly suggest you take a few minutes to listen to me. Otherwise, I wouldn't put a dollar down on your odds of surviving the next week."

CHAPTER EIGHT

Cecily slowly opened the door to her father's house, still not sure she'd made the right decision when she'd chosen to invite Thierren back to her place. She was still furious with him for expressing such blatant doubts in front of all the other dragons, but at the same time, they had a long history. She respected him and knew that whatever he had to say, it would be exactly what he believed. He didn't pull any punches, nor did he have secret agendas. Unlike a lot of the other *factionnaires*, with Thierren, what you saw was what you got.

"Do you want something to drink?" she asked as she hung her jacket on the tall, wooden coat rack that stood just inside the front door. She was determined to appear normal, though inside she was reeling, her defenses crumbling rapidly.

Had things really gotten that bad that quickly, or had she just been oblivious for too long?

Was her life really in jeopardy?

And if it was, why? As this afternoon had proven, she was far from a threat to anyone's bid for power.

Or was Thierren just overstating things, going for the effect? That wasn't like him, but as she was finding, everything changed when a shot at the throne was in the mix.

He hung his coat next to hers and then answered, "I don't know," with a grin that was one hundred percent Thierren. "Are you planning on poisoning me?"

"I suppose that depends on what you have to say."

"I think I'll pass, then."

"Suit yourself," she said with a shrug. "We can talk in here." She led him into the parlor that rarely got used.

As soon as they entered the small, fussily decorated sitting room off the foyer, Thierren closed the doors with a solid thump. She raised an eyebrow at him, but it was his turn to lift and lower his shoulders. "There are a lot of people who work in this house. I don't want—"

"I'm not my father. I employ only three people now, and they all live off-site. We're alone here."

As soon as she said the words, Cecily regretted them. Maybe it would have been smarter to let Thierren believe there were others around. It certainly would have been safer.

But she was being stupid. This was Thierren. He'd played hopscotch with her when she was a child, had held her when she'd gotten her first skinned knee. No matter how treacherous the times were, there was no way he would hurt her. He just didn't have it in him.

"Look," he said with a grimace. "I'm really sorry that I didn't stick up for you at the meeting today."

"It's fine." She didn't want him to know how much it had hurt her that not one of the three dragons she'd expected to support her claims had done so. Besides, she shouldn't complain. She'd wanted to know where she stood. It wasn't Thierren's or Gage's or even Wyatt's fault that where she stood was absolutely nowhere.

That was her father's fault and her own. People treated her like she was nothing, like she was incompetent, because that was how she had acted for so long. Sitting inside this house, simpering and wearing pretty dresses because that was what her father had wanted from her. She'd brought this on herself.

Still, it would have been nice if one of the few people she considered a friend, one of the few people whom she thought knew the real her, had given her the benefit of the doubt. Then again, this whole week had been a learning experience for her. Not a good experience, but a learning one nonetheless.

"No, it isn't. I understand that you felt abandoned in there today—"

"I was abandoned. You walked out on me." To hell with the stiff upper lip; she wanted to know why he'd done what he'd done. "How could you have done that? I know I made a mistake, but, really, Thierren, couldn't you have at least given me a chance to explain?"

"I could have, but it wouldn't have done you or me any good. I can't afford to be associated with you right now. None of us can, not if we want to help you. Julian's out for blood, and if he can't have yours, he'll settle for whoever steps in front of the sword."

She ignored the new pang of hurt his words caused her and focused on the important part of his statement. "So, you sacrificed me in an effort to appease him."

"It wasn't like that!"

"It was exactly like that," she snapped. "But, out of curiosity, how exactly is denouncing me in public part of a plan to help me?"

"Come on, Cecily. You know better than that. You can't just walk into the Dracon Club and think you're going to be able to change things overnight. Thousands of years of tradition and law have gone into the way things are done in this clan."

"I know that!"

"Do you? Do you, really? Because the way you're shaking things up, it seems like you just got here. Acel and Remy will never go for what you're proposing, not if you're the one proposing it. And if they don't follow you, neither will Luc nor Etienne nor even Blaze. And without them, and with Julian gunning for you, you've lost the *Conseil* before you've even gotten a running start."

"They're only five *factionnaires* out of fourteen. I don't need them."

"That just shows how naive you are. This isn't a democracy. Voting numbers don't mean shit here. We follow the king—"

"The king is dead, in case you haven't noticed! I'm the closest thing we've got, and while I admit I'm a disappointment, I still think some kind of leadership has to be better than nothing at all."

"That's just it. You're not a disappointment. You're becoming exactly what some of us have been waiting for you to be. But, Cecily, you're still a woman. You can only do so much, no matter how strong and smart you are. Not just with the *factionnaires*, but with the entire clan. Very few of the civilians will ever accept you as queen, not without a husband."

She shook her head as her stomach revolted violently at what he was implying. "I'm not marrying Julian. Even if I could imagine—for one second—tying myself to that man, I wouldn't do it. He's exactly what the clan doesn't need right now. He's cold-blooded and merciless and has a secret agenda about a mile long. He is *not* what is best for this clan."

"I'm not disagreeing. I've always thought your father was wrong to try to force him on you—you know that. But what if you don't have to marry Julian?"

"What do you mean? I know my father has used me as a bargaining chip for years, but I thought it was understood these past couple of years that he had decided to give me to Julian."

"He had. But, as you so eloquently pointed out a few moments ago, your father is dead. Any agreements, any wishes he had, died with him."

"So what are you saying? That I should marry one of the other *factionnaires*, even after what happened this afternoon?"

"That's exactly what I'm saying. If you have a husband who is more open-minded about the lines of succession, one who understands you and believes in the vision you seem to have for the clan, the two of you can move the Wyvernmoons in the right direction. In the direction you want us to go."

"It's not about wanting it," she told him impatiently. "Continuing on our current path means annihilation. I can't believe you don't see that."

"I do see it."

His instant acquiescence made her a little uneasy, when she'd expected to feel nothing but relief. But that was just her being weird after what had happened at the meeting—she should be glad that someone was finally seeing things her way. So instead of questioning his seemingly lightning-fast change of heart, she simply said, "Good. Because I refuse to sit by and watch as we destroy ourselves."

"I feel exactly the same way. That's what I've been trying to tell you."

"It didn't exactly seem that way in the club."

"I already explained that. You were going about things the wrong way back there."

"And you think you know the right way?"

"I do, actually."

"Really? So should I draw names out of a hat until I hit on someone whom I can actually stand and who can stomach being married to me, as well?"

"I don't think you need to do anything that drastic," he said with a smile.

Warning bells went off in her head at the smooth seduction of his grin, then started clanging at top volume when he shifted his weight so that he was sitting close enough for their thighs to brush. She told herself she was being stupid, even as her heart stuttered in her chest. After all, they'd sat like this many times through the years. Tonight was no different.

Except then he reached for her hands, brought them to rest on his knees. The warning bells turned to shrieks even before his thumbs started to stroke across the back of her hand, again and again.

"What are you doing?" she demanded, trying to pull her hands back from his grip. Inside her, her dragon woke up with a vengeance, snarling and growling at Thierren when it usually tolerated him. If she was completely honest with herself, she would admit that the beast had never particularly liked her friend, but that had never mattered to her before. Thierren had been nice to her when no one else had, when there'd been nothing to gain from it.

Or, at least, when she'd thought there'd been nothing to gain. Now she wasn't so sure. Hadn't she just been thinking yesterday that he was the one dragon she didn't have to worry about? That he had no illusions—or delusions—about marrying her to get his hands on the crown?

Could she really have been so mistaken?

Had she put more faith in him than he deserved?

God, she hoped not. She wasn't sure she could take it if that was the case. She'd trusted Thierren for years, had told him her secrets when she hadn't been willing to tell anyone else. If all of those meetings, all that friendship, had just been leading up to a marriage proposal, she wasn't sure she'd be able to take it. Not without crying—or at least not without taking a swing at him.

"Cecily," he crooned, leaning down so that his lips were only a few inches from her cheek. As he did, she felt the last little bit of hope inside her dissipate. So much so that when he opened his mouth and started to speak, his words weren't even a surprise.

"You know, I've never had any interest in being part of the royal family. I've never wanted the responsibility that comes with ruling a clan—that's not really my thing. But I feel like I don't have a choice—"

"You have a choice," she interrupted.

"What?" He looked confused, and she realized she'd thrown him off his spiel.

"I said, 'You have a choice.'"

"I know that. But I can't just leave you to struggle through this on your own. We've been friends for a long time. I need to step up now and let you know that I'm here for you, any way that you need me to be."

"Any way that I need you?"

"Yes."

"Including going beyond the normal boundaries of friendship? You would take your affection that far?"

"For you? Absolutely."

The words were sweet, exactly what she might have wanted to hear yesterday or last week or last month. But two days spent with her father's *factionnaires* had made her more cynical, less naive. And if that hadn't done the job, the calculating gleam in Thierren's eyes certainly would. Though he was doing his best to look soulful, she swore she could see the avarice in his gaze.

The betrayal cut like a knife. Not for him or her or the situation they now found themselves in, but for the relationship she had once believed they'd had. For the friendship she had once valued above all others.

This time when she tugged at her hand, he let it go—probably because he thought she wanted to throw her arms around him and thank him from rescuing her from the big, bad wolves. Or, to be more precise, the bigger, badder dragons. But she was no damsel in distress, not anymore, and if he thought she was going to latch on to the first offer she got, then he was sadly mistaken.

"I appreciate that, Thierren. I really do. As this . . . situation unfolds, it's going to be important for me to know who I can trust."

He blinked a little at her tone, and she didn't blame him. It wasn't one she'd ever used with him before—wasn't one she could ever remember using with anyone, actually. "I'm glad I can put your mind at ease," he answered, but his smile was a lot more unsettled than it had been just a few minutes before.

"Oh, you definitely did that. I'm so glad I can count on your support from this point forward. It will make it so much easier to convince some of the other *Conseil* members."

"Yeah, of course." He cleared his throat. "But I was kind of hoping to make my support for you a little more public."

"More public than a *Conseil* meeting?" She widened her eyes as she spoke, deliberately playing into the misunderstanding. She wanted to hear him say it—a part of her still wanted to believe in him, and she needed to plainly hear his betrayal, just to make sure she wasn't making another mistake. "I don't think we need to advertise that I'm taking over to the entire clan, not yet. As you said earlier, some might not be ready to accept a female ruler—especially some of the older dragons."

Now he looked pained, his smile definitely strained around the edges. "That's not what I meant. I was thinking along the lines of something more formal, more permanent."

"Oh, really? Like what?" *Don't say it, don't say it, don't say it,* she pleaded with him silently. *Please let me have misread the signals. Let me have made some terrible mistake.*

But then he said it—the words she'd been dreading since he first took hold of her hands. "I think you should marry me, Cecily."

She reared back in pretend shock. "Marry *you*? I thought you just said that you didn't want to be king."

"I didn't. I mean, I don't. But I can put aside my own desires and do this for you. I'd never turn my back on you when you need me."

He wrapped his arm around her shoulder and she nearly puked on his shoes. It was bad enough that he wanted to marry her to cement his own position in the clan. It was another thing altogether for him to treat her like she was a brainless loser who was too stupid to see the writing on the wall.

She was torn between raking her talons down his face and telling him to go to hell. She wanted to do both, wanted to draw his blood so badly that she could barely breathe with the desire for it. But that wasn't the way to get ahead with the Wyvernmoons, not with her father's *Conseil* and not with him. He'd approached her like a gentleman—or the closest thing a slug like him could manage. It would be bad form to respond as anything less than a lady.

"That's—that's a very kind offer, Thierren." She stumbled over the lie, got the words out from sheer will alone. "But I couldn't ask you to make a sacrifice like that for me."

He reached up, ran a soft hand down her cheek. "It's no sacrifice, Cecily. I want to do this."

Damn right, he does. So much so that he was champing at the bit, impatience in every line of his body. As if talking to her, let alone wooing her, was just a waste of his time on his mad dash for the grand prize. That she had gone from being someone this man sought out to talk to, to nothing more than a means to an end infuriated her all over again. A way for him to get the power she had never had a clue that he craved.

Unable to bear his touch a second longer, she stood up abruptly. For one moment, she saw a flash in his eyes, a fleeting glimpse of the impatience and annoyance she could feel seething right below the surface. And then it was gone, smoothed away like it had never existed, and that, more than anything else, was the death knell for his suit.

He was faking everything. The affection, the concern, the care. Faking it all in an effort to get a ring on her finger—and one on his. The royal ring, to be exact. How stupid to find out that she had been hoping, even through this whole conversation, that he at least felt *something* for her, as she did for him. Not romantic love, as that had never been between them. But was affection too much to hope for, in all the time they'd spent together? All the discussions they'd had?

In losing her father, had she really lost everything else, as well, *everyone* else, as well? It seemed like she had, only she'd been far too stupid to realize it. That thought grated above all others.

Turning her back on Thierren, she walked to the window. Looked out at the dark night and tried to fight the sudden hatred for the Dragonstars that welled up inside her. In killing her brother, they had done this to her. In killing her father, they had taken away any hope she might have had for a normal relationship—not even a sexual one, but *any* normal relationship.

A part of her wanted to lash out at them, to hurt them as they had hurt her, and to hell with what was best for the clan. The *factionnaires* would love it, and it might actually get her some support from them.

She could put together the biggest war party yet, could throw some of her own formidable magic behind it, could . . .

She cut off the rest of the thoughts before they could fully form. What was the point, anyway? Going after Dylan or his mate or his council, for that matter, wasn't going to bring her father back. Nor was it going to change the situation she now found herself in as she attempted to navigate through the sudden avalanche of interest and nefarious intentions that seemed to be assailing her from all directions.

Thank God she'd been raised in the Black Hills, where avalanches were fairly common in the wintertime. She'd learned early on how to survive in an inhospitable climate.

She turned back to Thierren with a smile on her face. "You've given me so much to think about, I can scarcely wrap my mind around it." She crossed to him, extended her hands and then forced herself not to flinch when he took them. "I knew I could count on you to have my best interests at heart, to try to help me when so many of the others were calling for my blood."

The bastard didn't even have the grace to look uncomfortable when he nodded and squeezed her hands. Instead, a smile bloomed across his face—the first real one she had seen all night. It only made her angrier.

"I'll always look out for you, Cecily. I've been doing it your whole life, after all."

No, he'd been looking out for himself her whole life. It was amazing how this new side of him tainted every memory she had of him. "I know you have, Thierren, and I can't tell you how much I appreciate your honesty. But I need you to go now. I have a lot to think about—"

"Don't think too long, Cecily. They won't wait forever, and you don't want to end up at Julian's mercy—either in the *Conseil* room or as his wife."

Annoyed beyond measure at his attempt to rush her, she let a little of her true emotional state shine through for the first time. He blinked, seemingly taken aback by the malice glittering behind her royal smile. She was glad of it, liked this proof that Thierren didn't know her nearly as well as he thought he did.

"Oh, don't worry about that. I have absolutely no intention of ending up in a position where Julian has power over me. No intention at all." She opened the parlor door and waited with thinly veiled impatience for Thierren to walk through it. "Now I must ask you to leave. I have much planning to do, and I'm afraid I can't do it with you here."

"But, Cecily, I had hoped that we could reach some understanding tonight—"

"Oh, I understand perfectly, Thierren."

Her oldest friend blanched. "What do you mean by that?"

She pretended to be confused. "That you've explained things admirably, of course. Why? Did you think I meant something else?"

He stumbled through some ridiculous explanation, but she was no longer listening. She escorted him to the front door, suffered through a hug from him when all she really wanted to do was slide a dagger between his ribs, then all but shoved him out the front door.

She slammed it behind him. Then locked it for the first time that she could remember.

CHAPTER NINE

Cecily leaned against the door she had just slammed and tried to pretend that her heart wasn't breaking wide open. It didn't work—but then, she hadn't really expected it to. After all, she'd never been the most accomplished liar, and no amount of self-denial was going to change that. Not now that she knew where she stood. Not now that Thierren had shown her exactly how unimportant she was in the grand scheme of things.

The only thing that mattered to him or to any of the others was the fact that she'd been born a Fournier. Any affection she had imagined that they held for her was nothing more than an illusion—and one they couldn't keep up as their own ambitions started to overrule their common sense. She'd thought it was her fault they had walked out this afternoon, that it was because of her mistake. But the truth was, they'd been waiting for an excuse to make her look like a fool. That she had handed it to them was her fault. That they had wanted it to begin with was completely theirs.

Sinking into the leather wingback chair that had stood next to the front door for as long as she could remember, she looked around the house that had always been much more a prison to her than it had ever been a comfort. It was beautiful, pristine, elegant to the extreme. The colors were understated but rich—golds and browns with accents of ivory and rich, dark green. Thick rugs covered gleaming wood floors, and heavy tapestries hung on the walls, side by side with original paintings by famous French Impressionists in ornately gilded frames.

It was a showplace, a modern-day castle with twin purposes: to boast and to intimidate. God knew it had fulfilled those purposes well—at least in her case. She'd been intimidated by this house practically from the time she was old enough to walk. Certainly from the time her mother had died. Everything here had a place, from the furniture to the dishes to her father and brother. She was the lone outsider, the one possession of her father's that had never quite been able to fit in.

Was it any wonder, then, that months after his death she still hadn't found her bearings?

Her shoulders slumped and Cecily buried her head in her hands as she tried to ignore the doubts that were crowding in on her from every side. Maybe she really was making an ass out of herself with her crusade to bring peace to the Wyvernmoons. Maybe she was as naive, as stupid, as the members of the *Conseil* seemed to think she was.

But whatever she was, whatever she knew or didn't know, she was certain that things couldn't go on this way. They just couldn't. If the clan was strong, if business as usual was moving along on a fairly even keel, maybe she could fight this fight. Maybe she could even win it. But time was a luxury that was not on her side, a luxury that wouldn't be on her side until she found a way to control the different factions all vying to take over.

And since they obviously weren't going to unite under her, there really was only one answer. She would have to take a husband. She would have to provide the clan with a king.

The thought of how badly she had failed—and how much she was going to have to give up because of that failure—grated and burned until she was half-mad with pain and sorrow. Everything she had, everything she was, longed to escape from her duty and all the agony and uncertainty and responsibility that came with it.

Maybe I could. The thought crept inside her slowly, so slowly that it took her a minute or two to really register it. When she did, she froze. Her mind flooded with what her life would be like if she simply took herself out of the game. If she just flat-out refused to play anymore.

Excitement welled up inside her at the thought of such freedom, and instantly Logan's face popped into her head. He was rogue, completely free from responsibility to a clan. Master of his own fate. And he was happy—she could see that in his smile, see the joy shining from his eyes when he spoke to her. She wanted to be like him, without a care in the world. And, after her fantasy last night, wanted to be with him, as well. So much so that she had reached for the door handle before the idea had fully formed in her head.

No more would she do what they wanted her to do just because they wanted her to do it.

No more would she be moved around just to make their lives easier.

From now on, she would do what *she* wanted to do, and to hell with the consequences.

Why shouldn't I? she wondered fiercely. She hadn't been brought up for this. Her father had not once looked at her and told her that she needed to be ready to rule in case something ever happened to Jacob and him. In fact, if he had a grave, the old man would be rolling in it at the very thought.

And yet . . . and yet, really, what alternative was there for her? Did she really want Logan's life? Did she really want to go rogue? Have nowhere to fit in, nowhere to call home? She might hate this house and everything it stood for, but it was still her home. A place where she could go when she wanted to get away from the prying eyes for a little while.

What would she do if she no longer had it?

What would she do, really, if she no longer had *anywhere* to belong?

Besides, who did the clan need more than its princess?

She thought back to the encounter she had had the week before, the one that had lit the fire under her desire to be a true queen. A civilian woman had come up to her to beg her pardon for her husband. She had pardoned him—of course she had, he'd done nothing wrong but take things into his own hands when the clan had failed him and his wife—but neither her father nor the *factionnaires* had cared about him or his family when the case had come up for trial. They had ignored them, tossed them aside like they were little more than garbage.

Like they were nothing more than pawns who existed for the *Conseil*'s amusement and abuse.

It had bothered her, angered her, made her determined to be more than an ineffectual figurehead for her people. Little had she known that, within days, the *Conseil* would have turned her into a pawn for much the same purpose.

The horror of that dawning knowledge hit her hard and she slid off the chair, not even noticing when she hit the ground hard. Wrapping her arms around her knees, she started to rock. And let the idea, the dream of being free, go before it had a chance to take root.

She wasn't going to turn rogue today or ever. Wasn't going to give up her clan or her position. Not because she needed or wanted the life of luxury provided to her by her birth and last name, but because as much as she tried to pretend otherwise, her people needed her.

Which meant that she was going to take the only road open to her. She was going to get married. She was going to pick a *factionnaire*, elevate him to king and spend the rest of her life working behind the scenes to make her people's lives better. The dream she'd had of ruling as queen, of one day finding a man who would rule alongside her equally, was just that: a childish pipe dream. It would never have worked out, and it was better that she realize it now, before she'd completely alienated every man on the *Conseil*.

Too bad she hadn't realized it before every single one of *them* had alienated *her*.

The idea of taking one of them for a husband physically hurt her, made her ache in a hundred different ways. It also begged the question— whom should she choose?

Not Julian, obviously, as he would rule the clan, and her, with an iron fist.

Not Acel and Remy, who were both too old for her, not to mention too mean.

Not Thierren, who was already drunk on the power of being her friend. His abuses of the position might be different from Julian's or Acel's or Remy's, but they would occur nonetheless.

Wyatt, she wondered, with his good looks and charm, both of which hid a wicked temper and a dark past?

Dash, who made almost everything a joke but who hadn't seen the need to stick around and back her up that afternoon?

Or Gage? She shuddered at the thought of being married to the man who had been a combination big brother/father figure for her entire life. Just the idea of the intimacy required of such an arrange-ment made her queasy—especially since she would be required to pro-vide the next heir to the throne.

And yet Gage was truly the only one who had not spoken against her. The only one who had held his tongue as she had bumbled through the motions of trying to take over the clan. And he had been the last one to leave the room that afternoon.

He hadn't helped her, but he hadn't actively sabotaged her, either.

She snorted at the thought. What a way to pick a husband—not based on mutual affection or attraction or even common goals, but on who had not actively tried to hurt her in the last week. God, her life had deteriorated even more than she'd thought.

If it was to be Gage, then . . . If it was to be Gage . . . Her stomach twisted, threatened to revolt, but she breathed through her mouth until the nausea passed. If it was to be Gage, then she would have to recon-cile herself to the idea of him touching her, kissing her, making love to her. If he was to take control of the warring factions of the clan, theirs would have to be a real marriage in every way.

But how could it be when the idea of being with him left her not just cold, but physically ill? Oh, he was good-looking, smart, even charming when he wanted to be. But he was also a man she had considered family for far too long.

Is this how it's going to be, then? she wondered feverishly. Would she have to give up any chance of experiencing passion or lust or truly magnificent sex? She had dreamed of finding a mate for decades, had dreamed of finding a man with whom she could willingly, openly share her body and her heart.

Now, however, she was going to be forced to settle for a man who desired her even less than she desired him.

She tilted her head back. Rested it against the wall and closed her eyes. Unbidden, an image of Logan rose behind her closed lids—huge and warm and so sexy that he made her toes curl and her mouth water. It had been amazing to be touched by him, held by him, kissed by him. Amazing and wonderful and so hot that it had sparked a fantasy unlike any she had ever experienced before.

A tingling started in her lower abdomen at the reminder of how she had spent a large portion of the previous night, and then the sensation spread through her breasts and her sex until she was all but squirming with the need it evoked. The idea that she was going to have to give up all that passion, that she was going to have to live the rest of her life without ever finding out what it meant to be made love to by him—

No, damn it! Just no! She sprang to her feet, stormed out of the house before she was even conscious that she had moved. But as she shifted—her clothes falling away as the dragon emerged—she knew exactly what she wanted to do. What she was *going* to do.

She took to the sky in a headlong flight, speeding through the starry night with renewed strength and purpose and focus. She would mortgage her future, settle for a passionless marriage and an empty crown, all in an effort to save her clan. But she would be damned if she was going to do any of that before she'd found out what it was like to truly touch someone and be touched by him. And not anyone, either. It was Logan her body burned for, and Logan she would have, at least once, before she had to lock herself and her passions away forever.

"I have to admit, I expected better progress from you," Shawn said seconds after he flashed into existence about five feet away from where Logan was sitting, trying to get a grip on the anger working its way through him.

"Keep doing that, asshole, and you're going to end up getting gutted," Logan growled. But he relaxed his fingers, slid the dagger that was never far from him back into its sheath. As he did, he forced his mental patterns back to normal. It took a few seconds, as he'd been prepared to dig into the enemy's brain and rip it to shreds at the first sign of trouble.

"Geez, you're losing your touch. Usually you know I'm coming to see you before I do."

"So sue me. It's not exactly easy to keep up the mental connection across a thousand miles."

"Yeah, but I've seen you do it over much longer distances before. You must be getting old."

Logan ignored him. Hoped if he didn't talk to him, his friend would go away.

But Shawn had always been notoriously thick-skinned, and this was no exception. Settling down on the ground next to where Logan crouched, he stretched out his legs in front of him before flashing in two bottles of beer. He held one out to Logan.

Logan looked at the bottle for a minute, then shook his head before taking it. "Should I ask where these came from?"

"My refrigerator," his friend replied with an affronted look. "I'm not a thief."

"You don't think it's going to look funny—two beers out here in the middle of nowhere, floating in midair, since we're currently invisible?"

"Jesus, what put that stick up your ass today? I'm shielding them, so relax."

Logan popped off the top, then took a long swig of beer, wondering how long it was going to take Shawn to spit out whatever it was he had come to talk about. He figured less than a minute.

But a few minutes passed with Shawn doing nothing more than companionably drinking his beer. So Logan turned his attention back to the asshole who had just made Cecily a proposal she had damn well better refuse. He figured she would, despite what she'd said when she'd shown him the door. The vibes rolling off her had been absolutely frigid. She'd been polite to the bastard, but she'd seemed upset by what he had to say, and Logan hoped that meant that she had seen through that whole smarmy act of his.

He'd wanted to delve inside her head and see what she was thinking, but the shields of that guy—Thierren—had been almost impenetrable. It had taken all of Logan's considerable talent to eavesdrop on his thoughts and the conversation, and he didn't have enough power left over to tap into her thoughts.

Thierren's thoughts hadn't been all that illuminating, at least not in terms of helping out the Dragonstars. They had, however, given Logan insight into how the *factionnaires* viewed Cecily. Within two minutes of being in Thierren's head, he'd wanted to beat him, and everyone else on the *Conseil*, into unconsciousness. Men who treated women like these guys did—who thought that badly of them—deserved to have their asses handed to them.

Logan scanned the areas around Cecily's house, then widened his search, but the bastard had disappeared. Either he wasn't thinking about anything, which Logan could believe, as he hadn't exactly seemed like the sharpest tool in the shed, or he was deliberately shielding.

Despite his opinions on Thierren's intelligence, Logan had the feeling it was probably the latter. Which meant he'd either felt Logan's scan, which he really hoped wasn't the case, or he was with someone who had enough psychic talent that he'd felt the need to completely block himself.

Shit. That was all he needed to deal with—another psychic dragon. His shields were excellent, but there was always somebody better out there. His life depended on the fact that a Wyvernmoon wasn't that somebody.

More than a little pissed off, Logan gave up looking. Though he kept the top layer of his consciousness focused inside the compound, he turned the rest of his attention to Shawn. His friend's unnatural silence was freaking him out. Finally, when he couldn't take it anymore, he demanded, "So, what are you doing here?"

Shawn shrugged. "I came to check up on my best friend. Is that not allowed?"

"Not when I'm supposed to be a rogue dragon, without friends or clan affiliations. And you practically have *Dragonstar* stamped on your forehead."

"Don't worry about it. No one's out there right now."

He didn't argue, because he knew Shawn was right. He'd done a scan right before he'd arrived. The only thing currently moving around on the mountains was the wildlife.

"So, seriously, how's it going?"

Logan shrugged. "As good as to be expected, I suppose."

"Really? Because you've been gone more than a week and you're still sleeping in the hills instead of on the Wyvernmoon compound. Is that psychic mind meld of yours not working?"

"I think you have me confused with Spock from *Star Trek*. I don't even know what a mind meld is."

"Don't go getting all technical. You know what I mean."

"I'm working on it. Things are complicated."

"Really? Do tell."

"Shawn—"

"Come on. You know I like to live vicariously through you," said the dragon, who spent most of his life juggling five women at a time, as well as some of the Dragonstars' most dangerous assignments.

Logan snorted. "I think you have that backward."

"Maybe. But it still looks like you need some help out here. So what can I do? Spill."

"I finally found my in. It's just going to take a couple of days to make it work."

"Oh yeah? What's her name?"

"I didn't say it was a woman."

"What do I look like—an idiot?" Shawn reached over and shoved his shoulder so hard he would have toppled over if he hadn't been expecting it. "Who is she?"

Logan took another sip of his beer. Weighed the consequences of letting Shawn in on his plan. Then shrugged. His king needed to know what he was up to, and telling Shawn was as good as telling Dylan. "Cecily Fournier."

Shawn choked on his beer, spewing the cold liquid all over the ground in front of him. "Are you fucking kidding me?" he demanded. "Your *in* is the fucking Wyvernmoon princess herself?"

"Can you think of anyone better?"

"That depends on whether you want to survive. The woman was raised by Silus, Logan. There's no way you can trust her."

"I don't have to trust her to do what needs to be done. I just need her to trust me."

"Yeah, but—" Shawn shook his head, then picked up a rock and threw it as hard as he could. Logan watch it soar through the air before finally bouncing off the Wyvernmoon safeguards.

"That was smart. Why don't you just hand them an engraved invitation if you're so eager to get caught?"

But Shawn wasn't listening. "Man, come on. If she finds out you're double-crossing her, she'll rip out your entrails and feed them to the fucking vultures."

"She'd do that, anyway, whether she invites me into the clan or someone else does."

"Have you never heard of a woman scorned? Dude, there's death. And then there's praying for death because the torture's so bad. Guess which side of the line a betrayed woman stands on."

An image of Cecily's face as he'd last seen it—through Thierren's eyes—flashed through his head. Young, vulnerable, and so despondent that it made him hurt for her, she had looked nothing like he'd expected Silus Fournier's daughter to look. There wasn't a hard edge showing, and while he told himself it was because she was a consummate actor, the little skitter of uneasiness working its way down his spine said something very different.

Was he making a mistake using Cecily? He hadn't thought so when he first met her, but now he wasn't so sure. Not that it mattered, he supposed. Whether he used her to bring down the clan or whether he used someone else, the result was going to be the same. Cecily would lose everything, and on this Shawn was absolutely correct: she would never forgive him.

But he wasn't going for her forgiveness. How she felt shouldn't matter to him one way or the other. The fact that it suddenly did . . . Yeah, the fact that it suddenly mattered made him very, very nervous.

He glanced over at Shawn, only to realize his friend was watching him with shrewd eyes. *Fuck*. Shawn was his best friend, and sometimes even he forgot that beneath the happy-go-lucky attitude was a force to be reckoned with. He braced himself for whatever was coming, knowing whatever Shawn decided to say, he wasn't going to like it very much.

But the other shifter just shook his head and grinned. "I guess you know what you're doing, right?"

"Right." He relaxed a little at Shawn's obvious understanding. "Absolutely. I know exactly what I'm doing."

"Yeah, that's what I figured. That's how you always play, isn't it? Go big or go home."

Shit. Fuck. Goddamn. There it was, and he'd walked right into it. They both knew that if things played out the way Logan wanted them to, he wouldn't be going home ever again. Hell, he wouldn't have a home to go to.

Dylan tolerated a hell of a lot, but blatant disobedience of this magnitude—not to mention the destruction of an entire clan when some of the members were innocents—was not one of them. If the Wyvernmoons didn't kill him, he'd be damned lucky if Dylan didn't do the job for them.

"Is that why you came out here?" He shoved to his feet, strode away. "To rub my nose in it?"

Shawn was right behind him, grabbing his arm and spinning him around so quickly Logan didn't even have a chance to react. Damn, the fucker was fast.

"You don't have to do this." Shawn looked him straight in the eye, and his face was more serious than usual. "You can go in there, steal the data and blow up the lab. That's enough. More than enough, considering they'll kill you if they catch you. You don't have to throw your whole life away—"

"I watched Marta die! And Michael! And how many others because of this goddamn virus and these goddamn motherfuckers who seem to think they have the right to play God? I can blow up the fucking lab today, but that doesn't mean they won't come up with something new, something worse, tomorrow. These bastards have no fucking honor, and they don't give a shit who they hurt. They need to go down and go down hard, or we will spend the rest of our goddamn lives looking over our shoulders and watching as our clan mates die." He knocked Shawn's hand off his shoulder and stumbled back a few steps.

"Gabe lost it when Marta died—he fell apart like nothing I've ever seen before. And Quinn? What do you think would have happened if he hadn't found a way to save Jasmine? He was on the brink, man. You know that. Not only would we have lost a friend; we would have lost the best healer the clan has. How many other people have to die before it's enough?"

"Dylan—"

"Dylan's a king. He can't make this kind of decision. He's too goddamn honorable."

"You're honorable, too, Logan. I think you've forgotten that."

"Bullshit. I'm a king's bastard who's spent the last four hundred years looking for a place to fit in. I'm practical. Honor is the least of my worries."

"Goddamnit!" Shawn roared as the last vestiges of good humor evaporated. "You need to listen before it's too late!"

"No. You need to listen and you need to hear me. It's already too late. I'm doing this, and when it's done, the Dragonstars will be safe. That's all that matters." He turned away, looked straight out into the darkness and willed his words to be true.

"And what about you?" Shawn asked.

He shrugged. "What about me? I'll be fine. I always am."

"No. You just think you are."

"Damn it, Shawn! I—" He turned around to let his friend have it, but Shawn was gone. He was, once again, completely and totally alone.

CHAPTER TEN

He wasn't here. Cecily had landed in the middle of her clearing, after working up a whole speech for Logan during the flight from her house. But now that she was here, standing next to what were obviously his tent and other possessions, he was nowhere to be found.

And wasn't that just typical? Her father had tried to sell it, but she couldn't even give her virginity away. She supposed the joke was on her.

She shifted back to her human form and prowled around the camp, trying to work off a little of her angst from her overemotional state. It didn't work. Not when Logan's unique scent still lingered in the air. Her beast picked up on the sea-and-peppermint smell right away, and Cecily drew it into her lungs. Wrapped it around her and promised herself that everything was going to be all right.

He couldn't have gone far or been gone long. Plus, the fact that all of his things were here meant that he obviously planned on coming back. But when would he back? Her beast wailed, itchy and desperate inside her.

It was a question she couldn't answer, so she ignored it. If her dealings with the *factionnaires* had taught her nothing else, they had taught her not to fret about things she couldn't change.

That's why she was here, after all. Why she had come looking for Logan when, really, this was the last place she should be. But she couldn't help herself. She wanted him, and while there were a lot of things she wanted that she now knew she'd never get—peace for her clan, prosperity, a rational *Conseil*—sleeping with Logan was one thing she did have control over. It was one thing she could take for herself before giving everything she had, everything she was, over to her clan.

As she walked from one end of the camp to the other, she ran over the possibilities for where Logan could be. He could be sightseeing—maybe he'd gotten a sudden hankering to see Mount Rushmore. Though he didn't exactly strike her as the tourist type, she'd been wrong about a man before. Fourteen men, to be exact, so what was one more in the grand scheme of things?

And if he wasn't off doing the tourist thing, maybe he was around her still. Hiking, swimming in the lake he'd shown her yesterday, or maybe just going for a short flight to stretch his wings.

If she really wanted to meet up with him tonight, she had two choices: she could go looking for him or she could pull up some ground and wait for him to return.

The first option seemed vaguely desperate to her. Okay, it seemed completely desperate; nothing vague about it. And while she was desperate, it wouldn't do to let him know that. Not if she wanted a shot at keeping the upper hand with him.

For a second, she flashed back to the fantasy she'd had the night before, the one that had seemed so real she had woken up with sore muscles and tender nipples. If Logan was even half as dominant as she imagined him to be, then she was going to need every advantage she could muster.

She shivered at the thought, a thrill of heat working its way through her at the idea of being at Logan's mercy. She'd never fanta-sized about anything like that before, would never even consider giv-ing herself over so completely to any of the Wyvernmoon men she knew. But there was something about Logan, something about the way he held himself, something about the mixture of kindness and dark-ness in his eyes when he looked at her, that told her she would be safe with him. Or if not safe, then at least unharmed. That was not a feeling she had ever had around her father's *factionnaires*.

For one second, thoughts of her future crept in, but she shoved them away. There would be plenty of time for her to think about that later—an eternity, really. Tonight she would think only of what she wanted and needed.

Tired of walking the same stretch of ground over and over again, and growing cold without her clothes or dragon's skin to keep her warm, Cecily stopped in front of Logan's meager possessions and looked them over. His black sleeping bag was rolled up tightly and rested against one of the outside poles of the tent.

Before she could think twice about manners and the inappropriateness of touching anything that belonged to him, she grabbed it. Unzipped it and spread it out on the ground. Then pulled one side over her and prepared to wait for him to return, no matter how long it took.

Logan landed a couple of miles away from the clearing where he'd been sleeping, just in case he'd been followed from the Wyvernmoon compound. He didn't think he had been—he'd done numerous scans while he was there and on the way back to ensure that he had gone undetected. But he'd learned many, many moons ago that it was better to be safe than sorry.

He shifted as soon as his feet hit the forest ground, then began the trek back to his campsite. He'd left his pack at the campsite without bothering to get dressed. It wasn't like there was anyone out there to see him, and he was too tired, hungry and completely out of sorts to worry about clothes. His conversation with Shawn had put him in a lousy mood, one he figured was going to linger for quite a while. Damn it.

The worst part was, he knew Shawn was right. He was letting himself get too interested in the dealings here, letting himself think far too much about Cecily. If he wanted to do the job he'd come to do, then he needed to remain unemotional. Uncaring. Blank when it came to things like the clan children—or its princess.

He also needed to stop dwelling on the future. He'd set his course, had decided on his goals, and he wasn't going to let anything shake those up. Not his weird attraction to Cecily Fournier, and not his desire to return to the Dragonstars someday.

He sighed at the thought, started to run a hand through his hair before—once again—remembering that he had cut it all off. Fuck. When was he going to adjust to this new role he had decided to play? When was he going to remember that the Logan Kelly, who had lived with the Dragonstars for the past hundred years, was going to cease to exist after he did what he'd come here to do? There was no way Dylan was going to let him back into the clan after he'd so blatantly defied orders, and there was no way he'd be able to look the other sentries in the eye, anyway.

Oh, Shawn understood where he was coming from, but, then, Shawn was different. He had a past even darker than Logan's, and he understood that sometimes it wasn't enough to just send a message to your enemy. Sometimes you had to crush them so completely that it never again occurred to them to come after you.

Lost in thought, he was only a few hundred yards from camp when he felt the intruder. Freezing where he was, he did a quick scan of the surrounding area, trying to figure out where the other dragon was lying in wait for him.

He didn't feel anything threatening coming from the surrounding trees or any of the other areas he had scouted when he first decided to set up camp here. Didn't feel any malice directed at him at all.

Which was strange, as he knew someone was up here with him. He could sense the other dragon on a psychic level, could feel him or her on a physical level. Worse, everything inside him shouted that the intruder was Wyvernmoon.

For the second time that night, he unsheathed the dagger he always kept strapped to his thigh; then he took a few more cautious steps toward the clearing where he'd been sleeping. The presence of the other dragon grew stronger, though he still wasn't picking up on any desire to kill him.

Suspicious, annoyed, determined not to be caught unawares, he took a long, slow sniff of the air. As he did, every muscle in his body stiffened.

It was her. Cecily. She had come back to him. She'd promised him that she would, but after what had passed between them the night before, he wasn't sure that she'd have the nerve to follow through on her promise. But here she was at his camp. He would recognize the sweet, caramel scent of her anywhere.

His dragon burst back to the surface at the thought, its scales rippling along his skin as it fought to get out. Fought to get to Cecily and her own beast. He was a little surprised at the thing's reaction, if he was honest. Tired from the long flight, it had curled up inside him and started to snooze the second he shifted back to human form. But one sniff of Cecily, and it was suddenly wide awake and raring to go.

Much like me, he acknowledged ruefully, his dick so hard that he was going to have trouble walking if he didn't get into that clearing soon. It was a good thing he'd sped up the second he realized it was her. He needed to see her, to touch her.

His beast roared its approval, and Logan nearly stumbled over his own feet in his haste to cover the last few yards between him and the clearing. Though it took only seconds, it seemed to take forever as his head filled with all the things he wanted to do with her. To her.

He wanted to run to her, to rush to her, to grab her and bend her over the closest rock and fuck her from behind like the animal he was.

He wanted to scoop her up in his arms and caress every part of her, to kiss and lick and nibble at her until she melted for him with a soft sigh of surrender.

He wanted to stretch out on the ground with her on top of him, to cup her full, beautiful breasts in his hands and toy with her nipples as she rode him hard.

He wanted her so badly that his hands were already shaking. It felt strange—he'd never been this aroused before with so little provocation. But, then, Cecily's existence, her proximity, the passionate nature he had discovered in her the night before, were provocation in their own way.

He had enough brain power left, barely, to force himself to stop at the last tree before the clearing. This could be a trap, after all. *She is the enemy,* he reminded himself, no matter how much he wanted to fuck her. She could slide a knife right between his ribs and smile at him while she was doing it.

He didn't think she would, but he'd been wrong before about his enemies and his women. He couldn't afford to make that same mistake with Cecily. Not now, when he was finally so close to getting the in to the Wyvernmoons that he'd been scheming and waiting for.

He scanned one more time and came up with nothing. Dropped all but the innermost layers of his mental shields and still came away empty-handed. She wasn't really thinking about anything, was just lying there in his sleeping bag, in a dreamy, half-awake state that he longed to be a part of.

Finally, as certain as he could be that she wasn't there for any reason beyond the obvious, he stepped into the clearing. Both man and dragon preened at the sight of her there, waiting for him on the closest thing to a bed that he currently had.

He walked over to her slowly, making no effort to disguise his approach. He didn't want to startle her, after all. Not now, when he was so close to his goal. But Cecily didn't move, even when he stood over her, and a little spurt of alarm worked its way through him. Had his scan been wrong? Was she hurt somehow?

"Cecily." He called her name as he crouched over her, reached out a hand to stroke her cheek. The skin was warm, supple, and his beast—coiled to attack at the threat of her being hurt—relaxed at the feel of her.

Her eyes opened slowly, dreamily, and she looked so inviting lying there, her long blond hair spread around her like a halo, that it took all his willpower not to jump on her and take her like the starving man he suddenly was.

"Logan." Her smile was soft and sweet, as was the hand she reached up to brush against his chest. "You're here."

"I'm here," he agreed, his voice hoarse. "And so are you."

"I've been waiting for you."

"I can see that."

She flushed a little, her skin turning that same milky pink it had the day before. It made him want to lap her up one slow lick at a time. His dragon roared its approval, and, unable to resist, he leaned down and nuzzled the silky skin beneath her ear as he pushed the unzipped sleeping bag out of the way.

Her breath caught and her hands came up to clutch at his head, to hold him in place. Logan grinned at the thought, more than happy to stay exactly where he was for, say, the next century or so. He nuzzled her again, then swirled his tongue behind her ear.

She gasped, arched, and her hands trembled in his hair. His arousal shot through the stratosphere at the obvious signs of her arousal. She was incredibly responsive, even more so than she'd been the night before, when he'd used his mind to bring her to orgasm, and he was dying to get inside her. To see how she reacted when he was actually making love to her.

At the same time, though, he wanted to take things slowly, to explore every part of her that he could. To find every sweet spot on her body and make her as crazy for him as he was for her.

He pulled away reluctantly, gratified by her small whimper and the way her hands tried to hold on to him. "It's okay, *A stor.* I'm not going anywhere."

He shifted, lowered himself to the ground beside her, then stretched out on his side so that he was facing her, their bodies only inches apart. She smiled at him, a tremulous curving of her lips that worked its way inside him and melted his heart just a little, when he would have sworn such a thing was impossible.

"I was afraid you wouldn't come back," he said, then immediately regretted the impulse. What was wrong with him? He was supposed to be exploiting her vulnerabilities, not showing her his own.

But she didn't move to take instant advantage of his admission, didn't do anything but reach out and stroke a hand over the roughness of his chin. He hadn't shaved in a couple of days, and suddenly he wished that he had. He didn't want to scrape her sensitive skin with his stubble.

"I couldn't stay away," she answered, rubbing her knuckles against his unscarred cheek.

"I could shave," he offered. "If it's bothering you—"

"Are you kidding? I love the way it feels. I want to feel it against—" She broke off, her eyes shifting away shyly, and his temperature skyrocketed.

"Where?" he demanded, grabbing her chin between his thumb and forefinger and tilting her head until she was once again looking him in the eye. "Where do you want to feel it?"

She shook her head, her little white teeth biting down on her lower lip in embarrassment or nervousness or some other emotion he couldn't quite put his finger on.

"Cecily," he asked again, and this time even he could hear the dragon in the deep gravel of his voice. "Tell me."

"I can't." Her voice broke. "Don't make me say it."

He swore at the vulnerability in her eyes, at the shyness that was so shocking in another shifter. He must have spent too much of his time in recent years around dominant, confident females. He'd forgotten what it was like to be with a woman who wasn't clawing his back as she told him exactly what she wanted from him.

Before Cecily, he would have sworn that was exactly what he liked in a woman, but there was something about her reticence that turned him on harder and faster than any woman ever had before.

"I'm sorry, *A stor.*" He brushed a soothing kiss over her forehead. "I didn't mean to push so hard."

She shook her head. "Don't apologize. I'm the one who—"

He stopped her with a kiss. And though he wanted to devour her, to thrust his tongue into the honeyed recesses of her mouth and take everything she had, he kept it soft, sweet, and, he hoped, a little comforting. She deserved that much after the way he'd come at her the day before down by the lake—and, later, in her thoughts.

He'd been a selfish asshole with her, he realized, as he soothed her nerves away with tender kisses to her cheeks, her forehead, the corner of her mouth. He'd been so caught up in his own needs and desires that he'd forgotten what the instant attraction between them must be like for her.

She was young, less than an eighth of his age, so she had to be relatively inexperienced sexually—at least compared to him. Which meant that for her to give her body to him—a man she didn't know very well and who wasn't of her clan—was probably already stretching her comfort zone. He needed to take it easy with her.

But it was hard to remember that and even harder to do it when her body arched against his and he could feel the heat rolling off her in waves that called to him and to the beast inside him. Her breasts pushed against his chest, and he could feel her hard little nipples digging into his muscles there. It was making him crazy with the need to be inside her.

Her needs aren't the same as mine, he reminded himself viciously. *At least not yet.* He needed to pet her and tease her and take it slow if he had any hope of raising her desire to the fever pitch his was already at. Reining in his need—and the dragon that was prowling just beneath his skin, watching, waiting for its chance to get to her—Logan took a deep breath. Then reached for her, praying his control was as good as he thought it was.

CHAPTER ELEVEN

T hough she knew it was silly to be so nervous, Cecily trembled at the dark intensity in Logan's gaze. He'd been nothing but gentle with her, nothing but tender and sweet and respectful, and still she was shaking so much she was afraid she'd come apart in his arms. Which was stupid, because she wanted this. Badly.

She was the one who had come to him, after all.

The one who had sought him out.

The one who had climbed into his sleeping bag wearing absolutely nothing.

So why, when he was giving her exactly what she knew she wanted, was she suddenly so close to losing her nerve?

He reached for her and she braced herself, expecting him to grope her like all the men who'd come before him. She hadn't had many dates in her life, and most of those had been spectacularly unimpressive. So unimpressive that she hadn't even let the men kiss her good night. But there had been a few she had liked enough to kiss and let them touch her. Every single one of them had gone straight for her breasts, squeezing and pinching until she'd felt bruised with their attentions.

Though Logan hadn't tried to touch her breasts yesterday—at least not anywhere but in her fantasies—she still couldn't help tensing. She wanted to skip this part, to go straight to the sex. Somehow she knew he would make that part of it good for her.

Determined to curb her impatience and her fear, Cecily braced herself for the foreplay she figured Logan would insist on. But when he touched her, it wasn't with the firm grip she'd been dreading. Wasn't even with his whole hand. Instead, it was one lone finger. His index finger.

He started in the center of her forehead, with a touch so light she could barely feel it. Then skimmed, slow and straight, over her nose to her lips. He paused there for a moment, ran the tip of his finger back and forth across her lower lip until she started to tremble with something other than nerves.

Unsure of herself but unable to stop, she darted her tongue out and licked his finger. He groaned then, his eyes darkening to a deep maroon that was unlike anything she'd ever seen before. His breathing quickened, and she was sure that he would start to rush, but he didn't. Instead, he slicked his finger across her lips a few more times before trailing it across her cheek to her ear.

Tenderly, slowly, he traced the outer shell. She shivered at the unfamiliar feeling and the delicate sparks his touch sent shooting through her body. He grinned and spent at least a minute toying with her ear and the slender gold loop that dangled from her lobe.

From there, he looped and swirled his way down, pausing at the hollow of her neck to feel the crazy pounding of her heart. She reached for him, circled his waist with her arm and snuggled a little closer to the enticing heat of him.

He did move then, sliding his arm under her head so that his thick, hard bicep made a pillow for her. He curved his body so that he was touching her from her neck to her toes, then slid one heavy leg between hers so that her upper leg curled over his hip.

She gasped at the intimacy of the position, at the way his huge erection was nestled against her sex. They were both naked, and she knew if he wanted to, Logan could slip inside her with one quick thrust of his hips.

But he didn't. Once he had her positioned where he wanted her, he didn't move at all. Didn't try to touch more of her. Didn't do anything but look at her. Her whole body was shaking now, more from arousal than fear, and she closed her eyes, hoping she could calm down a little if she wasn't looking at him.

"Look at me." His voice was hoarse, the words hard-bitten and raw.

Her lashes fluttered and then she was staring directly into those mystical eyes that seemed to see every part of her. "Don't close your eyes again," he said. "I need to see, need to know that I'm pleasing you. That I'm not frightening you."

"You aren't." She grabbed his hand, tried to put it on her breast, her earlier misgivings forgotten in her need to make him happy. "I'm ready for you."

Logan laughed, and she felt the vibrations all the way through her body. His cock jerked against her and she gasped, her body straining against his in an effort to get even closer. "*A stor*, I can feel you." He flexed his hips a little so she knew what he was talking about. "You're nowhere near ready."

She blushed. "I'm sorry."

"Don't be. I'm enjoying like hell getting you ready."

And then that diabolical finger of his was back, drifting from her collarbone to the curve of her shoulder.

Down her arm to her elbow, her forearm, her wrist.

Over her hand to her hip, her outer thigh, the back of her knee.

He paused, took a minute to gently toy with the tendons there. Pleasure shot through her, powerful, intense, overwhelming, and she convulsed, her leg tightening on his hip.

"You like that, hmmm?" He repeated the movements, and she was so caught up in the amazing feelings winding their way through her that she couldn't answer.

Her lack of response didn't seem to bother him, though, at least not based on the way his cock twitched against her. She moaned at the sensation, felt herself grow damp at the obvious sign of his desire for her. And nearly sighed in relief.

Surely, he would notice her wetness now.

Surely, he would decide she was ready.

Again she braced herself for the feel of him entering her. Again it didn't happen. Instead, that damn finger of his made its way up the back of her thigh to her ass. He used his whole hand then, molding her, squeezing her, massaging her, before skimming his finger along the crack of her ass from the top to the very bottom, where he toyed with the damp lips of her sex.

She moaned—she couldn't help it—as she tangled her fingers in his hair. "Logan," she breathed, her voice so shaky that his name was almost unrecognizable.

He leaned even closer, so that his lips were only a hairsbreadth from hers. "Yes, Cecily?"

"I don't . . . I can't . . . I want—"

"What do you want, *A Ghra*?" His finger delved between her cheeks and she startled, her leg tightening on his thighs.

"I just—" She paused, moaned, as he rested that finger against her anus and began to stroke. He didn't delve inside, just circled her again and again until she was as close to insane as she'd ever been. "Aren't you going to make love to me?"

"I thought that's what I was doing."

Her hands slid up and grabbed on to his shoulders as her hips thrust gently against his. "You know what I mean!"

"I do." The words came out as a growl, and Cecily's heart jumped to her throat as she realized Logan wasn't nearly as calm and relaxed as she'd thought he was.

"Then do it. Please. I need—" She stopped, still unable to vocalize her needs. *How do people do this?* she wondered. *How do they look at someone and tell them their most intimate desires?* She needed to try again; she knew it. If she didn't, Logan might not—

"I know what you need," he answered, rolling onto his back and taking her with him so that she was stretched out, full body, above him.

She'd barely had a chance to absorb the fact that she had six feet, seven inches of hot, rock-hard male below her before he was moving again. Sliding her up his chest a little until her breast was level with his mouth.

He lifted his head then, nuzzled the soft underside of her breast before pressing wet, openmouthed kisses wherever his mouth came into contact. Which was everywhere.

She gasped as he got closer to her nipple, the kisses getting longer and sexier as he slid his tongue out and circled her areola again and again. He made sure not to touch her nipple, though, no matter how much she arched and wiggled against him.

She arched and wiggled a lot.

Minutes passed that felt like hours as he kissed and licked and stroked first one breast and then the other. Over and over he moved between them until she was sobbing his name and her dragon was clawing at the inside of her skin in an effort to get out. It was as crazed as she was by what Logan was doing to her and the proximity of his own dragon, which Cecily could occasionally see peering out at her from Logan's crazy, lust-darkened eyes.

Fleetingly, she wondered whether he could see her dragon, as well. And if he could, did it excite him as much as the sight of his did her? Then the thought was lost as a wave of need—powerful, overwhelming, indefensible—swept through her. She shuddered with it, bucked against him, lost the last remnants of her pride and begged.

"Please. Logan, please." It was a whisper, as her voice had all but deserted her, but Logan heard it. His eyes burned a fiery red and he pulled her head down to his.

"Please, what? Tell me what you want, Cecily. I need to hear you say it."

Her hands shifted until they cupped his head and she pulled him up to meet her breasts again. "Please touch my nipples. Lick them. Suck them. Do whatever you want. Just do something!"

His mouth slammed down over the tip of her breast and he closed his teeth around her nipple. She screamed, her hands tangling in his hair as she held him to her. He licked and sucked, even nipped at her a little, before running his tongue over the hardened bud to soothe the luscious pain that came from feeling his teeth.

A delicious, exciting pressure built inside her, grew hotter and hotter, took her higher and higher. She rocked her hips against him, pressed her breast even deeper into his mouth and wondered if it was possible. Was she really going to come from just the feel of his mouth on her breast? Was she really that far gone? Was she—

Oh, God, she was. She really was. Her breathing got faster and faster, the tension built higher and higher, until she was almost there. Almost there, almost, one more touch and—

He lowered his head, let her nipple pop out of his mouth, and she screamed, her entire body shuddering with the frustration of being denied the release it so desperately needed.

"Logan, Logan, Logan," she chanted his name as her nails dug into the taut muscles of his shoulders. Tears poured down her face. "Please don't leave me like this. Don't leave me like—"

"Ssh, *A stor*, it's okay." He stroked a soothing hand down her spine, but his touch only made the tension screaming through her even more unbearable.

"It's not, it's not, it's not." She thrust her hips against him again and again, desperate for him to do something, anything, to put her out of her misery. "I have to—"

He must have realized just how close she really was, because at that moment, he sucked her nipple deep into his mouth at the exact same moment his thumb found her clit.

She screamed again, jerked against him, and he stroked and sucked, stroked and sucked. Once, twice, three times, and then she shattered, her body jerking and trembling and wiging out in fifteen different directions as pleasure unlike anything she had ever imagined burst through her.

It was overwhelming, insane, never ending and terrifying, so terrifying that she tried to jerk away from Logan's touch when she couldn't take it any longer. But he wouldn't let her go, kept his mouth and hand moving in a rhythm that wrung every ounce of unbearable sensation out of her.

Finally, finally, when she was certain she was going to go insane from the pleasure of it all, he released her nipple, his hand tangling in her hair as he dragged her mouth down to his.

Gone were the soft, relaxed kisses of earlier, and in their place was a ravenous hunger that enveloped her completely. He angled her mouth above his and thrust his tongue deep inside her, so deep that she felt his teeth biting into her lips. The sliver of pain whipped through her and shot her up and over again into another orgasm before she'd even had time to come down from the first.

She wasn't frightened this time. Logan was there to catch her, his hands racing up and down her spine as their kiss went on and on and on. His tongue was everywhere—on the roof of her mouth, against her cheek, on the sensitive bit of skin between her upper lip and gum, sliding over her teeth. He was insatiable and the kiss lasted forever, stoking the flame inside her so that she never really had a chance to come down from the orgasms he'd already given her.

She couldn't believe it, didn't understand how she could feel so satisfied and so needy at the same time. But when Logan's hands fastened on her thighs, adjusting her and spreading her legs so that her knees came down on either side of his hips, pleasure streaked through her all over again. Red-hot and so overwhelming that, once again, she didn't know what to do with it.

But somehow instinct took over and she scrambled into a sitting position. Unwilling to relinquish her mouth, Logan came with her. Wrapping her arms around his neck, she held on tight and let him do whatever he wanted to her mouth.

His tongue swept against hers and she responded in kind, stroking him with her own tongue in the way he'd taught her. She loved kissing him, loved the way he felt and tasted and smelled. Loved the fact that he couldn't get enough of her mouth, either. She could stay like this forever, kissing him, tasting him, while her breasts rubbed against the strong muscles of his chest and her sex slid over his hot, hard cock.

It felt like an eternity had passed, felt like only a few seconds, when Logan wrenched his mouth from hers. "Jesus, Cecily, you're making me crazy. I don't want to stop kissing you long enough to get inside you."

"Don't!" she gasped, grabbing his head and dragging his mouth back to hers. "Don't stop." She lifted up a little so that her mouth could reach his, and in doing so was completely spellbound by the realization that one shift of her hips would slide his erection deep inside of her. In this position, he could do nothing to slow her down.

With that thought in mind and her mouth still locked desperately on his, she aligned her body so that the head of his cock was directly below her sex. Then, telling herself that any pain she felt would be worth it when Logan was finally buried deep inside her, she began to lower herself directly onto him.

The head of his cock slid over her labia, began to push into her pussy, and she cried out, shocked at how good he felt against her. She shimmied her hips, pushed a little harder, and he slipped inside another inch. She could feel him there, feel the walls of her vagina clamping down on the tip even as her body screamed out for more. She widened her legs even more, pressed down a little harder, and was shocked at the lack of pain.

She'd heard horror stories about this moment for years from female dragons that she'd grown up with about how terrible, how painful, how awful it was. But with Logan, it didn't feel awful. It felt amazing. Maybe this first time wouldn't be nearly as uncomfortable as she'd feared. Maybe her friends had just been trying to scare her. *Or maybe,* she thought as she circled her hips on his erection, *maybe their first lovers weren't anywhere as wonderful as Logan.*

Suddenly, his hands grabbed her hips, stopped her from moving. She didn't want to stop, but when she tried to jerk free of his grip, he held her in place. "What are you doing?" she demanded, her hips bucking against his hold in an effort to take more of him. "Why are you stopping?"

"You're a virgin?"

CHAPTER TWELVE

Cecily froze at his incredulous question, and Logan swore that the top of his head was going to blow off. Closing his eyes, he tried to deal with the disbelief racing through his system.

She couldn't be a virgin.

She could not be a virgin.

She. Could. Not. Be. A. Virgin!

But the look on her face said that the thoughts he'd overheard as they'd been making love were right on. Cecily had never had a lover.

How was that even possible? Especially at her age, when she had to have gone through at least two heats by now, and in the dragon shifter community, where sex was incredibly common—not to mention how they found their mates. How on earth could she possibly be a virgin?

It made no sense.

At the same time, it made perfect sense. Especially if he took into consideration the easy way she blushed and the way she had such a hard time vocalizing her sexual needs. He had put it down to shyness, or gentility based on her royal heritage. It had never occurred to him that both had been due to total and complete sexual inexperience.

And he'd just come at her like a sexual steamroller, riding right over any questions or objections or concerns she might have had. *Jesus.* He was a bigger asshole than he'd ever imagined.

Opening his eyes, he found Cecily still poised above him, eyes wide and lower lip sucked between her teeth. She looked incredibly uncomfortable, like she'd rather be anywhere else but on his lap at the moment, and he wondered why she hadn't gotten up. And then he realized his fingers still had a death grip on her hips.

He let go so fast that she lost her balance and ended up splayed flat on her back. *Terrific.* Now he wasn't just insensitive, he was also a total bastard. It was exactly what he'd always aspired to be.

She scrambled to her feet, her arms crossed in front of her body, and he realized, with a blank sort of shock, that she was suddenly embarrassed of her body in front of him. He sprang up, then picked up the sleeping bag they'd both been lying on. He held it out to her.

She took it, wrapped it around herself. She was so short that the thing actually covered everything vital. It also made her look like she was wearing an extra-wide tire, but he figured now wasn't the time to point that out.

They stared at each other for a full minute, the silence between them so awkward that he had as much trouble holding her gaze as she had holding his. Especially when he thought of all the things he'd done to her body, both last night and tonight. Was it any wonder she looked like she was on the verge of passing out? Both times he'd taken her up and over so quickly that she'd barely had time to figure out what was going on.

Shit. If he could reach his own ass, he would kick it. Hard.

"So, umm, I'm going to go," she said, inching toward the other side of the clearing.

He paused before answering, certain he hadn't heard her right. "You're going to *what*?"

"I need to go. I have things that need to be taken care of back at home."

"You're just going to take off? Before we even talk about this?" Holy shit, had those words just come out of his mouth? When the fuck had he turned into a teenage girl? The next thing he knew, he was going to end up whining about . . . whatever it was teenage girls whined about these days.

"I think it would probably be best."

"For whom?"

"What do you mean?"

"Who would it be best for? I think we should at least work through this, don't you?" Jesus, he was in worse shape than he'd thought. *Let it go already, man.*

But he couldn't let it go, not when he could still taste her, and his dick was still hard enough to pound nails.

A spark of temper lit those fabulous violet eyes, burning away the bruised look that had been there since she'd scrambled to her feet. "What's there to talk about? You found out I was a virgin and couldn't get away fast enough. I think that pretty much sums it up."

He stared at her in shock. "Are you insane? You think that's why I stopped?"

"Well, what other reason could there be? I was more than willing, in case you missed that."

He allowed himself one brutal, frustrated yell, then did his best to rein himself back in. "I feel like we're in the middle of a bad farce."

"Well, I'm glad you're amused."

She turned to go and he rushed after her, using the superfast speed that made him such a good sentry. He knew if he let Cecily walk away right now, he'd never see her again, and that was completely unacceptable. On a number of levels.

He grabbed her elbow. She turned on him and shoved him hard. She was dragon strong, so he definitely felt the blow, but it wasn't enough to move him—or to make him let her go.

"Don't touch me there!" she exploded, nearly wrenching her arm out of the socket in an effort to get away from him. "I'm so sick of men who think they have the right to manhandle me just because they want to."

He dropped her arm, insulted. Took a few giant steps back. "Man-handle? I wanted to make sure you were all right—that's all."

"It's not your business if I'm all right. I'm not your business at all. Who the hell do you think you are?"

"Who the hell am I? I'm the man who just gave you three orgasms."

"Well, whoop-de-do!" She twirled her finger like a merry-go-round. "Am I supposed to thank you for them?"

She was furious now, her face alight with the thrill of battle as she advanced on him. All that gorgeous hair of hers was streaming behind her in a tangled mess, and the sleeping bag had slipped so that one perfect breast was peeking out from above the black fabric. She looked amazing. Passionate. Gorgeous. As different from the picture he'd had in his mind of the Wyvernmoon princess before coming to South Dakota as she could get.

His dick hardened all over again—not like it had ever completely gone down—and for a second, all he could think about was how to get her over him again. Or under him, if that would make her first time easier. He liked to think he was a flexible man.

"No. But I don't think that means you should attack me, either!"

"Attack you? Attack you?" She all but leaped across the last few yards separating them. "You want me to attack you?"

"I don't, no," he said. But it was too late. She shoved him again, and this time he let her move him a few feet, hoping it would calm her down if she thought she'd actually been able to inflict some damage.

It didn't work.

Not sure what to do to relax her, but knowing he needed to do something or she was going to fly away from him as fast as her wings could carry her, he reached out to her. Tried to get inside her mind. But she was locked up tight, so tight that he couldn't help wondering if she had some psychic abilities of her own.

He wouldn't be able to get inside her head unless he dropped all his shields, and he didn't want to risk that, in case she did indeed have some psychic talent. He hadn't been able to pick up on any, but he didn't want to end up with a brain the consistency of oatmeal, either. And he had been wrong before. Obviously, or Cecily wouldn't be standing in front of him, looking like she wanted to smite him.

Pissed off that he couldn't use his abilities to figure out what the hell was wrong with her, he lost it when she shoved him a third time. Gently grabbing her arms, he twisted her so that her back was resting against his chest. She struggled against him, but he kept her arms pinned over her chest so that she couldn't move.

"Stop it!" she said, twisting and turning in an effort to get away. "You're hurting me."

"No, I'm not." But he loosened his grip a little, just to make absolutely certain that he wasn't.

"Logan, I'm serious. Get away from me!" Her dragon's talons punched out through her fingertips and clawed him. He cursed but kept his grip on her, even after he had started to bleed.

Pissed off himself now, he allowed his beast one really loud roar. It didn't so much as make Cecily blink, but, then, with the way she was going at him, he hadn't really expected it to. *So much for the shy, retiring type.*

Furious, frustrated, at his wit's end, he let her go abruptly. She stumbled, would have fallen if he hadn't reached out and caught her. He let go as soon as she was steady and the sleeping bag fell to the ground between them. Suddenly, it felt like they were right back where they'd started before everything had gone to shit around them.

"Come on, Cecily." He sighed in exhaustion. "This is stupid. Is it really so much easier to fight with me than it is to just tell me what's got you so upset? Please? How am I supposed to fix it if I don't have a clue what I did to piss you off this badly?"

The fight suddenly went out of her, the light inside her dying at the same time her shoulders slumped. It made him feel like an even bigger asshole than he already did. "Or not. If you want to leave, I won't try to stop you again."

Unsure what else to do, he turned around and started back across the clearing toward his stuff, more than aware that if she flew away, she took his best access to the Wyvernmoons with her. It took a minute, but she followed him, the sleeping bag once again wrapped around her.

"Why did you stop?" she asked his back.

He turned around. "What?"

She was bright red again, and he was filled with a strange and dangerous tenderness for her, one that he couldn't afford to feel but somehow couldn't stop. Before he knew what he was doing, he held out an arm to her. She walked straight into it and he pulled her against his body. She was so short that her head nestled against his chest, and he brought a hand up to stroke her hair.

"You stopped when you found out I was a virgin," she repeated, and though her words were muffled against his chest, he heard her perfectly. "Why?"

"Why wouldn't I?" He pulled away, tilted her chin up so that he could look at her beautiful face. "What kind of an asshole do you think I am?"

"One who left me more aroused and sexually frustrated than I've ever been in my life," she retorted.

"Is that what this is all about? *Your* sexual frustration?"

"You just left me like that!"

"How the hell did you think I felt?" He gestured to his still-blatant arousal.

"That's your own fault. I was more than willing—"

"We were going way too fast. I was going to hurt you, and I didn't want to do that. If you'd told me sooner, I would have done things completely different."

"Oh." She paused. "It didn't hurt. I kept expecting it to, but it didn't."

"That's because we hadn't gotten very far. I promise you, if you'd given it a couple more minutes—or a couple more inches—it would have hurt like hell."

Her lips twitched. "So you weren't stopping completely?"

He laughed. "Are you kidding me? We've been fighting for twenty minutes, and still the only thing I can think about is getting you back on top of that damn sleeping bag. There was no way I was going to stop for good. I just needed to take a breather, to calm down a little bit."

"Oh," she said again. "Well, then, I'm sorry."

"I'm sorry, too. I probably could have explained a little better, but between the shock and the fact that I was about two seconds from slamming myself inside you, I wasn't exactly at my most coherent." It was his turn to pause, and then—because he couldn't help himself—he asked, "Why are you still a virgin?"

"In case you haven't noticed, it's a lot harder to get rid of it than one might imagine."

"Bullshit." He pulled her into his arms. "My reaction notwithstanding . . ."

She shrugged, looked away like it was too hard to say what she needed to if she could see his face. "My dad liked to use me as an enticement so others would see things his way. He'd promise me to one of his business allies or his *factionnaires*, pitting them against each other to get what he wanted. But it only worked if I never actually had a chance to *be* with any of them."

Shock kept him quiet for long seconds. When he was finally able to wrap his mind around what she was saying, he asked, "Your father used you as a bargaining chip? What the hell is this, the Middle Ages?"

"Don't look so shocked. It happens to rich young women all the time."

"Yeah, but not to dragons—at least none that I've heard of before this. I thought we were more civilized." But as soon as he spoke, bloody images flashed through his mind of Dragonstar clan members dying of the virus manufactured on the Wyvernmoon compound, a virus he was pretty damn sure had been invented—or at least heavily invested in—by her father. If a man was willing to kill his own species in such a horrible manner, why should Logan be surprised that he had no compunction about using his daughter any way he could to get what he wanted?

Her thoughts must have been running along similar lines, because she whispered, "You'd be surprised what one dragon will do to another."

Obviously. The whole Dragonstar clan had been blindsided. But would *she* be surprised? That was the fifty-million-dollar question.

Not that he had any room to be talking, he supposed. He was about to take a woman's virginity, knowing even as he did so that he was actively working to betray her. So what did that make him? Somehow, he didn't think the fact that she seemed eager to get rid of it would absolve him of guilt.

Disgusted with himself and the whole situation, Logan still knew himself well enough to figure out that he wasn't going to walk away. Not when he wanted Cecily so badly that he could barely keep himself from grabbing on to her and dragging her to the ground. And not when having an in with her might be able to save Dragonstar lives.

He was damned if he did and damned if he didn't, so he might as well enjoy himself on the way down. As long as he made sure that she enjoyed herself, as well.

Bending down, he started to smooth the sleeping bag back into place. But then he got a look at her face, and realized what had seemed so natural earlier had suddenly become awkward.

Determined not to lose this chance to have Cecily, but also determined to make her first time as easy and good for her as he possibly could, he forced a grin he was far from feeling. Then said, "How about I race you to the lake?"

Cecily was running full-out, but she could hear Logan gaining on her. He'd given her a ten-second head start, which she'd used to her advantage, but she had a feeling that in a couple of seconds any progress she'd made was going to be moot. Sure enough, she had barely taken another step when she felt his warm breath on the back of her neck.

Not willing to give in so easily, she didn't bother to waste precious seconds looking back. Instead, she ran another few yards, waiting for him to pass her. He did, and a few seconds after that, she veered off the main path onto a shortcut she often took. By the time he figured out what had happened, she'd be almost to the lake.

When she ran the rest of the way without pursuit, she figured she was right, and when she came out of the trees right next to the waterfall, she was feeling pretty smug. At least until she glanced across the lake and saw Logan lounging on a large, flat rock.

"Hey!" she exclaimed. "How'd you get here so fast?" She knew he was faster than she was, but her shortcut had shaved at least four minutes off her time. There was no way he was fast enough to have beaten that.

He just wiggled his eyebrows and pretended to twirl a fake mustache. "I have my ways."

"You cheated!"

"That sounds like the pot calling the kettle black," he said with a laugh. "Where did you go, anyway?"

"This is my mountain. I know all the shortcuts."

"Maybe not all of them."

She considered that. "Maybe not."

He'd risen and circled the small lake as they talked so that he was standing only a few feet away from her by the time she conceded defeat. He was still naked and more aroused than ever. She couldn't help looking her fill, but then what red-blooded woman would blame her? Even with the scar on his cheek, the man was closer to perfect than she had ever imagined possible.

He interrupted her perusal to ask, "So, do you like what you see?"

"Don't even go there. You know exactly how good-looking you are. There's no way I'm going to pander to your swollen ego."

"There's only one thing about me that's swollen right now, and I was kind of hoping you would pander to it."

"Seriously?" she asked. "That's the best you've got?"

"Hey, cut a guy some slack. All the blood in my brain has drained about three and a half feet south."

She pretended to think over his dilemma. "I can see where that might be a problem."

"It *is* a problem. A big problem."

"Looks more medium-sized to me, but, then again, my whole life I've been told my standards are too exacting."

"Hey! That's not very nice."

"I'm sorry. I thought you wanted honesty."

His eyes narrowed as he started toward her. "You're going to pay for that."

She retreated quickly, but within seconds he had her cornered between his big body and the lake. "Okay, okay. I'm sorry." She held up a hand. "I was just joking."

"That didn't sound very sincere."

"It's hard to sound sincere when you're threatening to toss me in an ice-cold lake! Besides, it's not like you could possibly be insecure in that area."

"No, but it's nice to hear that occasionally." He stepped closer.

"Hey, what are you doing? I already admitted I was wrong."

"Yeah, but I thought we'd already established that I don't play fair."

"Logan, no!" She backed up right to the edge of the rocks. "The water's freezing right now."

"Then I hope you're a fast swimmer." He moved to grab her, and she feinted left before moving right. But he was ready for her, and within seconds she found herself cradled in his arms.

He started to swing her. "One, two, three."

"No!" She grabbed on to his neck, determined to take him with her, but he stopped just shy of dangling her out over the water. She looked at him curiously.

He winked. "You didn't think I was actually going to throw you in, did you?"

"Of course I did!"

"I wouldn't do that to a lady."

"Oh, well. Thank you, then. I appreciate that." She loosened her arms from where she'd been clutching on to him, feeling strangely disappointed that he hadn't carried through with the threat. Which was stupid, considering how cold the water was around here in October. But after the intensity of the past half an hour, she'd really been enjoying this playful side of him.

But the second her arms released his neck completely, she was soaring through the air, straight at the deepest part of the lake.

She had a second to process the shock of being double-crossed, and then she was shifting. By the time her toes touched the water, she was dragon, and she used her wings to propel her straight back into the air before she had gotten more than her ankles damp.

She landed right next to him, back in human form, a superior smile on her face. Logan gaped at her in shock, and she couldn't resist rubbing it in. "Nice try, Slick." She reached out and playfully punched his shoulder. "Let me know when you're ready to play with the big girls."

"Believe me, I'm ready." He grabbed her arm and gave it one sharp tug. She tumbled against his chest, which was exactly what he'd intended. "How did you do that?"

She didn't pretend to misunderstand. "I've always been able to do it. It's a gift."

"I'll say. I like it."

"That's what all the guys say."

He growled, low and deep. "What guys?"

She laughed, spun around in a quick, delighted circle. How had she gone through her whole life without realizing how much fun it was to tease and play? Now that she'd discovered it, she had no desire to ever go back to the joyless existence she'd been living for so long.

"Chill out, Logan. I was joking. God, you're easy."

"That's what I've been trying to tell you. I'm incredibly easy." He paused. "Speaking of which, are you going to take advantage of my easiness anytime soon?"

"I already tried that. You ran away like a scared little girl."

"I promise to do better this time."

"I don't know. You look pretty wimpy. I'm not sure you could handle me."

It was his turn to laugh. "Try me."

She pretended to think about it. "I'll tell you what. I will have my wicked, wicked, *wicked* way with you *if* you put your money where your mouth is."

His eyes darkened, and when he spoke, he sounded like he'd swallowed about ten pounds of gravel. "What do I have to do?"

"I thought that was obvious. You've got to catch me."

She shifted in an instant, then launched herself straight into the sky.

CHAPTER THIRTEEN

Logan stood by the edge of the lake, staring up at Cecily in awe as she streaked through the skies in dragon form. She'd told him that she had always been able to shift that quickly, but he figured a part of him disbelieved his eyes—at least until she'd done it again.

Still, he wasn't one to let his shock and marveling keep him on the ground, not when catching her meant he'd finally be able to get rid of this hard-on he'd been sporting for what felt like forever. Besides, two could play her game.

Throwing every ounce of mental acuity he had behind it, he shifted as fast as he could. It was nowhere near as fast as what Cecily could do, but he was up and flying in a little under two minutes, which was pretty much a record for him. And then the chase was on.

She had a hell of a head start, and in dragon form they were a lot more evenly matched than they were as humans. Which meant that no matter how hard he tried, he couldn't quite catch up to her as she streaked and rolled and zoomed through the sky around him.

He almost got her when she flew extra close, but right before they collided, she somersaulted away and then went into a steep dive that was beautiful to watch even as it gave him a little bit of a heart attack.

Pull up, Cecily! he sent to her mentally. When she didn't immediately obey, just turned to stare at him with wide dragon eyes, he yelled it at her again, even as he raced toward her. *Damn it, Cecily, pull the fuck up.*

She did and narrowly avoided crashing into a sheer wall of rock. He shuddered at her close escape, then took off after her, determined that playtime was over. *That's it,* he projected into her mind again. *Let's land.*

But you haven't caught me . . .

She spoke back to him, and the second he heard her voice in his head, he nearly fell out of the sky. It was like that sometimes, albeit rarely. But it did happen that he was completely overwhelmed from the feel of someone's mind brushing against his own. He'd lived long enough to know that it usually only happened with people who were going to be important to him. Which was the last thing he wanted to think about right now, but there it was.

For one brief second, Cecily's mind completely opened to him— spreading out before him like a beautiful, golden map. She shimmered with light and incandescent joy, determination and a conviction that was rare to find. At the same time, there were hints of fear and resignation— he could see the darkness of the emotions marring the purity of the rest of her mind. She was at a crossroads and desperately afraid of taking the wrong path.

He raced to get closer to her—mentally and physically. Tried to throw himself into the psychological chart of her mental processes laid out in front of him, so that he could have a better idea of what was going on inside her and the Wyvernmoon clan. But the second he tried to touch it, to touch *her*, the map disappeared.

Desperate to get his hands on her now that he'd seen what was inside her, Logan sped up, arrowing straight at Cecily. Using every ounce of speed and strength and concentration he had, he tackled her in midair, sent her sprawling. And then the two of them were rolling and spinning through the air, their bodies winding around each other.

Hi, there, she told him as she stopped trying to flee and simply surrendered her body into his keeping.

Hi there, yourself. His beast reveled in the feel of hers wrapped around it, and so did he. The trust implicit in the act, the way she'd left both her jugular and her underbelly open to him, got to him in a way little had in a very long time. Dragons rarely let themselves be that vulnerable, and the fact that she'd made the conscious decision to leave herself that way with him stunned him.

It also shamed him. How could it not? Oh, he would never go for her jugular, never physically hurt her—he couldn't after everything they'd already shared. But that didn't mean he wasn't going to destroy her in the end. After all, he couldn't let anything stand in the way of bringing down the Wyvernmoons—even the best, most exciting sex of his life.

His dragon guided hers safely to the ground, then watched as she shifted—once again in the blink of an eye. As she turned human, he marveled at her, at the absolute control and impossible amount of talent it took to be able to do that, especially since she'd already shifted from one form to the other multiple times that day. Usually, the more a dragon shifted, the more exhausted he or she became and the longer it took to complete the change.

Which boggled the mind, if he really let himself think about it. If this was how fast she shifted after having done it so many times, what the hell was she like when she was fresh? Both man and beast were dying to find out.

Then he was shifting and it was nowhere near the quick, sparkly process her transformation had been. This was his sixth shift of the day, and his body let him know in no uncertain terms that he was overdoing it. Slow and clumsy and much more painful than usual, he was practically on his knees by the time it was over.

He looked up to see Cecily staring at him with worry and guilt in her eyes. His heart pounded a little heavier as he wondered just what was making her look like that. Did she know more about who he was than she had originally let on? His blood ran cold at the thought, and he automatically reached for his dagger, only to remember that he had taken it off earlier so as not to scare her.

But then she was rushing to him, her hand soft on his back as she helped him climb to his feet. "Why didn't you tell me that you had already shifted so much today? I would never have taken off like that!"

"I wanted to see you fly. You're beautiful and talented and great fun to be with in the air."

Her cheeks turned that pale pink color that drove him wild, and before Logan made a conscious decision to do so, he was pulling her against him. Lowering his mouth to hers and taking her lips in a kiss that was both tender and ravenous. He wanted her—God, did he want her—and though it had been only a few hours, a few days, it felt like he'd waited forever to have her.

As her mouth met his, her tongue darting out to brush tentatively against his, he told himself to take it slow. That they had all the time in the world. That there was no rush. This was her first time, and it was both his responsibility and his privilege to make sure it was good for her, especially after the way he'd gone at her earlier, like an out-of-control, semi-desperate man out for one last joyride.

Pulling away, he led her over to the sleeping bag he had smoothed out earlier. Laid her on the silky black fabric and then just looked at her for a minute, trying to etch every second, every memory of this time, deep into his brain so he could pull it out later and examine every nuance of it. Despite everything the future held, deep inside, he knew this was going to become one of his favorite memories.

Stretching out beside her, he reveled in the feel of all that silky skin and wild, sexy hair as it brushed against his body. Cecily was all woman—lush and round and so soft and fragrant that just a look, just a touch, brought him right up to the edge of his control. And when she leaned forward, brushed his lips with hers, his dick hardened to the point of insanity.

"Do you have any idea how much I want you?" he asked, cupping the back of her head to keep her lips against his.

"Probably not half as much as I want you," she answered, her tongue licking across his bottom lip.

"Don't bet on it." His hands tightened in her hair of their own volition, pulling her closer to him so that he could delve inside her mouth like he so desperately wanted to.

Cecily nearly went into sensory overload when Logan's mouth crushed against hers. It felt so good to be held by him, kissed by him, that a part of her wanted to crawl onto his lap and never, ever let him go.

Of course, she knew that wasn't practical, despite how close she felt to him right now, despite the fact that he was the only man she could imagine giving her virginity to. She barely knew him. And what she did know of him did not lead her to believe that he was the happily-ever-after type.

Not that she expected him to be or even wanted him to be. It was just that when he held her and kissed her, he tasted like forever, and things got all mixed up in her head. *But I can deal with all that later,* she told herself. Right now she wanted nothing more than to rub herself against him and take everything, anything, that he wanted to give her.

Logan chose that moment to nip at her lower lip, and she gasped as every thought she had melted into oblivion. She could think later, reason later. Right now all she wanted to do was feel.

He nipped at her again and she parted her lips for him, let him slide his tongue deep inside her as he so obviously wanted. He stroked his tongue against hers, circled hers, before beginning a series of slow in-and-out movements that made her crazy even as she moved to meet him thrust for thrust.

He growled, low and deep, when she mimicked his motions, and delight streamed through her at the proof that he was as affected by her as she was by him. Thrusting her tongue into his mouth, she toyed with him. Slipped and slid against him with glancing touches. Played with him. Teased him. Tormented him as she savored the sweet and salty flavor of him.

He broke away with a groan, rolled onto his back. His chest rose and fell rapidly while his hands fisted the sleeping bag.

Fear that she'd done something wrong swept through her—maybe Logan didn't like women who tried to take control—and she leaned over him with a worried frown. "Did I do something wrong?" she asked, holding her breath as she waited for him to answer.

He barked out a laugh. "God, no. You're doing everything right. So right that I'm afraid I'm going to lose it like some fifteen-year-old-kid with his first girl."

She grinned, liking the sound of that. "That's okay with me, since you're my first."

"That's the point. I need to do this right, take care of you, and all I can think about is getting inside that hot little body of yours and taking you until you pass out from the pleasure."

Her whole body turned hot at his words, her nipples tightening so fast that they actually hurt. "Is that even possible?"

He rolled over so that she was buried beneath his huge, rock-hard body, though he kept most of his weight balanced on his elbows. "Let's find out."

Lowering his head, he took her mouth in what he intended to be a sweet, gentle kiss.

A slow kiss.

A kiss that would gradually stoke the fire between them until Cecily forgot the nerves she couldn't quite hide and lost herself in the pure pleasure of making love.

That's what he intended, but the second her arms locked around his neck, he was lost. The pleasure wrapped around him, enveloped him, the taste and scent and silken feel of her taking him to the brink of his control all over again. He couldn't move without wanting her, couldn't breathe without needing to be inside her. He was on fire, and the only way to survive was to plunge himself inside her until she burned right along with him.

He was shaking by the time he lifted his mouth from hers to trail wet, openmouthed kisses across her cheek to the sensitive skin behind her ear. He dallied there for a moment, teasing her, just for the pleasure of hearing her gasp and moan. And then he was moving on to the long, slender column of her neck and the sweet curve of her shoulder.

He nipped and kissed, licked and sucked his way down her arm. Paused at her wrist and flicked his tongue back and forth over her rapid pulse before moving on to the soft flesh beneath her thumb. It was one of his favorite parts of a woman, and he spent a couple of minutes just kissing the fleshy part of her hand before sinking his teeth into it in one quick bite.

She cried out, jerked against him, while her free hand clutched at his hair. Loving the feel of her long, slender fingers scraping against his scalp, he laved the small hurt with his tongue until he was sure that the sting had dissipated. Then he pressed a kiss right in the center of her palm, savoring her soft, supple skin and the sweet lilac scent of her.

She moaned a little, so he lingered, gently licking the spot he'd kissed until she cried his name on a broken breath. God, he loved the way that sounded. Loved knowing that he was bringing her pleasure, and in some heretofore unexplored caveman part of him, loved knowing that no other man had ever heard her make those sounds.

Reaching up, he pulled her hand from his hair and started all over again on the left side.

She was losing her mind. There was no other explanation for the fact that she felt hot yet cold, fragile yet strong, drained yet so full of electricity that she figured she could power a small South Dakota town for at least a week. She couldn't breathe, couldn't think, couldn't do anything but feel as Logan took her apart one slow kiss at a time.

She never knew anyone could be so patient, never knew anyone could be so thorough. It was like he had all night, like the huge erection she felt against her leg didn't matter to him. Like she was the only thing that mattered. She couldn't imagine what he found so fascinating about her, but she wouldn't trade this pleasure for the world.

As soon as he let her go, she wrapped herself around him and pulled him down to her so that she could explore the taste of him, as well. But he was having none of it. She'd gotten only one quick taste—a long swipe of his collar bone—before he was pushing himself off her. "None of that, darlin'," he said with a rakish grin that shot heat straight to her sex.

"But I want to touch you, too."

"Not yet." He softened the rejection with the brush of his lips over hers. "I'm too close to losing control."

"It doesn't feel like you're too close. You're torturing me."

"I'm making love to you, darlin'. That's not even close to torture."

"Easy for you to say," she grumbled, a little shocked at how whiny and out of sorts she sounded. But, damn it, she was beginning to think he was never going to make love to her. "I feel like I'm going to explode at any second, Logan."

He grinned. "And I've barely gotten started."

"You can't mean that. I'm going to die if you leave me like this."

"Don't worry about it. I know CPR." He shifted so that his mouth was on the same level as her abdomen.

She had more to say to him, but then he circled her navel with his tongue and she forgot how to speak. His hands came up, cupped her breasts, moved in the same gentle circles as his tongue. She arched her back, tried to get him to move upward toward her waiting nipple, but he seemed determined to drag this out until she really did have a heart attack.

Just when she was on the brink of impatience, he brushed his mouth over her nipple, darted his tongue out and licked her, before blowing a slow, steady stream of air across the aching bud.

She did scream then, her breathing coming faster and faster as she waited for him to do it again. He made her wait, one second, two, and then his mouth was on her. His hands kneaded her breast as he sucked her nipple deep into his mouth and then nipped at her, using his teeth and tongue to sting and soothe and deliver more pleasure than she'd ever dreamed possible.

Her dragon roared and scratched as it struggled for a way to break through, to get to the surface and to the man who was slowly, inexorably driving her out of her mind. But Cecily wouldn't yield, wouldn't give herself over to the change. There was no way she was missing one second of this incredible, mind-bending pleasure.

Logan moved from one breast to the other, one nipple to the other; sucked her hard one second and then barely touched her the next. She never knew what he was going to do, never knew what kind of pleasure to expect, and it kept her on the edge of the precipice, even as it took her higher and higher and higher.

And then, before she knew it, he was shifting again, kissing his way down her breasts as his hands moved over her abdomen and then lower, his fingers dancing over her mons and the soft curls there.

"Open your legs for me, Cecily," he murmured, his voice low and deep and sexier than she had ever heard it.

For the first time since they'd started this, nerves assailed her. Her thighs trembled as she tried to work up the courage to open herself to him completely, to let him into this most sensitive, private place. He didn't rush her, didn't try to coerce her, didn't grab on to her thighs and open her himself. He simply waited, his whiskey-colored eyes fastened on her.

Slowly, so slowly she wasn't sure she was even doing it, she spread her thighs apart. Then held her breath and waited as his gaze shifted from her face to her sex. He didn't touch, didn't race to the prize, just spent long, leisurely seconds looking his fill. Her entire body was shaking and her heart was beating way too fast by the time he reached a single finger toward her and began to stroke.

"You're so beautiful here," he said, and it was almost a growl. "So pink and dewy and goddamned beautiful that it hurts to look at you. I want to be inside you so damn badly that I'm about to lose my fucking mind."

They weren't love words, weren't the words she had dreamed of hearing from her lover, but they were real and honest and so sexy that she felt herself surrender once and for all.

"Take me," she begged, arching to meet his finger. "Please, Logan. I need you so badly that I can't stand it. Please make love to me. Please."

He groaned, then lowered his head so that his tongue could replace his finger on her soft, slick folds.

She jumped at the unfamiliar caress, then melted as he swiped his tongue over her labia a second and then a third time. It felt nothing like she'd ever imagined, nothing like she'd ever dreamed about. It was hotter, wetter, sexier and more pleasurable than she might ever have guessed.

He pressed his face against her sex, inhaled. Then his fingers shifted lower, clamped down on her thighs to hold them open for him, and he thrust his tongue deep inside her. She screamed and bucked beneath him, her hands tangling in his hair as she lay back down and stared at the endless, starry sky above her. Never had it looked so rich, so dazzling, so unbelievably perfect.

When she couldn't take it anymore, when her body was on the brink of shattering into a million irretrievable pieces, he stopped. Withdrew. And his tongue went from driving deep to fluttering silkily over her mons, her labia, her clit.

As his tongue flicked back and forth across her clit, he slowly slid one finger inside her. She stiffened at the invasion, at the feel of him deep inside her. Then he bent his finger just a little so that it pressed against the front wall of her vagina, and she shattered, just like that.

There was no slow buildup to orgasm, no gently increasing tension. She just exploded as pleasure, white-hot and unbearable, poured through her.

"Fuck, Cecily," Logan groaned, even as he slid a second finger into her. "You feel amazing. I could stay here forever, making you come over and over again, and die a very happy man."

She licked her lips, tried to talk, but her voice was broken, her ability to breathe nearly gone. She was simply lost in sensation, the rhythmic contractions inside her stealing everything from her but the pleasure.

"Stop," she gasped. "Please, Logan, you have to stop. I can't take this."

"You can take it," he growled against her pussy. "You can take this and more, Cecily. You can take everything I want to give you."

"Logan, you have to stop. You have to stop." She was crying in earnest now, the pleasure so overwhelming that everything else had ceased to exist. Suddenly, she didn't know how much longer she could survive without him inside her.

He seemed to read her mind as he slowly slid up her body, delivering kisses on every body part he could reach before he finally claimed her mouth. Her hand came up to cup his cheek and he visibly melted a little as her fingers stroked tenderly over his scar.

"Are you ready?" he asked hoarsely.

"Yes!" Her hips bumped against his. "Yes, Logan. Yes, yes, yes!"

"Then kiss me again."

Her lips met his ravenously, her tongue tangling with his as he used his hand to line up his cock to the entrance of her pussy. And then he started a slow, inexorable push inside her.

She gasped against his mouth, her eyes going wide, but he slid his free hand up to cup the back of her head and keep her in place. Then he slid his other hand between them and circled his thumb around her clit.

She jerked instinctively, her hips bumping against his, and he slid inside another inch. He stroked her again, and again she lifted her hips, taking more of him. Over and over he played with her clit, advancing inch by slow inch until he came up against the fragile membrane that signified her virginity. She shuddered a little, cried out, but he seemed determined to bring her only pleasure. He pinched her clit between his thumb and middle finger and then used his index finger to rub her to climax.

The second he felt her start to come, he pushed forward, thrusting himself through the barrier and all the way inside her until he was buried balls-deep.

Only then did he rip his mouth from hers. "Are you okay?" he demanded.

She didn't answer. Her head was thrashing back and forth against the sleeping bag while her hands clutched at his hips and her body shuddered underneath his. "Cecily?" he asked again. "Cecily, answer me!"

"Do it!" she growled, her dragon so close to the surface that she could feel her talons digging into his skin. "Just fucking do it, Logan. You're killing me!"

Her words were all the answer he needed, and he started to pull out, slowly at first as her raw, newly discovered muscles clamped down on him. Lowering his head, he licked across her nipple and she gasped, her body instinctively arching against his. And then he was back in. He pulled almost completely out again, moved slowly forward. Pulled out, moved forward. Pulled out, moved forward until Cecily was once again on the edge of orgasm.

Her hands were all over him, racing over his back, clutching at his ass, tangling in his hair as her hips moved beneath his with more and more surety. Moving his hand between them again, he rubbed her clit at the same time as he told her, "Let go, Cecily." His voice was so low and guttural, she barely recognized it. "Let me feel you come, darlin.'"

She gasped, wrapped her legs around his upper thighs and pistoned her hips against his. His eyes crossed, and she felt his restraint shatter. Grabbing her hips, he thrust himself inside her hard. She screamed and started coming. The rhythmic contractions set him off, his orgasm roaring through him like a goddamn locomotive. Cecily clutched at his shoulders, tried to pull him down on top of her. He let her, and as her hard nipples brushed against his chest, he gave himself over to his release and came and came and came.

CHAPTER FOURTEEN

Cecily lay under Logan, her mind racing and her body trembling with aftershocks. She'd fantasized about this moment for years, had imagined what it would be like, had even masturbated with it in her head. But nothing—nothing—could have prepared her for what it had been like to have Logan make love to her.

Like she'd been caught in the heart of a category-five hurricane.

Like she'd been run over by an eighteen-wheeler.

Like . . . like the most considerate lover on the planet had taken incredible care to make sure it was the most amazing, memorable experience of her life.

Sighing, she snuggled into Logan, loving the fact that he was still above her, still in her. Though he'd come, he was still hard, and each breath she took rubbed him against her G-spot, sending thrills of pleasure sparking through her.

"Am I hurting you?" he asked, pushing up to his elbows so that he was no longer crushing her with the weight of his heavily muscled, six-and-a-half-foot frame.

"No," she said, feeling oddly bereft. She could breathe better now, but she missed the comfort of having him surrounding her on all sides.

The thought should have alarmed her—after all, she couldn't afford to get attached to Logan—and maybe it would later. Right now, she felt amazing. Like she could hike the entire Black Hills or fly around the world without stopping, or just lie here and bask in the afterglow with her wonderful, sensitive, incredibly talented lover.

The latter, she decided with a secret grin. She was definitely going to do the latter.

And maybe, if she was lucky, they would never have to get up.

Despite her protests and the way she clutched at his hips to keep him close, Logan slowly rolled off her. Afraid that it was over, that he would want her to leave now that they'd finally made love, she turned her head so he wouldn't see the stupid, irrational tears she couldn't seem to stop.

But she should have known better. He pulled her against him, throwing one of his legs over hers as he put two fingers under her chin and forced her to look at him.

"What's wrong?" he demanded with a swift, indrawn breath at the sight of the tears on her face. "Did I hurt you?"

She shook her head, unable to speak around the sudden lump in her throat.

"Then what's wrong? Tell me. I can't make it better if I don't know what I did."

"Nothing." She finally forced the word out past her too-tight throat. "You didn't do anything wrong."

"Then why are you crying?" He touched a tender fingertip to her eye, brushed away a tear.

"I don't know. I guess it's just too much. You know? Too much pleasure, too much emotion, too much . . . I don't know how to say it."

He nodded, settling back on the ground and pulling her body tightly against his. "I guess it's pretty overwhelming, losing your virginity after nearly fifty years."

"I think it's more that it was pretty overwhelming losing my virginity to you." She paused, embarrassed but wanting him to know how much his care meant to her. "You were really good to me. Thank you."

"It was no hardship, believe me." Twisting so that he was flat on his back and she was sprawled above him, he brought her mouth down to his. "You were pretty amazing yourself."

She all but preened at the compliment. Laying her head on his chest, she listened to the steady beat of his heart. And told herself that for now—just for the next few minutes—the future could wait.

He didn't want to get up. The realization hit Logan right about the time his brain truly started functioning again. Which, he was the first to admit, was quite a while after he'd finally managed to roll Cecily on top of him.

She felt good there, like she belonged, and he couldn't remember the last time he'd felt this relaxed. Even in New Mexico, the closest place he'd ever had to a home, he was always on edge. Always waiting for the other shoe to drop. How was it that lying here, with Cecily's head pillowed on his chest and her fingers drawing small, feather-light circles around his navel, he was able to breathe? Just breathe.

By all rights, she was his enemy. If she knew who he really was, she wouldn't get within a hundred yards of him, unless it was to plunge a dagger into his chest.

And yet it felt right to lie here like this, his arms wrapped around her, his legs tangled with hers, and a new erection rising insistently between them. God, she'd just about killed him, and already he was dying to get inside her again.

"Hey, what are you so pensive about?" she asked sleepily, her entire body wrapped around his, like she couldn't stand the idea of letting him go. Normally, that was his cue to head for the hills, but he was already in the hills, and neither he nor his dragon were in any mood to go anywhere else.

He told himself it was because he needed her to make his plan work, but even as he made the excuse, he knew better. He wasn't moving because cuddling with Cecily, just cuddling with her, felt better to him than sex had with any other woman.

It was a scary thought, one that he didn't want to so much as acknowledge, let alone deal with, so he pushed it to the back of his mind. For now, he would just enjoy the afterglow, and for once let tomorrow take care of itself. Or not. There were worse things than dying after a bout of truly fantastic sex. He was just glad he hadn't hurt her.

Cecily shivered as a light breeze blew past them, and he wiggled her around until they were both inside the sleeping bag and she was wrapped more securely in his arms.

She gave a little mew of complaint, then said, "I'm not a rag doll, you know."

"I know," he agreed, giving in to the urge to deliver a lingering kiss to her lips. "You've got too many curves for that." He ran a hand over her lush ass to demonstrate the point. As he did, he tried to ignore how much he liked the fact that there wasn't a part of her that he wasn't touching.

"Yeah, well, no matter how much I exercise, I can't seem to get rid of them."

He jerked her back a little so he could look her fully in the face. "Why would you want to do that?" he asked, scandalized. "You look gorgeous the way you are."

"Yeah, that's me. A regular fashion plate." There was an underlying bitterness to her words that was hard to ignore, but when he started to ask her what she meant, she shook her head. He frowned, not liking how easy it was for her to shut him out. He didn't push it, though. How could he, when he had more secrets than the CIA?

In the end, he didn't say anything and neither did she. Minutes passed, and still he felt no desire to put any distance between them. Instead, he just lay beneath her, stroking every part of her he could reach: her hair, her shoulder, the small of her back, her inner thigh. After a lifetime of harshness, he couldn't get enough of her softness, and every part of her body seemed to hold some new mystery he wanted to explore.

In the end, though, his stomach growled, and she giggled. "I guess that's my cue to get up, huh?" She pushed up to a sitting position, one that had her straddling his hips with the perfect heat of her sex resting right against his cock.

It took all his willpower not to grab her hips and guide her sweet pussy down over him. He was dying to be inside her again, but figured she'd probably had enough for a while. Because she was a dragon she healed quickly, but she hadn't shifted yet. Nor had she eaten, neither of which was an optimum situation for healing. She was probably sore, especially since he hadn't taken it easy on her at the end, despite his best intentions.

"Are you hungry?" he asked, but she wasn't listening. Her eyes had gone all foggy and her breath broke as she rubbed herself against him.

He did groan then, and slid a finger into the soft nest of curls at the apex of her thighs. Found her clit and circled it gently with his finger.

"Logan," she gasped, her hips rocking against his hand to increase the contact. "I need—"

"Ssh, baby. I'll take care of you." He pinched the small bundle of nerves between his thumb and middle finger, watching her face to figure out just how much pressure she needed. When she sucked her lower lip between her teeth to stifle a moan, he knew he had her, and he began to tap her clit softly with his index finger.

It took only a minute to bring her to the edge. And then with a twist of his wrist and the press of his palm against her sex, he took her all the way over, his eyes fastened on her beautiful face as he did so.

"God, they should bottle you," she said a couple of minutes later as she slid off him onto the ground.

"I could return the compliment." He held a hand out to her. "Need some help getting up?"

She laughed. "Getting up, staying up. My legs feel like Jell-O."

"Trust me. I won't let you fall."

———————

Logan's words echoed between them as Cecily put her hand in his huge one and let him pull her to her feet. She started to make some joke about trusting him farther than she could throw him, but the smile on his face had suddenly frozen. She wasn't sure what was responsible for his lightning-swift change of mood, but figured it was probably her. Maybe he'd expected her to make him come, as well, and since she hadn't . . .

Not that she wouldn't have liked to. He was the one who had jumped to his feet as soon as the tremors had stopped rocketing through her. If he'd given her a little recovery time, she would have been happy to return the favor.

She glanced down at his cock, which was still long and hard despite everything they'd spent the past two hours doing. Her mouth watered, and for a moment she wondered what he'd do if she dropped to her knees and took him in her mouth. She wanted to taste him, to explore him, to learn him as he had learned her.

She started to reach for him, but he had already opened his backpack and pulled out a pair of sweatpants and a T-shirt. He tossed her the shirt before pulling on the sweats. She felt the rejection like a slap.

She felt stupid, and she really, really hated feeling like that. But she'd brought it on herself—she'd entered into this fling with Logan without figuring out what the rules were. It was no wonder she'd somehow put her foot in it. Why were relationships, even casual relationships, so difficult to figure out? If sex didn't bring with it such incredible, unbelievable pleasure, she would understand the appeal of celibacy. No messy emotions, no awkward silences, no strange signals to figure out.

Logan went over to a cooler he'd set between two trees, pulled out a bottle of water, and held it out to her. "I'd take you out to dinner, but as you seem to be without your clothes, we'd probably get some funny looks."

"Oh yeah." Instead of putting on the shirt, she held it out to him. "I should probably get going, let you get something to eat and get settled for the night."

He shot her a strange look. "I am settled for the night. I thought we both were."

"I'm not sure—" She stopped, unable to put her confusion into words and too afraid of assuming and making another blunder.

"What's wrong, Cecily?" He came back over to her. "You don't want to stay?"

"I don't want to inconvenience you . . ."

"We just had earth-shattering, world-altering sex. Believe me, if ever there was a time for you to inconvenience me, this would be it." He took the shirt from her hands and gently tugged it over her head. "Not that you are. I'm just saying you could, if you wanted to."

"Oh. Okay, then." He winked at her, and she swore she was dazzled by the light in his whiskey-colored eyes. God, she needed to get a grip. He was a rogue, just passing through. And she had a duty to her clan that had nothing to do with him.

"What do you want to eat? I've got sandwich stuff and sandwich stuff."

"Sandwiches it is, then." She followed him back to the cooler, twisting the cap off a bottle of water as she went. "So, it was, umm, earth-shattering for you, too?"

"Well, I'm a big guy. The earth shatters around me pretty easily."

She froze, started to stutter out an excuse to flee, when she saw him looking at her with a wide grin on his face. "You know, one of these days, your teasing is going to get you clawed."

He gestured to the scar on his face before reaching for the bread. "How do you know it hasn't already?"

"Well, if you got that from teasing some poor woman, then you totally deserved it." She reached into the cooler and pulled out an apple. Then asked, "*Is* that how you got it?"

"What do you think?"

"I have no idea."

"A guy's got to have some mystery, doesn't he?"

"Somehow I don't think a lack of mystery is your problem. I've been around you for how many hours, and I still know almost nothing about you."

"Yeah, well, you kept my mouth busy for most of the hours, so I don't think that really counts."

He handed her a sandwich and she took it, feeling strangely shy considering all the things she'd let this man do to her not even an hour before. She'd had no trouble talking to him before they'd made love, but now, suddenly, every time he opened his mouth, she flashed back to all the ways and places he'd kissed her, licked her, touched her. It made her hot to think about it, but it also made her feel incredibly vulnerable.

Is this how everyone feels when they had sex for the first time? she wondered. *Like they've opened up a door inside themselves that can never be shut again?* She didn't regret being with him—how could she, when Logan had been so sweet and tender and exciting? But at the same time, there was a part of her that wished he hadn't been her private rebellion. A part of her that wished even a little bit of her time with him could be real.

But she was just being stupid. How many women dreamed of having a lover like him, one who cared more about her pleasure than he did his own? She was no expert, by any means, but she had trouble imagining any of her father's *factionnaires* treating her with even half the kindness and consideration and adoration Logan had. He'd made her first time absolutely perfect.

Then again, maybe that was the problem. She knew this couldn't last, knew she couldn't have him for more than this one night. When she left here, it was to go back to the compound and ask another man to marry her. A man that she knew, without a shadow of a doubt, could never make her body respond as Logan had.

Logan interrupted her self-examination by grabbing her hand and dragging her across the clearing to the big, flat rock that was her favorite place on the mountain. It overlooked the entire valley down below, let her see miles and miles in the distance. She always came here to think because it was one of the few places that helped her put her problems in perspective. Not even a warring clan seemed so bad when you were looking out at something so huge and incomparable.

He sat down in the center of the rock and then pulled her onto his lap. And she sat, wrapped in his arms, eating the sandwich he'd made her, and tried to figure out how the hell she was going to get through her wedding night with Gage.

"So, what is it you want to know about me?" Logan asked after they'd both finished their dinner. "I was just joking about that whole mystery thing."

Everything. The thought popped into her head, and she barely kept herself from blurting it out. She didn't need to sound like a sex-crazed groupie, after all. Although now that she thought about it, she had to wonder if there was a Logan Kelly fan club somewhere, filled with women he'd ruined for any other lover. She almost asked him, but then figured a question like that right out of the gate might end their conversation before it ever got started.

"How *did* you get that scar?" She reached up and brushed soft fingertips across it. He didn't flinch, but the look in his eyes told her better than any words could that he really didn't like her touching it.

She just wished she knew if it was because the scar bothered him or because he considered it off-limits to her.

He didn't answer for such a long time that she figured he wasn't going to at all. Trying to decide what she wanted to ask instead, she was caught completely off guard when he said, "I did it to myself."

Shock ricocheted through her. "What? Why?"

He shrugged. "Duty? Restitution? Both?"

"I don't under—"

He pressed a soft kiss to her mouth. "You already got two questions. Now it's my turn."

"I didn't realize there was a limit. I thought you said I could ask anything."

"You can." His hand snuck beneath her shirt, rubbed against her lower back. "But there are rules."

"Oh, really? And would those rules happen to have anything to do with where your hand is at this exact moment?"

"Perhaps."

"That means 'definitely.' Okay, lay them on me."

"Well, to begin with, for every question you ask, you have to pay a toll." She arched a brow. "A toll?"

"Exactly." His hand crept lower.

"But I don't have any money," she said, making her eyes deliberately wide. "I came here with nothing but a few purple scales and a tail."

"I like your tail." His fingers stroked against the cleft of her ass.

"I got that impression." She grabbed his hand, put it back in her lap. "So, about that toll?"

"Oh, right. The toll." His eyes were dark and heavy lidded, and just a glance at them made her so hot and trembly that she thought she might come right there in his lap. "For every question you ask, I get to do one thing to your body. My choice."

"Really? Okay . . . what happens if *you* ask the question?"

"Same rules, of course. If I ask the question, I get to do one thing to your body. See how it works?"

"What I see is that the odds are completely stacked in your favor."

"That's the way I like them."

"I just bet."

Could he look any more wicked than he does at this moment? she wondered. It was a full moon, and the light of it seemed to have unerringly found him. It was glinting off his gold hair, making his eyes shine and his skin glow. And his smile, that wild, self-deprecating little smirk of his, all but begged her to wipe it off his face—in the most satisfying way possible.

He must have sensed her thoughts, because the smile faded into a snarl, one that said he would like very much for her to do exactly what she'd been thinking about.

With a growl that sank deep inside her, he lifted her up and turned her to face him so that her legs straddled his and his cock was pressed tightly against her pussy. He was hard again—or maybe she should say *still*—and she decided her questions could wait. She loved talking to him, but if she had only one night with him, she knew exactly how she wanted to spend it.

Logan, however, seemed to have a different idea. Though his breath was hot against her cheek and his hips were rising and falling ever so slightly—just enough to rock their lower bodies together—he seemed in no hurry to take her again. Instead, he said in a voice so low that she had to strain to hear it, "It's my turn for a question. What's it like to be a princess?"

"Not everything it's cracked up to be," she answered immediately. "Until recently, my only job was to look pretty and smile at the right times. So now that I'm involved in the day-to-day running of the clan—or trying to be, anyway—things are different."

"Harder?"

"God, yes."

"So would you give it up if you could?" His lips were right next to her ear now, so that when he spoke, the soft exhalations of air danced over her sensitive earlobe and sent shivers up and down her spine.

She melted at the sensation, her body sagging against his as need, fresh and overwhelming, wound its way through her. "Would you?" he asked again.

"Would I what?" Her voice was shaky.

"Would you give it up?" There was an underlying seriousness to his tone—and the question itself—that snapped her out of her sensual fog.

"No. It may be difficult and terrible and like herding rabid wilde-beests most days, but it's my duty. My family is dead. I'm the last Fournier alive. I have to take care of my clan."

He didn't say anything to that, didn't do anything, and she couldn't help thinking that the game had turned awfully serious awfully fast. Part of that was her fault, but at least part of it was his. What was it she'd said that he hadn't liked?

But when she started to ask him, he distracted her by lifting up the hem of her shirt far enough to bare her breasts. "What are you doing?" she squeaked.

"Fulfilling the rules of our agreement, of course. I asked three questions, so I get to kiss three parts of your body."

"I thought you were joking about that."

"Do I look like I'm joking?"

No, he didn't. He looked more intense than she had ever seen him, and when he blinked, she swore she saw his dragon staring out at her. But before she could comment on it, his mouth was on her nipple, and he was rolling it gently between his teeth.

She gasped, and he raised his head to grin at her. "That's one."

"I might not make it through two more." There was no way to hide the fact that she was wet and trembling, not when she was on his lap and he was so attuned to every sigh and gasp.

She had just begun to hope he was going to press his advantage when he pulled back and dropped a chaste kiss on first her right cheek, then her left.

"Your turn to ask a question."

She blinked at him, still a little hazy from the feel of his mouth on her breast. She forced herself to get it together. "How old are you?"

"Three hundred and ninety-seven."

She nodded, having expected as much. Though he didn't seem to have the old-fashioned attitudes shared by much of the *Conseil*, there was something about him that said he'd been around for a good, long while.

"How many of those years have you been rogue?"

He stiffened against her, and she figured he was going to refuse to answer. But he surprised her when he said, "I left my clan when I was ninety-six."

"Why'd you leave?"

"Because they wanted me to do something that went against what I believed in."

The words hit her like arrows, reminded her forcefully of the battle she was presently waging with her clan, or at least parts of it. "Was it wrong?"

"Wrong?" he asked with a furrowed brow.

"What they were asking you to do. Was it wrong?"

"It wasn't right. At least not in my opinion, and I couldn't go along with it."

"So you left."

He nodded. "So I left."

She liked his answer. Partly because she knew exactly what he meant, and partly because it was honest, forthright and moral. She hadn't had contact with any of those virtues in quite a while, and though she'd known she'd missed them, she hadn't realized how much until he'd given them to her again.

"It's my turn to touch you," she said, her fingers itching to explore his gorgeous, golden skin.

"That's not how the rules work."

"Yeah, well, I didn't really like your rules. So I'm changing them."

"You can't do that."

"Watch me." She leaned forward and licked him from his navel to the hollow of his throat. She nearly moaned at the fresh, salty taste of him, and when his cock twitched beneath her, she wondered if he tasted the same there as he did everywhere else.

He groaned, thrust his hands into her hair and tugged. Not hard, but just enough to let her know that he was still in control of the situation. She hid her smile against his chest and decided not to disabuse him of that notion. At least not yet.

Though she did whisper, "It's your turn to ask a question."

"Thank God," he rasped. His hand ran in circles on her back, giving her goose bumps but comforting her at the same time. It was a weird combination, one she had no experience with whatsoever.

"What's it like to be a Wyvernmoon?"

She was surprised by the question, especially coming from him. He'd chosen to be rogue, had spent the past three hundred years on his own. So why this interest in what it was like to be a member of her clan? Unless . . . "Are you asking about my clan in particular, or do you just want to hear about what it's like to be a part of any clan?"

"Both, I guess." He paused, cleared his throat. "What's it like to know where you fit? To have absolutely no doubt about where you belong?"

She would have laughed if the look on his face hadn't been so absolutely serious. She was the last one to talk about belonging. Most days she felt like she'd been dropped in the middle of her clan by an alien ship, and knew that many of her *factionnaires* felt the same way about her. Fitting in wasn't exactly her strong suit these days.

But it had been once, and she could tell Logan's question had been serious. He really did want to know.

"It feels like home, I suppose. Warm, welcoming, a little stifling at times. But a clan is like that, isn't it? They have a series of expectations for you, and sometimes you meet them and sometimes you don't. But no matter what, you belong."

"So you belong with the Wyvernmoons?"

"Absolutely." As she said the words, she reaffirmed that they were true. "I spent a long time living down expectations of me, and now that I'm living up to my own expectations for myself, it's difficult. But it's worth it—it's *so* worth it—when I think about the members of the clan who don't have a voice, and how I have to be that voice for them. I may not fit in right now, I may still be searching for my spot among the

Wyvernmoons, but I know it's there. It has to be. They're my clan and I belong with them."

He nodded, but didn't ask any more questions. She waited for him to take his "toll," but he seemed too wrapped up in his own thoughts to go there right now. Which was fine with her, because the control he had over her body was, frankly, a little scary. A part of her felt like she would follow him anywhere as long as he kept giving her such amazing pleasure.

"Is it my turn to ask a question?" she asked.

"It will be," he answered, coming back to reality. "As soon as I kiss you."

It was the only warning she got before his lips descended on hers, devouring whatever she was going to say.

She responded instantly, like her body was wired for the taste and feel of his. Parting her lips, she smiled a little as his tongue slipped inside to tangle with hers. Gone was the urgency from earlier, the blind desire to mate. In its place was a tenderness she'd never felt before, a need to please him in the same way he had pleased her.

But before she lost herself in him completely, there was one more thing she wanted to do. Reluctantly pulling away from him, she took a deep breath. Waited for her heartbeat to settle and her brain function to come close to approaching normal.

Logan smiled at her, all heavy-lidded eyes and dark, dangerous desire. But when he started to kiss her again, she forced herself to hold a hand up and say, "Wait. I don't want to stop yet."

"Believe me, darlin', stopping is the last thing on my mind."

"No, I mean I have one more question."

"Now?" he demanded incredulously.

"Yes, now! If I don't ask now, you'll have me naked in ten seconds and then I'll forget my own name, let alone anything else important."

"Fine, go ahead. But just to clarify, I would have had you naked in two seconds."

"I look forward to experiencing that," she said, then paused as she tried to gather her wits about her. She was going to need them here, now and certainly by this time tomorrow. But there was no easy way to say this, especially since he was probably going to laugh her off the mountaintop. But she wouldn't be able to let the idea go if she didn't at least ask. "Do you want to come home with me tomorrow? I mean, to try out the Wyvernmoon clan? To see if maybe you could find a place with us?"

CHAPTER FIFTEEN

"What did you just say?" he asked, incredulity in his face and voice, along with something else. Something she didn't quite recognize but made her nervous all the same.

"I said, why don't you come back to the Wyvernmoon compound with me? Not to stay, I mean—I know that you don't want to stay anywhere too long. But while you're here in South Dakota, for however long that may be, you're welcome to come home with me. Well, not with me, but to the compound. We have a few different places you could stay. There's a small bed-and-breakfast, or you could stay with . . ." She was babbling. Completely, one hundred percent babbling—and making a total fool of herself.

She hadn't meant to, but he'd looked so surprised and then so amused that she hadn't been able to stop herself from filling up the silence between them before it could grow awkward. She hated awkward silences, hated how they made her feel and really hated how they made other people feel. In fact . . . *In fact, now I'm babbling in my head,* she told herself. How ridiculous was that?

"Never mind," she told him. "It was a stupid idea. I just figured if you were going to be here longer than a few days, you might appreciate a bed. It's getting colder every day now, and soon there will be snow on the ground—"

He pulled her into his arms and kissed her. Long and sweet and leisurely, it shut her up like nothing else could have.

When he lifted his head a minute later, she breathed out a huge sigh and said, "Thanks. Sometimes I have a hard time stopping once I've started."

He smirked. "I noticed that. In fact"—he reached down, cupped her ass and brought her lower body into stark contact with his—"I have the same problem."

"I meant talking. I have trouble stopping talking."

"I knew what you meant, I just liked my interpretation better. And"—he laid one finger on her lips when she started to interrupt—"I really appreciate the invitation. I would love to come stay for a few days, if you'll have me—and if you'll let me stay with you."

"Oh. Right. Of course." Giddiness worked its way through her at his words, calmed her down, even as excitement burst through her like the cork in a champagne bottle. "I would really like it if you stayed with me."

"Now, isn't that a coincidence? So would I."

"I suppose I should warn you: things are kind of a disaster right now."

He stilled, looked at her with inquisitive eyes. "What do you mean?"

"It's just that since my father died, everything has been really messed up. I'm trying to fix it, but we're not like a lot of the other dragon clans. Women can't inherit the throne, and so no matter what I do, nobody takes me seriously. They know I don't have any real power."

Logan didn't answer, just stroked a soft hand down her spine that she knew was meant to comfort her. It only made her feel more awful, though, for dumping all over him. When he'd fucked her, he probably hadn't figured he'd have to listen to her whine about her problems, as well.

"I'm sorry." She pushed away from him. "You don't want to hear this. The only reason I brought it up is I figured you'd probably pick up on some of it, anyway."

"Don't worry about what I want to hear. If you want to tell me, tell me. I'm a good listener."

She studied him for a moment, trying to decide if he was sincere. But he looked genuinely interested, not to mention concerned, and she so wanted someone to talk to. Not someone to solve her problems, necessarily, just a sounding board she could vent against. Someone who didn't care about her clan one way or the other and was a neutral party.

So she told him—not everything, obviously, as she would never reveal any information that could hurt her clan. She might like Logan, she might trust him with her body, but trusting him with her clan was an entirely different thing.

When she told him about choosing a husband, he drew back a little and she laughed. "You don't have to look so scared, you know. You're safe. My husband needs to come from the Wyvernmoon."

"I wasn't scared," he answered, but his shoulders relaxed quite a bit.

When she was done, they sat in companionable silence for a few minutes. And then he said something so quietly that she had to strain to hear it. "I can help, you know."

"Help? What do you mean?"

"I'm good at bringing order to chaos. I've pretty much spent the past three hundred years as a kind of security specialist. I can help fix some of the problems with your clan, if you want me to."

He didn't look at her when he was talking, and she didn't know whether that was because he really wanted to help her or if it was because he didn't. She started to dismiss his offer—the last thing she needed to do right now was muddy clan politics even more—when the little devil she was just discovering inside herself sprang to the surface.

Why shouldn't she muddy the waters? Why shouldn't she stack the deck a little bit in her favor? The *factionnaires* were complacent, power hungry, and completely certain that they held the upper hand. And while they might be right, wouldn't it be interesting if she threw another man into the mix? One who was strong and virile and intelligent. One whom she was obviously sleeping with.

It would upset the dynamics, get the *Conseil* thinking, which just might give her an advantage for a little while. If they thought she was wrapped up in her new boyfriend, they might let some things slip that would help her figure out how to defuse the tensions with the other clans. Or they might see Logan as a threat to their own bids for the throne. And if that was the case, all kinds of interesting things might happen.

She looked at him thoughtfully. "What kind of help are you offering?"

"What kind of help do you need?"

"Being a princess is pretty isolating—I hear only what they want me to hear or what they think I want to hear, not what's really going on. If you're a security expert—"

"I am."

She nodded. "Could you help me figure out what is really going on? I know my *Conseil* is lying to me. I know there's a lot more to the stories they're telling me than what they're admitting. I need to know what else there is. And I need to have someone at my back who I can trust."

She leveled a serious, take-no-shit look at him. "Can I trust you to be on my side? Can I trust you not to fuck me over?"

"I'm sleeping with you, aren't I? Not them."

"This has nothing to do with who I'm sleeping with, and I think you know that. If I bring you in, not just as a lover I've invited to stay for a few days, but as someone who can help me unravel the lies and conspiracies that are all around me, you need to be loyal.

"I'll pay you whatever you want, but I'll expect you to stay until I no longer need you—even after we've stopped sleeping together. If you're not interested, I understand. But if you want to stick around for a while, maybe rest up from all your wandering, then this might be a way you can do that."

He didn't say anything for a long time, then asked, "If I say yes, how do you know you can trust me?" His voice was studiously casual, but she heard the steel underneath it.

"I'm a pretty good judge of character. And besides, it's not like I'm going to give you the keys to the kingdom on your very first day. We can try it for a few days, see how things go, and then we can both decide if it's something we want to continue with. How's that sound?"

"It sounds good."

"Okay, then." She held out a hand to shake, but he smirked at her.

"Business or not, I think we can do better than that, don't you?"

And then he was pulling her into his arms, and pulling the shirt she was wearing over her head. "Hey!" she said a little breathlessly as desire slammed through her. "I liked that shirt."

"I'll give it back. I promise." He fastened his mouth on her collarbone. "Later—I promise. Much, much later."

"But we should probably talk about things. You should know what you're getting yourself into."

"Right, absolutely." He skimmed his mouth across her throat, over her shoulder to her breast, where he pressed small, hot kisses all the way around her nipple.

"Are you—are you even listening to me?"

"Of course I am. You want to tell me what I'm getting into."

"Yes. Exactly. I—"

"What you're not understanding, though, is that the only thing I'm interested in getting into right now is you." His mouth fastened on her nipple, and her legs buckled. She stumbled against him and he grabbed on to her upper arms, held her in place while he rolled his tongue back and forth over her. Sensual heat streaked through her at the contact, and she closed her eyes, nearly lost herself in him. Only the fact that she wanted a chance to make him as crazy as he was making her gave her the strength to push him away.

"Where are you going?" he asked, the look in his eyes quizzical as they both stood there, panting and shuddering.

"I want my turn," she said. "You've been making love to me for hours, and I've barely had the chance to touch you."

He swallowed convulsively. "I didn't realize you wanted that chance."

"Are you kidding me?" She eyed his huge, tattooed body. "You're like my own personal playground."

"Well, by all means, then, darlin'. Have your fun."

She started with his chest, stroking her fingers over the thick, hard muscles there that felt so different from the soft curves of her own body. The entire right side of his torso was covered with those gorgeous tattoos, and she traced them with a delicate finger, exploring the swirls and sharp edges before putting her mouth on the one just under his pec and licking delicately.

Logan groaned, his hands fisting in her hair. "Darlin', if you're sore, then you need to tell me now, before we go any further."

There was a tenderness between her legs, no doubt about it, but the promise of the incredible pleasure he gave her—and the pleasure she so desperately wanted to give him—rendered obsolete the thought of any discomfort.

She followed the long, curvy stripe of the tattoo across his body and down his side to nuzzle his hip area before swiping her tongue down below the waistband of his pants. He jerked, his fingers tightening against her scalp, and she reveled in the fact that was finally stretching the control he'd kept such a tight leash on while he'd been making love to her.

"Baby—" His voice broke, and he had to clear his throat before he could start again. "You didn't answer me. Can you take me again?"

She knelt and nipped at the flat, ripped muscles of his abdomen before lifting her head to give him her most seductive smile. "I would love to take you again." Then she gave one quick tug, and his sweatpants dropped to his ankles.

He kicked them off with a growl, but she barely noticed. She was too transfixed by the sight of his cock, up close and right at eye level. He was huge, but she'd already known that from how he felt inside her. She licked her lips, enthralled by the idea of tasting him.

Reaching out, she ran her index finger over the broad mushroom head, wiped away the drop of pre-ejaculate already glistening there. Then, lifting her eyes to his, she slipped her finger into her mouth and licked it clean.

"Fuck, Cecily. You're killing me here."

"Killing you?" She raised an eyebrow. "I've barely even gotten started."

"It doesn't matter. I want you so bad it's killing me not to lift you up, wrap your legs around my waist and shove my dick deep inside you."

She melted at the thought, desire soaking her pussy and making her want exactly what he did. But not as much as she wanted to feel him, to hold him in her hand, to taste him.

"You know what they say, don't you, Logan?" She touched the very tip of him again, wiped up another drop of precum, and swirled it softly around the head of his penis.

"What—what do they say, Cecily?" His voice was hoarse, his hands rough, and she knew she was getting to him. Good. He more than deserved it after what he'd put her through earlier. "Payback's a bitch."

"Fuck! Don't toy with me. I'm too hot."

"You certainly are." Moving slowly, a little unsure of what she was doing but wanting to explore every part of her lover, she cupped his testicles in her palm and then squeezed very gently.

Logan's breath broke on a long exhale, but he didn't move to stop her, so she spent a few minutes just exploring him. He felt like velvet here, soft and spongy and gently ridged where the skin bunched up. Her fingers traced over every part of him, nudging and prodding and stroking until his breath was bellowing in and out of his lungs, and touching was no longer enough.

Leaning forward, she nuzzled him, absorbing the musky smell of him deep inside her even as she blew softly on his sensitive skin. His thighs tensed and he jerked against her. She could almost feel the beast rising in him, could almost feel the fire sizzling through his bloodstream.

She wanted to taste him, to stroke him with her tongue, to know what it felt like to take him deep in her mouth and suck him to orgasm. Knowing that he had some psychic ability, based on the way he'd spoken to her telepathically when they'd been flying above the lake, she sent her thoughts to him. Let him see everything she wanted to do to him. With him.

He groaned, long and low and deep, and then growled, "Do it. Do it right fucking now."

She laughed. She couldn't help herself. The idea that she had driven this magnificent man to the brink of his control was intoxicating. Overwhelming. And so addictive that she wondered if she would ever be able to let him go. Pushing the unwanted thought to the back of her head, she leaned forward—urged on by his tight grip on her hair—and delivered one long, slow lick across the head of his cock.

He grew longer and thicker before her eyes, and when she did it again—to reward him—his entire body shuddered in reaction. His cock pulsed and jerked against her cheek and she felt—literally felt—the ecstasy raking down his spine with fiery talons. He'd opened up his mind, let her in, and suddenly she was feeling not just her pleasure in touching him, but also his pleasure in being touched.

It was unbelievably erotic, and her own sex pulsed until she burned with the same need to come that was blanketing his mind with a red haze.

Come up here, baby, he whispered in her head. *Let me love you. Let me take care of you. I promise I'll take the hurt away.*

His voice was so low, so seductive, so compelling that she was halfway to standing before she realized what he was doing—taking control of her mind, of her body, of her very soul. And though she trusted him more than she'd ever trusted another man, she wasn't ready to yield control. Not now. Not yet, when she had barely gotten a taste of him.

Sinking back to her knees, she wrapped her hand around the base of his cock and slowly stroked up to the velvet tip and then back again.

Up and back. But it wasn't enough, not to put out the flames rippling along every nerve ending in his body, and not enough to satisfy the curiosity that blazed inside her, hotter and more all-encompassing with every second that passed.

Leaning forward, she wrapped her hands around his strong, hair-roughened thighs and gently stroked his sac from behind. He cursed, dark and desperate and vicious, but he didn't try to block her, didn't try to stop her from seeing the power she had over him at that moment.

And then he was sending her a picture of her sucking his long, glorious cock deep inside her mouth, his fingers tightening in her hair as he guided her mouth where he needed it to go and his powerful body shuddering while ecstasy claimed him.

It was her turn to moan, her turn to shudder as broken breaths ripped through her. She couldn't wait any longer, couldn't tease him the way he had teased her. Instead, she took him in her mouth, sliding him so deep that he bumped the back of her throat.

She sucked gently, trying to find her rhythm, trying to decide what he liked and how the whole thing worked. Then pulled back until he was almost out of her mouth.

He groaned and tugged at her hair, and she followed his cues, her tongue stroking in circles around him while she slid him back in again. When he was all the way inside her mouth, she looked up at him, wanting to see what his need looked like.

His face was white, his jaw clenched, lines of desire etched deeply around his mouth. His eyes were closed, but she was in his mind, could see what he was feeling. His lust was rising, his desire hitting the point of no return, and she loved that she could do this to him. Loved that her mouth and body could bring him to such a conflagration of need.

She wanted more, wanted everything. If she had only a little while with Logan, she would take every new experience he granted her and run with it, savoring it as fully as she possibly could. She wanted to please him, to give him everything, to mark him so that he remembered her long after he was gone.

His cock jerked inside her mouth, leaked a little, and she swiped up the pearly drop with her tongue. Savored the warm, earthy taste of him, and the knowledge that she was slowly driving him beyond his control. Hunger ripped through her at the thought, sharp and overwhelming. She wanted to know everything about him, to see and feel and taste his reaction to her.

Pulling back, she delivered a series of long, lingering licks to his cock. She stroked along the broad head with her tongue, circling it and exploring the little slit at the front before she curled her tongue around him and slowly sucked on just the tip, as she would a cherry Popsicle.

He trembled against her, his dick jerking and throbbing against her lips, and she expected him to take control. Expected to feel his hands tighten in her hair as he slammed himself as far into her mouth as he could go. The thought excited her, and she squeezed her legs together in an effort to assuage the ache that was building even as she stoked the flame of his need higher and higher.

But he didn't take control, didn't try to seize the moment from her, though it cost him. She could see the stress it caused him to hold back, to let her explore him at her own pace, to let her take as much or as little of him as she wanted.

Suddenly, she wanted all of him, everything, and she dug her nails into the backs of his thighs to let him know she was serious. His eyes flew open, found hers, and that's when she took him in. Slowly, so slowly that she could feel each ragged breath he took, she drew him into her mouth. His hips jerked hard against her, the muscles of his thighs turning to rock under her fingers. Even his testicles drew closer to his body in reaction.

Need exploded through him, ravenous, rampaging, and his lust fed hers until she was so far gone she could barely think. She was going on pure sensation now, sensation and heat and an instinct as old as dragons themselves.

She ran her tongue up and down his shaft, circled it again and again as she teased the sensitive spot at the underside of his tip that she had discovered only a few minutes before. Then she drew him deep again, sucking strongly and then softly, strongly and then softly, in a rhythm she hoped was making him as crazy as it was making her.

"Cecily." This time when he said her name it was a demand, and she knew he was running out of patience. She could feel it in the way his hips moved against her, sense it in the whispers of thought—of desire—he sent streaking through her mind. Taste it in the rich liquid leaking over her tongue each time she took him in.

"Shit. Fuck. Darlin', you can't do that. You're going to make me come. You're going to make me—"

She wanted him to come, wanted to taste him as he splashed into her mouth and down her throat, wanted to feel the spasms work their way through him as he gave his body completely into her keeping.

She sent him her desires on the same mental path he'd used with her, sent him the images and an impression of her wild, aching need.

He groaned, and she swore the hands in her hair had turned to talons. He was close, on the very edge of his control, and she wanted to push him over. Wanted to see what would happen when Logan finally let go completely.

He was on fire, every part of him burning up at the feel of Cecily's gorgeous, talented mouth on his cock. She was kneeling before him, and something about seeing her like that—seeing the cool, haughty princess so determined to give him pleasure—absolutely blew him away. He was afraid to let her, afraid of losing control and hurting or frightening her. But her mouth felt so good and he was so far gone that it was almost impossible for him to remember that less than two hours before, she had been a virgin.

Shifting his weight so he was balanced on the balls of his feet, he tugged on her hair until her mouth was at just the angle he needed to blow his mind. And then he fucked her in the mouth, hard and fast and deep. Again and again he thrust into her mouth. Again and again she took him. And the pleasure built until he was nearly insane with it, until he was desperate and driven and almost feral with the need to spill himself inside her warm, sweet mouth.

There was a roaring in his ears, a fire in his blood, and suddenly, lightning was sizzling along every nerve ending in his body. His eyes flew open, met hers, and he could see it in her. There was electricity in her eyes, power she'd pulled from the very universe itself and was now feeding to him one small spark at a time, until his entire body was electrified with more pleasure than he had ever imagined possible.

The suspicion that she was an element, a stormcaller, ripped through him, and the look of her there—wild and wicked and so wonderfully comfortable with her power—sent him careening over the edge. He pumped into her mouth once, twice, then came in a huge flood that had him gasping and jerking against her as he emptied everything he was, everything he had to give, as deep inside her as he could get.

CHAPTER SIXTEEN

The compound was a mess.

The civilians were half-starving.

The security was a joke.

The infighting between the few soldiers he *had* run across was a nightmare.

And he was really beginning to think that all he had to do was sit back and watch as the whole thing self-destructed. Which he might have been okay with if the lab wasn't the one place on the compound that was guarded like Fort Knox. And if Cecily wasn't working herself into the ground trying to get the *factionnaires* to man the fuck up.

God, this was a fucking nightmare of epic proportions. He'd been a sentry for nearly a hundred years. He'd spent the other two hundred years since he'd left Ireland making money by helping other clans figure out their security woes. He could do what he'd promised Cecily he would. He could help her fix things.

That was the whole problem. Walking around here for twelve hours, seeing the people suffering—part of him *wanted* to help her fix things, not because he gave a shit about the future of the Wyvernmoon clan, but because somewhere up on that fucking mountain, Cecily had slipped under his defenses. She'd gone from being a means to an end to being his lover, and every instinct he possessed screamed for him to take care of her. For him to help her any and every way he could.

Except helping her was the exact opposite of what he'd come here to do.

Jesus, he was so fucked.

The beast inside him didn't care. Though it had been completely loyal to Dylan for a hundred years, somewhere in the past seventy-two hours, it had switched allegiances. Now, besides watching Cecily with sharp talons and hungry eyes that had him walking around hard all the time, it also wanted to take care of her.

To comfort her.

To hold her and whisper sweet things to her until she believed that everything was going to be all right.

But it couldn't do that—*he* couldn't do that. Because the sad fact was, in Cecily's world, nothing was ever going to be okay again. Not if he did his job right.

And he always did his job right.

Oh, the *factionnaires* had watched him with blood in their eyes when Cecily had introduced him as her new bodyguard at the Dracon Club the first morning. But he was relatively free to walk the compound, and no one had stepped forward publicly to demand that he be fully and properly vetted—a fact that truly surprised him. He had spent a day and a half on his laptop, making sure his background check would pass muster before he even met Cecily. If they had a security expert as good with computers as he was, Logan knew he might run into difficulty, but he had gambled on the fact that a clan as archaic as the Wyvernmoons wouldn't have anyone like that.

He'd been right. But the triumph he'd expected to feel never materialized, only this omnipresent guilt that was eating him alive.

Logan slammed a door on it, knowing there was no way he could function if he let himself dwell on the absolute despicableness of what he was doing. Cecily had asked him to come back with her because she'd thought he would make a powerful ally. Instead, he was the most competent of enemies.

He didn't have time for this. He needed to get his head in the game, or even the most incompetent *factionnaires* might actually be able to pull one over on him.

For the second time in the past ten minutes, he scanned the area directly around him. And smiled grimly as he realized a third *factionnaire* had joined the two who had been following him. The sniveling Thierren had finally decided to join the party. He'd wondered how long it would take.

He did a light scan of the other two men's brains, picked out their names as easily as he would red jellybeans out of the jar on Dylan's desk. Remy and Acel. And, fuck, were they pieces of work. He'd thought Thierren was bad, but ten seconds inside their brains had him desperately craving a shower.

These were Cecily's *factionnaires*? These amoral bastards whose only allegiance was to themselves? This was who she was counting on to help her get her clan back on track? No wonder she'd offered him a job qualifications unseen. A baboon would be better than these assholes.

He shook his head. Since she was keeping them, either she was a lot more naive than he'd thought—which was saying something—or she had a plan that he had not yet been able to piece together.

He was leaning toward the latter option, simply because he had trouble imagining her thinking—even for a second—that these guys were trustworthy. They would slit her throat in a second if it would get them what they wanted, princess be damned. It was her good luck that they felt they needed her—as a figurehead and as a means to ascend to the throne.

Of course, his arrival had put a neat monkey wrench in their plans, which was why three of them were trailing him right now. Not to stop him from messing with the compound or its people—the sad fact was, they couldn't give a shit about anything but their own power—but to eliminate him as a threat.

His hands went to two of the daggers he carried close to his body, even as he wondered if he should end this now. The only one doing any kind of shielding was that asshole who had tried to hit on Cecily the night before. The other two were ripe for the picking—he could rip their brains apart in ten seconds flat. Which might be a viable option if it wouldn't tip his hand.

No, it was better for him to stick to the game plan. To do what he'd come here to do. Even if it would give him an incredible amount of satisfaction to turn Remy's brains into pudding, especially with what he was thinking. Though a part of the asshole's brain was focused on bringing down Logan, another part was wrapped up in thoughts of Cecily. He wanted her naked, tied up and at his mercy, and fantasized about keeping her that way until she figured out who was boss.

Logan's dragon's talons punched through his fingertips and he could feel himself on the brink of losing control. Though he could definitely see the pleasure to be had from keeping Cecily bound and naked, he would never do anything to hurt her if he had her that way. This asshole wanted to rape and beat and threaten her into submission.

He had a particularly blatant fantasy that involved Cecily and a whip, one that flayed the skin off her tender back until she bled and begged him to stop. Only he wouldn't until she was a bleeding, quivering, humble mess.

The beast inside Logan roared in outrage at the image, and his human side wasn't far behind. He wanted to crush the bastard, to rip him apart for even daring to think that he had the right to imagine touching Cecily, let alone hurting her.

Infuriated, he struck without thinking, ripping through Remy's mind with the finesse of a jackhammer. Over his dead body was this motherfucker going to get his hands on Cecily. *Over my dead fucking body.*

Remy screamed, his hands clutching his head as Logan tore through his brain like a conquering army. By the time the man had fallen to his knees, Logan had shredded his nucleus accumbens—the pleasure center in his brain, responsible for sexual arousal—and done a damn good job of messing with parts of his cerebellum, namely the areas responsible for coordination and making the muscles work together. Let the sadistic motherfucker try coming at Cecily—or any other woman—now.

Acel and Thierren stopped to help their friend, but he could feel the suspicion rolling off them in waves. He'd been a good half mile in front of them, and while they'd thought he was unaware of their bumbling attempts to follow him, that didn't mean they wouldn't put two and two together sometime soon. Which was the last thing he needed right now.

Figuring he should beat it from the vicinity before he blew whatever semblance of a cover he had, he sped up a little bit. Swerved onto a side street, then swerved onto another one, until he was all but buried in the maze that made up the area of the compound that housed civilians.

As he walked down the streets, he felt his skin crawl, especially when he glanced in the lit window of one of the houses and saw a man walking the floor, his infant daughter curled up on his shoulder. There was a look of such love on the man's face that Logan had to turn away.

A few doors down another light was on, and a couple sat snuggled on the couch, drinking wine and watching something on TV. They looked really happy together, completely content.

He started to walk even faster then, made sure to keep his eyes on the road directly in front of him. He didn't scan the area around him while he walked—even though not doing so was a rookie mistake. But he couldn't stand the idea of getting inside these dragons' heads, not when he knew he was on the brink of shredding their nice, normal, little lives for good. And why? Because they'd had the bad misfortune of being born Wyvernmoons.

Pissed off at himself and the whole fucking world, he didn't let himself think or relax—hell, he barely let himself breathe—until he was out of the neighborhood and back on the main road that worked its way through the compound. He had to stop doing this, had to stop second-guessing himself. Had to stop feeling guilty. He'd lay a hundred-to-one odds that not one of the bastards he was up against had ever felt guilty when they sent that damn virus over to the Dragonstars and murdered hundreds of his people in the most horribly gruesome way he could imagine.

Logan glanced at his watch. It was close to one now, and he knew Cecily was expecting him. His dick hardened at the thought of her, warm and willing and waiting for him. Not that his reaction was unusual. From the second he'd met her, he'd been aroused most of the time.

He found himself speeding up even more, anticipation beating through him with every footfall. He felt like a total pansy, but there was something inside him that wanted to see her.

He'd almost made it to Cecily's street when he heard them. Two dragons. Their words were spoken aloud at a distance, undetectable to a human ear, but manifesting as a steady, consistent buzzing in the back of his mind. He'd ignored it, tuned it out, because he was so caught up in thoughts of Cecily, but his dragon obviously thought it was important, because it kept dragging his attention back to the sound.

"Your plan isn't working. She isn't backing down. And now she's brought that mutt into the equation," the first man said.

"He's nothing to worry about. In fact, he could be good for us. If she's distracted by sex, she'll be less likely to clue in to what we're doing," the other said.

Logan closed his eyes, blocked out all the other background noise, and focused on trying to pinpoint the voices. It took a minute, because the two men had thrown a few stumbling blocks in his way. But like everyone else out here in this compound, they were too complacent, too sure of their own power and superiority to really worry about whether they were being overheard.

"But if she didn't end up with you, I wanted her to be mine," the first voice said. "I don't want her being fucked by that rogue. God knows where he's been!"

Anger helped him arrow in. *Eriq.* A face rose in front of him, smarmy and rodentlike, and his first impression of the *factionnaire* came back to him in a rush. Pretentious. Spoiled. Weak. Easily led. Not much of a threat, in the grand scheme of things.

But he must have misjudged the little weasel if he was out here in the dead of night, plotting against Cecily. But who was he plotting with? Logan waited for the other man to speak, to give away his location. When he did, Logan slipped inside his brain with the most delicate of touches.

"Can you stop thinking with your cock for two seconds?" the second man asked. "This is serious. We've finally got the chance to make our move, and you're worried about who the ice princess has taken into her bed?"

Julian. The second man was Julian. The realization sent ice slamming down Logan's back. He hadn't liked the man on sight—hadn't liked any of them, obviously—but not liking Julian didn't mean he was blind to the fact that he was one of the most accomplished *factionnaires* the Wyvernmoons had. The plot against Cecily, whatever it was, suddenly got a whole hell of a lot more concerning.

Eriq made a sound of discontent and Logan ran with it, filling his head with thoughts of how idiotic Julian was being, of how he thought he was entitled to so much more than anyone else. Truthfully, it didn't take much of a push from him. Eriq was weak enough that the accusations were right there on the tip of his tongue, anyway. He'd just needed the extra push to get them out.

"You want me to be the one to do this because you think you're so much smarter than I am!" Eriq whispered fiercely. "You're just going to sit back and watch them crucify me, and then you're going to get Cecily, the crown, everything."

"Don't be absurd." Julian's voice was bored, but there was an underlying tension to it that hadn't been there before. Maybe Eriq's paranoia wasn't misplaced after all. "What would I want with the crown, anyway? I'm quite happy working behind the scenes."

But he isn't, Logan realized, doing a quick scan of his thoughts. Julian was the kind of man who wanted all the accolades, all the praise. Nothing short of being king would satisfy him.

The thought of Julian married to Cecily enraged him, even more than the casually vicious way he spoke about her. As if she was nothing more than a means to an end. There was no way this guy was going to get that close to Cecily, no way he was going to be the next one in her bed after Logan vacated it. He'd kill the bastard first. Slowly and painfully.

Julian was skating on the very thin edge of his control and Logan knew it, but that didn't make him pull back as it normally would have. He pushed a few thoughts into Julian's head, and if he pushed a little too hard, then who was around to know? He did the same to Eriq, until the two partners were at each other's throats, accusations and curses flying between them, until he began to wonder if one of them was actually going to take a swing at the other.

He hoped so, and regretted that he wouldn't be around to see it. But he couldn't afford to be caught near them, not after what he'd just done to Remy. Besides, Cecily was at home, waiting for him, and he was in the position to know just how wrong Julian had been when he'd called her frigid.

Furious, guilty, besieged by the need to mark Cecily as his even as he worked to destroy her, he walked the last few blocks to Cecily's house in an agony of need. His dragon was right below the surface, ripping and tearing at him from the inside in an effort to get out. To get to her. The man might be confused, his loyalties torn, but the beast had no such compunction. It wanted nothing more than to lose itself in Cecily forever.

He slammed into the house with one thought on his mind: to get inside her as quickly as he possibly could. To fuck her as hard as he could, until he could no longer feel the different sides of his loyalty pressing in on him. He wanted to lose himself in her arms, in the pleasurable oblivion she brought him to so easily.

But he was barely in the door before he realized Cecily wasn't alone. She was sitting in the small, fussy room to the right of the foyer, her head bent low and her hands on the lap of a man who was sitting across from her.

The beast went insane and he didn't even try to hold it back. He couldn't. He was right behind it, ready to rip the intruder limb from limb for having the nerve to touch what was his. If this was another *factionnaire* trying to convince her to marry him, he was going to leave here in a body bag.

He'd only been in the compound for a little more than twelve hours and already he'd had more than enough of the sneaky bastards. The next one who so much as looked at Cecily cross-eyed—*and this one is definitely doing more than looking,* his dragon seethed, as the man brought her hand to his lips—was going down.

He leaped across the foyer in one bound, and landed at the doorway to the parlor with a solid thump. Cecily glanced up, startled, and he froze as he realized there were tears in her beautiful violet eyes. His dragon saw red, and so did he. He reached for the man, prepared to kill now and ask questions later, when a look of alarm flitted across Cecily's face.

She slipped between him and his prey, and the dragon snarled. Or maybe it was him; he didn't know. They'd become one—a red-hot, seething creature full of jealousy and animosity. He wanted the man across from him dead, and it only stoked his rage that Cecily had put herself between them to save the bastard.

"Logan." Her voice was low and urgent, but the hand she put on his chest was both cool and steady. "This is Sebastian. He's a waiter at the Dracon Club, where I took you earlier."

He didn't care if the guy was the winner of the year's Nobel Peace Prize. He had touched Cecily, *kissed* her, and he was going to pay for it.

He reached for Sebastian again, but the look in Cecily's eyes was so trusting, so much about him, that he calmed down a little. Or maybe it was the way her thumb moved in feather-light strokes up and down on his chest. Either way, her focus on him calmed him down enough that he could think. Rationalize. And smell the despair that was literally rolling off the other man.

Something was going on here, all right, but it wasn't what he'd first imagined. Putting a choke chain on his anger—and his beast—he wrapped an arm around Cecily's shoulders and pulled her tightly to his side. He was calm enough now to listen, but that didn't mean he wasn't going to make sure that Sebastian knew exactly who Cecily belonged to.

"He came to ask me a favor. I need to take care of it." She slipped out from under his arm and crossed the room. The dragon watched her intently, but she didn't touch the other man, didn't even come within two feet of him.

For the first time, he realized she held a small prescription bottle in her hand. As she dialed the number on the label, he finally trusted himself enough to relax the agonizing stranglehold he had on his beast—and his own emotions.

He relaxed even more as he heard her speaking quietly into the phone.

"Jacques? This is Cecily Fournier. How are you?"

She paused. "Good. I'm calling about Sebastian LeCroix's account. Do you know what I'm referring to?"

Another pause, longer than the first. "Good. I need you to help him for me. Whatever he needs. You know I'm good for it. Yes, for everything. I'll take care of it."

A short pause. "Thank you, Jacques. I appreciate all your help. Yes, you have a good night, too."

She hung up the phone and turned to Sebastian, who had tears running silently down his face. He grabbed her hands, kissed them again, and this time Logan realized he wasn't actually kissing Cecily. He was kissing the ring on her finger. He'd noticed it earlier, but hadn't made the connection, as Dylan didn't wear one and it had been centuries since he'd seen a ruler who did. Sebastian was kissing the royal ring, as subjects had in days of old.

"That's enough, Sebastian." Cecily brought her hand up to his hair, tenderly stroked the strands back from his forehead. But there was nothing sexual in her touch. It was more maternal, though the dragon standing in front of her looked like he was probably about fifty years older than she was. Still young, but nowhere near as young as she was.

"Go pick up the prescription," she continued, pulling her hand away from him when he seemed unable to let her go. "Then go home. Your family needs you."

The man nodded, mumbled his thanks again and again as he backed out of the room. At the front door, he bowed low before slipping out into the night.

Cecily turned to him as the door closed behind her visitor. "His daughter—" Her voice broke, and the tears from earlier were back. "His daughter is sick with the same genetic disorder his wife has, and the pharmacy wouldn't give him the medicine that helps keep her out of pain. He's in debt because of how much his wife's medicine has cost him through the years. His daughter is suffering, has been suffering for weeks, because he can't afford to take care of her."

She turned to him, buried her face against his chest even as she wrapped her arms around his waist. "How has it come to this?" she demanded. "How the hell did my father let our clan get into such bad shape that our people can't afford the most basic necessities? I can't believe all this has happened in just the five months since he died. He must have known about it, must have let it happen long before his murder. But why? What could possibly be more important than the people who depended on him?"

Her shoulders started to shake and he could feel her tears, warm and wet, through the front of his shirt. As she cried—not for herself or her father, but for her suffering people—the last ounce of resistance he had melted into nothingness. His arms came around her and he rocked her slowly, soothingly, as he tried to figure out what the hell he was supposed to do now. How the fuck was he supposed to betray a woman he not only liked and desired, but whom he also respected?

But how could he not, when doing nothing meant he would be betraying the king and the clan, who had given him refuge for nearly a century, made him one of their own?

Not sure what he was doing or why he was doing it, Logan pulled away slowly. Settled himself on the couch and then pulled Cecily down next to him. He turned so that he was looking straight in her eyes and then told her, "That's not the only problem you've got."

As he spoke, he felt his entire world—everything he'd always believed or stood for—come tumbling down around him. He was in uncharted territory, and it promised to be a very bumpy ride.

CHAPTER SEVENTEEN

Cecily stared at Logan, confused. "What do you mean?"

"Your defenses are shit. A child could find his way onto this compound without so much as raising an alarm."

"But that's impossible. My father's always had the best defense. Our safeguards are impeccable, and the *factionnaires*—"

"The *factionnaires* are too busy fighting over you and the throne to pay any attention to whatever duties they might once have had."

She shook her head. "That can't be. They couldn't be that stupid."

"Oh, sweetheart, I don't think you have a clue just how stupid those men are."

She flinched inwardly at his tone, and at the sarcastic way he'd called her *sweetheart*. She wasn't sure how she felt about this version of Logan. He'd come back from his walk annoyed—she'd seen it the second he'd walked into house. And then he'd caught sight of Sebastian and she'd really thought there was going to be bloodshed. He'd calmed down, but even as he'd comforted her, there'd been something different. Something missing from the fun, tender lover she'd had up in the Black Hills earlier that morning.

But that didn't mean she was going to let him see how disconcerted she felt, especially as he was ripping away the last bastion of security she had. If the *factionnaires* had really stopped guarding the compound, if they were really leaving all of her people unguarded, that meant she was way worse off than she had ever imagined. It meant that every single one of them—Gage, Dash, Wyatt, Dax—were all guilty of treason. And maybe even worse. She wouldn't know until she investigated.

Clearing her throat, she pushed away from Logan. She might be young and she might be naive, but she wasn't a little girl who needed to be comforted from bad news. If she ever had any hope of being queen, she was going to have to show everyone that she could stand on her own two feet.

"Tell me."

Logan raised an eyebrow at her harsh tone, but didn't comment. Instead, he launched right into a laundry list of security problems. "The safeguards were once excellent. I agree with you there. But times have changed. Areas have been breached, unraveled from within, maybe; I can't be sure. But they've never been reinstated, so there are huge gaps in the main protection surrounding the compound. Plus, there's no evidence of any patrol going on."

"Should there be? If they thought the safeguards were enough—"

"Safeguards are never enough," he said so firmly that she regretted speaking up and showing her ignorance. "For the simple reason that they aren't foolproof. What happens if someone breaches them? If there's no one patrolling the borders, who's going to stop them or at least sound the alarm?"

"And you think my father would have had these patrols?" Even as she asked the question, she knew the truth. Of course Silus would have had them. He was paranoid about security, and now that she thought about it, she realized that when her father was alive, she had barely been able to walk twenty feet outside without bumping into a soldier or *factionnaire*.

"Of course he would have." Logan echoed her own conclusions. "I'm assuming he wasn't a fool."

"He managed to hold on to his throne for more than four hundred years."

"Then he definitely wasn't stupid."

"Which means that someone has ordered the soldiers to step down and told them they no longer needed to patrol. But who would do that?" She reached into the heavy chest that doubled as a coffee table and pulled out a blanket. Suddenly, she was freezing.

"It had to be one of the high-ranking *factionnaires*. No one else could make an order like that stick."

"But what were they hoping to accomplish by it? I don't understand."

He studied her through narrowed, contemplative eyes. "How long have you been trying to take over the clan leadership?"

"Just a few days. And it's not going very well."

"Well, today's my first day here. Maybe this is a recent development. Maybe someone's trying to make you look incompetent."

Her stomach started churning sickly as she thought about that. "Would everyone have to be involved in a decision like this?"

"I wouldn't think so." He reached out, stroked a reassuring hand down her back. "Just one or two key players."

"But wouldn't the *factionnaires* notice, even if they weren't the ones who called a halt to the patrols? Wouldn't somebody say *something*?"

"That would depend. If this is a new development, then no. They might not have noticed yet. Especially the ones who are doing their jobs."

"What does that mean? I thought you just said no one was patrolling—"

"The borders," he finished for her. "I said no one is patrolling the borders. But there is one area on the compound that is heavily guarded, and I'm not quite sure what it is."

Something moved in his eyes as he spoke, a darkness that was so deadly, so without compassion, that for a moment she was frightened of it. Frightened of *him*. But then he blinked and it was gone as quickly as it had come, and she was left wondering if she was simply jumping at shadows.

"Where's the area?" she asked.

He didn't say anything for a minute, just stared at her, and she had the very uncomfortable feeling that she was being tested. But that was impossible. She was the princess here. She was the one who had invited him to stay with her. What went on in her clan was no big deal to him.

Finally, when a silence she didn't understand had stretched her nerves to the breaking point, he pulled a sheet of paper out of his back pocket. "Do you have a pen?"

She fumbled open a drawer and handed him a pencil. He took it and drew a series of connecting lines on the paper. When she looked more closely, she recognized some of the major streets on the east side of the compound.

"You walked all the way over there?" she asked, surprised.

"You told me to take a look around, to get a feel for the place. So I did."

"That wasn't a criticism."

He was too busy drawing a large building to respond. When he was finished, he held the rough sketch out to her. "It's that building, right there."

She stared at the place he was pointing to, more than a little perplexed. Checked the street names to make sure she was thinking of the right place. She was, which meant, "The lab? There's security around the lab?"

His shoulders seemed to relax a little, but she wasn't sure. Logan didn't give much away reaction-wise, so trying to figure out what he was thinking was a little like looking in a crystal ball. She was afraid she was seeing only what she wanted to see.

"There's a whole shitload of security around that building. The soldiers were three deep over there."

"But why?"

"It's your clan. I was hoping you could tell me."

She shook her head. "I have no idea. I mean, it's a medical facility. They're doing research . . ."

"What kind of research?"

"I'm not sure. My dad mentioned a couple of diseases last year. Said his doctors were getting close to curing two of the biggest diseases dragons can succumb to."

"And you believed him?"

"Why would he lie?" she asked, bewildered.

Logan didn't answer, but there it was again. That unflinching stare that seemed to see right inside her. "What?" she demanded when she couldn't take it any longer.

He shook his head. "Nothing."

"Well, obviously it's something. You keep looking at me like Satan has suddenly invaded my body."

He blinked, and for the first time since she'd met him, he looked genuinely uncomfortable. "Sorry."

She nodded. What else could she do when he was being so weird?

"Who's in charge of the soldiers?"

"I'm not sure." It killed her to admit that to herself and to him. Killed her that she thought she could be queen when she was so freaking incompetent that she hadn't even realized her people were vulnerable to attack from whoever happened to be flying by. "But I can find out easily enough." She reached for the phone.

He stopped her with a hand on her arm. "I don't think you should do that yet."

"Why not? I need to get someone on the borders. We can't stay unguarded like this, not with—" She stopped abruptly, not willing to air all of her clan's dirty laundry at the same time.

But he wasn't going to let her get away with it. "Not with what?" he demanded.

"We're on the brink of war with two other clans."

"Two?" He sounded incredulous, but it wasn't like she could take offense. She'd been pretty damn disbelieving herself when she'd heard the news.

"I know. It's insane, but yeah. Two clans are gunning for us, and I don't think we're strong enough to hold off either one, let alone both, if they chose to attack together."

"What's the other clan?"

"Other clan?" she repeated. "What do you mean?"

He shook his head, dismissed her question. "I meant clans. Which two *clans* are making noises about war?"

"The Dragonstars in New Mexico and the Shadowdrakes of San Diego. Do you know either one of them?"

"I know of them." He shrugged. "Both have a reputation for being pretty peace loving."

"Believe me, I am aware of that. Which is why I'm really afraid we're the ones in the wrong here. I've gone over a million different scenarios in my head, asked the *Conseil* to take me through even more, but everything boils down to the fact that we have somehow provoked them." Cecily pushed to her feet, went to stare out the window into the night.

As she watched, a shooting star streaked across the sky. Maybe if she closed her eyes and wished on it, the disaster looming over her clan would somehow disappear. She sighed. The time for wishing had passed. Now she just had to find a way to get her people through this. Somehow, she didn't think it was going to be as easy as it sounded.

"So, wise and mighty dragon of all things strategic, do you want to tell me where we go from here?"

Logan couldn't believe how defeated Cecily looked. Since he'd met her a few days before, he'd seen her look a lot of different ways: angry, shy, happy, aroused, even powerful. But never had he seen her look so down, like the weight of her world was on her shoulders and she couldn't find a way to carry it any longer.

She was standing by the window, head bowed, shoulders slumped, looking a lot more like a dog that had been kicked than she did the princess of one of the most fearsome clans in dragon history. He understood how she felt better than she could imagine. He was feeling like he'd been kicked himself.

But, then, betraying everything you believed in could do that to a man. The fact that he wasn't done, that he was going to end up betraying both Dylan and Cecily before this was over, was about as comfortable as a hot poker up the ass.

But he'd reached his limit of self-castigation. He could pick it up in the morning, but for now he was exhausted.

"We're going to bed," he said. "You look as exhausted as I feel."

She turned to him with a smile, but her lips were trembling and her eyes were sad. "Yeah, well, some dragon I know kept me up most of the night, doing things that are probably illegal in at least fifteen states."

"I was thinking more like twenty-eight or thirty, but I'll give you fifteen."

She laughed, like he'd hoped she would, and he crossed to her and started guiding her slowly toward the huge, circular staircase that started at the back of the foyer. "Where's your room?"

"Third floor."

"Can you make it, or do you need me to carry you?"

"I have made it up these stairs every day of my life since I learned how to walk," she told him indignantly.

"Okay, then. Carry, it is." He swept her into his arms and started up the stairs, amazed all over again at just how little she was.

"Logan! I said I can walk."

"I know. But why should you have to when I'm around? At least give me a chance to be good for something besides bringing bad news."

Her hand slid over his chest. "I can think of a few other things you're good at."

"You'll have to remind me what they are tomorrow."

"Tomorrow?" she said, her lips pursed in a little moue of discontent. "What if I don't want to wait that long?"

"Tough. You're dead on your feet."

"You shouldn't get to make that decision for me. I'm a grown woman."

"Okay, then. Go to town," he said as he slipped inside her room and deposited her gently on the bed. "I, however, am exhausted and am going to bed."

He slipped his shirt over his head, took off his jeans, and slid under the covers on the right side of the bed.

The second his body touched the cool cotton sheets, he knew he'd made the right decision. Yes, they had a lot to talk about, and yes, she had a lot to do if she had even a hope of getting her clan back in order. But none of it was going to happen tonight, and the sooner she figured out she couldn't do everything in one fell swoop, the better off she'd be.

She sighed, a purely female exhalation of annoyance that had him smiling despite the sleep that was already starting to claim him. "That's my side of the bed, you know."

"Tough."

She didn't say anything, and he started to drift. He didn't need long to recharge his batteries, just an hour or two. But he hadn't slept, really slept, in almost two weeks and he was so tired . . .

"Logan?"

"I'm moving, I'm moving." He scooted over, lifting her off her spot in the center of the bed and putting her down where he'd been lying just a few moments before.

"That's not what I meant."

"Now you tell me," he muttered without opening his eyes.

"Thank you for coming home with me." She rolled over, dropped a kiss on his cheek. "Thank you for staying with me even though everything is such a mess." Another kiss, this time on his forehead. "Thank you for taking such good care of me." A third kiss, on his chin. "And thank you for trying to help me find a way to help my people." One last kiss on the corner of his mouth. Then she curled up against his side, her head pillowed on his bicep. She was asleep before his head had stopped reeling from the chaste sweetness of her kisses.

As she started to snore, just a little, Logan's eyes popped open.

It didn't look like he was going to get any sleep after all. Not while his conscience was ripping him apart from the inside out.

CHAPTER EIGHTEEN

Cecily woke to pleasure. Incredible, all-consuming pleasure, and the feel of Logan between her thighs.

Struggling to wade through the layers of the most erotic dream she'd ever had, she propped herself up on her elbows and said, "Logan?"

"Ssh," he whispered. "Just relax."

"I hate to be the one to break it to you, but that's not exactly the way to get me to relax." Her hips jerked against his hands, which were braced on each side of her, as if to underscore her point.

"Maybe not, but it relaxes *me*."

"Well, then, by all means. I'd hate to stand in the way of that." She dropped back on the bed and reveled at the feel of his mouth on her inner thighs. "Relax away."

His laugh was low and sexy, the soft expulsion of air that came with it blowing right across the lips of her aching sex. She arched at the feel of it, trying to get closer to him. Trying to hold him so tight that she would forget that this thing between them was just temporary. That soon—sooner than she would like, certainly—Logan would move on. Without her.

It wasn't like she could say she hadn't seen it coming. He was a rogue dragon, for God's sake. His whole life was about drifting. The shock was that he'd agreed to stay with her for a while and help her get her clan back in order. The fact that it didn't seem like enough after spending three nights in his arms wasn't his fault. It was hers.

When she'd chosen him for her first lover, he had seemed the perfect choice. He was handsome, smart, sexy, and though he tried to hide it behind a gruff facade, unfailingly kind. Oh, he would probably never describe himself that way, but she saw it in him. It was hard not to when she thought about the tenderness and patience he'd shown when he made love to her for the first time. The way he'd been so incredibly slow, so incredibly tender.

His eyes had burned pure red for her and he'd been so aroused that he had been shaking, and still he'd made sure to put her first—as he had every time they'd made love since. And the way he'd switched from jealousy to understanding when he'd figured out that Sebastian was in trouble . . . the way he'd praised her for helping someone in need instead of berating her the way her father would have.

How on earth was she supposed to hold out against that? How was she supposed to hold out against *him*?

"You're not." His voice was little more than a rumble, but it pulled her out of her thoughts and had her staring at him, mouth open in shock.

"What did you just say?"

"I said, you're not supposed to hold out against me. I like that you can't resist." He lowered his head again and nuzzled her inner thigh, but she was scooting up the bed, putting a little distance between them as she reached for the bedside light and flipped it on. If she used her dragon sight like she had up in the mountains, she would be able to see him clearly in the dark. But she didn't want to do that. She had a feeling this was a discussion she was going to want to be 100 percent human for.

"How did you know what I was thinking?" she demanded.

He didn't answer, was too busy squinting at her through narrowed eyes to pay attention to her words. Obviously, he had been awake in the dark a lot longer than she had.

"Logan!" she said firmly, determined to get his attention.

"What?" He sounded harried and more than a little put out now, nothing like the man who had just been making love to her.

"I said, how did you know what I was thinking? You answered a question I never asked out loud."

"I did?"

"Yes, you did."

"Oh." He looked sheepish. "Sorry about that. Sometimes I have a hard time telling the difference."

"What? You have a hard time? What, exactly, does that mean?"

He shrugged, rubbed his eyes. When he looked at her, they were a lot clearer than they had been. "It's part of my skills. You know, kind of like how you can do that whole electricity trick you did up on the mountain."

She felt herself blushing. "You caught that, huh?"

"Seeing as how I was the one you were zapping? It was pretty hard not to."

"I wasn't zapping you!"

"Hey, don't worry about it. Believe me, I'm not complaining."

"I know you're not. I saw your face while I was doing it." She picked up the pillow that was next to her and threw it at him. "Don't think I don't know what you're doing."

"I thought I was making love to you." He slid up the bed, pressed a lingering kiss to her mouth. "I certainly hope you knew what I was doing."

"No, that's not what I meant. You're trying to get out of answering my question."

"I already answered your question." He skimmed his lips down her neck, pausing to trail kisses along her collarbone.

"No, you only answered half my question." But her hands were clutching at his hair, holding his talented, talented mouth in place. "You said it was part of your skills, but you never fully explained. What is it you don't want me to know?"

"Nothing. I'm an open book." She might have believed him, except his accent was back, heavier than it had ever been on the mountain.

"Of course you are. But you're written in Gaelic." She reached down, pinched his ass. "And that's not a language I can read."

He gave a long-suffering sigh. "You're not going to let this go, are you?"

"Nope. I don't like not being able to understand something about you. Especially something like this."

"Fine. You know how I can talk to you in your mind?"

"Like you did up on the mountain? Yeah. So?"

"That's not all I can do." He shrugged, and looked so uncomfortable that all the pieces fell into place.

"So you're seriously psychic? And what? You just decided to pop into my mind, uninvited, and eavesdrop on what I was thinking? That's how you could answer the question?"

"I wasn't eavesdropping. You were thinking really loud."

"Oh yeah. I'm sure I was." She poked him in the ribs and grinned when he wiggled uncomfortably. "I'll try to work on that from now on. You know, whisper my thoughts when you're around."

"Now you're just messing with me."

"You think?" She wrapped her arms around his neck, and this time she kissed him, long and lingering, just like he liked it.

When they finally surfaced, he was above her, braced on his elbows, and they were both breathing hard. "So, you're taking this pretty well," he said, sliding a few strands of hair out of her eyes. "I'm assuming that means you have some psychic dragons in the clan?"

"A few. When I was a kid, one of my close friends was psychic. She could do the same thing you can, just pop into someone's mind and pick out a thought."

"Yeah, well, I don't usually do that. It only happens when I'm really close to someone and . . . distracted."

"Really? I think I like the sound of that. I distract you?"

"*A Ghra*, you're about the only thing that distracts me."

"Oooh, I like that even more."

She wrapped her legs around his waist, rubbed her pelvis against his. "So, where were we before your little parlor trick so rudely interrupted us?"

"You're the one who turned on the light. And, besides, it didn't seem to bother you the last time it happened."

"Last time? You've read my mind before?"

"Not exactly." His grin was wicked, intriguing.

"So what, then?"

He didn't answer, but a second later she felt his mouth on her breast. Wet, hot, shockingly unexpected. And so skilled that she arched off the bed. Yet even as pleasure coursed through her, she realized that there was something familiar about this psychic touch that should be brand-new. That's when it hit her. "So that was actually you?" she demanded. "That night, when I was sitting by the pool? That was *you* making love to me, not a fantasy?"

"Maybe."

"But I didn't know you then. I mean, we'd met, but we hadn't . . ." She blushed, thinking of everything she'd let him do to her that night when she'd thought it was only her imagination. "You weren't anywhere near me. How did you get inside me like that?"

"I was having the same fantasy you were, I think. Or something pretty close to it, and somehow my mind found yours."

"Oh." She wasn't sure how she felt about that. "Does it happen often? I mean, do you regularly make love to women in their heads?"

"No. Of course not."

"Really?" She eyed him suspiciously. "I have a hard time believing that."

"I swear."

"Okay, I can handle that, then." She rolled him over so that she was on top of him, her legs straddling his hips. His erection nestled against her sex, and she rocked her hips. Shivered a little at the feel of the tip of his cock rubbing against her clit. "You were my first lover. I like being your first something."

His hands came up, cupped her breasts. Rubbed her nipples. "You're my first in a lot of things."

Her breath caught, though she wasn't sure if it was at the words or the sensations streaking through her. "Don't say that if you don't mean it."

"You think it's usual for me to nearly attack a man the second I walk in the door, just because he's touching my woman's hand?" He thrust himself against her, made her gasp.

"Is that what I am?" she asked brokenly. "Your woman?"

"Well, you're sure as shit not my man."

It wasn't the answer she'd been looking for, but it would do for now, especially with him hot and hard between her thighs, and with her orgasm already beckoning. "Make love to me, Logan."

"I thought you'd never ask."

His hand came up, curled around the back of her head, and pulled her mouth down to his. She'd expected it to be hard and a little frenzied, considering the size and scope of the erection resting insistently against her. But he took his time nipping at her upper lip, sliding his tongue along her lower lip and then into her mouth, stroking gently over her own.

As he kissed her, she inhaled the familiar, musky scent of him, and ran her hands over the smooth, thick muscles of his chest. She already knew his body as well as her own, and she paused to flick her nail against his nipple, just like he liked it.

He arched beneath her, murmured her name, and Cecily fought back a sudden, unexpected influx of tears. What was she going to do when he got bored and wanted to move on? How was she going to cope when he walked away, when all she wanted to do was hold on to him as tightly as she could? Her whole life, she'd been waiting for someone who got her, who laughed at her deadpan jokes, held her when the burden of her position got to be too much, woke her up in the middle of the night just because he couldn't wait until morning to make love to her. Now that she'd found him, how was she supposed to just give him up?

She knew he was wrong for her. He wasn't a Wyvernmoon, wasn't high ranking, didn't have much money or a prestigious job. But somehow that didn't matter when he was kissing her, holding her, loving her.

"Cecily, darlin', are you all right?" he asked as he gently ended the kiss. His eyes were quizzical as they stared up at her, his fingers gentle as they tilted her chin so she was looking him in the eye. She was stupid, worrying about a future that hadn't happened yet when she had him here with her right now. Sometimes the present was the only thing that mattered. She needed to remember that.

Curving her lips into a sassy smile, she drawled, "I'm better than all right. Or at least that's what you told me last night."

He laughed, as she'd intended, and she ducked her head to trace the strong lines of his chest with her tongue. He groaned, fisted a hand in her hair and tugged her face up to meet his.

"I'm the one who woke you up. We do it my way."

"We always do it your way."

"Is that a problem? I haven't heard any complaints." He slipped his hands up her stomach, removed the nightshirt he'd slipped over her head not that many hours before. Then skimmed his lips over her chest until he found her nipple and pulled it into his mouth.

She went weak, every bone in her body melting as his tongue rolled slowly over her. She arched her back, pressed herself more firmly against him and gave herself over to the sensations rippling through her body. She wasn't going to worry about the future right now. As long as she had Logan in her bed, she was going to stay firmly grounded in the present.

Shifting so that she was lying beside him on the bed, she leisurely licked up the right side of his body, her tongue following every curve and angle of his tattoos. She'd done it before, on the first night they'd made love, but since then he'd been the one in control. The one driving her completely insane. Tonight, now, she wanted to get a little of her own back. Wanted to make him as crazy as he always made her.

"Cecily, darlin', let me touch you."

"It's my turn to touch you. I want you to feel what I feel when you make love to me. I want to make you crazy." She sank her teeth into his pec, relishing the way he jerked against her mouth.

"I'm already crazy," he said, grabbing her hand and putting it on his thick, hard cock. He thrust against her and she wrapped her fingers around him, stroking him from the base to the tip.

"Cecily," he said, and it was a warning, one she had no desire to heed.

Instead, she leaned over him, trailed her tongue down his breast-bone to his navel. She circled his belly button, reveling in the fresh, clean, spicy taste of him. She loved doing this for him, loved kissing him and running her tongue over every part of his body.

"Lower," he groaned, his hands clutching at her as she ran her tongue along the light happy trail that ran from his navel to the thatch of golden pubic hair at the base of his cock. "Please go lower. I need you to touch me."

"What you need," she teased in between soft, slow licks, "is to get a little patience. I already told you, I want to play with you for a little while."

She covered his abdomen with little nips, pausing to sink her teeth into the taut skin that covered the six-pack he sported, before soothing away the sting with a swirl of her tongue. His fingers tightened in her hair as his body grew tenser and tenser, and for a brief moment she wondered if she should give in to him and what they both wanted. Already she ached for his touch on her breasts, her sex. But then she thought of the long, lonely nights she would have in the future after he left, and decided that he could suffer a little longer. If this was one of the only memories she was going to have, there was no way she was going to rush it.

Logan's hands fisted in the sheets as Cecily's mouth explored every inch of skin on his chest and stomach before dipping lower to nibble across his hip bone and down the outside of his thigh. She was everywhere and anywhere, except where he wanted her most, and the fact that the omission was deliberate was slowly driving him out of his mind.

It tormented him, the question of when she was going to stop playing, when she was going to relent and get serious and touch him the way he longed to be touched. As she spread his legs, her lips lingering on his inner thigh, he arched involuntarily, his cock begging for her attention. For her lips, her tongue, her sweet, sexy little mouth.

But she only laughed, then brushed her cool, soft fingers against him—once—before continuing on her journey down his body. She nibbled at his abdomen, ran her lips and tongue over his balls, dug her fingers into the back of his thighs as she brought him closer and closer to the temptation of her pretty pink lips.

He opened his mouth—to demand, to protest, to beg that she let him take her—but before he could do more than call her name, she leaned forward and slipped his dick between her breasts. Her elbows pressed tightly against her sides so that the sweet pressure of her breasts surrounded him, driving him so close to the brink that the world around him turned dark and fuzzy.

"Cecily." Her name was a prayer, a curse, a plea for mercy, but his dragon wasn't feeling merciful. He finally managed to pry his hands away from the sheets, only to end up with them tangled in her hair as she began to slide her upper body back and forth against him in a rhythm that was guaranteed to blow sky-high the last shred of control he was clinging to with bloody, battered fingertips.

"Cecily, darlin', sweetheart. Please. Please. Please." The words poured out of him, tumbling from his mouth one after another as he lost himself in her. As he gave every part of himself over to her. His brain, his body, his straining, aching cock. He gave her everything, and in return she gave him the most unbelievable pleasure of his life.

Electricity coursed down his spine, and he didn't know if it came from her or if it was just because of what she was doing to him. And in those crazy, lust-crazed moments, he didn't care. All that mattered was her. And when she lowered her head and took the tip of his dick in her mouth, nothing in his life had ever felt so good.

Arching into the wet heat of her mouth, he thrust his hips again and again. Begging her to take him deeper. To take all of him. He couldn't help it. Nothing in his long, long, long life had ever felt this good. Nothing would ever feel this good again. He was certain of it deep down in the soul he so rarely liked to think about.

She moaned deep in her throat, and that one sound, on top of everything else, sent him careening over the edge. He thrust furiously against her, driving his cock deeper and deeper into her mouth. Deeper and deeper down her throat as it closed tightly around him.

He tried to rein himself in, tried to stop himself from taking her like a madman. But he was in a frenzy, his dragon so close to the surface that he could no longer tell what was him and what was the beast.

He strained against her, desperate to get deeper, desperate for her to take every part of him inside her. His cum boiled up hot and uncontrollable. His hands clenched onto her shoulders, and for a minute he really did fear hurting her. But then she clutched at his ass, his thighs, pulled him even deeper down her throat as her tongue tickled the sensitive spot at the base of his head. He lost it completely and came apart in her arms.

His orgasm was a vicious explosion that took over every part of him until everything around him ceased to exist. Until the only things in the world were her and him and the incredible fire that burned between them.

Ecstasy consumed him, enveloped him, burned him alive with his own flame. With hers. And still she took him, swallowing every drop of his cum and then sucking him back to wild arousal.

Dazed, desperate, determined to get inside her before he turned feral, he turned her so that she was facedown on the bed, her hands wrapped around the iron slats of the headboard. Then he locked his hands over hers on the iron slats and positioned himself behind her. With one hard thrust, he buried himself balls-deep inside her.

She gasped at the invasion, but she was wet and hot and tight, so tight that he couldn't have stopped even if he'd wanted to. And he didn't want to stop. He never wanted to stop. He wanted to fuck her forever.

And that's what he did. Taking her from behind like the animal he sometimes was, he fucked her and fucked her and fucked her.

Fucked her until she came around his cock, her sweet body milking him like there was no tomorrow.

Fucked her until she bucked wildly against him and came again.

Fucked her until she screamed his name and begged for mercy.

And still he didn't stop. He couldn't. She had broken something open inside him, something that he had kept buried his entire life, and there was no shoving it back down. It was wild and feral and uncontrollable. And it needed her. Needed him to mark her, to claim her, to spill his cum so deep inside her that she would never get his scent out of her skin.

When she came for the fifth—or maybe it was the sixth—time, he slipped a hand down the curve of her ass and pressed his thumb inside her anus with one unapologetic thrust. She screamed his name, her lithe, strong body bucking beneath him as she came again.

He felt the contractions start deep inside her, and he knew, in that moment, that he was hers. That she owned him. That even as he took everything she had to give, he belonged to her.

The knowledge, combined with the incredible pleasure of her

orgasm, was too much. He couldn't hold on any longer, couldn't hold anything back. Grabbing on to her hips so hard that he was sure he left marks, he pushed forward at the same time he slammed her back against him.

She screamed, a loud, wild cry that raked down his nerve endings and pushed him right over the edge of the precipice. And then he was flooding her, his cum jetting into her in rhythmic pulses that gave her what he had never intended to give another person.

CHAPTER NINETEEN

When it was over, Cecily slid peacefully back into sleep and Logan just lay there, listening to her breathe for the longest time. In, out, in, out. She was so beautiful that it hurt to look at her, with her blond hair fanning out around her head like a halo. He wanted nothing more than to settle in next to her and stay there, touching her, cuddling her, loving her, for as long as she would let him.

Panic assailed him at the thought, gripped him by the balls and wouldn't let go. Forgetting his earlier wishes, he scrambled out of bed and nearly fell on his ass in his desperation to get away from her—and his feelings for her.

His throat was parched from fear, and he walked toward the bathroom on trembling legs, calling himself a pussy even as he did so. He'd spent his life locked in battle, had fought more wars than he could hope to count, had taken on the world alone for centuries. And yet here he was, shaking because of one little dragon whose head didn't even reach his shoulder.

Flipping on the bathroom light, he found a glass sitting on the counter. He filled it with water, drank it all in one long gulp, though his hands were shaking so badly that he ended up spilling a third of it onto the counter.

He cleaned the mess up with a hand towel, then filled the glass again. Only after he'd finally succeeded in washing away the dryness coating his throat did he look in the mirror at the shuddering mess he had become. His eyes were dilated, his skin was pasty white and his breath was seesawing in and out of his lungs like he'd just run a half dozen miles or so full-out.

What was he going to do?

What the fuck was he going to do?

He couldn't have fallen for her, couldn't be in love with her. Doing so would be incredibly stupid, and while he was a lot of things, he was rarely stupid.

And yet feelings were building inside of him that were so real, so powerful, he couldn't deny them. There was this sense of rightness that he felt whenever he was near her. The need he had to hold her, to protect her, to make sure that no one—least of all those bastards her father had left in charge—ever had the chance to hurt her.

But how could that be? How could she have come to matter to him so much in such a short time? How could she have broken down every barrier he'd erected? He'd come to destroy her, goddamnit, to rip her clan apart, *factionnaire* by *factionnaire*. Brick by fucking brick. How could he have been so insane as to fall for her when he knew what he had to do?

But when he'd been sitting in that parlor with her that night, holding her while she cried for a little girl she'd never met, he'd known there was so much more to her than he had ever wanted to believe. It was bad enough that she kept him hot and hard all the time, that she made him lose perspective on things much bigger than the two of them, but when he saw how much she cared about her people, she melted him.

She fucking destroyed him.

He'd deliberately asked her about the lab, had watched her closely as she answered. Had waited for some sign of guilt, of remorse, of knowledge about what was going on there, but she'd been a blank slate. Two days ago, he would have believed it was because she was a hell of an actress. Tonight, he'd been afraid to hope that it was because she really didn't know anything about the virus or what her father had done.

And if that was the case . . . He let out a shuddering sigh. If that was the case, there was no way he should be able to look himself in the fucking mirror. Because then he was as bad as all of her *factionnaires*, huddling around her, keeping secrets and doing their best to destroy her in an effort to save themselves.

Sickened, disgusted and afraid for the first time in he couldn't begin to remember when, Logan bent over the sink and splashed water on his face. Tried to wash away his guilt and confusion as easily as he did the sleep from his eyes. It didn't work, but as he was drying off, he saw something in the mirror that sent his world spinning off its axis.

It can't be, he told himself as he squinted at the mirror. *It can't be,* he repeated as he looked down at his right arm in shock.

It can't be.

It can't be.

It can't be.

But it was. Jesus Christ, it really was.

His tattoos had changed, shifted a little, so that the jagged lines on his arm had somehow come together in a faint band around his bicep. A mating band.

The first of the three that formed when a dragon met the woman he was destined to be mated with for the rest of his life. When complete, they would lock he and Cecily together for the rest of their very long lives.

He stared at the intricate black ring in disbelief, shocked at how beautiful it was. He'd seen them before, of course, on his mated friends' arms, had always known that they were incredibly artistic, but he'd never realized just how gorgeous they really were. Probably because he'd never paid much attention to them before, and because the band had never been his. Or maybe it wasn't the band that was so beautiful, but the feelings that brought it forth.

Unable to stop himself, he traced the band with his finger, learning all of its twists and turns. It was surprisingly delicate—like Cecily—yet sturdy, too, the links and connections well-defined.

He told himself to stop looking at it, to pretend he'd never seen it, but he couldn't stop touching it. It felt amazing. Warm, mystical, welcoming. It felt like Cecily. It felt like he'd always imagined home would feel, if he ever managed to find it.

How could he have known? How could he possibly have guessed that after four hundred years he would find his home? Here in the middle of enemy territory.

The thought jerked him out of the fantasy he hadn't even known he'd been weaving and landed him in the middle of reality with a solid thump. He was an idiot, a fucking idiot, to get caught up in the magic of it even for a second when he knew the truth.

This story didn't have a happy ending.

How could it? He had lied to her from the very first minute he'd met her, had accepted her invitation into her clan with only one goal on his mind: to destroy everything she wanted to save. And even if he didn't, even if he went against every instinct he had and settled for simply destroying the lab, he couldn't take back the fact that he had lied to her. Had betrayed her trust. Had coldly and deliberately used her.

Besides, he couldn't just let everything else go. Not after meeting her *Conseil* and getting up close and personal with so many of her *factionnaires'* thoughts. Cecily might not be the evil incarnate he'd once imagined her to be, but the people she was surrounded by were. There was no way he could leave her with any of them alive. Every single one of the *Conseil* had to go—including those who Cecily considered her friends.

No, there was no future for him and Cecily. Despite the fact that he wanted her like he'd wanted no other woman, despite the fact that he had fallen in love with her, despite the fact that he was well on his way to respecting her and what she was trying to do, he couldn't pretend that everything was going to be all right.

If he stayed with her, if he stayed here and abandoned the Dragon-stars, he would forsake every ounce of self-respect he had. If he tried to make it work, if he destroyed the lab in secret and killed off her *Conseil* the same way, and then she somehow found out, he'd be dooming her to only half a life. After they'd bonded completely, after their mating was complete, if she found out that he had betrayed her, it would destroy her. Mates didn't betray each other, didn't lie to each other, sure as hell didn't build a life on deception.

No, he couldn't do it. He couldn't finish the process, couldn't let the bond complete itself. If he did, they'd both be damned. And while he already was, he could not stand the thought of bringing Cecily down with him. Which meant there was only one thing for him to do.

He had to lock his feelings for Cecily away, hide them so far inside himself that even he forgot they were there. If he did that, if he succeeded in convincing her that he didn't care about her, then the mating ring would fade and Cecily would be all right. She could marry someone else, have children with someone else, and never be the wiser. And while the thought of her letting some other man touch her made him furious, made him ill, the thought of destroying her was a million times worse. If he did anything else, if he tried to believe in fairy tales or the fact that she might someday be able to forgive him, then he would end up ruining not only his life, but hers, as well.

It was the right thing to do. Not the easy thing, but the right thing.

Dragging on a pair of jeans and a T-shirt, he slipped out of Cecily's room through the back patio door. With the wonder of the mating band still a fist in his gut, he didn't trust himself not to climb back into bed with her and make love to her until the bond was firmly in place and she was irrevocably his. So he'd spend the rest of the night wandering the compound and trying to figure out how to turn off his feelings for her once and for all.

And the next time he saw Dylan—if he ever saw his king again—

he would tell him that he was full of shit. Finding his mate was any-thing but wonderful.

In the meantime, he had something else to tell his king. Closing his eyes, he concentrated on building the mental bridge that would allow him to contact Dylan across more than a thousand miles. When he reached him, he settled down on a nearby bench and told Dylan all about the Shadowdrakes and their vendetta against the Wyvernmoons. By the time he was done, Dylan had already mapped out a plan on how the Dragonstars could ally themselves with the other clan.

When he was done, he figured he really had to hand it to himself. He'd been on the Wyvernmoon compound for a little more than twenty-four hours, and already he'd started the ball moving toward their ultimate destruction. And his own.

CHAPTER TWENTY

Cecily was in a crappy mood as she walked into the restaurant on the east side of the compound, where she was supposed to meet Gage. She was the one who had asked for the meeting, away from the west side of the compound, where the *factionnaires* usually hung out, and she needed to be on top of her game if she was going to win him over to her side. Yet she'd never felt worse.

After making love to her so completely that she had *cried*, Logan had been nowhere to be found when she woke up. She'd waited for him for hours, even as she told herself she wasn't. When he hadn't shown up by ten o'clock, she had even tried to reach out to him telepathically. But he hadn't answered her, and he hadn't returned before she had to leave for her lunch meeting at one o'clock with Gage, and now she was beginning to feel like a three-day stand.

Which was fine. It wasn't like Logan had made any promises to her, after all. But he should have been honest with her. He should have told her how he felt, not made love to her like she was the only woman in the world. Maybe she was overreacting—maybe he had another explanation for where he'd run off to—but she didn't think so.

Add to that the fact that she'd been digging through her father's office and found a series of bills that amounted to millions of dollars, all from a research lab she'd never heard of. When she'd called the number, it had been disconnected, with no forwarding number, which seemed odd, considering it was the kind of place that should want clients to be able to find it. Especially if those clients had given millions upon millions of dollars.

She'd planned to ask Logan to look into it, but since he was nowhere around, she was going to have to figure out how to do it herself. She was starting with Gage, because, along with Julian, he had been her father's second-in-command. She figured if Silus had been draining the clan's coffers, Gage was one of the few who might know why.

Not that she really needed the why, she supposed, but she couldn't help it. Her father had been working on something big toward the end of his life. She'd known that, even though he had never trusted her enough to let her see it. This lab, this money, had to be related to that. And if it wasn't, she wanted to know what the hell it was.

Gage stood when she approached the table, dropped a swift kiss on her cheek before helping her tuck her chair into the table. His solicitousness surprised her. Though he'd always treated her like that, lately she'd felt more like a plague sufferer around him than a beloved friend.

"Hi, Gage. How are you?" she said as she laid her napkin on her lap.

"I'm . . . cautiously optimistic," he answered, with a sparkle in his eye that she hadn't seen for a long time.

"Really? You want to tell me why? Because I have to admit that optimism is not exactly what I'm feeling at this point."

Before he could answer, the waiter approached and poured her a glass of the wine Gage had ordered while he'd been waiting for her. She figured it said a lot about her life of late, and just how much things had deteriorated between them, when she took one look at the open bottle and wondered if it was safe to drink or if he had poisoned her.

And this was the *factionnaire* she trusted most. The one she had planned on asking to marry her to give the clan a king. God, her life really was shit, wasn't it?

"You're a woman, Cecily. I told Silus he underestimated you, but your father was a stubborn man. He wouldn't deviate from his own ideas to save his life. I often asked him why he even bothered to have a *Conseil*."

"And what did he say?" she asked.

"That it was a status thing. Any king worth fearing had a group of ruthless and powerful advisors next to him that his enemies could point at with fear."

"Nice man, my father."

Gage shrugged. "He wasn't all bad."

"Maybe not, but I'm having a hard time seeing the good in him these days."

"You're not the only one."

His response surprised her, and she studied him for a minute, trying to read the handsome face that was almost as familiar to her as her own. But nothing seemed out of place. Gage's long-lashed blue eyes shone with sincerity. His full lips smiled convincingly—she even caught sight of the dimple at the corner of his mouth that she had teased him about when she was a teenager. There were no new lines of strain or worry, no circles beneath his eyes to signify sleepless nights. Nothing at all that said he'd been staying up late worrying about the clan, as she had.

Which, she supposed, was an answer in itself.

Deciding to lay all her cards on the table in an effort to gauge where he stood, she reached into her purse and placed the file folder she'd found that morning on the table between them.

"What's this?" he asked, taking a lingering sip of wine, as if to tell her that her earlier suspicions had been completely unfounded.

"I was hoping you could tell me. I found it in Dad's study and can't seem to figure it out."

Gage glanced at the thick pile of papers. "They're invoices."

"I know that, Gage. Invoices that total close to forty million dollars. That's a pretty big expenditure for the clan, and I was hoping you would be able to tell me what it went toward."

He shook his head, shrugged. "They look like lab invoices to me. Maybe for equipment or something?"

His voice was sincerely puzzled, his eyes appropriately shadowed. But she'd known him long enough to know that when he rubbed a finger over the bridge of his nose, there was more to a story than he wanted to say.

She thought about the information Logan had given her the night before, and took a shot in the dark. "Do these invoices have something to do with why our lab is so closely guarded?"

His eyes shot to hers. "What do you know about the lab?"

And I've got you, she thought triumphantly. "What do *you* know about the lab?"

"It's not my really my area. Wyatt, Dax and Dashiell are in charge of security over there. You should probably talk to them."

She made a mental note of the names, and didn't know whether she should be pleased that her three favorite *factionnaires* were still doing their jobs when everyone else seemed to have decided that duty could go to hell, or if she should be upset that they were obviously involved with something that Gage was doing his best to keep quiet.

"I will. But you were my father's second-in-command. I have a hard time believing he spent forty million dollars last year alone, and you didn't know anything about it. Just like I can't believe that a smart, experienced guy like you doesn't think it's odd that the lab is locked up tighter than the White House. And I know you, Gage. I've known you my whole life. If you think something's odd, you don't stop digging until you get to the bottom of it."

He drained his wine, but she noticed that he didn't pour himself another glass, even though it looked like he could use it. The words on a bumper sticker she'd seen once came back to her. *Just because I'm paranoid doesn't mean they aren't out to get me.* "Come on, Gage. Tell me what the hell is going on. You owe me that much."

The waiter picked that moment to come up to take their orders, and Cecily considered waving him away. But she changed her mind at the last second, decided it might be best to let Gage stew. So she spent a few minutes talking to the waiter, listening to the day's specials and then asking himself a few questions about himself, his family. Trying to get a good idea of how the regular dragons in the clan were doing.

As the waiter was leaving with their orders, she instructed him to take the wine and throw it away. Gage didn't argue, and her heart cracked wide open. This was the man she had planned to ask to marry her? The man she'd wanted to make king? The hero worship she'd had for him since she was ten years old died a painful death.

"It was just a few sleeping pills. I didn't want to hurt you."

"Just get me out of the way for a while. Why?"

He shook his head. "I don't think it matters now."

"Says the man who didn't almost end up passed out in his fettuccine."

He didn't answer for the longest time, and when he finally did say something, it had nothing to do with the fact that one of her oldest, dearest friends had just tried to drug her insensate.

"Don't go near the lab, Cecily. It's not a good place for you."

"Why not?" She leaned forward and whispered fiercely, "What's in there that has you so afraid? What has my father done, Gage? What have *you* done?"

"I haven't done anything." He slid back from the table so fast his chair hit the ground hard. "There's no way I'm taking the blame. Not for this. I did your father's dirty work for nearly five hundred years, but this . . . this is pure evil. I never had anything to do with what went on in that lab. You remember that."

He stormed out of the restaurant and she was left staring after him, completely bewildered. And more than a little frightened.

Pure evil? What the hell had her father been up to?

And why had Gage tried to drug her?

Logan had just knocked out one of the guards and slipped into the lab when a wave of psychic energy hit him hard enough to scramble his brain. At first, he'd figured it was a booby trap, meant to attack any outsiders who actually found a way into the lab. But a quick glance around told him no such alarm had been triggered. He was safe, undetected—at least for now. Which was a good thing, as it was two in the morning and his shields were down, all of them, his brain completely exposed as he tried to figure out exactly what the hell was going on in the lab.

He'd spent most of the day outside the large, unimaginative-looking building, observing the comings and goings and anything else he could see. As he'd waited, he'd reached a few conclusions. The first one was that for a lab that was manufacturing a deadly virus of biblical proportions, there were an awful lot of people walking in and out of the place. The second one was that the security had more than doubled since he'd been there the night before, especially around the south side (which was why he'd come in on the north side). He wondered if it was attributable to his attack on Remy. Had they traced it back to him? And if so, why hadn't they come after him?

The third thing he'd figured out was more an educated guess based on observation. Something big was going on in there, and whatever it was was big enough that more than half of the *factionnaires* had been by to check up on it. He'd watched nine of them stroll through the large doors at the front of the lab, and none of them had come back out. At least not while he'd been lying out here in the middle of the bushes.

Of course, he had been gone for an hour when he had picked up on an incredible amount of distress from Cecily. He'd tried to ignore it, as he had her psychic calls earlier in the day, but when he'd realized she was both devastated and confused, he hadn't been able to stay away.

After his disappearing act that morning, she hadn't exactly been overjoyed to see him, which he should have been happy about. But the whole mating thing was a tricky one, and no matter what he had told himself the night before, it drove him—and his beast—nuts to know that he'd hurt her.

She had still been interested in his skills, however, and she'd shown him the invoices she'd found. It had taken all his willpower to keep it together when he realized that he was holding in his hands the name of the company that had helped Silus manufacture the virus that had killed Quinn's brother, Gabe's mate, Dylan's niece and so many other Dragonstars. His beast had screamed for vengeance, and he'd filed away the names on the invoices, to be dealt with later.

He'd told her he was working on infiltrating the defenses of the lab and he wasn't exactly sure what was going on there—which was true, strictly speaking. After all, he'd spent the past sixteen hours trying to figure out what new atrocity was going down in there. She hadn't tried to stop him, had, in fact, encouraged his quest. That openness was just one more reason he couldn't believe—wouldn't believe—that she knew anything about the virus.

Suddenly, a psychic war cry rang through his head, digging sharp talons into his brain. It was followed by the screams of what had to be close to two hundred healthy dragon shifters as they ripped through the magical safeguards that surrounded the compound.

Dylan's plan must have failed, if he'd even had time to implement it. A quick psychic probe told him that the Shadowdrakes had arrived, and they were loaded for dragon.

Though none of the San Diego dragons had gotten to the lab yet, he could sense them flying through the town, slicing down Wyvern-moon clan members wherever they found them. And while he might have agreed with what they were doing even just a couple of days before—and had spent the past decade imagining being part of a similar war party—his first thought now was of Cecily.

He was up and running before the thought had fully formed, skidding around corners and hoping he wouldn't run into anyone as he retraced his steps as fast as he could. She was alone at her house, defenseless except for her beast, and though she was incredibly fast, her dragon was no match for the highly trained ones that were pouring into the compound.

Cecily! He called out for her, but it was her turn to ignore him. Or at least that's what he hoped she was doing. Her house was situated in the center of the compound. Surely none of the attackers had gotten to her yet. *Cecily, damnit, I'm not joking! Answer me!*

He was almost to the door when he sensed a huge group of shifters walking toward him from an intersecting corridor. Swearing mentally, he started feeling doorknobs, looking for an unlocked one that he could slip behind unnoticed. If he got caught now, they'd never let him go, and Cecily would be on her own out there.

He got lucky on the fourth door he tried, and he scanned the room as he stepped inside. It was empty, and he hoped he was in the middle of some janitor's closet that no one ever went into.

He wasn't. Instead, he'd stumbled into a room with a number of lab tables and three sophisticated computer setups. He really hoped that none of the people walking toward him wanted into this room.

Figuring he should at least try to take advantage of the situation, he sped down the aisle to one of the computers. In the back of his head, he kept his scan going across the compound, looking for Cecily's energy. He needed to find her so that when he left this room in a few minutes, he would be able to go right to her. He refused to believe that he was going to be stuck in here for the duration.

The computers were all password protected—big surprise—but he whipped out the small tablet computer he carried with him everywhere and quickly connected it. Then he sent out a mental SOS to Shawn. There wasn't anything the guy didn't know about computers, and if he couldn't break these passwords, no one could.

Shawn answered right away, pissed off and sleepy. *What's up, man? I just got to sleep. Is everything okay there?*

Logan explained the situation as succinctly as possible.

Give me a minute.

I haven't got a minute. Didn't you hear what I said?

Well, find one. I'm a miracle worker, but I'm not God.

Within moments, he saw the screen on his computer change as Shawn seized control of it. It flickered through about seven different screens as Shawn did whatever it was that he did and Logan watched the door impatiently, prepared to rip to shreds the brain of anyone who opened the door in front of him.

No one did, but by the time Shawn said *I'm in* about three minutes later, Logan's nerves were shot. His brain was filled with images of what was going on outside the lab in the compound, and from everything he could pick up, it seemed that the Shadowdrakes had beaten him to the draw. They were launching a full-scale war on the compound, and every dragon whose brain he brushed seemed to have two objectives: kill as many Wyvernmoons as they could and get to the lab.

Good, he told Shawn, as he disconnected his computer and shoved it into his bag while he ran. *Now figure out what the fuck is in there and let me know. Something big is going on, and I'm hoping you can figure out what. If we've got any luck at all, that computer is part of the network.*

With any luck at all, Shawn agreed. *Trying to get into it was no walk in the park, so maybe we'll get lucky.*

Maybe.

Logan listened at the doorway—he used both his ears and his psychic sense—and heard nothing. Yanking it open, he took off full speed down the hallway, determined not to answer any questions that came his way. But somehow he managed to make it all the way outside without seeing anyone, and once his feet hit the ground, he poured on every burst of speed he had. Cecily was out there somewhere, and he would get to her.

He started shifting while he ran. It was difficult and painful and something few dragons could do, but the ability had served him in good stead through the years. He only hoped it did this time.

He launched himself into the air at the same second he finished shifting and flew hell-for-leather toward Cecily's house. Two Shadow-drakes intercepted him about halfway there, and though he didn't want to hurt them—they were just defending their clan against the virus as much as he was—he couldn't take a chance on them slowing him down. If they had gotten this far into the compound, then some-one could have gotten to Cecily. And he knew with utter certainty what they would do to the Wyvernmoon princess if they could get their hands on her: the same thing he would have done before he'd met her.

One barreled straight into him and sent him careening through the air. He dove, tried to avoid them, but they weren't going anywhere—which was exactly what he had expected.

Focusing his power, he lowered his guard and reached out, isolating their specific brain patterns from all the others pouring in on him from all sides. Then he struck both of them at the same time, not destroying part of their brains as he had with Remy, but rendering them uncon-scious with a powerful psychic blow he designed specifically for them.

They were out instantly, and he took off, not bothering to hang around to make sure they spiraled safely to the ground.

He was at Cecily's house in less than three minutes, and Logan called to her from within the beast. *Cecily! Cecily, where are you?*

She didn't answer, and he flew straight through the big glass door of the house and into her family room, convinced he would find her locked in a struggle for her life or already dead on the floor. He found neither, though he wasted precious seconds zipping through the house, looking for her. Once he realized she really wasn't there, he headed for the Dracon Club and prayed like he hadn't in centuries.

He was bleeding from where he'd plowed through her glass door, and hoped he wasn't leading a trail straight to her for the Shadow-drakes to find. But he was going to have to take his chances, because there was no way he was stopping to check the damages. He had to get to Cecily, had to make sure his mate was alive.

But when he got to the Dracon Club, it looked like a full-scale war had broken out. Dragons—Wyvernmoons and Shadowdrakes—were fighting everywhere he looked. Some were in beast form, some in human, and the battles were fierce. He didn't know enough Wyvernmoons yet to be able to tell them apart on sight alone, and there were too many of them to distinguish by scent. Which meant he had no idea which clan was winning or losing. He knew only there were an awful lot of bodies strewn in his path.

Frantic now, he searched the parking lot and street for glimpses of Cecily's purple scales or blond hair. He saw neither, and finally landed outside the club with some vague idea of shifting and heading inside to comb the club for her. Because if she wasn't here, then the sad fact was that he had no idea where she was. He might have fallen in love with her, but he had known her for only a few days, and that wasn't long enough for him to even begin to hazard a guess about where she would go during an attack.

As he shifted into human form, he narrowly avoided being hit by a blast of energy flying from one direction and a fireball coming from another. Ducking behind one of the few cars in the parking lot, he finished the change. But as he headed for the door at a dead run, he was distracted by a huge bolt of lightning that split the night sky in front of him neatly in half.

Thunder cracked directly above him, so loud and powerful that it shook buildings and set off car alarms. Wind shrieked through the streets, sharp and wet and fast. It pummeled everything in its path, and Logan felt the sting of it against his own naked skin. It was followed by another powerful blast of lightning and the sound of two dragons screaming in pain.

In that moment, he flashed back to Cecily's mountain, when she had used her hands to shoot sparks into him that brought his pleasure to a fever pitch. He remembered thinking then that she was a storm-caller, but it hadn't been the time to ask her for clarification. He had

246 · TESSA ADAMS

forgotten about it in the heat of everything else that had happened afterward.

Now he wondered if she was the only one of her kind in the Wyvernmoon clan, or if there were others. Either way, he figured it was his best bet to find her, and he sprinted toward the lightning even as the dragons closest to it ran away.

A moment later, he looked up and up and up and there she was. At the top of a three-story building, her hair blowing wildly in the storm she had created while her eyes glowed a dark, eerie purple. Her arms were raised high as lightning exploded all around her. She seemed to almost pick one of the bolts out of midair and then hurtle it toward three Shadowdrakes who were trying to get away.

They weren't that lucky. Her blast hit them dead-on, and they went flying. As they did, he swore he heard her laugh, low and long and exhilarated. She was riding high on the storm she'd called to her, absorbing it into her very being until her entire body seemed to glow. Yet even as he watched, two men sneaked up behind her. He saw their shadows loom large in the bright yellow globes of the streetlights, and he started to run, convinced that no matter what he did, he wouldn't get there in time.

CHAPTER TWENTY-ONE

Cecily! He screamed it into her head as he ran for the front door of the building, knowing he could run the stairs faster than he could shift at this point. She didn't answer, and he was afraid she was too high from riding the storm to even hear him. He ran even faster, terror a rampaging beast inside him as he strained to get to her.

He took the stairs four at a time, screaming for her the entire way up. When he finally got to the roof—maybe ninety seconds after he'd first seen the men looming over her—he was terrified of what he would find. Breath sawing out of his lungs, dread a red haze before his eyes, he burst through the door onto the roof, screaming in rage. He was prepared to take the bastards apart piece by piece for daring to touch his woman.

But he'd worried for her for nothing. Cecily had them on the ground at her feet, caught in a maelstrom of wind and rain and lightning. They were alive, but he could feel their alarm, feel their horror all the way across the roof.

She might not have been able to beat them in hand-to-hand combat like some of the female dragons he knew from the Dragonstar clan, but, then, she didn't have to. This power of hers, it was incredible. Unbelievable. He'd never been more proud of her, his dragon preening inside him, proud of itself for choosing such a strong, powerful mate.

"I'm sorry I couldn't answer you," she said, her voice hoarse with the effort to be heard above the storm she was controlling. "I was in the middle of something."

"I can see that." He grinned at her, fought the urge to pull her into his arms and kiss her right there in the middle of the storm, in the middle of the battle. "You have quite a few tricks up your sleeve."

"Yes, well, a woman has to have some mystery." She threw his own words back at him, then turned to look out at the street below them. The fight was still going strong, and up here, for some reason, it was a lot easier for him to tell who the Wyvernmoons were and who the Shadowdrakes were. Maybe because he was standing next to the Wyvernmoon princess and she was, in essence, connected to them all. Whatever it was, he'd never had an easier time distinguishing clan affiliation.

"Over there," he yelled, pointing at where three Shadowdrake males had a Wyvernmoon female cornered. As they advanced on her, the battle raging around them seemed to be the last thing on their minds.

Even as Cecily pulled down more lightning, he thrust his mind into the first one's head. What he found in there was evil, disgusting, the dragon's desire to humiliate and debase the woman in front of him an all-consuming fire in his brain.

For the first time, he wondered about the logic of the Dragonstars forming an alliance with the Shadowdrakes. Any leader who would allow his men to rape defenseless civilian women during battle was not the kind of leader Dylan would need—or want—to associate with.

As the bastard reached for her, talons extended, Logan didn't hesitate, didn't try for finesse—not with the other two bearing down on the helpless woman, as well. Instead, he honed his will to a blade, raking it through the man's brain and shredding everything he came into contact with. Blood was leaking from the man's nose and ears and mouth before Logan dropped him, dead, on the street.

He aimed for the second man's mind, but Cecily was already there, a thin stream of lightning heading straight toward the two men. The woman was facing them and was obviously familiar with Cecily's abilities, for she scrambled as far backward as she could. The men started to follow her, but before they could move, Cecily's electricity blasted them off their feet.

"Good job," he said, and this time he did pull her into his arms and kiss her. He couldn't help it. His complete and utter relief that she was safe was so overwhelming that he couldn't speak of it. Couldn't do anything but pour his feelings into the kiss and into her.

She clutched at him, returned the kiss for a moment, then shoved him away. "They got through because there were no guards, no *factionnaires*, watching our borders. They were able to hurt my people because someone called the guards off on purpose, left us open to this attack."

"Yes." He couldn't sugarcoat it for her, knew that she wouldn't want him to, anyway.

Traitor. The word hissed from her mind to his.

"Yes."

"I want him found and imprisoned." Her voice was flat and emotionless, colder than he had ever heard it. "I want him dead."

Though he'd known they were coming, and though he hadn't been the one to leave the compound defenseless, he felt her words like blows deep inside him. He wasn't a traitor, as his loyalties had never lay with her, but that didn't mean he hadn't betrayed her. Didn't mean he wasn't going to betray her more before this whole nightmare was through. He couldn't stand the idea that one day soon she would feel about him the same way she felt about the Wyvernmoon who had sold out her people to the Shadowdrakes.

But there wasn't time for that now. The battle raged on, people dying all around them, and Cecily needed his help. He wouldn't let her down, not now. Not this time.

Standing with her on top of that building, he fought side by side with her. Not because he cared about saving what Silus had built out here in the middle of South Dakota, but because he had faith in Cecily.

In who she was and in what she wanted to create. No matter what he'd thought when he'd come here, she was not her father's daughter.

There was no way he could make things right for Gabe or Dylan or Quinn. No way he could make things right for the hundreds and thousands of Dragonstars who had lost loved ones to Silus's evil creation. But that was one man and his corrupt council. That wasn't the entire clan.

It wasn't the poor woman down there who had nearly been raped and murdered simply because she was a Wyvernmoon. It wasn't Sebastian, who was just trying to make ends meet in a clan that had forsaken him for so long. And it wasn't Cecily, with her beautiful smile and even more beautiful heart. With her plans and determination and hopefulness that she could somehow buck thousands of years of tradition and save her home. Save her people.

Logan! Shawn's voice ripped through his head, coming at him from the psychic bridge he had built between them hours before. *Are you in the lab?*

No. We're under attack from the Shadowdrakes. My guess is that Dylan's attempt to reach out to them today failed, he said, tongue firmly in cheek.

But Shawn wasn't in the mood to joke. *It didn't fail. Rafael simply said he wasn't sure an alliance between the clans was going to be necessary. I'm assuming this is what he meant.* A pause. *Are you okay?*

Just dandy, he answered as he grabbed Cecily and hit the deck in an effort to avoid an energy blast aimed straight at them. It missed, but only by inches, and the resulting explosion rattled every bone in his body.

He rolled off Cecily slowly. "Are you okay?" he demanded.

She was still trying to catch her breath, but she gave him a thumbs-up sign.

"Stay down!" he ordered fiercely, as he crouched and looked over the edge of the buildings. But no one was paying attention to them. One of the *factionnaires*—Wyatt, he thought—had gutted the bastard who had sent the blast toward Cecily. He hoped none of the others down there had that particular power.

Logan! The roar came down the bridge. *Are you all right?*

It was Dylan this time, and it had been a long time since he'd heard his king so frantic. But, then, Dylan had never been very good about sitting back and watching while any of his people were in danger. With her courage and determination to do right by her people, Cecily reminded Logan of his ruler.

I'm fine. We're fine.

Dylan paused, and Logan could almost feel him evaluating the *we* he had just used. But the king didn't comment on it. Instead, he said, *Good. Because you need to get back to that lab. Now.*

Chills went through him at Dylan's tone—a combination of cold, calculating rage and a fear the other dragon shifter couldn't quite hide.

What did Shawn find?

They've created a strain of the virus based on the main DNA strands that all Dragonstars share. Quinn was speaking now. *They've done the same for the Shadowdrakes.* He paused. *Do you know what that means, Logan?*

Spell it out for me.

It means that all our research is useless, as is the vaccine we've been developing based on our own antibodies. Useless. They have a weapon that, if released, will kill every single man, woman and child with Dragonstar DNA.

His world imploded. Right up there on the rooftop, as the battle raged around him in all directions. It simply crumpled in on itself and took a huge part of him with it.

He sank to his knees beside Cecily, stared at her, and wondered—just for a moment—if she knew. If everything had been an act and she'd known what was going on in that lab all along.

No. He wouldn't believe that of her. Not of Cecily. He couldn't believe it of her—not if he wanted to survive.

Still, he found himself turning away from her, angry with her even though he knew the mess they were in wasn't her fault. She simply hadn't known. But a part of him felt betrayed, anyway, wanted to know *why* she hadn't known. Why she hadn't been aware of what was going on right under her nose.

I'm going to head back to the lab, he told Dylan.

Good. We're leaving now. We should be there in a few hours.

No! I don't want you here, don't want you anywhere near the virus!

That's not your choice, Dylan answered.

Fuck that. You want to chance bringing it back to the caves? On your clothes? Your shoes? Stay put, goddamnit. I'll take care of it.

Be practical. You can't bring the lab down alone, Dylan said.

Watch me. Very deliberately, he broke the bridge between them. He was the only psychic in the group—without him holding it up, there would be no communication. Dylan, as king, had the power to communicate telepathically with each of his sentries, but not over great distances. He was on his own.

He turned to Cecily. "I have to go."

"What? Now?" She looked at him like he was insane.

"Something big is coming."

"Bigger than this?" She gestured to the fight going on beneath them.

"Yes."

"Then I'm coming with you."

He shook his head. He didn't want her anywhere near the lab. He had to move fast if he wanted to get it done before the other Dragonstars showed up; he wasn't stupid enough to believe that an objection from him would keep them home. But that meant the lab, the virus, everything had to be gone before his king and fellow sentries made it to South Dakota. He might have broken the bridge between them, but he knew Dylan well enough to know that his king was already on the way. Logan was determined that there should be nothing left to threaten him—or any of the other Dragonstars—by the time he arrived.

"No. You need to take care of your people. They need you."

"*You* need me." She grabbed on to his arm, put her face right next to his. When he shook his head, she said, "At least tell me where you're going."

What was he supposed to say? He didn't have time to explain, and even if he did, he wouldn't. He didn't want to give her time to warn anyone at the lab. She might not condone the virus, but there was no way she would condone the killing of that many Wyvernmoons, either.

He didn't like it much himself, knowing he was probably going to get some innocents in the blast. But he couldn't worry about that now, couldn't let it get to him. Besides, if they worked in the lab, they had to know something was up with all the secrecy, had to know something about this damn virus. They'd brought about their own destruction.

"There's something big going on at the lab," he told her. "I'm afraid the Shadowdrakes are gunning for it."

"The Shadowdrakes?" Her eyes grew wide. "You know more than what you're telling me, don't you?"

"Cecily." He grabbed her hand, but she shook him off.

"I knew it. I saw your face when I showed you those invoices. You know what they've been up to and you didn't tell me."

A blast of fire came soaring over the side of the building, nearly singeing off what little hair he had left. Things were getting worse out there, and if he didn't leave now, he was going to be pinned down on this roof for the duration. "I can't do this now!" he roared. "I have to go."

"So go!" She shoved him away from her. "Do what you have to do. But when this is all over, you're going to answer to me, Logan Kelly!"

In that moment, she looked every inch the queen, and he knew when the battle was done that he would indeed answer to her. And in doing so, would lose her forever.

"Fine. But you need to get out of here, too. It's too dangerous for you."

The look she gave him was imperious, commanding, royal. "You don't get to tell me what I need to do. Go. Take care of whatever it is that's so important to you that you can't share. But don't presume to tell me what to do or how to take care of my people."

Another energy blast came hurtling at them, and Cecily slammed her hand out, met it with a blast of lightning so powerful that the energy dissolved in midair. Then she quirked a brow at him. "Go, Logan. I don't need or want you here." And then she turned her back on him.

Leaving her there on that roof was the hardest thing he'd ever done. He wanted to grab her and pull her to safety, to stash her somewhere where no one and nothing could ever hurt her again. Wanted to force her to look at him, to talk to him, to forgive him for what he'd done and what he was about to do.

But in that moment, he couldn't touch her. She was the queen and she was doing what she had to do—fighting to keep her people safe. He couldn't interfere with that, couldn't make her stop any more than she could turn him from the course he was on.

He took one last look at her, and then he ran.

CHAPTER TWENTY-TWO

For the second time that night, he shifted on the run. Flew back to Cecily's house and got the bag of explosives he'd picked up for just this occasion. Then headed for the lab as fast as he could fly. But with every flap of his wings, something inside him was telling him to stop, to go back to her, to make things right with Cecily before it was too late.

He ignored the feeling, focused on everything he had to do in the next hour. He shoved the future, whatever it might be, to the back of his mind. He would figure out what happened next after he ended the malignant evil of the virus once and for all.

He landed about 250 yards from the door he'd broken into earlier, and just observed for a second. Everything was quiet and there were no Shadowdrakes in sight, but he knew better than to assume that meant anything. Dragons were sneaky—he should know.

The guards were still in place around the perimeter, and, in fact, it looked like security had again doubled in the time he had left to check on Cecily. He wouldn't be able to go ten feet without tripping over one of them.

Fuck. Time for Plan B.

Ducking behind a clump of big trees, he shifted as quietly as he could. Then pulled some clothes out of his bag and dressed quickly. He strapped on his daggers, tucked his Glock in the back of his jeans and then slung his scoped rifle over his shoulder. It was going to take some doing to get into the lab this time around, but he would get in there. The fate of his entire clan rested on him not failing here, not failing now.

He took a few steps forward, went over his planned distraction in his head, then whirled around as a twig snapped behind him. His gun was in his hand, cocked and ready to fire, before he realized that the person standing behind him wasn't an enemy. It was Shawn.

"What the fuck are you doing here?" he whispered viciously.

"You didn't think I was going to let you have all the fun, did you?" Shawn's voice was light, but the look in his eyes was completely deadly. There would be no reasoning with his friend tonight.

"You know you could be exposed to the damn virus, don't you?" Logan demanded severely.

"Yeah, well, everyone has to die sometime." He pulled out his own gun. "Do you have a plan?"

"You mean besides blasting the motherfuckers to kingdom come?" Shawn's grin was fierce. "Yeah, besides that."

"Not really, no."

"Okay, then. We go on three."

"I was joking, asshole." Logan pointed to the back of the clinic. "I want to do a quick sweep of the perimeter. They've added guards since I was here earlier, which is understandable, considering they're under attack. But the door I want to go in"—he pointed to one on the far left of the building, as far from the actual lab area as it could get—"is over there. I think it's our best chance of getting in undetected."

"All right, then. Let's do this thing."

Logan glanced at the bag on his friend's shoulders. "What's in there?"

"I assume the same thing that's in yours. Enough C4 to blow a hole in the world."

Then Shawn dropped to his belly and began to inch forward, using the low bushes around the area as cover.

Logan moved about twenty feet to Shawn's right and did the same thing. He wasn't sure how long they would go unnoticed, but he wanted to stay inconspicuous for as long as possible. It upped the odds of them bringing the entire thing down.

No one gets out, Shawn. He sent him the order. *We don't know who knows what, and we sure as shit don't have time to sort it out. If they're in the lab or around it, they die.*

Damn straight.

Okay. Just wanted to be sure we were on the same page.

We are. A pause. Then: *There's a guard directly in front of me.*

I see him. Give me a minute to get in position and then give him something to look at.

I'm on it.

Logan scooted forward a few inches at a time, until he was within a couple of feet of the guard. The man looked bored, half-asleep, but he was carrying a weapon that could do a lot of damage.

Now, Shawn.

Shawn rustled a few leaves, let the red light on his scope flash for just a second. The guard straightened up, pointed his gun at where Shawn had been only moments before, and started forward tentatively. He'd taken three steps when Logan grabbed him from behind and slit his throat before he could so much as whimper. He let the guard fall where he stood.

One down; forty-three to go, came Shawn's ironic whisper.

For the next fifteen minutes, they repeated the same scenario over and over. Sometimes Shawn was the bait, sometimes Logan was, but by the time they reached the lab, they'd left a string of bloody bodies behind them. More than once he'd had to use his psychic powers to rip their minds apart, but he'd tried not to do it too often. It took a lot out of him, and he had a feeling he would need every ounce of strength he could muster before this night was through.

Okay, almost there, said Shawn, yanking a computer out of his bag.

Too bad you can't just blink yourself in.

I don't blink. Besides, even I can't get through security like this. At least not without a little help. Logan watched in awe as his friend whipped up the lab blueprints and security codes.

Where the fuck did you get that?

The computer you hooked me into was one of the security ports, Shawn answered as his fingers flew over the keys. *Give me a minute and I'll get the door open for us.*

And to think I was just going to blast my way in.

Yeah, well, I've always had more finesse than you. And this way, we maintain the element of surprise.

Provided nobody steps in the blood out there.

Naturally.

Logan gave Shawn the minute he'd asked for as he concentrated on laying charges every few feet along the back of the building, especially the spots where he knew there were support beams.

You ready? Shawn asked.

Yeah. He stuck the detonator in his front pocket.

Shawn pressed a button on the computer and Logan heard the side door click open. He opened it slowly, slid in, then waved Shawn inside with him. They were exactly where he'd expected them to be, on the administrative side of the building.

We need to find the supercomputer, Shawn said. *I want to download as much information from it as we can.*

I don't know if we have that much time.

We need to make the time. If someone manages to slip out, or if someone has already sent something to someone they know outside this lab, if one of these bastards took his work home with him one night, then parts of the blueprint for this virus could already be floating around out there. We need as much information on it as we can get.

Logan cursed, low and long, furious with himself that he hadn't thought of the arguments Shawn was bringing up. *Okay, then we split up. If you have the blueprints, I assume that means you know where the Cray supercomputer is located.*

It's in the room right at the heart of the building.

It'll be the most heavily guarded, so we go in there together. Then, while you're downloading what you need, I'll lay the interior charges. But we have to do this quick. The window of opportunity is not that large. Someone's going to discover those bodies any minute now.

So stop wasting time and let's go.

They made their way down the hallway, not taking the time to hide. The place was crawling with guards in civilian clothes, and Logan was counting on the fact that he and Shawn were shifters and could give any challengers pause. Hopefully, it would take them a couple of seconds to figure out that they didn't belong, and a couple of seconds was all they needed to take care of the problem.

They were almost to the main labs before they ran into trouble. Two guards were patrolling the corridor in front of a huge meeting room, a fact that piqued Logan's curiosity even as he told himself it didn't matter. He nodded to Shawn, and the two of them let loose their daggers at the same time. Shawn's caught one guard in the eye, straight to the brain, while Logan's sliced the other guard's jugular.

Messy, Shawn said, as they retrieved the knives.

So sue me. He paused, sent out psychic feelers. We need to move now.

As they picked up the pace, he got one good glimpse inside the meeting room. There were about twenty people inside, chief among them Julian, Luc, Etienne, and Gage—all Wyvernmoon *factionnaires.* The bastards.

It took only another minute for them to get to the lab. Shawn had his computer in hand, and Logan left him to it as he picked up both bags of explosives and started laying charges where they would do the most damage.

Within seconds, Shawn had unlocked every door in the wing, and Logan was inside the labs. In one he found a couple of huge jars of alcohol, and he carried them with him, dumping some of the flammable liquid over every piece of electronic equipment he could find. He had enough C4 to blow this place sky-high, but he wanted to make sure that whatever was left burned completely.

Four times he ran into lone researchers. With the humans, he simply ripped through their brains, shredding them. With the two dragons, both of whom had mental shields, he didn't waste time trying to break through them. Instead, he just slit their throats.

Within ten minutes, he was back outside the supercomputer room, waiting for Shawn. *Are you ready? We need to blow this thing!*

Almost. I've routed it to do a massive info dump to Phoebe's Cray in New Mexico. But I don't want to leave until it's done.

How long is that going to take?

It's going to take as long as it takes, Shawn snapped. *Back off. I've already got the charges laid on the computer, so any information in here should disappear once everything goes boom.*

Okay. Logan took a deep breath, tried to calm himself down. He wanted to get this done, wanted to get the info back to Phoebe, wanted to get Shawn the fuck away from the lab before everything blew. He'd put extra explosives and fuel in the labs that contained live cultures of the virus, so that everything in there would incinerate instantly, but he didn't want to take any chances with Shawn. He wanted his best friend as far away as possible before this thing blew to hell and back.

He scanned the area mentally and froze as he picked up on two people in the hallway next to him. He tried to scan them, but they were blocked, which meant they were dragons. And their shields were a lot stronger than any he had seen in the lab so far.

Hurry up. We've got a problem out here.

It's done, it's done. I'm heading for the door now. What's the problem?

Logan ducked into the lab at the last second and stopped Shawn from hitting the hallway at a dead run. Putting up a quick mental block so that whoever was passing wouldn't sense him or Shawn if they had powers similar to his own, Logan watched as two huge men in military gear turned the corner.

Shadowdrakes, Shawn said.

Yeah, I think so, too.

No. I recognize them—they're Shadowdrake sentries. What the fuck are they doing here?

The attack on the clan. It's just a distraction. They're doing the same thing here that we are. Trying to kill the virus before it kills them.

Do you blame them?

No. But I don't relish trying to explain to them that we're on the same side.

Shawn snorted. *Especially since you stink of sex with the Wyvern-moon princess.*

Logan ignored him. They've got to know we're here. The explosives are everywhere.

True. So let's blow this pop stand, in case they decide to set off the fireworks before we can make it outside.

Good point. He headed into the hallway, his hand on his gun. He didn't want to shoot the Shadowdrakes, especially if they were there for the same reason he and Shawn were, but he wasn't going to make himself an easy target.

The two dragon shifters whirled around the second he and Shawn hit the hallway, and in a second they were all staring at one another, guns raised and fingers on the triggers. He saw the glimmer of recognition in their eyes the moment they realized who they were dealing with.

"When's it set to blow?" one asked him.

"I'm taking it down in five minutes, so you're going to want to get out," Logan responded.

"We need longer. We've got to download the information."

"We have no time for that."

"Make time, or the four of us are going to die right here."

Fuck. Fuck. Fuck. Fuck. Fuck. Fuuuuuuuuck.

Well, that's eloquent, Shawn said.

Fuck you. It wasn't that he was afraid to get into it with the Shadowdrakes, because he wasn't. He already had their shields half unraveled, and in another minute he would be able to kill them with a thought. But that wasn't the point. They didn't want anything more than what he and Shawn wanted—to ensure that their clan could fight this virus if it somehow managed to survive. He didn't begrudge them that.

"I'll give you eight minutes," he said, setting the detonators in his pocket. "Starting now."

The other men were already moving.

And then he and Shawn were hurtling down the hallways. He was getting Shawn as far away from this goddamn death factory as he could, and he could only pray that it was enough.

They hit the side door at four minutes and counting, and hit the woods behind the lab a minute after that. Shawn slowed down, turning to look at the lab.

"What are you doing? Keep going!"

"I need to see it blow. I need to know it's finally over."

"Goddamnit, Shawn. The virus—"

"Will incinerate in the fire. You know that. You made sure of it. I need to see it, Logan."

Because he understood, because he had the same feeling, he didn't say anything else. Just stood in the woods with Shawn and waited for the world around them to blow up.

CHAPTER TWENTY-THREE

Cecily felt the explosion a second before she heard it. The ground beneath her feet rumbled, and she had a moment to think, improbably, of earthquakes before a deafening roar filled the air. A bright glow burned against the night sky to her left, and she knew.

Logan had blown up the lab. She wanted to blame it on the Shadowdrakes, knew they'd had at least as much opportunity as her lover had had. But deep down inside, she knew it hadn't been them. Logan had done it.

The knowledge was one more blow in a day full of them. The attack was over, the remaining Shadowdrakes taking to the air a few minutes before, as if they had known that the lab was going down. As if destroying her father's shining glory had been their purpose all along.

And maybe it had been. She didn't know what went on there, because no one had ever told her. She'd planned on finding out, had been on her way to the lab to investigate when news of the Shadowdrake attack had found her and she'd returned to help fight in the only way she knew how.

The provocation for this unending war between her clan and the others had been in that lab. She knew that now, but it was too late for her to do anything with that knowledge. She looked around at all the dead at her feet. It was way too late.

And Logan—was he one of them? It was obvious to her now—when it no longer mattered—that he had come to destroy her clan, destroy her. Was he a Shadowdrake? It made sense, but she had seen him kill some of the attackers today. Had seen him defend Wyvernmoon lives against the Drakes, which seemed impossible if he was one of them. Was he Dragonstar, then? It made a twisted kind of sense.

He had betrayed her, had come into her life for the express purpose of destroying her clan—and her—from the inside. It was a good plan. A very good plan, and one she couldn't even fault him for. Not when she was the one who had invited him in. The one who had given him means and opportunity on a silver platter. She had to assume her father had given him motive.

So, what now? she wondered as she fought back the tears that were incredibly close to the surface. She wanted nothing more than to retreat to her house, to bury her head and pretend that the past week hadn't happened. She wanted to curl up on Gage's lap like she had as a little girl and ask him for advice. He would know what to do.

But she couldn't forget that he had tried to drug her that afternoon—an attempt to keep her out of the way of the battle, she could only assume. Just like she couldn't forget that he had been in charge of security assignments for years. It had passed to Julian a couple of years ago, but the guards still respected Gage. Still listened to him. And if he told them to take a couple of days off, to leave their posts undefended, that was exactly what they would do.

He had turned traitor. She didn't know why, didn't know when. But she would find out. After she dealt with the crisis caused by this latest attack.

And deal with it, she would. Queens didn't run away when things turned to shit around them. She'd wanted to take control of her clan, had wanted to fix what was broken. Now she had to live with her mistakes and the people she had let die because she had clued in to what was going on too late to save them.

The guilt of her failings burned like acid.

Not knowing what else to do, she walked through the streets with the emergency workers, looking for survivors of the bloody battle. There weren't nearly as many as she'd hoped there would be. The Shadowdrakes had been thorough. And though there were empty spaces on the street from where Shadowdrakes had fallen during battle and then disappeared, as their death magic flashed them home, there were many more spaces taken up by Wyvernmoons. Everything she'd done had been too little, too late.

She turned the corner, hoping for relief, and only found more bodies. Looking over them, she froze, as she saw Sebastian laying in the street, his neck broken and his eyes staring vacantly into the night.

The tears came then. She couldn't stop them, couldn't fight them as she stumbled through the bodies of the dead. Maybe it wasn't the right look for a queen, maybe she was making the biggest mistake yet, but she had no more fight in her. Not right now.

Even knowing it was useless, she checked Sebastian for a pulse. Nothing. She reached up, gently closed his eyes, and prayed that his wife and child were still safe at home.

"Help me," a faint voice said, and Cecily looked around wildly, searching for the person who was still alive in the midst of all this destruction. She found the young boy, no more than eighteen or nineteen, trapped beneath a car one of the Shadowdrakes must have rolled during the battle.

"I need help over here!" She raised her voice as she ran, made sure it carried to the various rescue workers. As soon as a few started for her, she crouched down beside the boy and stroked his hair. "Help's coming. I promise."

His pupils were dilated with shock, his skin so white that she was amazed there was any blood left in him. "What's your name?" she asked.

"I'm James."

"Hello, James. I'm Cecily."

"I know who you are. You're the new queen. My mom was very excited when she saw you up there fighting today."

"Your mom? Is she around? Can I get her for you?" Cecily looked up and down the desolate street.

"She's over there." He nodded toward one of the small shops that lined the street. *The bakery,* she thought. "They got her at the very beginning of the attack. I dragged her inside, tried to help her, but I'm not a healer. She died hours ago."

If she'd been standing, her legs would have gone out from under her. God, how much more was she supposed to take? How much more guilt could sit on her shoulders without crushing her completely?

"I'm sorry, James." She reached for his hand, held it, because she could do nothing else. "So sorry that I couldn't save her."

"You didn't kill her. The Shadowdrakes did."

And then he didn't say anything more, because the emergency crew shifted the car off his leg and the pain made him pass out in her arms. His leg was crushed and bleeding in three places.

"Can you save him?" she demanded of Lucy, one of the clan healers. The other woman had crouched beside his leg and was running her hand over the pulverized bones.

"Save him? Absolutely. Save his leg? I don't know. We need to get to the clinic, where I can work on him."

Cecily stepped back so that they could get James on a stretcher. "I want to know what happens with him. Call me after you're done and let me know what he needs, and I'll make sure he gets it."

Lucy eyed her curiously for a moment, but then James moaned and she began to see to him, administering to his pain. Cecily backed away and let them do their jobs.

She stayed on the street with the rescue workers—with her people—for hours. Dawn came and went and the sun was directly overhead before they had found all the survivors and cleared away the dead. In the middle of the search, Wyatt, Dax and Dashiell had found her, looking exhausted and banged up, but alive.

She froze at the sight of them, overwhelmed by the knowledge that they had not hidden away like so many of her father's *factionnaires*. They had stayed and fought with her, with her people, even though they'd known it was a losing battle. That loyalty, in the wake of so much pain and betrayal, did what nothing else had been able to do. It brought her to her knees.

Dashiell was there in an instant, pulling her up and into his arms. "A queen doesn't belong on the ground," he murmured softly in her ear as he began striding down the street with her, Wyatt and Dax on either side of them.

"Yeah, well, I'm just a princess," she answered, laying her head on his chest, because suddenly she was so tired, she could barely think. "And not a very good one, at that."

"I don't know about that." He stroked a soothing hand down her back. "You've exceeded my wildest expectations."

She didn't exactly consider that a compliment, seeing as how the clan was currently in ruins. If this exceeded his expectations, she couldn't help wondering just how badly he'd expected her to mess up.

"What are we going to do?" she asked. "I should know, but I don't. How do we come back from this? What do we do?"

"First thing we do is get some rest," Dax said softly. "And then we regroup and see where we stand."

"Where we stand?" she choked out. "Please tell me where, exactly, we stand, considering you're the only three *factionnaires* who bothered to stick around to fight. I knew they were bastards, but even I couldn't have imagined this level of betrayal."

"It gets worse," Wyatt told her. "Gage is dead. He was killed in the lab blast. From what we can piece together, some of the others were there, as well—Julian, Etienne, Acel, Thierren. We're not sure who else."

"Are they dead, as well?"

"We can't find their bodies, and a few of the survivors said they saw them fleeing into the hills."

Cecily nodded, unsurprised. "What was in that lab, Dash?"

She felt him tense underneath her, saw Dax and Wyatt do the same. "Don't you think I have a right to know? I watched my people die because of it tonight, and we're at war because of it. Surely I need to know what's been going on there."

Dash shook his head. "We're not sure. We've been shut out of the place for two years now. Silus let only a precious few into that lab, and we weren't among the chosen."

"Still, you have a good idea. I know you do. What kind of weapon was he building?"

"He wasn't building anything. He was using the best scientists in the world—human and dragon—to manufacture some kind of virus," Dax told her grimly.

"Virus? Like biological warfare?"

"Exactly."

She was glad Dash was carrying her, because she knew she would have ended up on the ground a second time. She'd known her father was a bastard, known he hadn't cared about anything but himself, but this? This was beyond anything she could ever have imagined. "How did the Shadowdrakes know about it? Was there a leak?"

"You could say that," Dash answered. "I don't have proof yet, but I'm pretty sure he'd been using it on them."

For long seconds, she forgot how to breathe. And then she was struggling against Dash, demanding that he put her down. "You're telling me that you've suspected for years—"

"Months. We've suspected for months," interrupted Dash.

"Whatever! You've suspected for months that we were engaging in biological warfare against other North American dragon clans and you didn't bother to tell me?" Her voice had risen to a shriek, but she couldn't help it. Would the lies never end?

"In our own defense," Wyatt said coolly, "up until a few days ago, we didn't know you'd care. And for the past week, ever since you started talking diplomacy, we've been trying to get proof for you. We couldn't let you go to the other clans completely uninformed about what was causing the war."

"And yet you treated me like shit in the meetings. Made me feel like a bumbling idiot."

"Damn straight. There was no way we could publicly take your side—not until we'd found out what we needed to know."

"What about what I needed to know? This is why we're at war, why the Shadowdrakes and the Dragonstars keep coming at us. Because we're attacking them with this monstrosity."

"Yes." Dash's face was grim, his eyes pained as he refused to meet her eyes. She turned and started walking again. They were almost at her house, and she could feel exhaustion tugging at her, along with an overwhelming horror. Her father had been an even bigger monster than she ever could have imagined. And her ignorance of his actions wasn't an excuse.

For five long months, she'd been a party to the most despicable crimes imaginable—war crimes, really—and she hadn't even cared enough to get involved. She'd known something was wrong. Not this wrong, but still, she'd known things were bad. And she hadn't tried to fix it.

No wonder Logan betrayed me.

The last thought brought crippling pain, so crippling that she almost fell while climbing the stairs to her front door, and would have if Dash hadn't reached out and grabbed her arm to steady her.

"Thank you," she murmured, pulling away from him as soon as it was polite to do so. She felt dirty, disgusting and evil. Physical contact was suddenly too much for her to handle.

Turning to look at the three *factionnaires* that had been loyal to her through everything, she forced a smile she was far from feeling. "Go home. Get cleaned up. Get some food and some sleep. We'll meet back here tonight around nine o'clock to start trying to figure out what to do. I don't want to wait until tomorrow. Not with everything that's still unsettled."

"We'll be here," Dax told her.

"Good. I do have one favor to ask. I know you're all exhausted, but I need to know about the others. I need to know where every *factionnaire* is and where his loyalties lie. If they're not with me, fine. But are they with Julian or Acel or someone else? They won't let this go unchallenged, and we can't afford to be caught unawares again. Or everything we fought for today will be for nothing."

Choked up all over again but determined not to show any more weakness in front of them, she turned and let herself into the house. Closed the door behind her and rested against it, too exhausted to go any farther. She wanted to cry, but she was too numb. Her tears had all dried up somewhere on that street, surrounded by the bodies of the people she was supposed to take care of. She felt like it was the end of the world.

Through sheer will alone, Cecily made it to the sofa in the parlor. She kicked off her shoes and had started to curl up when her instinct for self-preservation kicked in—about five minutes too late. She whirled toward the door, already reaching for a storm, for lightning, before her dragon registered who was in her house.

Despite everything that had happened, Logan had returned to her.

CHAPTER TWENTY-FOUR

He'd never seen her look worse. Covered in blood and God only knew what, with her hair hanging in tangles around her head and her eyes bruised and sad-looking, she was a far cry from the woman he'd left on that rooftop a few hours before. A far cry from the woman he had met—and made love to—on a mountain that suddenly seemed thousands of miles away.

"Are you hurt?" he asked in a voice that was much harsher than he'd wanted it to sound. But it had just occurred to him that all the blood on her might not belong to other people.

Her spine stiffened at his touch, her chin coming up in a way that screamed *Go to hell*. Not that he hadn't been expecting it, but it still hurt—whether he had a right to feel that way or not.

"Do you care, or are you just putting on a show for your little friend?" Her eyes shifted toward the foyer, where Shawn was currently standing, trying to look as inconspicuous as possible.

Gesturing for Shawn to come forward, he said, "Cecily, this is Shawn. Shawn, Cecily."

"Nice to meet you." Shawn inclined his head respectfully. She ignored him.

"He's—"

"Dragonstar. I can smell it on him. And I assume you are, too?"

He was having a hard time meeting her eyes. It was a new feeling, and one he was definitely not enjoying. "I am."

"Well, thank you for all your help with the Shadowdrakes earlier. I appreciate it. Now get the hell out of my house."

Had he thought she looked defeated earlier? Dirty or not, covered in blood or not, she now looked every inch the queen he knew she was destined to be. "Cecily, let me talk to you. Please—"

"I think I've got a clear enough picture about what you were doing, thank you. Please show yourselves out."

She turned and headed for the stairs, and Logan couldn't help the hopeless surge of fear inside him. She was slipping through his fingers like he'd always known she would, but he wasn't ready for it. Wasn't ready for what they had to be over. Wasn't ready to say good-bye to her yet. *Not yet. Please, not yet.*

"It's not what you think—"

She whirled on him, eyes narrowed and fire dancing across her fingertips. "It's exactly what I think, and we both know it. You were using me to destroy my clan. I get it. I even understand why you felt you had to do what you did."

"You do?" Out of the corner of his eye, he saw Shawn slipping toward the front door. He didn't blame his friend—if he could walk away without this confrontation, he would do it in a heartbeat. Looking at Cecily so angry, so hurt, was killing him.

But he couldn't just walk away, not like he'd planned all along. Not without talking to her and telling her how he felt about her. He didn't deserve it—hell, he knew he didn't deserve it—but he wanted another chance with her.

"I know why you came here. And I want to apologize to both of you." Her voice carried true and clear across the huge foyer—and made Shawn freeze with his hand halfway to the door.

"I didn't know about the virus until tonight. I still don't know everything about it or why my father created it, but I know that it's awful and that he used it against you and the Shadowdrakes. I'm so very, very sorry."

Logan didn't know what to do, didn't know what to say. He looked at Shawn, saw that the other shifter looked as baffled as he felt. "You don't need to apologize to us."

"Yes, I do." Her voice cut like a scalpel, and he couldn't help feeling like she was excising all the strings of their relationship so that there was nothing left between them. "My clan, my responsibility. My father has been dead for only five months, but from what I understand, Dragonstars have died during those five months, courtesy of some of my *factionnaires.*

"I can't replace what you lost, can't undo what was done. But I can apologize and tell you it will never happen again. Even if something is salvageable from the lab you blew up, even if the knowledge is stored somewhere else, I promise you, the Wyvernmoons will not bother you again. Please convey my deepest regrets to your king."

"Goddamnit, Cecily! Don't do this!" He was across the foyer in one leap, standing at the bottom of the stairs, looking up at her. Pleading with her. He didn't care what it looked like, didn't care that he'd lost his legendary detachment, didn't care about anything or anyone but Cecily. "I'm sorry. I didn't mean to lie to you."

"That's exactly what you meant to do. It's why you came here, why you had sex with me, why you accepted my offer to join us." Her voice broke. "And I played right into your hands. I fell for you, hard, and gave you everything you wanted. Access to my people, access to my compound, access to the lab. I trusted you completely. That was my fault, that I was so dazzled by your smile and the first sex of my life that I gave you carte blanche. It was a very un-queenlike thing to do."

Behind him, he heard the front door open and close, knew that Shawn had left to give them some privacy. "I didn't know you when I put the whole plan in motion, didn't know how brave and honest you were going to be."

"I know. I already told you, I don't blame you for how this came about. If someone was doing that to my people—" She stopped, her voice giving out, and the obvious manifestation of her pain nearly shattered him. "If someone was doing that to my people, I would do everything and anything I could to stop them."

At her words, the knot inside him relaxed a little, even as his dragon warned him that he wasn't out of the woods yet. The thing paced right below his skin, its claws digging in a little more with every step it took. It was angry at him, too. Angry that he'd hurt its mate. Angry that he was still at the bottom of the stairs instead of pulling Cecily into his arms like both he and his beast so desperately wanted.

"Then we can still be together. If you understand why I betrayed you, then we can work this out." He hated having to say it out loud, hated how vulnerable he felt at that moment with her standing above him, watching him with unreadable eyes. But he had to try. He had to make her see that they belonged together, even after everything that had passed between them. Maybe because of what had passed between them.

"I said I understood why you came here, why you did what you did to get into the clan. What I don't understand is why you didn't tell me later, after we got back to the compound. You know me—or, at least, I thought you did. You made love to me, held me, listened to me while I talked out my fears and hopes for my clan, all the time knowing you were going to betray me.

"You promised to be loyal to me, promised to help me, and instead you made me look like a fool. You let me introduce you to the *Conseil*, knowing how badly I was struggling to gain their respect, and you didn't care how that made me look."

She reached up, brushed a stray tear off her cheek, and he felt the pain of it deep inside himself. "But even that I could forgive. Even that I might be able to get past. I'm that pathetic, and I love you that much. But I can't forgive the fact that you believed I was capable of this, that you thought—after knowing me, after *fucking* me—you really thought that I could kill children. That I could set a virus on your clan and sit back and watch while it annihilated you."

Panic was a trapped animal inside him, knocking down all the barriers he'd kept between himself and the world for longer than he could remember. "It wasn't like that, Cecily. I swear to you, I didn't think you had done it."

"Bullshit! Don't lie to me anymore." She was screaming now, tears pouring unheeded and unchecked down her face. "I can't take it. Can't you see how this is ripping me apart? But you know what? I refuse to take responsibility for this. You're the one who thought I was a monster and slept with me anyway. You're the one who planned on betraying me all along, but took my virginity anyway—an extra fuck-you to me and the Wyvernmoons. And you're the one who came to this house and let me fall in love with you, even knowing how it was going to end. That I can't forgive you for. I *won't* forgive you for it. Good-bye, Logan. Don't let the door hit you in the ass on the way out."

Sorrow held him frozen in place for long seconds as she swept up the stairs and onto the landing above. But then he was running, taking the stairs three at a time in his effort to get to her, to make her understand.

"Cecily, I love you." He grabbed on to her elbow, turned her to face him. Shook her in his desperation to make her understand. "Yes, I lied to you. Yes, I used you to get in here. Was it right? No. But when I devised the plan, I wasn't thinking of right or wrong. I was thinking that I couldn't stand the idea of watching one more of my people die, paralyzed, bleeding out, in pain so excruciating that nothing could help him.

"I wanted revenge." He shrugged, afraid that he was only making things worse but unable to lie to her anymore. "I wanted to stop what was happening, needed to stop it like I hadn't needed anything since I escaped from my clan in Ireland more than three hundred years ago. But at the same time, I wanted to make those responsible for killing my clan mates as miserable as they had made us through the years."

He shoved a shaking hand through his hair. "I don't know that you can understand it if you haven't lived through it, haven't seen it. But one of my closest friends lost his wife and daughter. Dylan MacLeod lost his sister and niece. Our healer, Quinn, lost his brother and a lover. We all lost friends. We all stood by and watched them die in the most awful way possible. Hell, yeah, I wanted revenge. I wanted it so badly I could taste it—almost as badly as I wanted to ensure that not one more Dragonstar died a victim to that goddamn virus."

"I can understand that—"

"No, you can't. If you haven't seen it, if you haven't stood by someone's bed as they're organs liquefied in front of you, then no, you can't understand it. And when it happens again and again and again and there's nothing you can do to stop it, nothing you can do to keep the people you love safe, it's torture. I had to try to stop it. I had to come here and blow that fucking death factory to kingdom come. I had to, Cecily."

She was trembling, her arms were wrapped around herself like they were the only thing stopping her from shaking apart. "I already told you that I don't blame you for coming here." She was crying so hard he could barely understand what she was saying. He wanted nothing more than to take her in his arms, but knew she wouldn't thank him for it.

"Maybe you don't, but I need you to understand why I did it." He was shaking now, too, afraid that he was going to break down and cry like a total pussy. But he could feel her slipping away from him and it was killing him. *Killing* him.

"After we'd made love, after I got here, I knew you couldn't be behind the virus. You didn't have it in you. But by then I cared about you so much that I couldn't tell you. I was afraid you'd kick me out, that you wouldn't give me a chance to explain. And I didn't want to lose you. I couldn't lose you, Cecily."

"You never had me, and I sure as hell never had you. All that's between us is lies."

"That's not true." He reached up, ripped the sleeve off his shirt. "Look at these, Cecily."

"I've already seen your tattoos."

"But have you seen how they've shifted, changed, in the past few days? Have you seen the mating bands?" He grabbed her hand, put her fingers on his shoulder. Shuddered when he felt her cool fingers tracing the intricate black circles. There were three now, and nothing had ever felt so right. Even as his entire world was collapsing around him, the fact that she was there, touching him, touching the bands that showed that they were intrinsically linked, lit him up deep inside like nothing ever could.

She was staring at him in wonder as she slid her hand over the tattoos again and again, and he knew he wasn't the only one who felt the joy, the astonishment, the absolute perfection of being mated.

But then she jerked away, and the absence was a physical blow. He reached for her with his mind, needing to touch her. Needing to connect. But her shields were up, so high and so tight that he knew there was no way he could get in—not even if he opened himself completely, left his mind completely undefended.

He did it anyway; he couldn't help himself. The world outside her house crashed in on him, echoes of pain and death and fear nearly crushing him. It didn't matter. Nothing mattered but showing her what was inside him.

Her eyes widened, he felt a stirring in his mind, and for a second he thought she would let him in. But then she was gone, stumbling down the hall away from him. "It doesn't matter," she whispered.

Desperate, frightened, furious, he went after her. Grabbed her arms and yanked her against him. Heat, shocking and powerful, leaped between them. "Tell me this doesn't matter," he whispered. "Tell me you don't feel the same way I do."

She shook her head. "Logan, don't—"

But he couldn't help himself. He lowered his head, touched his mouth to hers. And then he was kissing her, his lips moving frantically on hers, his tongue thrusting into her mouth as he tried to get inside her any way that he could.

Her hands came up, tangled in his hair, held on to him as tightly as he was holding on to her. Their tongues met, dueled, stroked frantically over and against each other, and he never wanted to let her go. He wanted to kiss her like this, hold her like this, forever.

She didn't feel the same way, though, and within seconds she had wrenched herself from his grip. "No!" she said. "I won't let you do this to me. I can't."

"Cecily, I'm sorry. I'm so fucking sorry—"

She shook her head. "It doesn't matter. It would never work. You're Dragonstar; I'm Wyvernmoon. You have responsibilities in New Mexico; I can't leave South Dakota. My clan needs me and I have to focus on them. I can't be with you, not when I can't trust you."

"You can trust me—"

"Good-bye, Logan."

"Damn it, Cecily. You can't stay here alone. Unprotected. You're a sitting fucking duck for whatever bastard wants to seize power from you."

"Have I somehow given you the impression that I'm incapable of taking care of myself?"

"That's not what I meant. But, Cecily, the *factionnaires* are ruthless, and most of them are still alive. You're not safe. They will come for you, and they will try to kill you. You need someone to watch your back."

"Maybe I do. But you're not that someone. You'll never be that someone." She walked into her bedroom, turned and barred the doorway with her body to keep him from following her. "I mean it, Logan. I want you to leave. I don't ever want to see you again."

His entire world felt like it was falling down around him, and he wanted to fight for her. Wanted to beg her to give him another chance.

But he could tell it was no use, not now, when her eyes were so haunted and resolute. Not now, when she looked like he felt—like nothing was ever going to be okay again.

Turning, he walked slowly down the stairs and out the front door, wondering how he was ever going to find the strength to leave her. Or to live the rest of his life without her.

CHAPTER TWENTY-FIVE

When the doorbell rang, Cecily looked up from the table where she, Dax and Dashiell were going over the damage estimates from the Shadowdrake attack. Infrastructure-wise, things weren't as bad as they'd thought they would be, but the casualty rate was much higher than she had feared.

In the week since she had demanded that Logan leave, she and the three *factionnaires* who were still loyal to her had done their best to get things moving again. Businesses were open, the hospital and clinics were working around the clock and evidence of the battle had been completely cleared away.

But her *Conseil* was shattered. Gage had died in the Shadowdrake attack. She later heard that he'd instigated the process to shut down the lab once and for all. She felt a little better knowing that her oldest and dearest friend hadn't completely betrayed her—that in his own way he'd been looking to end the war between the clans—but it hurt that, like Logan, he hadn't felt he could talk to her. Hadn't felt he could trust her to do what was right.

Because she was Silus's daughter? Or because she'd spent most of her life being weak? It was probably a combination of both, and it killed her to think that so much of this could have been avoided if she'd simply stepped forward sooner after Silus's death. If she had tried to take the reins when her father's funeral pyre was still warm, instead of trusting in his *factionnaires* to do what was best for the clan. It was a mistake she'd learned the hard way not to make again.

The very hard way.

But she would find a way to put things back together, even if it killed her. She owed it to her people, and to all of the Fournier rulers who had come before her.

She knew it wasn't going to be easy—Julian, Acel, and the others were seeing to that. They were trying to get her people to rally around them in an effort to seize control from her. So far, most of her people were sticking by her, but part of her wondered if it was only a matter of time before they turned against her. She wouldn't blame them. God knew she had made a mess of almost everything she had touched so far.

That was going to change—and it was going to change soon. She knew that if she wanted to solidify her people's belief in her and her right to be queen, she was going to have to go back to her original plan. She was going to have to pick a husband, would have to give her people a king.

A huge part of her was revolted by the idea. Party because it both-ered her that even in the twenty-first century, her clan didn't believe a woman could be trusted to rule, and partly because after Logan, she could not imagine letting another man close to her. Though they had been together only a few short days, though he had betrayed her in the most terrible way possible, she missed him.

She cried herself to sleep at night, filled with an overwhelming longing for him that she couldn't deny.

She woke in the dead of night, her hand searching for his warmth on the cold, empty bed.

She woke in the morning, plagued by nightmares of her people dying, of Logan dying, more exhausted than she had been when she went to sleep.

And though she knew she needed to get married—needed to pick

Dax, Dashiell or Wyatt for a king—the thought made her physically sick. Not that they wouldn't make good kings. She believed they would, especially Wyatt, who was an incredible strategist and also one of the most compassionate men she'd ever met. But the idea of being touched by him, by being touched by any of them, left her beyond cold.

But it needed to be done—and soon. She needed to be pregnant, needed to provide her clan with an heir, preferably male, to give everyone a tangible reminder that things were back on the right track. If she had to sacrifice her happiness to do it, if she had to give her body to a man she would never want as much as she wanted Logan, it was a small price to pay for the deaths and mistakes she was responsible for.

With the decision made, she looked up in time to see her new butler and security expert, David, walk into the room. But instead of escorting Wyatt, as she'd anticipated, he was leading Julian, Antoine, Etienne and Luc into the room.

Dashiell leaped across the table, knocking over his chair in his haste to put his body between hers and the four traitorous *factionnaires*. Dax was only a split second behind, but it was just long enough for Julian to pull a knife from his waist and send it spinning across the room.

It nailed Dax in the throat, and Cecily watched in horror as he went to his knees. His hands came up automatically, yanked out the knife. Blood gushed from the open wound.

She started to get up, to run to him, but Dashiell shoved her toward the patio door. "Run!" he said in a fierce undertone, even as he shot a huge fireball straight at Julian.

The other dragon deflected it easily, sent one of his own hurtling back. Dashiell jumped out of the way and it crashed into the china cabinet, where her favorite antique Limoges china resided. The cabinet shattered and glass flew everywhere.

Desperate to end the fight so she could get to Dax, she reached for the electricity that always pulsed right below her skin. Grabbing on to it, she shaped it superfast, then sent it soaring across the room at Julian. He was so busy defending himself from an attack by Dashiell that he didn't see it coming, and it struck him straight in the chest. He went down, hard.

She turned to the other three, realizing for the first time that Luc had a small syringe pressed to David's neck—which explained everything she needed to know about why he'd let the four defectors into the house.

She had an instant to wonder what was in the syringe—something awful, judging from the uncharacteristic look of terror on David's face—and then Dashiell went down, felled by a powerful energy blast from Etienne. A quick glance told her he was stunned, not hurt, and she let loose with another flash of lightning, aiming it at Etienne instead of Luc, as she was afraid she might jostle him and he would stab David. But Antoine was waiting for her and he deflected her blast, sending all of her power spinning back toward her.

She jumped out of the way, shifting in midair and landing less than a foot from Antoine. Bending forward, she did something she had never in a billion years imagined she would ever do: she wrapped her mouth around his head and picked him up, then shook him back and forth until she heard his neck crack. Then she dumped him on her dining room floor and ripped open his stomach with her long talons.

Whirling away from him, she saw Dashiell and Etienne rolling across the floor. She leaped at them, ripped Etienne off Dashiell with her mouth, then watched as Dashiell—whose gift was the ability to flow through matter—plunged his hand straight into Etienne's chest cavity and ripped out his heart.

She dropped Etienne, then went after Luc, who had knocked David to the floor. But Dash beat her to him, sending a powerful fireball his way. It missed, and he fled. After a cursory look at the room to make sure the other three dragons really were finished, Dashiell took off after him.

Cecily shifted back to human form, and, unmindful of her naked form, ran to Dax and David. But they were both beyond help. Horrified at how easily their lives had been snuffed out, she sank onto the carpet between them. She couldn't stop trembling, and for several long seconds, was convinced she was going to throw up.

Taking a few deep breaths, she somehow managed to keep her stomach from revolting, but it was close. She sat there, shocked and shaky, trying to focus on what she needed to do. Everything around her seemed fuzzy, and whatever it was that she should be doing had escaped her.

But there was a little voice inside her screaming that she needed to get up, needed to check on Dashiell, needed to make sure he and Wyatt were safe. She stumbled to her feet, headed for the patio door.

She never got there. She had almost made it to the patio when Julian's hand wrapped around her ankle and jerked. She hit the ground hard, kicked out with her free foot and caught him straight in the face. But she was barefoot and at an awkward angle, and the blow didn't have nearly as much impact as she had hoped it would.

And then he was on her, scrambling up her body to wrap his hands around her throat, cutting off her air. "You could have made this easy, Cecily. You could have come to me and this never would have happened," he growled, his fingers tightening even more.

He was sitting on her chest now, and she felt something pop deep inside her as she bucked underneath him, clawed at his hands, pounded on his chest, all to no avail. Tried to conjure up an energy blast, but had nothing to feed it with. Her own energy was fading fast, the world around her turning gray, and she knew if she didn't do something right then, he was going to be right. She was going to die, and he was going to be left in charge of her clan.

The thought gave her the extra burst of magic she'd been searching for, and as she felt her hands light up with electricity, she threw every ounce of strength she had left behind them. Then grabbed on to Julian for all she was worth, closing her eyes and praying as his body jerked and spasmed above her.

His hands loosened from around her throat, and she drew a huge gulp of air into her lungs, making sure to keep both of her hands in contact with him as she did. He was gasping now, his skin turning blue as she shot volt after volt of electricity into him. They were still pressed together, and she could feel his heart stutter against her chest, but it didn't stop. She was almost out of power, her last-ditch effort to save herself not enough.

Even worse, she could see Julian rallying. See him pushing off the effects of the electricity even as she gave him the last few weak volts that she had left. His fist came up, plowed into her face, and she felt the sickening crunch of bone as it connected with her nose.

"Now you die, bitch." His hands tangled in her hair and he lifted her head up, then hit it against the wood floor. Lifted it up, hit it again. She could feel the world fading around her, knew she was blacking out. She fought it, knew that if she gave in, she would never wake up again. As he lifted her head a third time, a picture of Logan's face rose in her mind. Scarred, tired, and so beautiful she was nearly overwhelmed. *I'm sorry,* she told him telepathically, sending the thought out into the universe and trusting that it would somehow find him. *I'm sorry I wasn't strong enough to understand. Sorry I wasn't strong enough to forgive you.*

Then she closed her eyes, knowing there was nothing else she needed to do. She felt bad for her clan, prayed that somehow Dashiell and Wyatt would be strong enough to stand against Julian. But she couldn't do anything else and she knew it. She'd given it her best shot, but she was fading fast . . .

Suddenly, Julian was ripped away from her, along with a few sizable chunks of her hair. There was a loud thump, followed by a low, feral growl that chilled her blood. That little voice in her head had started screaming at her, telling her to get away, but she couldn't move.

Couldn't scramble away as her twitching legs wanted so desperately to do. Couldn't even bring her hands up to shield her face. It was all just too much effort. She was cold, so cold . . .

Another loud growl and a wet, sucking sound convinced her to open her eyes. But what she saw convinced her that she was hallucinating. Logan was there, right in front of her, half-man, half-dragon, caught in midshift. His face was twisted with more rage than she had ever imagined possible. And he was ripping Julian apart with his bare hands even as he continued to shift back to human.

Seeing him made her heart hurt, even if he was a figment of her concussion-addled imagination. Tears slowly leaked down her face. She closed her eyes just as Logan became fully human. A second later, an unholy scream rent the air, along with the sound of blood spattering and two loud thumps, one right after the other.

And then Logan was there, holding her hand, his hand smoothing over her forehead. "It's okay, Cecily. Hold on, *A Ghra*. Hold on."

He felt so real, sounded so real, that she somehow found the strength to lift her hand and touch his cheek. The scar felt rough and bumpy under her fingers. As his own hand came up to cover hers, she wondered if maybe it wasn't a dream after all.

"Logan?" she whispered through lips so dry she felt like she'd been wandering through his New Mexican desert. Her eyes fluttered open.

"I'm here, *A Ghra*. I'm here. I'll get you help."

"Are you . . . real?" she asked.

His face twisted in pain, even as he leaned down to brush his lips over her forehead. "I'm as real as they get, sweetheart. Now, just hold on for me a little longer."

But it was getting harder and harder to breathe, the blackness that had loomed for so long taking over, though she longed to stay with him. *I love you*, she told him just before she let go. If these were her last minutes to live, she was going to make them count. *I'll always love you.*

As Cecily's mind slipped from his, Logan lost his tenuous grip on sanity. He dug in, held on to her with every ounce of strength he possessed. She wasn't leaving him, not now. Not when she should still have a long, long life stretching in front of her.

Shawn, he screamed. *Hurry up! I need Quinn. I need—*

I'm on my way to get him, Shawn answered, and Logan got the impression he was rushing through town toward the clinic. *We'll be there in five minutes.*

She'll be dead in five minutes.

Fuck. Hold on to her. I'm coming.

What the hell do you think I'm trying to do? Logan demanded, but Shawn was gone, his attention solely focused on getting to Quinn. Logan tried to help him out, to tap into Quinn's mind, as well, so that he knew to be ready for Shawn, but holding on to Cecily was getting more and more difficult.

He could feel her slipping away, could feel the light inside of her dimming. If Quinn didn't get here soon—

No! He couldn't think like that. He couldn't, not if he wanted to remain sane. And he had to keep it together. For the first time since they'd met, Cecily truly needed him. He wouldn't fail her, no matter how much it hurt to see her like this.

But her breathing was becoming more and more labored, her pulse weaker and weaker. Logan felt the mating bands on his arm begin to burn, and he knew. He knew he was going to lose her.

Letting out a roar that shook the very foundations of the house, he placed his hand over her heart and willed every ounce of strength and energy he had straight into her. He couldn't heal her, couldn't fix what was broken inside her like Quinn could, but he could damn well give her as much of his life force as her body could take. He wasn't psychic for nothing.

She didn't respond, though, and he was scared to death it was too late. That he hadn't given her enough, that he wasn't strong enough to hold on to her. But he wouldn't give up—he couldn't. Shawn and Quinn would be here soon. He just had to hold on to her for a little while longer.

He lowered every barrier he had, every shield that kept the outside world from pressing in on him, and concentrated on connecting with her faded, foggy mind. As he did, the world around him threatened to close in, to take him under with her, but Logan ignored it the same way he ignored the blood dripping down his face from the nosebleed the psychic overload caused. Nothing mattered but Cecily, and he would gladly give his life to hold her to this earth. He poured every ounce of energy he could into her mind until he had nothing left. Until he was lying on the floor next to her, his own heart stuttering in his chest.

And still it wasn't enough. Still she was disappearing right in front of him. The knowledge shook him, shook the formidable will that had been a part of him for as long as he could remember.

Don't you dare die on me, Cecily! You stay with me. Use some of that crazy strength of yours to hang on to me just a little longer.

There was no response, no answering glow that came when her mind reached for his. He rolled over, rested his forehead against hers, told himself—and her—that no matter what happened, he was going to be with her. He'd never leave her again, even if it meant following her from this life to the next. Especially if it meant that. No way could he live without her. No way would he even want to try.

It had nearly killed him when he'd heard Dashiell's cry of alarm. To know that Cecily was in danger and that he was too far away to help her had been torture of the worst kind. During the entire flight from the mountain, where he'd been staying in a futile effort to feel close to her, he had cursed himself for not being closer. For not sticking by her side no matter what she said.

He'd known Julian was going to attack, had felt it in every bone in his body, and still he had left her alone and unprotected. That she had asked him to made little difference—he had failed his mate, failed Cecily, and now she was paying unthinkable consequences.

Rolling over so that his arm was draped over her waist and his forehead nuzzled against her temple, he tried to fight the encroaching lethargy. If he gave in, he knew he'd lose his grip on Cecily, and she would float away from him forever.

Live, Cecily, he pleaded with her. *For me. For us. Please don't give up. Please don't leave me here—*

Quinn and Shawn flashed in, and the Dragonstar healer took in the situation at a glance. Moving to the other side of Cecily, the side Logan wasn't pressed full length against, he ran his hands over Cecily's heart.

Save her, Quinn! He didn't have the strength to speak, so he sent the thought from his brain to Quinn's.

"I'm trying, damn it. Don't let go of her."

I won't.

Already he could feel Quinn's healing presence, could feel the heat and peace that emanated from within Cecily just from the superficial contact. Quinn pressed down on her chest, and Logan felt him discover the shattered ribs, the punctured lung, the internal bleeding. Felt, as he started to heal her from the inside out, his energy slowly, painfully mending what was broken inside her.

It went on for what felt like hours, what probably was hours, as Quinn sought out every injury. The healer cursed silently when he got to Cecily's head, and Logan felt a moment of intense panic. What kind of shape was she in if Quinn—

"Don't speculate!" The order was sharp, bitten out. "I'll take care of her."

It was the reassurance Logan needed, ragged though it was, and he felt himself relax just a little, especially when he could feel the way Cecily's breathing eased and her heart beat a little stronger.

But when Quinn finally pulled away from Cecily, she was still unconscious, her spirit still flickering. "Don't stop!" he croaked, pushing himself to a sitting position to stare angrily at Quinn. "She's still too weak."

Quinn shook his head, his mouth grim when he stared at Logan. "I'm good, but I'm not a miracle worker. That's all I can do today. If she hangs on, if she makes it through tonight, I'll go back in tomorrow and try again. Her injuries are intense—especially the brain injuries—and I can only force so much healing at any one time."

"But what if she dies before you can heal her more?" Logan demanded as he felt his own heart stutter, nearly stop. "What if—"

"No *what if*s." Quinn squeezed his shoulder tightly. "Let Shawn take her back to New Mexico and into my clinic. We'll get her hooked up, and I'll stay with her. I promise Jasmine and I will do everything we can to make sure she's all right."

It wasn't the full assurance Logan had been looking for, but he knew it was the best he was going to get. Standing up with help from Shawn, he lifted Cecily in his arms. Then he nodded to Quinn as Shawn put a hand on both of their backs, pulling the four of them into a close-knit triangle.

"Thanks for coming," he told Quinn. "I know it couldn't have been easy—"

Quinn shook his head, waved off the thanks. "This is what I do, man. Besides, she's yours, and that trumps Wyvernmoon any day."

Logan nodded, because the lump in his throat had grown so large it was impossible to talk over it. And then Shawn flashed them home.

CHAPTER TWENTY-SIX

Cecily woke up slowly in an unfamiliar bed. Machines were beeping all around her, and some of the most intense sunlight she'd ever seen was streaming through the window in the corner of her room.

Where am I? she wondered as she struggled to get her bearings. There was an IV in her hand, and it seemed that the machines—and their beeping—were all correlated to her.

Hospital. She was in the hospital. *But why? And where—*

A sharp stab of pain shot through her head as she remembered Julian on top of her, remembered not being able to breathe as he sat on her chest. Remembered thinking, for certain, that she was going to die . . .

So why hadn't she? Who had saved her? And where had they brought her? The rusts and golds and purples that decorated the room weren't the colors of the hospital on the Wyvernmoon compound. In fact, the way they all blended together reminded her of pictures she'd seen of desert sunsets—

Logan. He'd rescued her. Had swooped in and killed Julian before the bastard could finish her off completely. Which meant she was probably in New Mexico with the Dragonstars. *As a prisoner?* she wondered. *Or as a patient? Or both?*

She looked around the room, desperately hoping that Logan would suddenly just be there. But the chair near her bed was empty, as was the small cot lining the wall across from her. She was on her own.

Not that she'd expected things to be any different. Just because he'd saved her life, just because she'd apologized to him, didn't mean Logan had forgiven her. Her clan had done some terrible things, and she had let them. Things that she didn't blame Logan for holding against her, especially after she'd been unable to forgive him for his duplicity.

Understanding didn't mean she was just going to wait around here like a sitting duck, however. If Dylan was anything like her father, she had no doubt that whatever punishment he came up with for her would be utterly and completely diabolical. She couldn't afford to stay here and be tortured, no matter how much she, as head of the Wyvernmoons, might deserve it. Her clan was in chaos, her people leaderless, and she needed to get back to them. Needed to assure them that she was alive, that they weren't alone. That they could get through this together.

Sitting up, she swung her legs shakily off the side of the bed. The room spun around her and she took a minute to get her bearings before she attempted the next step. If she was a prisoner—and she had to believe that she was—then she was going to have to be fast. Once she started stripping off the sensors and whatever else was attached to her, she was going to have to get it all done in a few seconds. That would give her time to shift, and, if she was lucky, get out the door before anyone wised up. Before Logan or his king came looking for her.

Her resolve weakened at the thought of Logan, her stupid heart beating double time in the hope of seeing him again. Her head might be telling her she needed to get the hell out, and quickly, but her heart was screaming for her to stay. Even if it meant she was a Dragonstar prisoner. Even if it left her clan without a queen. She needed Logan, wanted him, more than she had ever needed or wanted anything in her life.

I can't let that matter, she told herself fiercely, scooting forward so that her feet rested firmly on the ground. *I can't let anything matter except getting out of here.* She pushed herself slowly to her feet, ignored the fact that she was trembling and her head felt like it was going to split open at any second.

Once she got herself to a standing position, Cecily tried to shuffle a few steps, but the room spun around her. Stopping, she closed her eyes and took some deep breaths as she waited for the nausea to pass. Only it didn't pass, and she was forced to swallow rapidly, again and again, to keep herself from throwing up.

Damn. She was well and truly screwed if she couldn't so much as walk across the room without seeing stars. Fear started to crawl up her spine as her stomach tied itself in knots. How was she going to escape? How was she going to get back to her clan if—

The door opened slowly and Logan pushed his way in, a duffel bag in one hand and a cup of coffee in the other. He looked so good, so healthy and beautiful and welcome, that she felt more stupid tears well up in her eyes. Jesus, if things continued this way, she was going to need to bring Kleenex boxes in by the truck full.

Logan's eyes widened when he spotted her, and he was across the room in one leap, his duffel bag lying forgotten on the floor as he reached for her. "What are you doing up? Are you insane?"

His hand closed around her elbow, and then he was guiding her the couple of steps back to bed, helping her climb back on it, pulling the covers up to her waist. "I was only gone half an hour. When did you wake up?"

"I don't know. A few minutes ago."

He looked so good, she wanted to just sit there and drink him in forever. Whatever he'd done, whatever she'd done, didn't seem to matter at that moment. All that mattered was him and the fact that he was here, holding her hand, when she'd been sure she was never going to see him again. Sure she was going to die.

Whatever the future held for her, right now she wanted nothing more than to feel the hard press of him against her. To smell the warm, peppermint scent of him. And if he'd lean over just a little bit, she wouldn't mind savoring the taste of him, as well.

He obviously didn't feel the same way, though, because instead of leaning closer, he pulled away from her. She felt the rejection deep inside, felt the trembling burst of hope give way to abject despair.

"Don't do that," Logan said fiercely, bending down so that he was looking directly into her eyes. "I'm not leaving you. But Quinn needs to take a look at you. We've been waiting three days for you to wake up."

"I lost three days?"

"Yes." His hand grabbed hers, squeezed fiercely even as a very tall, very dark man with green eyes strode into the room. He was dressed entirely in black except for his white lab coat, and it did nothing to make him look more endearing. She'd always thought Logan looked tough, but this man was a total badass from the word *go*.

His eyes were kind, though, as they looked at her on the bed—or at least as kind as she had a feeling he got. "So, you ready to train for the Olympics, then?" he asked with a sardonic twist of his lips.

"Not exactly." She looked at Logan, baffled. *Who is he?* she demanded.

Your doctor. His name is Quinn Maguire.

He doesn't look like any doctor I've ever seen.

Maybe not, but he saved your life. Give him a chance.

She relaxed a little because Logan was totally comfortable in his presence. But it was difficult, as he was eyeing her like a bug under a microscope—and not a particularly interesting one, at that.

"Then perhaps you'd like to tell me what you were doing up and out of bed? It looks like you were trying for the fifty-yard dash."

"More like a thousand-mile marathon, but whatever works." She wasn't going to give him an inch, refused to let him see how unsettled he made her.

He grinned, shot Logan a quick smile. "I like her."

"Yeah, well, you can't have her. She's mine."

"That's okay. Jasmine would probably object if I brought her home, anyway."

Cecily's gaze shot to his as she tried to figure out what Logan meant by that. Had he forgiven her? Was he willing to go against his king and take her back? But she couldn't stand the idea of that, the idea of him giving up the only home he'd ever had.

Suddenly, Logan was there in her face. "Why don't you just settle down? There's plenty of time to deal with everything else, but right now you need to let Quinn look at you."

"Oh, by all means, don't let me interrupt," Quinn answered even as he walked forward, stethoscope at the ready. "I kind of like watching Logan melt like butter at your feet."

The next few minutes passed in a blur of confusion as Quinn asked her a bunch of questions about how she was feeling, filling her in on the extent of her injuries as he examined her. It seemed Julian had done even more damage than she'd first thought.

When he was finished examining her, he turned to Logan with a grin. "She's a little shaky yet, but that's to be expected. A couple more days and she'll be good as new—provided she doesn't try for that marathon she was talking about."

"She's not going anywhere," Logan answered, his hand squeezing hers in warning. "I'll make sure of it."

"Somehow I didn't think otherwise." Quinn gave her a quick wink before heading to the door. "I'll be back in two hours to check on her, so try to behave yourselves."

He shut the door behind him.

Cecily stared after him for a second. "He's different from our healers," she finally said.

"Because he looks like he belongs on a Harley-Davidson, or because he has no sense of decorum?"

"Yes," she answered.

Logan laughed. "You'll get used to him."

"Not if I only need to stick around a couple more days." She held her breath, waiting to hear what he would say. Praying it wouldn't be that she was under arrest and unable to leave.

In the end, he didn't say anything, but his smile dimmed considerably. "Is that what you want? To go back to your clan?"

"I have to go back to my clan. Everything is a disaster. I can't even imagine what's happened since I disappeared."

"I've been keeping an eye on it for you. I let Dashiell and Wyatt, both of whom survived that last attack, by the way, know you're safe for now. They've got everything well in hand, at least for a few more days."

"Good," she nodded. "Thanks."

Logan didn't say anything for a long time; then finally it seemed like something inside him burst and words just came tumbling out. "I want to go back with you."

"What?" she asked, shocked and a little spellbound.

"I know I fucked up, know I betrayed you and your clan. I'm sorry. I can't say I would take it all back because that lab—and everything in it—had to go. But the rest? The lies, the sneaking around, the betrayal? If I could do things over, things never would have turned out like this."

"I know. I never blamed you for the lab. If the virus was half as evil as you said it was, then it needed to go. I just wish I'd figured things out earlier. I would have had it destroyed months ago if I'd known."

"I know that now, and I'm sorry I doubted you. Sorry I didn't trust you."

"It's okay." She put a finger to his lips to stop the apology. His eyes closed and a shudder racked his body. "We both said and did things we regret."

His eyes opened at that, and they were so dark, the pupils so dilated, that she would have sworn they were black if she didn't know better. "Do you remember what you said to me right before you blacked out?"

She thought for a minute, shook her head. "No. I'm sorry. Everything's kind of a blur."

"Oh." He looked disappointed. "Never mind, then."

"No. Tell me what I said." She grabbed his hands, squeezed.

"You told me you loved me."

Her cheeks flushed, but she didn't take her eyes from his. This was too important, and she wasn't going to let fear or embarrassment or anything else get in the way of telling Logan how she felt. "I do love you, but you already knew that. I said that to you before . . ."

"Before you kicked me off your compound?"

"Yes."

"Is it true? Do you still love me, despite everything?"

"Of course I do, Logan. I didn't wait fifty years to fall in love just to turn it on and off like a faucet. I love you more than I ever imagined it was possible to love anyone."

"I love you the same way. And I know there's a lot of crap we have to work through, but I thought maybe if you loved me enough, we could work it out. I know you can't marry someone who isn't a Wyvernmoon—"

"Wait a minute." The room was spinning again, but this time it was excitement and not fear that was making everything look bright and shiny and just a little fuzzy as it whirled by. "Are you saying you want to marry me?"

"Of course I want to marry you. I understand about the king needing to be a Wyvernmoon, but if you don't marry anyone—"

"Oh, I'm going to marry someone. The clan needs a strong, united, married couple to lead it."

"That's bullshit. You're a hell of a leader, Cecily, all on your own." His face lit with temper. "And you can't tell me you love me, tell me you want to be with me, and then expect me to just step aside and let you marry someone else."

"Who says I want to marry anyone else?" she demanded. "In case you haven't noticed, I'm pretty good at breaking rules."

He looked wary. "What does that mean?"

"You know exactly what it means. You're screwed now, Logan. I'm going to marry you, and you're going to be saddled with the most miserable, fucked-up clan on the planet. And don't think you're just going to be a figurehead, either—you're going to help me get things back on track."

He grinned. "Are you asking me to marry you?"

"No. I'm telling you that you're going to marry me. You had your chance to get away, but that's gone now. You're stuck with me."

"Thank God!" He bent and took her lips in a kiss so tender and needy and loving that it had her breath catching in her throat. "But are you sure . . . ?"

She wrapped her arms around his neck and brought his mouth back to hers. *Life's too short to spend it lost in the past. I want to build a future with you, Logan. Let me do that.*

Logan wrenched his mouth away from Cecily's as a searing pain struck his arm. He looked at Cecily, unsure if he'd heard her correctly. Had she really forgiven him for betraying her? Had she really found a way to move past what he'd done, when he still couldn't? She held him even tighter, and he realized that she could. That she had.

He smiled. "I'm ready to get started whenever you are." Then he kissed her with all the pent-up pain and fear and remorse he had inside him. She tasted salty from the tears running slowly down her face.

"I'll never make you cry again, Cecily. I swear it. I'll never do anything to hurt you again."

She laughed and wrapped her arms around his neck, pulling him close. "Don't make promises you can't keep."

"I will keep that one. I swear."

"Never is a long time, especially when you're mated." She traced a finger lightly over his arm and he glanced down, shocked when he realized exactly what the pain he'd felt earlier had been from. All three of the mating bands were darker, thicker, so solid and tightly inter-twined that they looked like they could never be separated again.

Heat swept through him at the sight of them, at the knowledge that Cecily was finally his for good. Lowering his face to her neck, he felt tears well in his own eyes for the first time in more than three hun-dred years. He blinked them away as he steeped himself in the gor-geous scent of her.

"You're the most beautiful woman I've ever seen," he told her. "Not just on the outside, which is a pretty incredible package, I have to admit. But on the inside, as well, where it counts. I don't understand, coming from where you did, how you have such an unending well of goodness and compassion and forgiveness inside you."

"It's easy to forgive when you love someone, and easy to have com-passion for people when your own life is so full."

He nodded. "I'll remember that."

"Good. Now, are you going to make love to me or what?"

"This is a hospital, in case you haven't noticed. And you nearly died three days ago."

"Yeah, but I'm feeling much better now. You heard Quinn—I'm almost perfect."

"*Almost* being the operative word here. Now settle down and get some rest."

Her hand squirmed between them, started rubbing against his abdomen. "But—"

"Stop that!" He captured her hand, brought it to his lips. "There will be plenty of time for that later."

"Promise?" She pouted, but he could tell she was exhausted.

"I guarantee it. Now go to sleep."

Two days later, Cecily was out of patience with waiting—and so was he. Quinn had released her with a clean bill of health, and the plan had been for them to fly back to South Dakota that afternoon.

But the second she got out of the clinic, Cecily was all over him. Not that he was much better. He'd barely managed to shut the door of his small house before he pulled her into his arms.

Lowering his head, he kissed her, and the feel of her lips on his was like finding himself again—warm and familiar and so overwhelming that it cut him off at the knees.

He moved his hands to her waist, determined to be careful as he started to undress her. But he was strangely unsteady, and his fingers shook as he shimmied her jeans and panties down her legs. "I've missed you," he whispered. "Missed this."

"So have I." She arched against him invitingly. "So hurry, won't you? It's been too long since you've been inside me."

He sank to the floor at her feet, kissed his way up her beautiful calves to her knees and her inner thighs. "I want to play a little first." He buried his face against her pussy, inhaled the amazing, spicy scent of her.

Her hands twisted in his hair, tugged hard. "Play later. Fuck me now."

"Wow. You've really got that queen thing down these days."

"I do. And remember, if you don't please me, I can always have you thrown in the dungeon."

"You don't have a dungeon."

"True. But I can build one."

"I don't think that will be necessary." He contented himself with one long, lingering lick of her clit, then pulled her down on top of him. "Since you like being in charge so much, you can take me this time."

Her eyes widened as she stared down at him, knowing how hard it must be for him to offer her that. Logan lived to be in control—in the bedroom and out of it. For him to so easily offer to let her control things between them, even in bed . . . It meant more than she could tell him.

So she concentrated on showing him, lowering herself slowly onto his cock until he was buried all the way inside her. Until they were one.

She rode him slowly, sweetly, loving him with her body the way he always loved her. She wrapped herself up in him, immersed herself in the feelings and the heat that arced between them with each slow rise and fall of her body on his.

Deep inside, need was urging her to go faster, to take him harder, but she wanted this time to be languid, lazy, loving. She wanted it to be perfect.

His hands came up, caressed her breasts, played with her nipples, before slipping between her legs to caress her clit. He arched his back, drove himself deeper, did everything he could to get her to speed things ups.

But she wasn't ready to come yet, wasn't ready for this perfect moment to disappear. "Not yet," she said, gasping as he stroked her higher. "Please not yet. I don't want this to end."

He laughed, and she felt it inside her, a little burst of sensation deep in her pussy.

"Cecily, *A Ghra*, didn't we just decide that this was never going to end?"

She bit her lip, looked down at her lover with his gorgeous face and ruby eyes, which had turned the intense red of his dragon. "Promise?" she whispered.

His face turned serious. "I swear it."

"Then take me, Logan. Make me yours forever."

Logan didn't need a second invitation as he pistoned his hips beneath hers, driving himself deeper, deeper, deeper inside her. Driving himself as deep as he could go, so deep that she could never get him out.

Her hands found his, her fingers tangling with his as they rose and fell against each other. Sweat poured off him, off her, and when her breath broke, he knew he wasn't going to be able to take it any longer.

"Come for me, Cecily. Now! Come for me now!"

She did, her body clenching around his in rhythmic contractions that took him the rest of the way to paradise, and he emptied himself inside her in a series of long, shuddering pulses.

When it was over, she collapsed on top of him and he wrapped his arms around her, told himself he was never going to leave her again.

She was his. His woman, his mate, his home.

He laughed a little at the realization, pure joy flooding through him.

And when her lips met his, he reveled in the fact that after four hundred years and four continents, he had finally found a home.

ABOUT THE AUTHOR

Tessa Adams lives in Texas and teaches writing at her local community college. She is married and the mother of three young sons.

If you enjoyed *Forbidden Embers,*

look for the other tantalizing books

in the Dragon's Heat series by Tessa Adams,

all available now from Heat.

DARK EMBERS

Like all dragons, Dylan can procreate only with his destined mate—for whom he's searched five hundred years. His dark, rampant sexual appetite has earned him quite the reputation, all in the pursuit of his one true match.

But his search is delayed when a deadly disease sweeps through the Dragonstars, and Dylan must venture to the human world to find a cure. He tracks down renowned biochemist Phoebe Quillum, never imagining the beautiful scientist will be the mate he's been seeking for centuries. But no sooner do they meet than Phoebe and Dylan are besieged by obsessive, overpowering sexual desire.

Their passion turns to something truer—and they know in their souls and bodies that they're in too deep to get out. And when Phoebe is kidnapped by Dylan's oldest enemy, he must risk everything to reclaim the only woman he's ever loved, or his clan will be wiped out forever.

"A sexy and intriguing new world. I'm looking forward to seeing where Tessa Adams takes her dragons next."

—Nalini Singh, *New York Times* bestselling author

"A blistering-hot, fast-paced adventure that will leave readers breathless. Dylan and Phoebe have great chemistry and a romantic story that will captivate you and keep you turning pages long into the night."

—Anya Bast, *New York Times* bestselling author

"A fantastic debut . . . there was even a moment I felt myself get teary eyed—in an erotica, people!"

—Among the Muses

HIDDEN EMBERS

Quinn Maguire, healer of the Dragonstars, has been unable to find a cure for the insidious disease killing off his people one by one. Yet even in such dire circumstances, Quinn can't bring himself to approve when the head of the clan enlists Dr. Jasmine Kane for help. She is female. She is an outsider. She is human.

Decked out in black leather and a tough attitude, Jasmine clashes with conservative Quinn in more ways than one. But when he realizes she's his destined mate, Quinn doesn't know whether to rejoice or to rebel. While Jasmine makes him burn hotter than any woman ever has—dragon or human—their differences make a relationship impossible.

But when a rival clan infiltrates the Dragonstars, Jasmine becomes the first human infected with the disease. Now Quinn must do everything in his power to find a cure . . . before he loses the only woman he's ever loved.

"This second installment in the Dragonstar series is a glorious continuation of the first, filled with a fiery passion that's hot enough to set the desert sands aflame."　　　　—*Romantic Times* (4½ stars, Top Pick)

"A no-holds-barred epic romance where no emotion is left unscathed. . . . [Tessa Adams] is fearless as she rains down acute tragedy upon *Hidden*

Embers. I've read some tragic scenes in romance but I'm thinkin' that Adams takes the cake here. Girl had me in tears! From beginning to end, I was in love with this story!"

—Lovin' Me Some Romance (4½ stars)

"A super thriller that contains three fabulous subplots.... The lead couple is a delightful pairing of opposites who heat the pages when taking a respite from their save-the-clan quest."

—Harriet Klausner, Genre Go Round Reviews